CARROT CAKE
MURDER

Books by Joanne Fluke

CHOCOLATE CHIP COOKIE MURDER

STRAWBERRY SHORTCAKE MURDER

BLUEBERRY MUFFIN MURDER

LEMON MERINGUE PIE MURDER

FUDGE CUPCAKE MURDER

SUGAR COOKIE MURDER

PEACH COBBLER MURDER

CHERRY CHEESECAKE MURDER

KEY LIME PIE MURDER

CARROT CAKE MURDER

Published by Kensington Publishing Corporation

A HANNAH SWENSEN MYSTERY
WITH RECIPES

CARROT CAKE
MURDER

JOANNE FLUKE

KENSINGTON BOOKS
http://www.kensingtonbooks.com

ISBN-13: 978-7582-2961-8
ISBN-10: 0-7582-2961-5

First trade paperback printing: March 2008

10 9 8 7 6 5 4 3 2 1

Printed in the United States of America

This book is dedicated to Dale Constantine.

Acknowledgments:

Thanks to Ruel, my in-house story editor, research team, and cheerleader.
And to our kids who know that there is no substitute for butter.
Hugs to the grandkids as they try to convince their moms that carrot cake is a vegetable.

Thank you to Mary Ann Grossman who gave me the idea for the victim in this book.

Thank you to our friends and neighbors:
Mel & Kurt, Lyn & Bill, Gina & the kids, Adrienne, Jay, Bob, Amanda, Dale, John B., Trudi, David, Dr. Bob & Sue, Laura & Mark, Richard & Krista, and my hometown friends from Swanville, Minnesota.

Thanks to the Hannah fans at Mysteries To Die For for taste-testing the Viking Cookies.

Thank you to my Editor-in-Chief, John Scognamiglio. You're the absolute best.

The same goes for Walter, Steve, Laurie, Doug, David, Maureen, Magee, Meryl, Colleen, Michaela, Kate, Jessica, Peter, Robin, Lydia, Lori, Mike, Tami, and Barbara.

Thank you to Hiro Kimura for the incredible carrot cake on the cover.
And thanks to Lou Malcangi for designing such a delicious dust jacket.

Thanks also to all the other talented folks at Kensington who keep Hannah sleuthing and baking up a storm.

Thanks to Levy Home Entertainment for inviting me to the 2007 convention in Chicago. Not only did I have a great time, I met some really wonderful people!

Thank you to Dee for Alison Wonderland's stage name. Thanks to John for proofreading and for keeping my computer running. And thank you to Jill Saxton for catching more goofs than anyone else.

Thank you to Dr. Rahhal & Trina for all that you do.

Thanks to Mrs. Line for trying out so many recipes. And hugs to everyone who sent favorite family recipes for Hannah to try.

Massive hugs to Terry Sommers for testing all the recipes and trying them out on her family. Nobody's keeled over yet, right Terry?

Thank you to Jamie Wallace for keeping my Web site, **MurderSheBaked.com** up to date and looking great.

And many, many thanks to everyone who e-mailed or snail-mailed. Writing is solitary work, but when you invite me into your lives, you make me feel like family.

Chapter
One

The *Amen* couldn't come fast enough to suit Hannah Swensen. She was sitting in the third pew from the front of Holy Redeemer Lutheran Church in Lake Eden, Minnesota, and her ears were still ringing from the fifth and final chorus of *Jesu Priceless Treasure*. She thought she might have suffered a slight hearing loss from Marge Beeseman's attempt at a high *G*, but that wasn't her primary concern. Her eyes were trained on Reverend Knudson as he emerged from the small dressing room adjacent to the pulpit. He was wearing an ordinary suit, the type Doug Greerson, president of the Lake Eden First Mercantile Bank, wore every day to work. The minister's vestments had gone the way of his solemn manner, and he was smiling as he walked forward to informally address his flock.

An ecumenical fly droned its way from the open doors at the back of the church, alighting momentarily on Lutherans, Catholics, and Bible Church members alike. The church was packed this last Sunday in August, and much of that was Hannah's mother's doing. Delores Swensen had spent the previous evening on the phone, convincing scores of Lake Eden residents to attend Reverend Knudson's ten o'clock service.

Hannah turned to look at her mother. Delores was watching the reverend with the same intent gaze that Hannah's cat,

Moishe, employed to run surveillance on the chipmunk that
frequented the flowerbeds beneath Hannah's living room
window. The other occupants of the pew had also drawn a
bead on their minister in mufti. Hannah's two younger sisters, Andrea and Michelle, appeared mesmerized by his every
move. And their mother's business partner, Carrie Rhodes,
was clutching her hymnal so hard Hannah was afraid she'd
crack the spine. Even Carrie's son, Norman, looked nervous.
This was the showdown, the eleventh hour, the pivotal moment they'd all come to witness.

Reverend Knudson made his way to the head of the center
aisle with all eyes upon him. He was still smiling and he didn't
look as if he had an important announcement to make, but almost everyone in the congregation, members and visitors
alike, knew that he did. The reverend was about to tell them
that he planned to marry Claire Rodgers, owner of Beau Monde
Fashions, Lake Eden's only designer dress shop.

Startled by a poke in the ribs, Hannah turned to her
youngest sister. "What is it, Michelle?" she whispered.

"Two rows back on the other side," Michelle replied, her
voice so soft it was almost inaudible. Then she jerked her
head in the direction she wanted her oldest sister to look and
nudged her again.

Hannah turned around and gave a little gasp as she saw
the couple seated two rows behind them on the aisle. It was
Mayor Bascomb and his wife, Stephanie. And they were the
very couple Hannah had least expected to see at Holy Redeemer Lutheran this morning!

"Mother convinced Mrs. Bascomb to come," Michelle
continued, her lips close to Hannah's ear. "She didn't think
anyone would have the nerve to object to Reverend Knudson
and Claire getting married if they were here for the announcement. I mean . . . what reason could they give in front
of the mayor's wife?"

"Diabolical!" Hannah breathed, shooting her mother an
admiring look. Rumor had it that Claire had once been

Mayor Bascomb's mistress. No one could prove it, but some members of the congregation tended to look down their noses at Claire. It was the reason Hannah, her family, and the scores of people that Delores had recruited were here to support the reverend's announcement. There was no way Hannah and her extended family were going to let anyone throw a damper on this happy occasion.

"I'm delighted to see so many of you at services this morning," Reverend Knudson said, beaming. And then he proceeded to announce upcoming activities for the week. Hannah learned that Bible study would take place on Monday night, there would be a church rummage sale on Tuesday afternoon, they would hold twilight services on Wednesday at seven with choir practice immediately after the service, and Luther League would meet in the church basement on Thursday night. Friday evening was slotted for Lutherans Without Partners, a new singles club. There would be two weddings on Saturday, and the regular services on Sunday morning.

"And now, if you'll bear with me, I'd like to say something on a personal note. There is someone in this congregation who is near and dear to my heart."

Hannah nudged Michelle. This was it. Reverend Knudson was about to do it!

"That someone is Winifred Henderson, and I'd like to thank her for her years of service in the church nursery. Because of Winnie, many of you mothers have enjoyed worry-free Sunday church services, knowing that your children are well cared for and happy in the nursery. Even though we don't ordinarily applaud in church, I think Winnie deserves a standing ovation."

Hannah stood and applauded along with everyone else, and then she sat back down to wait for the last announcement. Reverend Knudson's eyes met hers for a moment, and then they quickly skittered away.

Uh-oh! Hannah breathed, coming very close to groaning out loud. There was only one reason for Reverend Knudson

to avoid her eyes. Claire had gotten cold feet and asked him
to delay the announcement again!

The reverend's hand began to rise in a signal for the or-
ganist to play the recessional. But Hannah was quicker, and
she shot to her feet. "Wait!" she said loudly. "I have an announcement to make."

All eyes swiveled in her direction, and Hannah came close
to wishing that the floor would open up and swallow her. But
something had to be done right now and she had to do it.
Reverend Knudson and Claire were perfect for each other.
And Claire was letting her fear of rejection stand in the way
of their future happiness.

"I know you're too modest to mention how hard you
work to keep all these church activities going," Hannah
began, making up a speech as she went. "I didn't realize it before, but you just told us about a meeting, or group, or event
every single day of the week. And you go to every one of
them. Not only that, you counsel people if they have a problem, you visit the sick at Lake Eden Hospital, and you or
Grandma Knudson are always available on the phone if we
need you. I know I speak for everyone here when I say that
we appreciate all the time and effort you spend looking after
us and the church."

"That's right," Marge Beeseman called down from the
choir loft. "We think you deserve a standing ovation, too!"

This is nice, Hannah thought as she applauded with everyone else. *They're in the mood to applaud, and they'll go right
on applauding when I throw them a curve.*

"Sometimes we take you for granted," Hannah continued.
"We forget that you have a personal life in addition to your
life as our pastor. And I know that's why you're not mentioning the most wonderful news of all." Hannah looked around
at the congregation. She had them on the edges of the pews.
Everyone was leaning forward, waiting. "And that wonderful news is that wedding bells are about to ring for you and
your bride."

If they lean forward anymore, they'll fall on the floor, Hannah thought fleetingly, noticing that people in the front pew were canting forward at close to a ninety-degree angle. But she went right on despite Reverend Knudson's startled expression. "I'm happy to tell all of you that she's a member of our own congregation. Since the Reverend is too shy to do it, I'm announcing that Reverend Knudson and Claire Rodgers will be getting married at Christmas! And I think our beloved minister and his bride-to-be deserve a standing ovation."

Of course they all applauded. They were programmed for standing ovations. And thanks to Delores and her phone recruiting, more people approved than objected. Now there was only one more thing for Hannah to do and that would be easy.

"I thought we should have a small celebration on this joyous occasion, so I brought several kinds of cookies and Edna Ferguson made coffee. There's juice for the kids, and everything's all set up on tables outside. Please enjoy yourself, and don't forget to tell Reverend Knudson and Claire how much you're looking forward to their marriage."

"Hannah?" Norman came up to her and slipped his arm around her waist. "That was just amazing what you did back there. You could sell kitty litter to nomads."

Hannah laughed. Norman had a way with words. "Thank you . . . I think. Did you happen to notice how fast the Old-Fashioned Sugar Cookies went?"

"They're almost gone. Decorating them with Claire and the reverend's initials was a brilliant touch."

"Thanks," Hannah said, knowing full well that Norman had caught her psychological ploy. Anyone who took a cookie with the two sets of initials encircled by a heart was giving symbolic approval to the marriage. "How about the Viking Cookies?"

"What Viking Cookies? The little sign is still there, but the plate's empty. And I didn't even get to taste them."

"Don't worry. I saved some for you." Hannah was pleased that the Viking Cookies were such a big hit. The recipe was a new one that Lisa had perfected and it was made with her favorite white chocolate.

Marge Beeseman came up to them with a huge smile on her face. "That was an excellent speech, Hannah."

"Thanks. I figured I'd better do something or Reverend Knudson would cop out again. Did Lisa tell you that we saved a few dozen cookies for this afternoon in case some of your relatives come in early for the family reunion?"

"She told me. And that's so sweet of you, Hannah. My sister Patsy and her husband are here already, and so is Lisa's oldest brother, Tim, the one who moved to Chicago."

"How many people do you expect?" Norman asked. Although he wasn't a Lake Eden native, he'd been here for almost three years now and he knew that Lisa's family was huge, and so was the Beeseman family.

"Almost all the out-of-town relatives sent in the card that Lisa and Herb mailed with the invitation. And some locals called instead of filling it out. As it stands right now, I think we'll be over a hundred."

"That's a big party!" Hannah said, wishing she'd saved more cookies. "Did Andrea find enough rentals for you at the lake?"

"I think so. And if we're a little short on room, we'll just double up. The Des Moines Beesemans are bringing their RV and there's room for three more in there, and the Brainerd Hermans are bringing an extra tent in case anyone needs it."

"Are you looking forward to seeing all your relatives again?" Norman asked.

"I'll say! There are some grandnieces and grandnephews I haven't even met yet. It's going to be the most wonderful week! There's only one thing I wish . . ." Marge stopped speaking and looked a bit wistful.

"What's that?" Hannah asked her.

"It's my brother, Gus. I was hoping he'd hear about the family reunion and show up."

"He didn't respond to the invitation?" Hannah was curious.

"He didn't *get* an invitation. I don't have an address for him."

There was a story here, and both Hannah and Norman realized it. Like a good, attentive audience, they remained silent and waited for Marge to explain.

"Gus left Lake Eden over thirty years ago, and no one's heard from him since. I hired a private detective to try to find him when my mother got sick, but he said Gus probably changed his name, and unless he knew what it was, he couldn't get a lead on him."

"Did you try a search on the Internet?" Norman asked.

"Herb did. There are some other August Hermans, but not my brother, Gus."

"He didn't tell anyone where he was going?" Hannah couldn't help but ask.

Marge shook her head. "He just disappeared in the middle of the night. He was staying with my folks at the time. All he took was a change of clothes and some money from the teapot on the kitchen counter." Marge must have seen their puzzled looks, because she went on to explain. "The teapot was a gift from one of my great aunts, the ugliest thing you ever saw! None of us drank tea, so we used it for the family bank when we were all growing up. We knew we could take money out when we needed it, and pay it back later, when we could."

"How much money did your brother take?" Hannah was curious.

"We were never really sure, but my father didn't think it was over a hundred dollars. Nobody ever bothered to count it. They just remembered how much they took so they could put it back."

Hannah did some fast figuring. "Bus tickets weren't that expensive back then," she said. "Your brother could have gone all the way to the west coast. Or to the east coast, for that matter."

"And he would have had seed money when he got there," Marge informed her. "I know my sister Patsy lent him some money about a week before he left town, and he borrowed some from me, too."

"Then his problem wasn't lack of money."

"No. He was living with Mom and Dad, so he didn't have to pay for rent, or food, or anything like that. I was living there, too. I had a job, but I didn't leave home until the next summer, when I got married."

"Was there any indication that he was going to leave?" Norman asked. "I mean, did he act restless or anything like that?"

"Not really. To this day, I don't know why he took off like that. I've been thinking about it ever since Lisa and Herb first mentioned having a family reunion, and I couldn't help hoping that he'd finally come home."

There was a moment of silence. Neither Hannah nor Norman was quite sure what to say. Then there was a honk from the street as a car drove up, a shiny new red car with a classic hood ornament.

"Nice car!" Norman exclaimed, eyeing the new Jaguar with obvious admiration. Then he turned to Marge. "One of your relatives?"

Marge gave a little laugh. "That's unlikely. As far as I know, we don't have any family *that* rich. Can you see who's driving?"

"It's a guy," Hannah told her. "Come on. Let's walk over to see who it is."

By the time they made their way to the street, the Jaguar was surrounded by admirers. They walked around to the street side, and Marge's eyes widened as she saw that her son was sitting in the passenger seat. "Herb?" she gasped. "What are you doing in there?"

"Hi, Mom. I took a quick run by the house to make sure no more relatives came in while we were at church, and look who I found waiting for us!"

Herb leaned back so that Marge could see the driver. "He said you probably won't recognize him, since it's been a really long time."

"Is it . . . ?" Hannah breathed, hardly daring to ask if Marge's wish had come true.

"Yes!" Marge was clearly ecstatic as she ran around the car to hug her brother through the open window. "Oh, Gus! I'm so glad you came home at last!"

VIKING COOKIES

Preheat oven to 350 degrees F., rack
in the middle position.

2 cups butter *(4 sticks—melted)*
2 cups brown sugar
2 cups white sugar
1 teaspoon baking powder
1 teaspoon baking soda
1 teaspoon salt
4 eggs—beaten
2 teaspoons vanilla
½ teaspoon cinnamon
¼ teaspoon cardamom *(nutmeg will also work, but
    cardamom is better)*
4 ½ cups flour
3 cups white chocolate chips *(I used
    Ghirardelli's)****
3 cups rolled oats *(uncooked oatmeal—I used
    Quaker's Quick Oatmeal)*

*** *Make sure you use real white chocolate chips, not
vanilla chips. The real ones have cocoa listed in the ingredients. If you can't find them in your market, look for a
block of white chocolate, one pound or a bit over, and cut
it up in small pieces with a knife.*

Melt the butter in a large microwave-safe bowl, or on
the stove in a small saucepan. *(It should melt in about 3
minutes in the microwave on HIGH.)* Set it on the counter
and let it cool to room temperature.

When the butter is cool, mix in the white sugar and the brown sugar.

Add the baking powder, baking soda, salt, eggs, vanilla, and spices. Make sure it's all mixed in thoroughly.

Add the flour in half-cup increments, mixing after each addition. Then add the white chocolate chips *(or pieces of white chocolate if you cut up a block)* and stir thoroughly.

Add the oatmeal and mix. The dough will be quite stiff.

Drop by teaspoons onto a greased *(or sprayed with nonstick cooking spray)* standard-sized cookie sheet, 12 cookies to a sheet.

Flatten the cookies on the sheet with a greased metal spatula *(or with the palm of your impeccably clean hand.)* You don't have to smush them all the way down so they look like pancakes—just one squish will do it.

Bake at 350 degrees F. for 11 to 13 minutes or until they're an attractive golden brown. *(Mine took the full 13 minutes.)*

Cool the cookies for 1 to 2 minutes on the cookie sheets and then remove them to a wire rack to cool completely.

Yield: 10 to 12 dozen delicious cookies, depending on cookie size.

These freeze well if you roll them in foil and put them in a freezer bag.

Hannah's Note: These cookies will go fast, even frozen. If you want to throw the midnight freezer raiders off the track, wrap the cookie rolls in a double thickness of foil and then stick them in a freezer bag. Label the bag with a food your family doesn't like, (something like BEEF TONGUE, or PORK KIDNEYS, or even LUTEFISK—it works every time.)

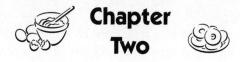

Chapter Two

Hannah stopped just inside her condo door and stared around her in shock. There had been a blizzard in her living room! Her wall-to-wall carpeting, normally a dark green color that she'd chosen because it reminded her of a lush green lawn, was covered with fluffy white snowflakes. Except it wasn't snow, and it wasn't flakes. And there was the empty couch pillow cover to prove it. Hannah picked up the cover and read the tag listing the contents. What she'd thought was snow was really the "unidentified fibers" Cost-Mart used as stuffing in their decorator sofa pillows.

"Moishe?" she called out, realizing that her orange-and-white feline roommate was nowhere in sight. He hadn't hurtled himself into her arms as he usually did when she came in the door, and that meant he was probably responsible. The pillow was a bit wet on the corner, from kitty saliva no doubt, and at least two paws' worth of claws had shredded the fabric to pull out the faux snow. The male companion who shared her home and her bed knew he'd done wrong and he was hiding somewhere, waiting for her to get over her initial shock and anger before he showed himself.

At least the pillow stuffing was easy to collect. Hannah got a garbage bag from the broom closet and began to fill it with the fluffy white balls. As she bent, retrieved, and stuffed, she thought about the very few times that Moishe had misbehaved.

A month or two after he'd decided to set up residence with her, Hannah had forgotten to empty his litter box when she cleaned the condo. Moishe had given her a one-day grace period, but the following night, when she'd come home from work at her bakery and coffee shop, she discovered that he'd accomplished the task himself and the litter was scattered all over the floor. At that late stage, it had been impossible for Hannah to tell whether her fastidious feline had gotten in to scratch it out, or whether he'd tipped the pan to dump it out and then righted it again. It didn't really matter in the giant scheme of things. She'd never needed another reminder to empty Moishe's litter box.

A more serious infraction had taken place a month or two after the litter box incident. Moishe had taken an immediate dislike to Hannah's mother, and he'd snagged several pairs of her real silk and really expensive pantyhose before Delores had decided that Hannah should visit her, rather than the other way around. Hannah liked to think that her kitty's dislike of Delores came from an effort to protect her from her mother's not-so-gentle reminders that she was over thirty, her biological clock was ticking, and she was still single. Perhaps that was true. Or perhaps Moishe simply didn't like the perfume Delores wore, or the pitch of her voice, or any of a hundred other things.

Hannah glanced at the deflated pillow casing. The litter box message and her mother's shredded stockings had been easy to interpret. This message was not so obvious. Did it mean that Moishe had suddenly developed an aversion to pillows? Although she'd never been to veterinary school, she didn't think it was common for cats to develop pillowphobia. Had Moishe objected to her color scheme for couch accessories and decided to let his preferences be known? The wine-colored pillow was intact, but he'd quite literally beaten the stuffing out of the light green pillow. Perhaps the light green color had reminded him of some traumatic incident in his kittenhood?

"Ridiculous!" she murmured under her breath. If there was a message in Moishe's pillow bashing, it probably had something to do with what was *inside* the pillow. Hannah let her imagination run wild. It was possible that a colony of bugs originating from the country that exported CostMart's unidentified pillow fibers had hatched.

Hannah glanced down at the fibers she'd tossed in the garbage bag. She didn't *see* any bugs. Could they be tiny, almost microscopic insects that would flutter around harmlessly for a day or two and then disappear? Or were they some type of science fiction worm that would invade her body, take over her mind, and . . .

A small pathetic sound brought Hannah out of her late-night horror movie scenario. Moishe was inching across the rug toward her, clearly unsure of her reaction but unable to stay away any longer from the mistress he loved. His expression was wide-eyed innocent, and it seemed to say, *What happened to that pillow? You don't think I did that, do you?* He reminded Hannah of her niece, Tracey, who'd come out of the kitchen at The Cookie Jar with chocolate smears on her face, insisting that she'd given a half-dozen chocolate chip cookies to a poor starving man who'd knocked at the back door.

"It's okay," Hannah said, cutting straight to the chase. "I know you shredded that pillow, and I'm not mad at you. I just wish I knew why you did it."

Moishe gave as close to a shrug as a cat could give, hunching his shoulders forward and then back. His tail flicked once and his eyes opened wide. Hannah thought he looked thoroughly bewildered. Perhaps he didn't know why he'd done it either, and she reached down to pick him up.

The moment she lifted him up into her arms, he began to purr. Hannah nuzzled him and gave him a little scratch behind the ears in the spot he loved. He licked her hand to show that he was grateful for her forgiveness. At least she *thought* it was to indicate that he was grateful. It could also have something to do with the fact that she'd packed up the leftover cookies and probably smelled like butter.

"Just let me finish up here," Hannah said, placing him on the back of the couch so that she could pick up the last few clumps of pillow innards. She tied the bag shut, placed it by the door so she'd remember to carry it out to the dumpster when she left for the evening, and beckoned to Moishe, who was watching her intently. "I bet you'd like lunch. I know I would."

After a quick survey of the pantry and cupboards, Hannah turned to her cat again. "How about Salmon Cakes?"

"Yowwww!" Moishe said.

Hannah took that as approval and she selected a small can of red salmon from the pantry. She opened it and dumped it into a strainer, removing the soft backbones and the dark skin for Moishe. Once she'd thoroughly drained the fish and flaked it, she cut the crusts from two slices of sourdough bread and tore it into small pieces. She'd just added the last few ingredients to the bowl when Moishe gave another yowl.

"Can't wait, huh?" Hannah glanced down at her pet. By some miracle, or perhaps it was a deliberate trick, her twenty-three-pound cat managed to look half-starved. If it was a trick, it was a good one. Hannah just wished that she could emulate it when she tried to wriggle into the bronze silk dress she planned to wear to the dance at Lisa and Herb's family reunion tonight.

Moishe gave another yowl, and it sounded so pathetic that Hannah surrendered and dumped the salmon bones and skin in his food bowl. While her cat attacked it with the same ferocity he would have shown to a small, furry rodent, she gave her bowl a final stir. She was just shaping the mixture into cakes about the size of a hamburger patty and preparing to fry them in butter when the phone rang.

Hannah turned to look at her pet. He'd lifted his head from the last of the salmon and was staring at the phone balefully. As it rang again, his ears went back and flattened against his head. The hair on his back began to bristle, and a low growl, more doglike than catlike, rumbled from his throat.

"Mother?" Hannah asked him, already knowing the answer. There was only one person in the universe who got such a negative response from her cat. Surprisingly, mostly because she didn't believe in ESP or any of its cousins, Moishe was right more times than he was wrong. It was probably Delores. Hannah reached for the phone, lifted it out of its cradle, and answered, "Hello, Mother."

"I wish you wouldn't do that, Hannah!" Delores gave her standard reply.

"Do what?" Hannah asked, even though she knew exactly what her mother meant.

"Say *Hello, Mother* before you really know who it is. What if it was someone else?"

"Then I'd be wrong."

"Yes. And you'd feel very foolish, wouldn't you?"

"Not really."

"Well!" There was a long pause while Delores considered it. Finally, she spoke. "You're right. You wouldn't. But I really wish you'd just say hello like a normal person."

"I know you do." Hannah felt a little niggle of guilt for annoying her mother. "It's just that I can't seem to resist."

Delores sighed so heavily, it sounded like a little explosion in Hannah's ear. "You do it because you know it bothers me, don't you?"

"In a way. It's become almost like a game. I say, *Hello, Mother.* You say, *I wish you wouldn't do that.* And I say, *Do what?* And then you give me a reason not to answer the phone that way. It's what we always do before we really start to talk."

"So it's our own private greeting? A mother-daughter ritual?"

"That's exactly right." Hannah nodded even though she knew her mother couldn't see it. There were times when Delores was amazingly perceptive.

"Then we'd better continue to do it, dear. Rituals are important. They're patterns for us to follow to bridge awkward moments."

"That's extremely insightful, Mother."

"Thank you, dear. I've been researching the English Regency period and the number of formal traditions they practiced was truly amazing. Did you know that the dress a debutante wore to be presented at court had to follow strict guidelines? And her curtsy had to be just so?"

"I didn't know."

"And did you know that the number of *removes* at a formal dinner was dictated by the family's social status?"

"No. What are *removes?*"

"They're similar to courses, dear."

Hannah nodded. Unlike some Regency conventions, this one was aptly named. When a meal was served formally, the server *removed* the plates from the previous course before presenting the next. And sometimes the plate or bowl had a cover that was *removed* with a flourish. "Are you doing this research for your Regency Romance Club?"

"Only partially, dear. And that reminds me . . . we're thinking about serving high tea as a fundraiser. Do you think you could help us with the pastries?"

"Sure. Have you set a date?"

"Not yet, but it won't be before Christmas. I'll do more research on exactly what they served and how it was presented. Perhaps, if they had scones in Regency times, Sally could make some of hers."

It was clearly going to be a long conversation. Hannah stretched out the phone cord, put a frying pan with butter on the burner, and turned on the heat. "I didn't know Sally made scones."

"Today was her first batch. She served them to us at brunch, and they were delicious."

"You went out to the Lake Eden Inn for brunch?" Hannah tipped the pan so the butter would melt faster.

"Yes, with all the relatives who arrived early for the reunion. Carrie and I were standing there talking to Marge after you left the church, and Gus practically had to invite us."

"Gus York? Or Marge's brother, Gus?"

"Marge's brother. He asked Marge to recommend a good place for brunch, and then he invited us all."

"That was nice of him."

Delores gave a little snort that Hannah could hear clearly over the receiver. "It was the *least* he could do. He practically broke Marge's heart when he left town in the middle of the night. And Marge's mother and father never stopped hoping that he'd come home. He was the youngest, you know."

"Why did he leave in the first place?" Hannah asked, holding the phone between her neck and her shoulder and cranking her head to the side so it wouldn't fall as she got her plate of uncooked salmon cakes and carried them over to the stovetop. She dropped them into the frying pan and stood back slightly to avoid being splattered by the sizzling butter.

"No one knows why he left, dear." Delores stopped speaking for a moment, and then she asked, "What's that noise?"

"What noise?"

"It's a frying noise. I'm on my cell phone, and it must need recharging. Anyway . . . the real reason I called is to ask you if you have any crackers."

Hannah glanced at the pantry. The door was ajar, and she could see a large package of assorted crackers sitting on the shelf. "I've got some."

"Good. Lisa needs you to bring them. Mike made his Lazy Day Pâté for the potluck tonight, but he doesn't get off work until six and he won't have time to run back into town for crackers."

"Consider it done. Anything else anyone needs?" Hannah flipped a Salmon Cake and it sputtered as it landed on its uncooked side.

"Just your Special Carrot Cake. Lisa and Herb were raving about it at the brunch, and everybody's looking forward to trying it."

"That's good to hear," Hannah said, flipping the other three Salmon Cakes.

"I'll see you there, dear. I've got to go now. That frying noise is getting louder, and I just know we'll get cut off."

Hannah said goodbye and rubbed her sore neck as she walked over to hang up the phone. She supposed she should have admitted that her stove was the source of the frying noise her mother thought was a waning battery, but her lunch was almost ready. Since it was past two in the afternoon and she still had to assemble several veggie and dip platters, there wasn't a lot of time to waste. She had just dished up her first helping and was placing it on the coffee table in the living room when her doorbell rang.

Hannah muttered a few choice words she never would have used around either of her nieces. Whoever it was had lousy timing. Then she picked up her plate (she knew better than to leave one of Moishe's favorite entrees within kitty reach) and carried it to the door. "Who is it?" she asked, rather than squint through the peephole.

"Mike. I need you, Hannah."

Those four little words were definitely the key to Hannah's heart. She couldn't resist a plea for help, even from the ugliest, meanest person in Lake Eden. And Mike Kingston was about as far from that description as you could get. He was ruggedly handsome, a tall Viking-type of a man, and although he was tough and fit and could pulverize an opponent in a fight, she was fairly sure there wasn't a mean bone in his body. "Come in," she invited, unlocking the door and holding it open for him.

"Thanks, Hannah. I had to run out here to talk to your downstairs neighbor, and I thought I'd drop by to pick up those crackers, if you've got them."

"I do. But Sue and Phil aren't in any trouble, are they?"

"Not at all. Phil witnessed an accident on the freeway when he was coming home from his night shaft at DelRay Manufacturing. I just took his statement." Mike glanced down at the plate in her hand and his eyes widened. "That looks good! What is it?"

"Salmon Cakes, hot off the stove . . . or the cell phone, in Mother's case."

"Huh?"

"I was talking to her when I was frying them and she thought . . . never mind. It's not important. Sit down and eat. I've got plenty for two."

There was a yowl from the feline who was watching Mike with half-narrowed eyes, and Hannah turned to reassure him. "That's two and a cat. I have enough for us, and for Moishe."

"You heard her. Relax, Big Guy." Mike gave Moishe a scratch under his chin as he sat down on the couch. Then he cut off a tiny piece of the Salmon Cake and held it out on the palm of his hand. "Here you go. This should tide you over until you get yours."

Hannah watched as Moishe licked it up daintily. She could hear him purring all the way across the room, and she ducked into the kitchen to dish up another plate.

"What's this sauce on top?" Mike asked when she emerged from the kitchen with her own plate. "It's great!"

Hannah didn't want to tell him, but she couldn't lie outright to a man she'd come within a hair's breadth of marrying. "It's one of Edna Ferguson's tricks," she explained, hoping he wouldn't ask for details.

"Tell me. Whenever I visit my sister, she sends me home with fried chicken. It gets kind of dry when I heat it in the microwave, and I bet this sauce would be good on it."

Poor handsome bachelor who had to bring home leftovers from his sister's table! Hannah almost felt sorry for him until she remembered that scores of Lake Eden ladies would jump at the chance to let him taste their home cooking. But he *did* need her, if only for cooking advice, and Hannah couldn't resist telling him the truth. "Okay, I'll let you in on the secret, but you can't tell anyone else."

"If I do, you'll have to kill me?" Mike quipped, flashing the mischievous grin that always made her feel weak in the knees.

"Oh, I wouldn't kill you. I'd lock you up in a closet and . . ."

Hannah clamped her mouth shut. Some things were better left unsaid.

"And what?"

"And leave you there until I decide what to do with you," Hannah finished her sentence with the best ambiguity she could think of on the fly.

"Okay. I promise I won't tell anyone Edna's secret. What is it?"

"Well, I usually make my own dill sauce with fresh baby dill, mayo, and a little cream, but it's better if you make it the night before, and I didn't know I'd be frying Salmon Cakes today."

"Okay. I've had your fresh dill sauce with your Salmon Loaf. It's great, but tell me what this is."

"Campbell's Cream of Celery soup."

"What?"

"It's Campbell's Cream of Celery soup, undiluted. It makes a good sauce in a pinch. Really. All you have to do is heat it in the microwave, and it's even better if you mix in a little dry sherry, but I'm helping Lisa with the potluck buffet tonight, and I thought I'd better not."

"What time are you going out to the lake?"

"Four. I'm stopping by The Cookie Jar first to pick up my cakes, and then I'm heading out. How about you?"

"I should be there by six-thirty as long as I remember to take your crackers with me. Save me a dance tonight, will you?"

"Absolutely," Hannah said, hoping her heart wasn't beating so hard that he could see it through the light sleeveless shell she'd worn to church.

"Tell Andrea, too. And Michelle. I'm crazy about the Swensen sisters."

Hannah smiled, but she would have liked it a lot more if he'd said that he was crazy about just her. Whatever. Mike was Mike, and you had to either take him the way he was or not take him at all.

SALMON CAKES

1 small can salmon***
2 slices bread, crusts removed *(you can use any type of bread)*
1 beaten egg *(just whip it up in a glass with a fork)*
1 teaspoon Worcestershire sauce *(or hot sauce, or lemon juice)*
½ teaspoon dry mustard *(that's the powdered kind)*
¼ teaspoon salt
¼ teaspoon onion powder
2 Tablespoons butter

*** Check the weight on your can of salmon. It should weigh between 7 ounces and 8 ounces—red salmon is best, but pink will do.

Open your can of salmon and drain it in a strainer. Remove any bones or dark skin. Flake it with a fork and put it in a small mixing bowl.

Cut the crusts from two standard-sized slices of bread and tear the middle part into small pieces. Add the pieces to the bowl with the salmon.

Add the egg and mix it all up with a fork.

Mix in the Worcestershire sauce *(or lemon juice, or hot sauce,)* the dry mustard, salt, and onion powder.

Stir it all up until it resembles a thick batter with lumps.

Divide the batter into thirds. *(You don't have to be exact—nobody's going to measure them when you're through. They'll be too busy eating them.)*

Spread a sheet of wax paper on a plate and pick up one of the lumps of batter. Squeeze it together with your hands to form a firm ball. Place it on the wax paper and flatten it like a hamburger patty. The patty should be about a half-inch thick.

Hannah's 1st Note: If you flatten your Salmon Cakes too much and you'd like to make them thicker, just go ahead. All you have to do is gather the batter into a ball again and start over.

Shape the other two lumps of batter into balls and then patties. Let them sit on the wax paper for a minute or two to firm up even more.

Melt the two Tablespoons of butter in a frying pan over medium heat.

Place the Salmon Cakes in the pan and fry them over medium heat until they're golden brown on the bottom. *(That should take approximately 2 minutes.)* Flip the patties over and brown the other side. *(Total frying time will be approximately 4 to 5 minutes.)* Remember that all you're doing is frying the egg. Everything else has already been cooked.

Drain the Salmon Cakes on a paper towel and transfer to a serving platter. Serve with Dill Sauce, or Edna's Easy Celery Sauce. They're also wonderful with creamed peas, or creamed corn.

Hannah's 2nd Note: When I do these for the family, I use my electric griddle and triple the recipe so I have nine Salmon Cakes. If you don't have an electric griddle or you prefer to use a frying pan, you can fry them and then put them in a single layer in a pan in an oven set at the lowest temperature to keep them warm until you've fried them all. Make sure to refrigerate any leftovers. I've put leftover Salmon Cakes in the refrigerator overnight and heated them in the microwave the next day for lunch. They're not quite as good as freshly fried, but they're still very good. (They're also good cold.)

Hannah's 3rd Note: You can also make Tuna Cakes, Shrimp Cakes, Crab Cakes, Chicken Cakes and any other "cake" you can think of. All you need to do is substitute 6 to 8 ounces of the canned, or cooked and chopped main ingredient of your choice for the salmon. (This is why I always keep a can of salad shrimp, a can of tuna, and a can of chopped chicken in my pantry.)

Yield: Serves 3 if you team it up with a nice green salad and a slice of something yummy for dessert. *(If you serve it alone, as a total lunch, it'll work for one person with a big appetite, one person with a little appetite, and a cat.)*

DILL SAUCE

Hannah's Note: This sauce is best if you make it at least 4 hours in advance and refrigerate it in an airtight container. (Overnight is even better.)

> 2 Tablespoons heavy cream
> ½ cup mayonnaise
> 1 teaspoon crushed fresh baby dill *(if you can't find baby dill, you can make it with ½ teaspoon dried dill weed, but it won't be as good)*

Mix the cream with the mayonnaise until it's smooth and then mix in the dill. Put the sauce in a small bowl, cover it with plastic wrap, and refrigerate it for at least 4 hours.

EDNA'S EASY CELERY SAUCE

Hannah's 1st Note: If you make your Salmon Cakes at the drop of a hat, the way I occasionally do, you won't have time to make the Dill Sauce. All Edna's Easy Celery Sauce requires is a can of cream of celery soup and some milk or cream.

Hannah's 2nd Note: The can of cream of celery soup should be in your pantry as a staple, along with a can of

cream of mushroom soup, and a can of tomato soup, and a can of cream of chicken soup. They're a good base for any sauce you want to make on the fly.

One can of cream of celery soup, undiluted *(10 to 11 ounces depending on brand name—used Campbell's).*
Milk or cream to thin

Open the can. Dump it in a small microwave-safe bowl. Heat it in the microwave until it's piping hot. *(Try 30 seconds and see if it's hot enough. If not, heat at 15-second increments until it is. Thin it with the milk or cream to sauce consistency.)*

Drizzle the sauce over the Salmon Cakes, sprinkle on a little parsley or fresh dill if you happen to have it, and serve immediately.

Hannah's 3rd Note: Edna tells me that you can also use undiluted cream of chicken soup (if you're using the chicken variation,) cream of mushroom soup, or cream of garlic soup. She also said something about cream of asparagus soup for Shrimp Cakes, but I haven't tried it.

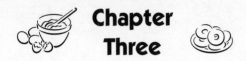

Chapter
Three

Hannah knew that if she had to hear one more chorus of the *Beer Barrel Polka,* she'd scream. It reminded her of the dance she'd shared with Marvin Dubinski only minutes before, and that wasn't a pleasant memory. Once dinner had been served and the dessert buffet had been set out on the bar, the dancing had begun. Hannah had danced nonstop for at least thirty minutes, going from partner to partner. Her first partner was Mike, and then Norman, followed by Bill, Lonnie, Mayor Bascomb, and Jon Walker. Her last partner, Marvin Dubinski, had finished Hannah off for the night. They'd danced to a polka, and Marvin had stepped on her feet a total of six times. Now she was hiding out in a booth with Marge Beeseman and her family, hoping that Marvin wouldn't spot her and ask her to dance any more polkas.

Mercifully, Frankie and the Frankfurters, the local band Lisa and Herb had hired for the dance, segued into a waltz. At least Hannah *thought* it was a waltz. It had a one-two-three, one-two-three rhythm, but the band played it so rapidly, most of the couples on the floor gave up trying to move to the music and came to a halt. The few that did attempt to dance whirled around as fast as the blades in the window fans, bumping into the stationary couples and making them scramble to get out of the way.

At least Frankie, if that really was his name, realized his

mistake. He led his group into a slower number, one with a cuddle-up-and-barely-move rhythm that restored order to the dance floor. Hannah tuned back into the conversation at hand, just in time to hear Marge Beeseman's question. Since Hannah was sandwiched in the big round booth between Marge and her brother, Gus, she had no choice but to be a party to their conversation.

"Did you find what you wanted to take from your old room?" Marge asked.

"Part of it. I couldn't find my favorite bedspread. I wanted to hang it on the wall in the guest bedroom. That has a western theme."

"Are you talking about the chenille one with Roy Rogers on it?"

"Yeah. The trunks were all labeled, and Lisa showed me the one from my bedroom. I thought it would be there, but it wasn't. I guess I'll have to go to some antique stores to find another one."

"That might be really expensive," Marge cautioned him. "Some of those old memorabilia items go for an arm and a leg."

"Doesn't matter. I don't mind paying for what I want. It's one of the advantages to having money."

Hannah was still watching the dance floor. The havoc was over, and the mirrored ball that hung from the ceiling rotated like the planets in the science project her father had helped her make in ninth grade. As the ball revolved, it sent beams of colored light down to illuminate the dancers who were now moving sedately. Since everything was calm, and there was no bump or tumble imminent, she turned her attention from the dance floor to Marge's brother, Gus. Hannah assumed that he was just trying to impress people, but he certainly mentioned money a lot!

Gus Klein was a handsome, well-dressed man in his fifties. Just an inch or so short of the six-foot mark, he had carefully styled dark blond hair with an elegant streak of silver over his left temple. The silver streak made him look distinguished, and Hannah suspected a beautician had placed it there. She knew she shouldn't make snap judgments, but he seemed to be a man who was all about appearances. Some people believed that if the package was appealing enough, it didn't really matter what was inside. Hannah was not one of them. Naturally, she preferred an attractive package, but it was what was inside that really counted.

What was inside Gus Klein? Hannah hadn't known him long enough to know, but he seemed a bit shallow to her, and she didn't like his continual bragging about his life in Atlantic City. He'd told them all that he had a standing appointment for a manicure at his office, he called in a masseuse when he felt tense, and when he entertained, he ordered food from the most exclusive restaurant in town and had it delivered to his penthouse condo.

She did know that Gus expected everyone else to wait on him. When Marge had asked him to join her at the buffet line, he'd told her he was too busy talking to some Brainerd cousins and practically ordered her to bring him a plate. The same thing had happened with the dessert buffet. It was as if his time was too valuable to stand in line like the rest of the relatives. He'd sent Lisa off to bring a sampler plate of dessert and coffee for the table, and then he'd passed out what he'd said were real Cuban cigars that he'd imported at great expense.

Hannah looked around for Andrea and spotted her on the dance floor with Bill. Andrea was the fashion expert, and Hannah hoped she'd assessed Gus's clothing. While Hannah didn't know a whole lot about men's attire, or women's either for that matter, she knew that the clothes Gus wore weren't mail order. They weren't mall clothing, either.

So what was the bottom line on Gus? Hannah thought about it for a minute. Most would say that he was handsome, charming, and sophisticated. And for those who didn't dig deeper, all of the above would be correct. But Hannah had the feeling that Gus was none of the above. She couldn't help but feel that he was playing a part, trying to appear urbane and elegant when he was really a beer-and-brat guy. Something wasn't quite right about Gus Klein's public persona, but she couldn't put her finger on what it was.

Hannah glanced at Marge. Lisa's mother-in-law was dressed to the nines tonight in an outfit that Hannah termed *aging hippie,* a phrase she'd never utter out loud for fear she'd hurt Marge's feelings. Some ladies liked to look sleek. Delores was a case in point. Her outfits were always tailored to embrace her perfect figure. Other ladies liked flounces, full skirts that swung out like cowgirls at a Saturday night square dance. Marge liked flutter. Butterfly wings and swooping fringes had nothing on her tonight. She was wearing a purple chiffon pantsuit that fluttered around her legs when she walked, and almost cleared off the table when she made a sweeping gesture.

Jack Herman, Lisa's dad, sat next to Marge. He looked handsome in dark slacks and a lavender shirt, but he didn't look happy. His lips were curved in a smile, but his eyes were angry and Hannah could tell that his smiling countenance was nothing but a polite gesture. Several times during the evening, she'd caught him glaring at Gus. Lisa had mentioned that there was bad blood between them, but when Lisa had asked her father what was wrong, he'd refused to discuss it.

Marge's twin, Patsy, looked so much like Marge that Hannah could believe the stories they'd told about how they used to play jokes on their dates by switching places halfway through the evening. There were ways to tell the twins apart, but only if they were standing side by side. Patsy's hair was slightly darker and she was a bit heavier than Marge. Marge's nose was a smidgen longer. Patsy's eyebrows were darker. It wasn't much of a yardstick to tell them apart, and Hannah was glad they didn't dress alike.

Mac, Patsy's husband, sat next to her. He was handsome

and athletic, and Hannah had caught several of the unattached women at the dance eyeing him appreciatively. Patsy had noticed too, but she didn't seem concerned. Either she trusted her husband completely, or she just didn't care. Hannah was betting on the latter since they were sitting right next to each other without touching. If her psychology professor at college was correct when he lectured on body language, the space between them spoke volumes about the health of their marriage.

"I don't think Mother bought your bedspread at a store," Marge said to Gus.

"She didn't," Patsy confirmed it. "I remember we saved box tops for her and she sent away for it."

"That's right! You know the type of thing we're talking about, don't you, Hannah?"

Hannah was jolted out of her musing and back to the scene by Marge's question. It was a good thing she'd been half listening to the conversation. While she'd much rather be ignored and left to her own thoughts, Marge obviously wanted to include her.

"I think I do," Hannah answered. "Andrea and I saved the little proof of purchase circles from something or other so that Michelle could have a fairy princess wand. All we had to pay was the postage and handling."

"Did she like it?" Patsy asked.

"She loved it. Unfortunately, the little bulb burned out the first week, and Dad couldn't find a replacement."

"That's probably what happened to your bedspread," Marge said to Gus.

"It burned out?" Gus gave her a little grin to show he was kidding.

"Close. It must have fallen apart when Mother washed it to store it in the trunk. But you said you found some things you wanted."

"I got some of my baseball stuff."

"The special bat Dad bought you when you made the team at Jordan High?" Patsy asked.

Gus nodded. "It was right on top, my Louisville Slugger, the one I used in high school. I hit my first home run with that bat. I couldn't find my glove, though." Gus gave a little chuckle. "Maybe that fell apart right along with my bed-spread."

"You could be right," Patsy told him. "Leather does that if it's not treated."

"And I know Mother didn't treat it," Marge picked up on her sister's comment. "She kept your old room just as it was for a couple of years, and then she packed everything up and put it in the trunk. Dad dragged it up to the attic, and I'm pretty sure they never looked at it again. It was just too painful, you know?"

Gus shifted a bit and Hannah could tell he was uncom-fortable. "Well, I'm glad they kept my things for me." He turned to Hannah. "Did you keep anything from your child-hood?"

"Let me think about that for a second." Hannah recog-nized his attempt to steer the conversation in another direc-tion. It was clear he didn't want to answer difficult personal questions. Hannah thought about thwarting his attempt, but Gus was looking at her the way a drowning man might look at a rescue vessel, and she simply had to help him out. "I still have the pink satin toe shoes I bought when I was a kid."

"Ballet?" Marge sounded incredulous. "I didn't know you took ballet lessons."

"That's just the problem. I didn't. When I was about eleven, I got the notion that if only I had the proper shoes, I could dance the lead in *Swan Lake*."

"So you got the shoes and discovered that you couldn't do it?" Marge asked.

"That's right," Hannah replied, dismissing it with a smile and a shrug, not mentioning the disappointment she'd suffered when she couldn't achieve *en pointe* without grasping the back of a sturdy chair and hauling herself up on it. She'd been so sure she was a natural in a field that had no naturals, only dedication, constant practice, and years and years of ballet training. But this wasn't the time or the place to bare her soul. It was best to make light of it "Another childhood dream fractured. You know how it is. But I *did* keep all the Degas prints my mother bought for me."

"So here we all are, reliving old memories," Jack said, staring directly across the table at Gus. "Remember Mary Jo Kuehn?"

The silence that followed Jack's question was so heavy Hannah imagined she could cut with a knife. She wasn't sure what it meant since she'd never heard of Mary Jo Kuehn, but everyone except Jack looked uncomfortable.

"I remember," Gus said, "and I'll never stop missing her. She was such a pretty girl. But I met another pretty girl today, Jack."

"Who was that?" Marge asked, seizing the opportunity to change the subject.

"Jack's oldest daughter, Iris." Gus turned back to Jack. "She doesn't look at all like you, so I guess she must take after her mother. And speaking of Emmy, you're here with Marge. Did you and Emmy get a divorce?"

Jack gave him a look that would freeze lilacs in July. "Emily is dead."

"I'm sorry to hear that." Gus sounded sincere to Hannah's ears. "How about your sister, Heather?"

"She's dead, too," Jack repeated, still glowering.

"Do you remember Mr. Burnside?" Marge trilled, and Hannah's eyebrows shot up. She'd never heard Marge sound so intensely cheerful before.

"Of course." Patsy sounded deliberately cheerful, too. "I thought I was going flunk algebra, but he took pity on me."

"You did all right," Marge reached over to pat her hand. "Did you enjoy the dessert buffet?"

"Oh, my yes! It's absolutely scrumptious. And your carrot cake . . ." Patsy turned to smile at Hannah. "I've always been known for my carrot cake, but yours . . . it's even better than mine. Mac had three pieces!"

"I had four," Gus declared, "and I want more." He turned and winked at Hannah. "I don't suppose you've got another cake stashed anywhere?"

"Actually . . . yes, I do. I was saving it for tomorrow, but I can always put it out if there isn't any left on the platter."

Mac, who was at the edge of the booth, stood up to look. "There's half a platter left."

"Gus just wants you to leave him a private stash so he can eat it later," Marge informed her. "He used to do the same thing with my Cocoa Fudge Cake. I always had to bake two, one for the family and the other one for Gus."

"You're right," Gus admitted. "I'm guilty as charged." He turned to Hannah. "Will you put away a plate of carrot cake for me?"

"Oh. Well . . . sure. How much do you want?"

"At least half a cake," Patsy answered for him. "That's what he used to ask Marge for. And in the morning, it was all gone. Gus was a midnight refrigerator bandit."

"So is Jack," Marge said, in an attempt to bring Jack into the conversation.

Hannah turned to look at Jack. He wasn't having it. He was just staring at Gus and glowering.

"I don't suppose you brought that Cocoa Fudge Cake tonight, did you?" Gus addressed Marge. Hannah was sure he'd noticed that Jack was glowering at him, but he preferred to ignore it.

"Not tonight, but I'm baking it tomorrow. I'll make an extra cake, just for you."

"For me and not for your boyfriend?" Gus glanced across the table at Jack.

"Jack isn't exactly my boyfriend, although I love him a lot. I always have and I always will." Marge shot Gus a level look and took a deep breath. Hannah suspected that she was debating the wisdom of saying more. "And speaking of love," Marge went on, "how could you leave Lake Eden in the middle of the night without saying anything to any of us?"

Gus reared back as if he'd been hit buy a salvo of enemy arrows. "I didn't do it on purpose, Marge. It was just that I had to go then. I don't have to explain myself to you or to anyone else."

"No, you don't," Patsy chimed in. "But you *should* have. It's too late for the people who loved you the most. Our parents are dead now. They deserved an explanation, or at least a good-bye before you left."

"They never stopped believing that you'd come home," Marge added. "And you never even wrote, or called, or anything. We saw their hearts break, and we want to know why."

Hannah's head swiveled to Gus. He looked horribly uncomfortable. For a split second she almost felt sorry for him, but what Marge and Patsy had said was true. Gus hadn't bothered to call, or write, or contact his parents in any way. And now it was too late.

Gus was silent for a moment. And then he leaned forward. "I couldn't," he said. "I had to prove myself first. And that didn't happen until a couple of years ago."

Hannah began to frown. Gus had been bragging about his nightclub business when she'd joined Marge in the booth. "But you said you were successful once your flagship, Mood Indigo, got off the ground. You also said that you paid off the money you borrowed to start it over twenty years ago. You could have come back then. Your parents were still alive."

Gus turned to her, and Hannah fought to the urge to shrink back. He didn't look happy that she'd caught him in an inconsistency.

"What is this? The inquisition?" He gave Hannah a look

intended to warn her off. "I didn't want to put the cart before the horse. There's no way I wanted to contact Mother and say I was a successful businessman and then fail in my plans for expansion."

"Expansion?" Mac leaned closer. "You have more than one nightclub now?"

"You bet. I've got four, and I'm thinking about expanding again. Atlantic City is a great place to own a nightclub, and they're popping up all over."

Mac leaned slightly closer to Gus. "You must be pulling in a good profit to think about opening another one."

"Oh, I am. You don't expand unless you've got the money to do it. That's what I meant about putting the cart before the horse. It always takes a while to get a new club going."

"The construction of the building?" Mac guessed.

"That and the fact you have to get the customers in and then keep them coming back. You definitely have to set aside a big budget for advertising."

"I like the name Mood Indigo," Marge said, and Hannah noticed that she squeezed Jack's hand. "Do all the others have a blue theme?"

Gus looked relieved now that they'd switched to a less personal subject, and he favored his sister with a smile. "It's clever of you to realize that. We play mainly blues in the clubs. And the décor in each club is a different shade of blue. There's Mood Indigo, you already know about that. And then there's the Aqua Room, Sky Blue Heaven, and Midnight Stars. I got that idea from the map of the heavens I used to have on my ceiling. It's one of the reasons I wanted to go through that trunk from my old bedroom. I thought I might come up with another name for a nightclub."

"True Blue," Jack offered. "Except that it wouldn't fit. You've never been true to anyone in your life."

"And you've never minded picking up the leftovers," Gus shot back.

There was a moment of silence when everyone just held

collective breaths. Hannah wondered if they would sit there forever, just wanting for that second shoe to drop. She hated to think of what might happen if it did. Jack was glaring at Gus. And Gus was glaring at Jack. This could be very awkward, especially since she was seated next to Gus.

"Excuse me," Hannah said. And the tension eased as everyone turned to look at her. "I think I'll check my cake platter to see if I need to cut more. Does anyone else want more dessert?"

"I do!" Marge seized the opportunity.

"Me, too," Patsy said, giving Mac a little nudge. "Come on. Slide out and let's get some more of Hannah's Special Carrot Cake."

Marge grabbed Jack's arm and almost pushed him out of booth. "Let's go, Jack. I need some more coffee."

Jack slid out of the booth and held out a hand to Marge. Then he turned to give Gus a final glare. "I'm out of here. And it's not a minute too soon."

And then they were gone, Jack, Marge, Patsy, and Mac. And that left Hannah alone in the booth with Gus.

"You're leaving, too?" Gus asked in a tone she couldn't quite read.

"Well . . . I should probably cut the last cake and refill the platter," Hannah hedged awkwardly. But then she took pity and said, "Why don't you come with me? I'll fix a plate of cake for you and you can stash it somewhere for later."

"Hold on a second. I'll be right with you." Gus popped what looked to Hannah like a pill in his mouth and washed it down with the scotch and soda Marge had gone to fetch for him earlier.

"Should you be drinking and taking meds at the same time?" Hannah couldn't resist asking.

"It's just an over-the-counter antacid. That pâté had too much horseradish for me."

Since they were sitting at the center of the horseshoe-shaped booth, Gus slid out from one direction and Hannah slid out from the other. Gus leaned over to retrieve his glass, and while she was waiting for him, Hannah looked out over the crowd. She was surprised to see Jack standing only a few feet away, holding Marge's arm while she exchanged a few words with another couple in a booth.

Hannah gave a little wave, but all Jack did in return was scowl. He'd obviously heard her talking to Gus, because the look on his face was disapproving. If she had to describe it, Hannah would say that Jack Herman looked as if he'd just overheard her making a pact with the devil!

HANNAH'S SPECIAL CARROT CAKE

Preheat oven to 350 degrees F., rack
in the middle position.

2 cups white *(granulated)* sugar

3 eggs

¾ cup vegetable oil *(not canola, or olive, or anything but veggie oil)*

1 teaspoon vanilla extract

¾ cup sour cream *(or unflavored yogurt)*

2 teaspoons baking soda

2 teaspoons cinnamon *(or ½ teaspoon cardamom and the rest cinnamon)*

1 ½ teaspoons salt

1 20-ounce can crushed pineapple, juice and all***

2 cups chopped walnuts *(or pecans)*

2 ½ cups flour *(don't sift—pack it down when you measure)*

2 cups grated carrots *(also pack them down when you measure)*

*** *That's about 1 ½ cups of crushed pineapple and a scant cup juice*

Grease *(or spray with Pam)* a 9-inch by 13-inch cake pan and set it aside.

Hannah's 1st Note: This is a lot easier with an electric mixer, but you can also make it by hand.

Beat the sugar, eggs, vegetable oil, and vanilla together in a large bowl. Mix in the sour cream *(or yogurt.)* Add the

baking soda, cinnamon *(and cardamom if you used it)* and salt. Mix them in thoroughly.

Add the can of crushed pineapple *(including the liquid)* and the chopped nuts to your bowl. Mix them in thoroughly.

Add the flour by half-cup increments, mixing after each addition.

Grate the carrots. *(This is very easy with a food processor, but you can also do it with a hand grater.)* Measure out 2 cups of grated carrots. Pack them down in the cup when you measure them.

Mix in the carrots BY HAND. Grated carrots tend to get caught on the beaters of electric mixers.

Spread the batter in your prepared cake pan and bake it at 350 degrees F. for 50 minutes, or until a cake tester *(I use a food pick that's a little longer than a toothpick,)* inserted one inch from the center of the cake comes out clean.

Let the cake cool in the cake pan on a wire rack. When it's completely cool, frost with cream cheese frosting while it's still in the pan.

CREAM CHEESE FROSTING

½ cup softened butter
8-ounce package softened cream cheese
1 teaspoon vanilla extract
4 cups confectioner's *(powdered)* sugar *(no need to
    sift unless it's got big lumps)*

Mix the softened butter with the softened cream cheese and the vanilla until the mixture is smooth.

Hannah's 2nd Note: Do this next step at room temperature. If you heated the cream cheese or the butter to soften it, make sure it's cooled down before you continue.

Add the confectioner's sugar in half-cup increments until the frosting is of proper spreading consistency. *(You'll use all, or almost all, of the sugar.)*

Hannah's 3rd Note: If you're good with the pastry bag, remove ⅓ cup of frosting and save it in a little bowl to pipe on frosting carrots and stems.

With a frosting knife *(or rubber spatula if you prefer)* drop large dollops of frosting over the surface of your cooled cake. I usually end up with somewhere between 6 and 12 dollops. The dollops are like little stacks of frosting—you'll spread neighboring stacks together, working your way from one end to the other, until you've frosted the whole cake. *(This dollop method prevents uneven*

frosting thickness and "tearing" of the surface of your cake as you "pull" frosting from one end to the other.)

If you decided to use the pastry bag to decorate your cake, mix most of the remaining frosting with one drop of yellow food coloring and one drop of red food coloring. Mix it thoroughly to make an orange frosting and pipe little carrots on top to decorate your cake. You can save a bit of uncolored frosting to color green and dab green stems on the large end of the carrots.

Chapter Four

When Hannah's alarm clock went off in her darkened bedroom, she rolled over on her stomach, clamped the pillow over her head, held it in place with her arms, and tried to block out the noise. She wasn't ready to get up yet, certainly not now, and maybe not ever. She'd just closed her eyes, she was very sure of that, and it couldn't possibly be time to get up, get dressed, and drive to work. Perhaps the power had gone off in the middle of the night, causing her alarm clock to malfunction. Or perhaps she'd goofed when she'd set it last night. Whatever the reason, she was absolutely certain it couldn't possibly be four-thirty in the morning.

She really should check on the time, but that meant she'd have to open her eyes. If she kept them closed, she might be able to drift off to sleep again. Quite clearly it wasn't time to get up. She wouldn't be this tired if it were. She assessed her level of exhaustion and decided it had to be two-thirty or three in the morning. If she'd gotten another hour or two of sleep, her eyelids wouldn't feel as if they'd been weighted down with hockey pucks.

Hannah gave a little smile under her protective pillow. How much did hockey pucks weigh, anyway? She seemed to remember that she'd looked it up once, and the regulation weight was between five and a half and six ounces. That was the NHL standard. Then there were the blue four-ounce training puck, and the two-pound steel puck that was used to increase wrist strength. There were also hollow, lightweight, orange fluorescent pucks that were used for road hockey and floor hockey. Roller hockey pucks were made of plastic in light, visible colors. They were available in yellow, orange, pink, and green, but red was the most popular color.

Hannah gave a little groan. Now that she'd recalled almost everything she'd read or heard about hockey pucks, she was wide-awake. And her alarm clock was still ringing. She had to reach out and shut it off. It would wake the neighbors if it continued to ring.

Her eyes popped open, and Hannah sat bolt upright in bed. Her alarm clock couldn't be ringing. It didn't ring. It beeped. Her *phone* was ringing, and that meant something was horribly wrong. Not even her mother called her before six in the morning!

Two-thirty. Hannah glanced at the lighted display on her clock as she reached for the phone by her bed. She snatched it from the cradle, her heart beating hard, hoping against hope that it was a wrong number and nothing awful had happened to her family. "Hello?" she croaked, quickly clearing her throat so that she could talk.

"Hannah?" a young female voice asked.

"Yes. Who's this?"

"It's Sue Plotnik from downstairs. Is everything all right up there?"

Hannah glanced around. Everything looked fine, and she was fine, too, if she didn't count the fact that her pulse was racing. "I'm fine, and everything looks okay. What's the matter?"

"We're not sure. The noise woke us up. Don't you hear it?"

Hannah started to ask what noise Sue was talking about

when she heard it, a low rumbling and thumping like an unbalanced load of clothing in a washing machine. "I hear it now. What is it?"

"Phil thought there must be something wrong in your master bathroom. The thumping is loudest when we stand in our bathroom and that's right below your bathroom."

"Hold on and I'll go check."

"Wait!" Sue sounded panicked. "Phil says not to go in there alone. He thinks maybe a burglar tried to get in your bathroom window and got stuck."

"That couldn't be it. Right after I moved in, Bill put locks on all my windows. They only open far enough to let the air in."

"Okay, then. I'll hang on while you go check, and if you're not back on the line in two minutes, I'll send Phil up with the extra key."

Hannah's heart was beating hard as she placed the receiver on the nightstand and headed for her bathroom. The door was open an inch or two, and the rumbling noise was loud. She really didn't know how she'd slept through it, but she supposed that if a person was tired enough, that person could sleep through anything. After a long night of studying when she was in college, she'd slept through a tornado siren. She hadn't learned about the tornado until the next morning, when she emerged from her apartment to find several large trees uprooted near the entrance to her building.

Hannah inched the door open and stepped cautiously into the bathroom. The noise was coming from her tub, and it sounded like thunder in the space that was enclosed by tile walls and glass doors that turned the tub into a shower stall.

Something was in there! By the dim nightlight she had plugged in by the sink, Hannah could see a dark blur racing around the enclosure. The glass door was open a few inches, but the dark blur passed by too quickly to identify. It was short and there was a scrabbling noise as it fought for purchase against the slippery sides of the tub. It had to be some kind of animal, smaller than a dog and about the size of . . .

"Moishe!" Hannah gasped, sliding the glass door open in time to see her feline rounding the back of the tub and heading for the faucets. He skidded to a stop, gave her a *Whatcha-want?* look, decided it wasn't something he needed to pursue, and began speeding around the bathtub racetrack again.

There was only one thing to do, and Hannah did it. She stepped into the tub and cornered him as he passed by the faucets again. "That's quite enough, Moishe!" she told him in no uncertain terms.

Moishe studied her expression for a moment or two, and then he jumped out of the tub and ran into the bedroom. Hannah slid the glass door shut and hurried back to the phone. She had some apologizing to do to her downstairs neighbors.

She had been asleep for all of three seconds when it happened again. Hannah got out of bed and dragged her cat out of the bathtub. She remembered sliding the glass door closed, and that meant Moishe had managed to claw it open. Sterner measures had to be taken.

This time Hannah didn't bother to shut the glass door. Moishe would only claw it open again. Instead, she closed the bathroom door and hoped that she wouldn't run into it when she got up out of the sound sleep she was hoping to get before morning. Unfortunately, it *was* morning. One glace at the lighted display of her alarm clock told her that it was ten after three. The term *hellcat* took on new meaning for her as she crawled into bed and attempted to go back to sleep for the hour and minutes that were left before her alarm clock went off.

She was just drifting off when she heard it, a determined scratching at the bathroom door. That conjured up visions of new paint jobs and perhaps even a new bathroom door in

Hannah's mind. Moishe obviously wanted to run more laps in the Bathtub Grand Prix, and he was bound and determined to claw, bite, or tunnel his way in.

Hannah gave a little groan and sat up. She'd been awakened from a sound sleep twice in one night by the ungrateful feline she'd taken in from the cold Minnesota winters, kept healthy with regular vet visits, and fed good nutritious food every day. She'd even bought him his own expensive feather pillow, and she let him snuggle under her comforter. She felt betrayed, and that made her angry, but getting annoyed at Moishe wouldn't solve her problem. She had to calm him down before he found another noisy pastime that would bother her neighbors.

There was only one action to take, one thing that would managed to calm her hyperactive pet so that he wouldn't cause trouble. She flicked on the light, shut off the alarm that would sound in a little over an hour anyway, and headed for the kitchen to put on the coffee. She'd pretend it was morning and feed Moishe. And once he was fed, he'd probably nap on the back of the couch. By then it would be too late for her to try to go back to sleep again, so she'd mix up a batch of Raisin Drops, the new cookie recipe her friend Lois Brown had sent her from Phoenix, and bake them when she got to The Cookie Jar.

RAISIN DROPS

Preheat oven to 350 degrees F., rack
in the middle position.

1 ½ cups raisins *(I've used regular raisins, and also golden raisins—they're both good.)*
1 ½ cups water *(right out of the tap is fine)*

---

3 ½ cups all purpose flour *(don't sift—just scoop it out and level if off with a knife)*
1 teaspoon salt
1 teaspoon baking soda
1 teaspoon baking powder

---

1 cup softened butter *(2 sticks, ½ pound)*
1 ½ cups white *(granulated)* sugar
3 eggs, beaten *(just whip them up in a glass with a fork)*
1 teaspoon vanilla extract

Approximately ½ cup white *(granulated)* sugar for later

Hannah's 1st Note: Hank, the bartender down at the Lake Eden Municipal Liquor Store, suggested that you could soften the raisins in brandy or rum, instead of water. (I used water.)

Put the raisins and the water in an uncovered saucepan. Simmer them on the stove until all the water is absorbed. *(This took me about 20 minutes.)*

Move the saucepan to a cold burner, or on a potholder on your counter, and cool the raisins for 30 minutes. *(If you're in a hurry, you can speed up this cooling process by sticking the pan in the refrigerator until the raisins are approximately room temperature.)*

In a medium-sized mixing bowl, combine the flour, salt, baking soda, and baking powder. *(I stir mine gently with a whisk so that everything's mixed together.)* Set the bowl aside.

Hannah's 2nd Note: I used an electric mixer for this part of the recipe. You can do it by hand, but it takes some muscle.

Cream the softened butter and sugar together until they're light and fluffy.

Add the eggs, one at a time, and beat until the mixture is a uniform color.

Take your bowl out of the mixer and blend in the raisins and the vanilla by hand.

Fold in the flour mixture carefully. The object is to keep the dough fluffy.

Put approximately ½ cup sugar into a small bowl. Drop dough from a teaspoon *(or Tablespoon if you want large cookies)* into the bowl of sugar. Form the drops into balls with your fingers and move them to a lightly greased *(I*

sprayed it with Pam) cookie sheet, 12 to a standard-sized sheet.

Bake the Raisin Drops at 350 degrees F. for 9 to 10 minutes, or until just lightly browned.

Lois Brown's Note: I bake just a few at first to make sure there's the right amount of flour. If they spread out too thin, add another Tablespoon or two of flour. I have been making this recipe for my family for 40 years.

Yield: 5 to 6 dozen deliciously soft raisin cookies.

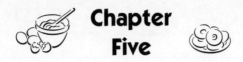

Chapter Five

Hannah lowered the driver's window of her cookie truck to enjoy the gentle breeze wafting off the far shore of Eden Lake. Even though the gravel road around the lake was showing wear from the tourists who'd towed heavy boat trailers and campers, she took the ruts at a fast clip to outrun the mosquitoes. She'd been through enough Minnesota summers to know that if she slowed to a crawl, the insects that some people called the Minnesota State Bird would descend on her arm in hungry hordes to gorge on a luncheon of A negative.

It was a perfectly lovely day. The air was scented with a wisp of smoke from a fisherman's shore lunch and a dampness that reminded her of wet swimming suits tossed over a porch rail to dry. The sun was almost straight overhead. When it reached its apex, the shadows of the tall pines that lined the lakeshore would be at their smallest, no larger than a dark circle on the ground around the tree trunks. It was the final Monday in August, and Hannah was playing hooky with her mother's blessing, an occurrence that had never happened during her school days at Jordan High. Delores and Carrie were also playing hooky. They'd closed their antique shop to attend the Beeseman-Herman Family Reunion and sent their assistant, Luanne Hanks, next door to Hannah's cookie and coffee shop. She'd arrived to take charge just as

Hannah was about to turn the CLOSED sign on the front door to OPEN, and now Hannah was free to enjoy this lazy end-of-summer day.

Since she was in no hurry, Hannah took the long way around the lake. Attending Lisa and Herb's family reunion would be fun as long as she didn't get buttonholed by Gus Klein again. She'd spent quite enough time with him at the dance last night.

Hannah let out a groan as she came around a curve and saw that the public parking lot was full. In addition to the relatives who were staying at nearby lake cottages, it appeared that everyone in town had driven out for the day's festivities. It wasn't surprising, considering the size of both families. Lisa was the youngest daughter in the large Herman family. Most of the children had stayed in the area and married into other large families. The same was true for the Beesemans. At last count, over a hundred people had arrived for the reunion.

Since there weren't any vacant parking spots, Hannah created one of her own. That was the beauty of owning a four-wheel-drive cookie truck. When the proper gear was engaged, her Suburban climbed up the three-foot berm of dirt surrounding the parking lot and found a semi-level spot on top.

Hannah took the time to spray on mosquito repellent, a precaution she'd learned early on in life. Then she retrieved the large box of cookies she'd packed to add to the lunch table. Kids loved cookies, and there were plenty of kids at the family reunion. She held the box with both hands, dug in her heels to walk down the berm, and then hurried toward the picnic tables by the shore where a crowd was gathering.

Loud, merry voices floated up to greet her. Hannah spied Lisa standing on top of a picnic table, holding a cheerleading megaphone to her lips. She was wearing a red T-shirt with the legend FAMILY IS EVERYTHING.

"It's time for the family portrait," Lisa called out. "We're going to have the lake in the background, so line up at the edge of the water behind the two chairs for your host and hostess. That's my dad, Jack Herman, and Herb's mom, Marge Beeseman. Norman and Herb will tell you what row you're in if you can't figure it out for yourself. We want the tallest in the back and the shortest in the front."

Hannah set the cookies down on the food table and headed for the shore to watch. She'd heard that Norman had offered to take the group pictures, and perhaps she could help.

"Hannah!"

Hannah knew that voice, and thankfully it wasn't Gus. "Hi, Mother," she said, turning to greet the fashionable, dark-haired woman who would die rather than exceed the petite dress size she'd worn in high school.

"Hello, dear." Delores steadied herself against her eldest daughter's arm and shook the sand from one white high-heeled sandal. "I wish I hadn't worn these today, but I didn't think the beach would be quite this sandy."

Hannah laughed. "It's a beach, Mother. By definition it's sandy."

"You're right, of course. But I didn't think it would be *this* sandy." Delores paused for a moment, and then she gave Hannah a smile. "Did you like the surprise we sent you this morning?"

For a brief moment Hannah was puzzled, but then she got it. "You mean Luanne. That was really thoughtful of you, Mother. I didn't think I'd be able to drive out here until we closed."

"Anything for my dearest daughter."

Uh-oh! Warning bells sounded in Hannah's head. Her mother wanted something . . . but what?

"I hope you can relax and have a good time today. You deserve a little break, Hannah."

The warning bells turned into klaxons, and yellow caution lights began to blink on and off. "Thanks, Mother," Hannah responded. And then, just because she couldn't resist, she asked, "What do you want?"

Her mother reared back in surprise. "*Want?* What makes you think I *want* anything? Just because I called you my dearest daughter and I said I you deserved to relax and have a good time doesn't mean I *want* anything."

"I'm sorry," Hannah said, backpedaling as fast as she could. "I thought there was something you wanted me to do for you."

"Well . . . now that you mention it . . ." Delores gave an elaborate shrug. "You could find Marge's brother Gus for me. No one's seen him since the dance last night. When he didn't show up for the family picture, they sent me to find him. But my shoes . . ." she glanced down at the stylish sandals. "They're just not suitable for trying to locate someone. You know what I mean, don't you, dear?"

Caught like a rat in a trap, like a fly on a sticky spiral of flypaper, like a deer in the headlights, like a moth fluttering helplessly against . . .

"Hannah?"

Delores interrupted her mental chain of similes, and Hannah focused on the here and now. Delores *had* wanted something, and now she knew what it was. "Okay, Mother." she said, bowing to the inevitable. "I'll go find Gus for you."

Nothing was ever easy. Hannah gazed around the small lake cottage. The only living creature inside was a small green frog hopping determinedly from the bedroom closet toward the kitchen alcove. Unless Gus had met a witch who'd turned him into the Frog Prince, he wasn't here. And since his Jaguar was still parked in the driveway, he'd gone somewhere on foot. But where? Eden Lake was far from being the largest body of water in Minnesota, but it would still take several hours to walk around the perimeter searching for him.

The frog gave a croak, and Hannah watched as he hopped up on the counter and into the sink. He landed next to what looked like a green-and-white capsule, and Hannah picked it up just in case it was something that could hurt him. There were markings, probably indicating the manufacturer, but they were so blurred Hannah couldn't read them.

There was no pill bottle on the counter, and the bathroom medicine cabinet had been empty and standing open when she'd checked the bathroom. She didn't know where the pill had come from, so she couldn't put it back. She supposed she could wrap it in plastic and toss it in the open suitcase that Gus had left on the bed, but the green-and-white capsule appeared to be a twin to the over-the-counter antacid she'd seen Gus take at the dance last night, and that meant it was probably expendable.

She glanced down at the capsule again, and her decision was made for her. The powder inside was already starting to leak out of the side. It was dissolving from the slight bit of moisture that had gathered in the bottom of the sink and there was no sense saving a dissolved capsule. She poked it down the drain so the frog couldn't get it, and ran some water to flush it down. That was when she realized that there were no dirty breakfast dishes. It was a cinch that Gus hadn't washed them. The dishtowel hanging on a rack by the side of the sink was bone dry.

"No dishes," Hannah said to the frog, who was looking at her with inscrutable black eyes. The frog didn't comment, not even a croak, as she opened the refrigerator door. A quick peek inside explained the absence of dirty dishes. There was no food. The only contents were a bottle of Jack Daniels and two cans of beer. There was nothing in the freezer compartment, either, except two trays of ice cubes, the old metal kind with the dividers between the cubes that nobody could pry up if they were filled too full. If Gus had wanted something other than a boilermaker for breakfast, he'd probably walked over to the Eden Lake Store to buy supplies.

Hannah ran a little more water in the sink for the frog and then she headed across the road to the store. It had been one of her favorite places as a child. The old-fashioned bell on the door tinkled as she pushed it open and stepped in. Some things never changed, and Hannah found that comforting. The interior of the store still smelled the way it always had, a curious mixture of ring bologna, dill pickles in a large jar on the counter, and elderly bananas that had gotten too ripe for anything except banana bread.

"Hello, Hannah." Ava Schultz came out from the back, pushing aside the curtain that concealed her living quarters from her customers' view. A small woman prone to quick movements and rapid speech, she reminded Hannah of a little brown wren, flitting from one part of the store to another and seldom lighting in one place for long. Ava had fashionably cut, perfectly coiffed, dark brown hair without a touch of gray. Delores and her friends were certain that, she wore a wig, since Bertie Straub, the owner of the Cut 'n Curl, insisted that Ava had never come in, not even once, to have her hair cut, styled, or colored.

"Hi, Ava." Hannah walked over to the main attraction, a shiny metal case filled with every available Popsicle flavor. "Anything new since I grew up?"

Ava gave a little laugh and joined her at the case. "See the three boxes in the middle?" she asked, pointing to them. "Those are Rainbows, Scribblers, and Great Whites."

"Never heard of them."

"Of course not. We didn't have them when you were a kid. All we carried then were the double pops in a variety of flavors."

"Rhubarb," Hannah said with a grin. "That was my favorite."

Ava's mouth dropped open. "They never made rhubarb!" she exclaimed. "You're pulling my leg, Hannah."

"You're right. I should have known I couldn't put one over on Winnetka County's leading Popsicle authority."

"I *do* like to keep up with it," Ava admitted. "The kids enjoy hearing about the new products, and they've got so many nowadays." She pointed to another box. "Look at those Lifesaver Super Pops. From the bottom up, they're pineapple, orange, cherry, and raspberry. And over here are the Incredible Hulks. They're part of the Firecracker Super Heroes series. The Hulk is strawberry-kiwi, grape, and green apple. They've even got Big Foot. It's cherry and cotton candy swirled together and shaped like a foot with a gumball. Get it?"

"Big Foot. Cute. Popsicles have come a long way since nineteen-oh-five when Frank Epperson left his lemonade and stir stick out on the porch and it froze solid overnight."

"You remembered!" Ava gave her the same smile a teacher might bestow on a favorite student.

"Of course I did." Hannah smiled back. Ava had told her the story enough times. But she wasn't here to discuss Popsicle history. She had to find out if Ava had seen Gus. "Did Gus Klein come in this morning?" she asked. "They're lining up for the family reunion picture, and they sent me to find him."

"I haven't seen him since he walked me back here last night after the dance. And before you can ask, it's not what you think. He just wanted me to open the store so he could get some milk to go with that carrot cake you gave him."

"So you opened the store for him?"

"Of course I did. A customer's a customer, even after midnight. He bought his groceries, and then we had a drink together and waited for the cars to clear out of the parking lot. He said he hid your cake behind the bar and he was going back to eat it as soon as no one else was around. I think that was so he wouldn't have to share. We went to school together, you know. Gus never was any good at sharing, not even in kindergarten."

Hannah thought about that for a moment. On the one hand, she was pleased that Gus liked her Special Carrot Cake so much that he hadn't wanted to give any away. On the other hand, she'd given him a half-dozen pieces, and he could have given one to Ava.

"Anyway," Ava went on, "he got the milk and some other groceries."

"Food for breakfast?" Hannah guessed, remembering the empty refrigerator.

"Not what a normal person would eat for breakfast, but that didn't surprise me. Gus was never what you'd call a normal person. From little on, he had his own style, you know?"

"What did he buy?" Hannah was curious.

"Sliced ham, bread, Swiss cheese, a half-dozen little packages of potato chips, and ten Milky Ways, the old-fashioned kind with the milk chocolate, not the dark. The last I saw Gus, he was heading back to the pavilion with his cooler and his sack of groceries."

"Cooler? What cooler?"

"Guess I forgot to mention that he bought one of those disposable coolers. I asked him why he needed a cooler when there was a refrigerator in his cottage, and he said it wasn't working right."

Hannah frowned. When she'd checked the cabin, the refrigerator had been working just fine. The ice cubes in the trays hadn't melted, and cold air had rolled out of the door when she'd opened it. Why would Gus lie to Ava about it?

"He was supposed to come back to pay me for the groceries this morning," Ava went on, "but he never showed."

Ominous music began to play in the recesses of Hannah's mind. It sounded like a cross between Bach's *Toccata and Fugue in D minor,* and the soundtrack of a bad horror movie. But she didn't have time to think about that now. "What time was it when Gus left here last night?"

"A little after one-thirty. I got ready for bed, that takes about ten minutes, and I looked at the clock before I turned off the lights. It was a quarter to two."

Hannah reached reflexively for her steno pad, the kind she

used for murder cases, but she quickly thought better of it. This was nothing more than a missing person, someone who hadn't shown up for the family reunion picture. Gus hadn't left for good, his car was still here, but he could have found a warmer, more hospitable place to sleep than the single bunk in his unheated lake cottage. There had been at least five dozen women at the dance last night. One of them might have thought a good-looking, middle-aged man like Gus was irresistible, especially since he wore expensive designer clothes and sported a Rolex watch and a diamond pinkie ring. Lake Eden women didn't meet many men who drove Jaguars and flashed around money at every opportunity. Gus could have asked one of the women for a late date, and she could have accepted. Then he could have waited with Ava until no one was around, gone back to collect the carrot cake, and walked to the woman's cottage bearing gifts of what appeared to Hannah to be picnic fixings.

The more Hannah thought about it, the more sense it made. Perhaps Gus and his lady friend had decided to skip the group photo this morning, and they were sitting at her kitchen table right now, eating a ham and cheese sandwich, and sharing the carrot cake . . .

". . . or not," Hannah muttered under her breath, and then she turned to Ava. "I'd better get going. They'll be ready to take that photo soon."

"I hope you find Gus. If you do, will you do me a favor?"

"What?" Hannah asked, knowing better than to promise blindly.

"Right after they snap that picture, grab Gus by the ear and march him back here to pay his bill. You can tell him I said that groceries don't grow on trees, not unless they're apples that is."

Chapter Six

There was only one logical place to look, and Hannah headed straight for it. The Lake Pavilion was clearly deserted. The sandy parking lot was empty of cars and contained only a crumpled cigarette pack, the remnants of what had once been a blue and white bandanna, and a neatly clipped coupon for a two-fer breakfast at Paula's Pancake House.

As she approached the entrance to the white clapboard structure, Hannah felt an odd prickling at the back of her neck. She'd experienced that sensation before, and it had preceded something unpleasant, something bad, something like discovering a body. She told herself that Gus was fine and she'd find nothing but the debris of a party inside, but her feet dragged a bit as she approached the front entrance.

Last night the pavilion had looked majestic, a gleaming white edifice in the moonlight with its open shutters spilling out warm yellow light into the humid blanket of summer darkness. Music had set up joyful vibrations in the walls, the wooden booths, the old chrome-and-black plastic barstools, and the revelers themselves, causing laughter and loud voices to peal out in a cacophony of raucous gaiety. Today it was . . . Hannah paused, in both mind and step, attempting to think of the word. *Sad.* The word was *sad.* The white paint was peeling, the shutters were warped from exposure to the elements, and there were a half-dozen brown beer bottles leaning up against the front of the building like tipsy sentinels. The party was over. Everyone had left. All that remained was the abandoned pavilion with its curling shards of paint.

Hannah tried the front door, but it was locked, just as she'd thought it would be. She knocked, calling out for Gus, but there was no answer. Someone else might have gone back to find Lisa or Herb to get the key, but Hannah had been born and raised in Lake Eden, and she knew all about the Lake Pavilion. In a town where Lover's Lane was regularly patrolled, and the parking lot at the rear of Jordan High was peppered with arc lights, the Lake Pavilion was the sole haven for teenage couples seeking privacy.

The shutter was at the back of the pavilion, the third from the corner. Hannah found the proper one, tugged on the padlock that had been rigged to open, and removed it. Gaining access to the pavilion was as easy as her high school friends had told her it was. She lifted the shutter and propped it open with the stick that was attached to the side of the window frame. The opening was a bit above waist height, but she managed to swing one leg up and over the sill. A moment later, she was sitting on the sill with both legs hanging down inside the building, preparing to push off with her hands and jump down.

She landed awkwardly, which wasn't surprising. She'd never been the athletic type. Since the shutter was at the back of the pavilion, not visible from the road, she left it open for illumination.

All was quiet within. The interior had an air of abandonment, and the only sign of life Hannah heard was the buzzing of several flies that had been trapped inside. As a child she'd believed that if she recorded the high-pitched buzzing of house flies and played it back ever so slowly, she'd hear tiny little voices saying things like, "Dig in. Hannah spilled strawberry jam on the kitchen table," and "Watch out! Her mother's got a flyswatter!"

A phalanx of giant trash barrels sat against the wall. Several were close to overflowing with plastic plates from the dessert buffet and Styrofoam cups with the remnants of coffee. Another barrel was marked with a familiar symbol, and it contained bottles and cans for recycling.

Hannah wrinkled up her nose. There was an odd combination of scents in the air, a spicy sweetness from the dessert buffet, the acrid scent of coffee that had perked too long in the pot, the lingering fragrance of perfumes and colognes, and the stale odor of spilled beer and liquor. Those smells were ordinary, what you might expect in a place where a large party had been held. But there was another scent under it all, cloying and sharp, and slightly metallic. It reminded Hannah of something unpleasant, something bad, something . . . but she didn't want to think about that now.

She fought the urge to dig in, to start picking up paper napkins, cups, glasses, and bottles, and stuffing them into the appropriate trash barrels. She reminded herself that Lisa and Herb had organized a crew of relatives to clean the pavilion this afternoon, and nobody expected her to do it. Her number one priority was to find Gus so that they could take the family picture.

A light breeze swept across the shaft of sunlight that streamed through the open window, setting dust motes twirling. As Hannah watched, several more flies buzzed by the beam of sunlight on their way to the mahogany bar against the far wall. The top of the bar was empty except for a brown grocery sack and a white, disposable cooler. It was obvious that Gus had been here. Perhaps he'd been so tired, he'd forgotten his groceries and his cooler.

Fat chance! Hannah's rational mind chided her. *He wanted those groceries. He asked Ava to open the store after hours for him. There's no way he would have forgotten them when he left.*

Another group of flies with the same destination in mind

flew in and headed straight for the bar. If this kept up, Lisa and Herb would never get the insects out in time for the slideshow they'd scheduled for tonight. Hannah hurried to the kitchen, soaked a rag with water, and grabbed a bottle of cleanser. They'd set out the dessert buffet on the bar last night, and it was apparent that whoever had wiped it down hadn't done a good job. She'd clean it thoroughly right now so that no more flies would come in.

Hannah had almost reached her goal when she noticed something. She stopped abruptly and peered down at the floor. The flies weren't the only insect group attracted to this particular locale. There was a line of black carpenter ants streaming toward the bar and disappearing behind it. They must be looping around because there was a returning line of ants and they were carrying morsels of something. Carpenter ants seldom foraged for food during the daylight hours, but their scouts must have discovered something tasty enough to call out the troops.

Hannah moved closer and let out a groan when she saw what had attracted the ants. They were retrieving sweet crumbs from a piece of her carrot cake. It had been dropped, frosting-side down, and mashed to a pulp by someone's heel!

For a brief moment, Hannah was livid. Gus had dropped a piece of her Special Carrot Cake and stepped on it. What a waste! But then she spotted something sticking out from behind the bar, something that looked like a shoe, on a foot, attached to a leg that was presumably connected to a person who was on the floor behind the bar. Hannah set the bottle of cleanser on the barstool as the ominous organ music that had been playing in her mind increased in volume, until the crashing chords almost deafened her.

"Oh, murder!" she breathed, hoping that her words weren't prophetic. But she recognized the shoe, the rich buttery leather that shouted designer footwear with an exorbitant price tag. And the trousers. They were part of an expensive suit that had probably cost more than she made all week in The Cookie Jar. She'd seen the outfit last night at the dance, and she knew precisely who had been wearing it.

Hannah took a bracing breath and made her feet move forward. Gus had come back to the pavilion to eat his cake, but he'd only enjoyed a bite or two before disaster had struck. And now, as Hannah stood there staring, he was lying face up on the floor with a bloodstain resembling a peony in full bloom on the front of his shirt.

Stabbed, or shot, Hannah's rational mind told her, but she ignored it. It didn't really matter what the murder weapon was. Gus was dead . . . or at least she thought he was dead.

Hannah tore her eyes away from the sight and focused on the area around Gus Klein's body. Pieces of her carrot cake were scattered on the floor, and the ants didn't seem to mind that there was a dead body in the middle of their picnic. Except for the cake and the ants, the floor was perfectly clear. Whoever had killed Gus had left nothing resembling a clue behind.

She shut her eyes, praying that she'd experienced a slight delusional episode, perhaps from lack of sleep. Then she opened them again to find that nothing had changed. Gus was still on the floor exactly where he'd been before, and there was no doubt in Hannah's mind that he was dead. His chest was perfectly motionless, and any fool could see that he wasn't breathing.

You should check anyway, the rational voice in her mind prodded her. *Think about how guilty you'd feel if he were still alive and you didn't call for help.*

"Right," Hannah said, swallowing hard. The last thing she wanted to do was touch another dead body, but the voice was right, she'd never forgive herself if Gus were still alive and there was something she could do for him.

Hannah glanced around. There was no pay phone in the pavilion. She patted her pocket. No cell phone, either. She'd left it at home again. That meant she *couldn't* call for help, so there was no need to . . .

So you can't call. So what? Ava's got a phone, and your legs aren't broken. If he's still alive, you can hustle yourself right over to the store and call from there.

"Okay, okay," Hannah answered the inner voice that sounded a whole lot like her mother's. "I'll check."

She swallowed again, took a deep breath for courage, and knelt beside Gus. She reached out with one hand to feel the pulse point at the side of his neck.

Nothing. Hannah pressed a bit harder. Still nothing. He was dead, all right, and it wasn't a pretty sight. She wanted to find something to cover him so the flies that were buzzing around couldn't gather. But that would be the wrong thing to do since she wasn't supposed to touch anything. Gus Klein hadn't stabbed himself in the chest so hard that he'd fallen backwards. This was a murder scene, and she had to call . . .

"Hannah?"

The voice startled her, and she shot to her feet. Herb was standing at the open window.

"You can stop looking, Hannah. We took the picture without Uncle Gus. Norman's going to stick around, so if he shows up later, we'll take another one."

"He won't show up." Her voice sounded strained to her own ears, and Hannah cleared her throat.

"What do you mean, *He won't show up?*"

Hannah cleared her throat again. "He's . . . he . . . call Mike and Bill on your cell phone, will you? It's important."

"Okay, but why?"

"They need to come out here. Uncle Gus is . . . gone," she forced out the words, knowing full well that the woman who hated euphemisms had just used one.

"You mean he left the family reunion without even saying goodbye?"

"Not exactly," Hannah said, sighing as she avoided yet another a direct answer. "Just tell them to hurry. And don't let anyone in until they get here."

Chapter
Seven

Hannah gazed out across the blue-green expanse of the lake. The sun was shining brightly, the water sparkled as she skimmed it with the tips of her fingers, and a light breeze lifted her hair from the nape of her neck. The warmth of the sun and the serene beauty of the lake was almost enough to erase the memory of Gus . . . almost, but not quite.

Norman rowed smoothly across the water. He'd been waiting for her when she left the pavilion, and he'd led her down to the water and launched the boat.

"Where are we going?" Hannah asked him. They were in the middle of Eden Lake, and she was glad to get away from the continual questions about what had happened, the speculation about who could have done such a terrible thing to Gus, and why.

"We're here." Norman dropped the anchor next to a huge bed of pink and white water lilies.

"Where's here?"

"Eden Lake's water lily garden. Marge told me her father added plants to it every summer."

"It's gorgeous. And all this time, I never knew it was here."

"Are you okay, Hannah?"

"I'm a whole lot better now," she said, admiring the water lilies. "All I need is a white dress and a straw bonnet with a ribbon around it and I could pose for Monet's *The Boat at Giverny*."

"Or the girl who's not paddling in Renoir's *The Skiff*. But I don't think she has a hat on."

"It's hard to tell with the impressionists. Of course I could always jump in and be a floating face in the middle of any of Monet's water lily paintings. It would be like *Where's Waldo?* and nobody would even spot me."

"Don't do that. Or at least don't do it before you have some lunch." Norman opened the hamper Hannah hadn't noticed before and took out two stemmed glasses. "Let's start with the drinks. Champagne? Or lemonade?"

"I think it'd better be lemonade. Mike hasn't interviewed me yet."

"Smart choice." Norman filled her glass with lemonade from the thermos he'd brought and handed her a sandwich. "Here. You need this."

Hannah accepted the sandwich and bit into it. "Egg salad. My favorite! And this is really good egg salad. Who made it?"

"I did."

Hannah looked at him in surprise. "I thought you didn't cook."

"I don't. But anybody can hard boil an egg, and the rest is just chopping it up, mixing it with other stuff, and spreading it on bread."

"Okay . . ." Hannah stopped and took another bite to be sure. "But this is gourmet egg salad. It even has bits of bacon in it. How did you make it?"

"I'm not sure. I just kept adding things until it tasted right."

"Well, please write it down the next time you make it. I want the recipe."

"Really?" Norman looked surprised.

"Yes, really. Egg salad is one of my favorite comfort foods.

If I eat it, I feel better. It's like macaroni and cheese, or chicken soup. It makes me feel warm and loved."

Norman smiled. "You *are* loved, Hannah."

Hannah wasn't sure what to say. She knew Norman loved her, and she loved him, too. She wanted to tell him she'd marry him and be with him always, but she couldn't. As long as she also had feelings for Mike, it wouldn't be fair to marry Norman.

Norman reached out to put an arm around her. "Sorry. I shouldn't have said that."

"I'm glad you did," Hannah said, reaching out to give him a little hug. And then she changed the subject. "Moishe was really crazy last night. I was so tired, I slept through the noise, but my downstairs neighbor called me at two-thirty in the morning."

"What was Moishe doing?"

"Racing around the tub in my master bathroom. He was making a terrible racket."

Norman began to frown. "Sounds like the Big Guy isn't happy. Is it because you've been gone so much lately?"

"Maybe. He also shredded my couch pillow and left little bits of stuffing all over the floor."

"*Definitely* not happy. I'd invite him out to play with Cuddles, but she's gone on vacation."

Hannah realized she hadn't really talked to Norman for at least a week. They'd both been so busy they hadn't had time to go out to dinner, or just sit over coffee and converse. "What's all this about sending your cat on a vacation?" she asked.

"Oh, I didn't send her. Marguerite dropped by and asked if she could take Cuddles to her friend's house for the week. Since she had Cuddles before I adopted her, I thought it was only fair. Her friend has an older male Persian, and everything's set up for cats. Marguerite thought Cuddles would be in her element."

"But what if she's not?" Hannah was a bit worried. Cats could be finicky about the company they kept.

"She's fine. Marguerite called me this morning to report."

"And if she hadn't been fine, you would have jumped in your car and driven up to get her?"

"Of course. I miss her a lot, but it's good for Marguerite to have this time with her. And after all, I promised we'd have split custody."

Hannah took another bite of her sandwich and gave a little sigh of pleasure. Norman just *had* to write down the ingredients! She'd never tasted an egg salad she liked better. "How about Clara?" she asked, knowing that Marguerite's sister was allergic to cats, dogs, birds, and a whole long list of other things. "Did Doc Knight find a better allergy medicine for her?"

"No, but Clara and Marguerite are taking separate vacations this year. Clara's going to a church retreat, and Marguerite's visiting her friend in Duluth."

"They've never done that before, have they?"

"No. Marguerite says they've always gone everywhere together, but it was Clara's idea to split up this year. Clara's crazy about Cuddles, you know. It's just that she can't be around her without having a reaction. She told Marguerite to bring Cuddles to the condo while she was gone, but Marguerite thought it would be easier to go to her friend's house."

"Kitty dander. It would take a professional cleaning crew to get all the allergens out of the condo for Clara if Marguerite brought Cuddles there."

"Exactly. So tell me more about Moishe. I know you've been gone a lot, but has anything else changed in your routine?"

"Not really, unless you count the cable."

"There's something wrong with your cable?"

"It still works, but our lineup's changed and they haven't sent a new cable guide. We've got over two hundred channels now, and I haven't been able to find Moishe's favorite."

"The Animal Channel?"

"Yes. Do you get it?"

"I get it, but I have a dish. How about Andrea?"

"They've got a dish, too. And Mother never watches it, so she's no help."

"You could always call the cable company and ask." Norman suggested.

"I will, if I ever get a couple of hours to spend on hold. I tried yesterday afternoon, but their business office isn't open on Sunday."

"I think I'm beginning to understand something here," Norman looked thoughtful. "Moishe's lonely because you've been gone so much, and he doesn't have his favorite television channel to watch. Is there anything else he doesn't have?"

"Mice. There's plenty to eat outside right now and the field mice won't come in until the first cold snap. And the maintenance guys replaced the weather stripping on all the doors and windows, so I don't have as many bugs."

"No Animal Channel, no mice, no bugs," Norman reiterated. "Maybe he's bored."

Hannah thought about that for a minute. "You could be right. But what can I do about it? I can't take him to work with me."

"I'll call around. Somebody's bound to know the new cable lineup. I'll get the number of the Animal Channel and tell you."

"That would be great!" Hannah said. Norman was always so good to her. "Maybe I should loosen a little bit of that weather stripping and let some bugs in for him."

"Don't do that. I've got another idea that might work. They're having a sale on Kitty Kondos at the pet store in the mall."

"What are Kitty Kondos?"

"They're three-story activity centers covered with carpeting. The base is the first story. It's a big tub-like thing that supports the rest of the structure."

"*Tub*-like?" Hannah gave a wry smile. "Moishe should like *that!*"

"True, but this tub is carpeted inside and out. He can race around the middle to his heart's content and it won't make any noise."

"That sounds good, especially for Sue and Phil. What's on the next tier?"

"It's the second story of the tub with an opening on both sides. A covered plank juts out and leads to a frame covered in carpet with all sorts of toys on strings. The clerk said she has one at home, and her cats just love to walk the plank and bat at the toys. And on the other side, there's a mesh hammock. She said it's a favorite nap place for older cats because nothing from the floor can bother them."

"And there's another story above that?"

"That's the penthouse, and there's a little outside staircase leading down to the floor. It's a faster exit than ducking down through the tubs."

"So how much does all this grandeur coast?" Hannah asked the important question.

"A dollar."

"*What?!*"

"That's what Moishe's will cost. I'm getting one for Cuddles, and if I buy two, I can get the second one for only a dollar. I was going to do that anyway and give one to Moishe for Christmas. But from what you've told me, I think he needs it right now."

Hannah's eyes narrowed. "Are you *sure* you're buying one for Cuddles and you're not just trying to help me out?"

"I'm positive. I've even got the color picked out. I thought blue would go best in the living room, and that's where I want to put it. She's already got the kitty staircase I built in the den."

The one you built for Moishe, Hannah filled in the unsaid

part of Norman's answer. He'd built the kitty staircase hoping that she'd marry him. And from what he'd said earlier, he still loved her even though she'd turned down his proposal.

"Well . . . if you're sure you're getting one anyway . . ." she said.

"I am. What color would you like?"

"You decide," Hannah told him, because it didn't really matter to her. Coordinating colors in her condo was not a high priority. There was also the fact that almost everything she owned came from the Lake Eden Helping Hands Thrift Store, and if she had a décor at all, it was economical eclectic.

"Okay, where do you want to put it?"

"You can decide that, too."

"How about right next to your desk in the living room? That way Moishe will have something else to do, and he won't bother you when you use your computer."

"Good idea," Hannah said, not willing to admit that the only time she used her computer was when Norman came over to give her a word processing or Internet lesson.

Norman stared at her for a moment, and then he shook his head. "There's something wrong, isn't there," he said, and it was more of a statement than a question.

"What could possibly be wrong? Didn't I just agree with everything you suggested?"

"That's just it. You agreed with everything I suggested. That's not normal for you, Hannah. I think you're still in shock."

"Maybe I am," Hannah said, and only after the words had left her lips did she realize that she was agreeing with him again. "I guess I must be," she concluded.

"Then you need a dose of your own medicine. Hold on a second and I'll get some."

Hannah watched as he reached into the picnic hamper and pulled out a covered cake pan. "Dessert?" she guessed.

"Yes, and you're going to love it. I had a piece while I was waiting for you to come out of the pavilion."

"It's chocolate!" Hannah started to smile as Norman removed the cover and she caught a whiff of the delightful aroma.

"It's Marge's Cocoa Fudge Cake."

"She mentioned it last night. And she said she was going to bake it today."

Norman dished it up on a paper plate and held it out to her. "I forgot forks. You'll have to pick it up with your hands."

"Not a problem." Hannah picked up the cake and bit into it. She gave a little moan of pleasure as she tasted it, and then she took another bite, a bigger one than the first. Once that was gone, she gave Norman a smile that came straight from her heart. "It's incredible!"

"Lisa gave it to me when she saw me packing up the picnic for you. She said you'd need chocolate."

"Oh, I do. I do!"

"She also said to tell you that Marge wrote down the recipe in case you want it."

"*In case I want it*? Of course I want it! Was there ever any doubt?"

"Lisa thought you'd like it. That's why she gave me both cakes. Marge made two so she could give one whole cake to Gus."

"Lisa thought we could eat *two* cakes?"

"No, but she thought seeing them out at the lunch buffet would make Marge sad."

"She's probably right," Hannah said, thinking about what Gus had said at the dance last night and how he was looking forward to a piece of Marge's cake.

Norman glanced at his watch and clamped the lid back on the cake pan. "Time to go, Hannah."

"Go where?"

"To meet Mike and Bill at the yellow cottage. That's where Patsy and Mac are staying. They volunteered to let Mike and

Bill use it as a temporary headquarters to interview the relatives."

"Now I get it." Hannah started to smile. "Lisa probably wants me to dish up that second cake for Mike and his team."

"That's right. She figured the endorphins in the chocolate would put Mike in a good mood and he'll be more likely to answer questions."

"What questions? It's the other way around. Mike's going to interview me. He'll be the one asking the questions."

"Lisa knows that, but she also knows you. She told me she knows that you get all the information you can so that you can investigate. She spent some time with Marge and Patsy this afternoon, and they all want you to help them. They said that the sooner you catch the killer, the faster everyone can get back to normal and enjoy the family reunion again."

"Then they're going on with the reunion?"

"Absolutely. They all got together and took a vote on it. People came hundreds of miles to be here, and it would be heartbreaking if they had to turn right around and go back home again. Granny Truog's here and she's over a hundred. This could be the last chance she has to see some of her relatives."

"Everything you said makes sense. It would be a real pity to call it off."

"So are you going to help Lisa out and take the case?"

"Why not?" Hannah asked, grinning as she threw her hat, the imaginary straw hat with a ribbon around the brim that she'd worn to pose for Monet, into the ring once again.

COCOA FUDGE CAKE

Preheat oven to 350 degrees F., rack
in the middle position.

Hannah's 1st Note: Marge says to tell you that she got
this recipe from two girls she met on the bus to Fargo,
Sandy and Patricia. They used margarine, but since Marge
is from a dairy state and she knows that there's no substitute for butter, she uses regular salted butter in her cake.
She says she made a couple of other changes too, but it's
been so long she doesn't remember what they are.

Before you start, grease and flour a 9-inch by 13-inch
cake pan. *(You can also spray with Pam or another nonstick cooking spray and then dust it lightly with flour.)*

2 cups white *(granulated)* sugar
2 cups flour *(don't sift—just level it off with a knife)*
_____

1 cup butter *(2 sticks, ½ pound)*
1 cup water
3 Tablespoons unsweetened cocoa powder *(I used
    Hershey's)*
_____

½ cup milk
1 teaspoon vanilla extract
1 teaspoon baking soda
2 eggs, beaten *(just whip them up in a glass with a
    fork)*

In a large bowl, stir the sugar and the flour together. Set it aside on the counter.

Put the butter, water, and cocoa powder into a saucepan and bring it to a boil over medium heat.

Pour the cocoa mixture over the sugar and flour, and mix it all up together. *(You can do this on medium speed with an electric mixer, if you wish.)*

Hannah's 2nd Note: Marge says you shouldn't be a neat-nik and wash your saucepan. If you make the frosting, you'll use it again.

Whisk the milk, vanilla extract, baking soda and eggs together in a small bowl. *(I used a 2-cup Pyrex measuring cup.)*

Add the egg mixture to the large bowl. Stir it until it's thoroughly incorporated.

Pour the batter into a 9-inch by 13-inch greased and floured cake pan.

Bake at 350 degrees F. for 20 to 25 minutes. When the cake begins to shrink away from the sides of the pan, it's done.

Hannah's 3rd Note: This cake is delicious without frost-ing, or just lightly dusted with powdered sugar. If you want a frosting, try the one below. Start making it 5 min-utes before the cake is due to come out of the oven and the frosting and the cake will be ready at the same time.

CHOCOLATE FROSTING

½ cup *(1 stick)* butter
3 Tablespoons unsweetened cocoa powder *(I used Hershey's)*
⅓ cup milk
1 one-pound box of powdered *(confectioner's)* sugar
1 teaspoon vanilla extract

Place the butter, cocoa powder, and milk in a medium-size saucepan *(The one from before that you didn't wash.)* Bring them to a boil, stirring constantly.

Remove the pan from the heat and add the vanilla. Stir in the powdered sugar, a half-cup at a time, until the frosting is thickened, but still "pourable." *(If that's not a word, it should be.)*

Pour the frosting on the hot cake, and spread it out quickly with a spatula.

Hannah's 4th Note: Interruptions happen and it's not always possible to finish the frosting at the same time you take the hot cake from the oven. For that reason I've come up with an alternative fudge frosting, one that can be poured over a piping hot cake, a warm cake, or a stone cold cake. Here it is:

NEVERFAIL FUDGE FROSTING

½ cup *(1 stick, ¼ pound, 4 ounces)* salted butter
1 cup white *(granulated)* sugar
⅓ cup cream
½ cup chocolate chips
1 teaspoon vanilla extract
½ cup chopped pecans *(optional)*

Place the butter, sugar, and cream into a medium-size saucepan *(You can use the one from the cake that you didn't wash.)* Bring the mixture to a boil, stirring constantly. Turn down the heat to medium and cook for two minutes.

Add the half-cup chocolate chips, stir them in, and remove the saucepan from the heat.

Stir in the vanilla and the chopped pecans, if you decided to use them.

Pour the frosting on the cake and spread it out quickly with a spatula. If you're pouring it on a warm cake or a cold cake, just grab the pan and tip it so the frosting covers the whole top.

If you want this frosting to cool in a big hurry so that you can cut the cake, just slip it in the refrigerator, uncovered, for a half-hour or so.

Hannah's 5th Note: Marge says that this cake smells so good, you might have to keep it under lock and key until it's cool enough to cut.

"Thanks, Hannah." Mike snapped his notebook closed to show that their interview was over, but when Hannah made a move to rise to her feet, he reached out to stop her. "Just one more thing."

"What's that?"

"You mentioned that you spent some time with the victim last night at the dance."

Through no choice of mine, Hannah wanted to say, but of course she didn't. "That's true. I told you I was sitting in a booth with Gus and his relatives."

"And they were discussing things they remembered from their childhood?"

"Right." Hannah glanced longingly at the cake that sat on the counter. She'd been closeted with Mike in the kitchen of the lake cottage for over thirty minutes. Normally, being closed up with Mike in an isolated cottage at Eden Lake might have been an opportunity for romance, but not today. Mike was all business. He was the detective, and she was the person who'd found the body. There were guidelines to follow, and Mike was following them.

"Would you like another piece of cake?" Hannah asked, hoping for the diversion of chocolate.

"No thanks. I gained half a pound yesterday and I've got to watch it. But you go ahead if you want to."

Hannah sighed. She could have used another piece of Marge's cake, but she didn't want to admit it in front of the man who curtailed his calories if he gained an ounce. "I'm fine. Did you have anything else you wanted to ask me?"

"Just a couple of things. Let's get back to the conversation you had at the dance last night. From what you told me, it sounds like it was a family discussion that didn't have much to do with you."

"That's exactly what it was, at least most of the time. Marge tried to include me, and so did Gus, but we didn't have a lot in common, especially when they started talking about the people they'd known in school."

"Did they mention anyone in particular?"

Hannah shrugged. "A couple of classmates that Mother probably remembers, and some teachers."

"And you didn't know any of the people they mentioned."

"Only the ones that still live in Lake Eden. And there weren't that many of them."

"So you weren't interested?"

"Not really."

"Then why didn't you make an excuse and leave?"

"I couldn't leave, not without asking them all to slide over and let me out. I was in the middle of a six-person round booth with Gus, Patsy, and Mac on one side, and Marge and Jack on the other."

"How long did you sit there?"

"Through two sets of music. That was probably between twenty and thirty minutes."

"Well, that's long enough."

Mike gave her one of his famous grins, the kind of smile that made her almost believe that she was the only woman in the world who mattered to him.

"Long enough for what?" Hannah gathered herself together enough to ask.

"Long enough to give me your take on the family dynamics."

Yellow caution lights began to blink in Hannah's mind, and warning bells sounded. "What are you asking?"

"I want your personal take on the victim. How did he get along with his long-lost family?"

Hannah hesitated. There was no way she wanted to mention the animosity she'd noticed between Jack and Gus. "I think he got along just fine," she said, "considering that he took money out of the family teapot and skinned out in the middle of the night to disappear for over thirty years. There were bound to be hurt feelings, especially since he didn't contact any family or friends during the time he was gone."

"I heard that the victim and Jack Herman were buddies at Jordan High. Did they appear to be friendly last night?"

Uh-oh! Hannah kept her expression carefully blank. Someone Mike had interviewed must have told him about the animosity between Jack Herman and Gus.

"Hannah?" Mike prompted.

Hannah conducted a lightning-fast inner debate and decided not to mention the fact that there had been some sort of problem between Jack and Gus. "I already told you, there were hurt feelings all around. And hurt feelings lead to resentment. The conversation I heard was polite, if that's what you're asking. But most of the time I wasn't personally involved, so I wasn't paying close attention."

"Do you think you would have noticed if there was any overt hostility?"

"Nobody came out and threatened anybody, if that's what you mean. And there certainly weren't any punches thrown, or anything like that." Hannah told herself she wasn't really being untruthful. After all, Jack hadn't threatened Gus, and they hadn't gotten physical. "When I found Gus, there was blood on his shirt," she said, deliberately steering the conversation away from Jack Herman. "Was he shot?"

"No."

"Then what was the murder weapon?"

"We're not sure yet. Doc Knight said it was something

long, thin, and sharp, like an ice pick or an awl. You didn't touch anything, did you?"

"I know better than that! It was clearly a murder scene. The only thing I did was feel for a pulse on the side of his neck."

"Then you didn't move him?"

"No." Hannah switched gears again. "I did notice one thing I thought might be unusual, especially now that you tell me it was a stabbing."

"What's that?"

"There wasn't very much blood, and I thought stabbing victims bled a lot."

"Not in this case. Doc Knight explained it to me. He said that if there are multiple stab wounds and the first few aren't fatal, the victim bleeds. In this case there was only the one wound, and death was almost instantaneous. Stab wounds don't bleed unless the victim is alive and his heart is still pumping. Gus died so fast, he didn't have very much time to bleed."

Hannah's stomach lurched, but she didn't want to let on that Mike's explanation had made her queasy. "I see. I really hope it wasn't my grandfather's."

"*What* wasn't your grandfather's?"

"The ice pick. If it *was* an ice pick, that is."

Mike looked a bit dazed. "You think the murder weapon belonged to your grandfather, personally?"

"No, not that. He gave them away at his hardware store for Christmas one year."

Mike flipped open his notebook and jotted that down. "Do you know who got them?"

"Almost everyone in town. People still had iceboxes in those days, and they chipped ice off the block for cold drinks."

"But everybody's got refrigerators now. Why would they still have ice picks when they're not needed anymore?"

"Ice picks come in handy for all sorts of things. I've got

one in my kitchen drawer at home, and I just used it to poke another hole in a leather belt."

"Yeah, that would work. I bought a leather punch when I went down a size last year. I didn't want to replace all my belts, so I poked another hole and made them smaller."

Hannah nodded, hoping he wouldn't guess that the hole she'd punched with her grandfather's ice pick was to make her belt larger.

"So what you're telling me is that there are a lot of similar ice picks floating around, and anyone in town could have one."

"Yes, but I don't know how many are left now. That was a long time ago, and they had wooden handles. My grandfather had them painted red and green for Christmas, and the name of his hardware store was stamped on in gold. If the handles broke or splintered, people probably threw them away. But if they were still in good shape, a couple of them could have wound up out at the lake cottages."

"Okay," Mike said, snapping his notebook shut again. "There's not much help there."

"Probably not. Did you find Gus's wallet?"

"Why do you want to know?"

"Because if you didn't, the motive could be robbery. Gus was flashing money around all night."

"Someone else mentioned that," Mike said, not saying where he'd gotten his information. "We recovered the victim's wallet. It was still in his pocket. And it contained a little over two hundred dollars."

"Good!"

"Why do you say that?"

"Because he owed Ava for the groceries he bought last night, and now she'll get her money. It's interesting that robbery wasn't the motive, though."

"We can't rule it out. It's possible that the thief didn't intend to kill him, and fled when he realized what he'd done."

"Or he was after something other than money. Gus was

wearing a Rolex and a diamond pinkie ring last night. When I found him, I didn't notice if he still had them."

"We recovered both of them, and Bill had the guys in robbery take a look. The pinkie ring's a fake. Everybody agrees it's paste. They're still not sure about the watch, so we're having a jeweler take a look at it."

"Why would Gus wear a fake ring?" Hannah asked him.

"Lots of rich people do. They keep the real jewelry locked in a safe and wear paste rings and fake watches."

"Why bother to buy the real stuff when you're never going to wear it?"

"Search me. Some people buy expensive jewelry as an investment. It's probably more interesting than buying a lot of stocks or bonds."

Hannah shrugged. "Maybe. So you think that Gus has a safe at home filled with real jewelry?"

"That's my guess. We'll have someone check it out when we get a minute. In the meantime, we're treating this like a routine homicide."

Was homicide ever *routine?* Hannah doubted it. But she chose not to argue the point with Mike. "Any suspects?" she asked instead.

"Everybody's a suspect until we start weeding them out. It all depends on where they were at two this morning."

"That's the estimated time of death?"

"Doc Knight puts it between one and three. And since Ava says he left her place after one-thirty, and he had time to eat a piece of your carrot cake and drink some milk before he died, we're asking everyone where they were between two and three in the morning."

"I was home at two-thirty," Hannah said, before he could ask, "and I can prove it."

Mike gave a little laugh. "Moishe's testimony doesn't count, Hannah. We don't speak cat down at the sheriff's station."

"Actually . . . it *does* count." Hannah was a bit disappointed that Mike hadn't drawn another conclusion about her middle-of-the-night companion. Or maybe she was pleased that he trusted her. She couldn't quite decide which. "Moishe was chasing around inside my bathtub, and Sue Plotnik called to ask me if everything was all right."

"I guess that clears you. There's no way you could have stabbed the victim, and driven home in time to take the phone call."

"Well *that's* a relief!" Hannah said, but Mike didn't react to her sarcasm. He just stared at her with a frown that knit his reddish-blond eyebrows.

"Why was The Big Guy chasing around inside your bathtub? Do you have mice?"

"No. And that could be part of the problem, right along with the fact that I can't find the Animal Channel on my new cable lineup."

"What do you mean?"

"I've been gone a lot lately, and Norman thinks Moishe's bored. When I came home from church yesterday, he'd ripped open one of my couch pillows and scattered the stuffing all over the rug."

"Maybe he needs a playmate. Why don't you ask Norman to bring Cuddles over to visit?"

"That would probably help, but Cuddles is up in Duluth this week, vacationing with Marguerite and her friend."

"Oh. Well . . . maybe I should drop by for a little cop-to-cat talk. I could tell him about bathtub noise abatement and willful destruction of couch pillows."

"Anytime," Hannah said, smiling at Mike's description.

"Anything else you want to know about the murder?"

Hannah blinked several times. Was she hallucinating, or was Mike actually offering to give her information?

"Hannah?"

"Actually . . . yes. It's been bothering me, and of course I didn't look. What was in that disposable cooler on the bar?"

"A bread wrapper with six ham and cheese sandwiches inside."

Hannah was puzzled. "You mean . . . already made?"

"Right. He must have put them together right there at the bar and stashed them in the cooler. I can't figure out why he'd do that, though."

"He told Ava that the refrigerator in his cabin wasn't working right," Hannah offered. "But I opened it when I went to the cottage to look for him, and it felt cool to me."

"You're sure?"

"Pretty sure. The ice tray was still frozen solid."

"Maybe it was cutting on and off. The old ones do that sometimes. The water in the ice cube tray would freeze right back up again, but he might not have wanted to take the chance with a ham and cheese sandwich, especially with mayo."

"There was mayonnaise?"

"Mayo and mustard."

The light dawned, and Hannah nodded. "I get it," she said, shaking her head.

"Get what?"

"That's one of the reasons he came back here, to use the mayo and mustard in the kitchen refrigerator."

"You know there was some in there?"

"Yes. We ran out of cream for the coffee, and I went to the refrigerator to get another carton."

"And you're sure he didn't buy the mustard and mayo at the store?"

"I'm almost certain. Ava's the type to keep a running tab in her mind, and she named everything he bought last night. She didn't say a word about mayonnaise and mustard."

Mike laughed. "So he took those from the pavilion refrigerator. That's pretty cheap for a man who flashes money around and wears a Rolex and a diamond pinkie ring."

"A Rolex that could be a fake and a diamond made out of paste," Hannah reminded him.

"That's true, but I already explained that. And that suit he was wearing didn't come cheap. Maybe he just forgot the mayo and the mustard. And then, when he started making his sandwiches, he looked around for some."

"Maybe," Hannah said, giving in because fighting about it would be useless. Perhaps that *was* what had happened. She had no reason to think otherwise.

"Okay." Mike gave her a warm smile. "Since you found the body, you don't need copies of the crime scene photos, do you?"

Hannah's mouth dropped open. What was Mike talking about?

"I can call you with the highlights from the autopsy report when it comes in."

"That would be nice," Hannah said carefully, still not sure why Mike was being so cooperative. She had a sneaking suspicion she'd be better off not asking, but she couldn't resist. "Why are you volunteering all this information?"

"Because you're going to get it anyway, one way or the other. There's no sense in trying to keep you from sticking your nose in my case, is there?"

Hannah thought about that for a moment, and then she shook her head. "No. Lisa already asked me to help catch the killer so all the relatives can relax and enjoy the reunion again."

"Okay, then. I've been thinking about it, and I'd rather have you share any information you learn with me. That way we won't be working at cross-purposes. And the only way you'll share with me is if I share with you. Isn't that right?"

"That's right," Hannah said, surprised that she could even find her voice to speak. Mike was actually sanctioning her sleuthing! Or was he? This could be some sort of a trick. She'd have to ask Andrea and Michelle what they thought of his proposal.

"Check it out with your sisters and see what they think,"

Mike continued, practically reading Hannah's mind. "Call me on my cell when you decide."

"Okay," Hannah said, pushing back her chair.

"One more thing . . . I'll give that cake to my team when they report back, but in the meantime, will you cover it for me? It's just too temping. I can smell it all the way over here and it's screaming, *Eat me! Eat me!*"

"I know exactly what you mean." Hannah clamped the cover on the cake pan and gave a little wave as she headed for the door. Was Mike serious about sharing his information? Or would he withhold crucial clues so that he could solve the case first? As she went out the screen door and started down the road to join the women who were counting on her to help them fix dinner for the reunion crowd, she had the uncomfortable feeling that Mike was playing some sort of game with her and he hadn't bothered to tell her the rules.

Chapter Nine

They were in the kitchen of Libby Thompson's cottage. Libby was Lisa's great aunt and her cottage was theirs to use for the reunion. It was a huge lime green monstrosity that had grown with the years until it took up three lots to accommodate the Thompsons, their children, the grandkids, and the great grandkids. Because the extended family was so huge and they all lived in the area, the cottage kitchen had been enlarged to hold two sets of double ovens, two stovetops, and two industrial dishwashers. With the exception of Sally's kitchen at the Lake Eden Inn, it was the largest kitchen at the lake and the perfect place for multiple cooks to prepare dishes for the potluck dinner.

"Oh, dear!" Marge said, looking worried.

"What's the matter?" Hannah asked her.

"It's this recipe. I'm just not sure it's appropriate."

Hannah glanced over at the recipe. It appeared to be similar to other hamburger-tomato-macaroni casserole recipes, and Hannah didn't see how it could be unsuitable. "It looks just fine to me. What's inappropriate about it?"

"The name. I mean . . . in light of what happened last night, I thought . . ."

"She's talking about Gus," Patsy spoke up.

Hannah moved over for a second look. She hadn't bothered to read the name before, and it was written in big block letters at the top of the recipe card. FUNERAL HOTDISH, it said.

"It's a really good hotdish," Marge went on. "I got the recipe from Joyce Fuechte. She's on the Funeral Committee at St. Peter's Lutheran in Swanville, and they served it at my cousin Ted's funeral when everybody came back from the cemetery. What do you think, Hannah? Should we use it?"

"I don't see why not. Just don't tell anyone what it's called."

"But what if they ask?" Patsy wanted to know.

"Make up something. I'm sure Joyce and the committee won't mind. You could call it Anniversary Hotdish. They probably serve it for anniversaries, too."

"That's a good idea," Marge complimented her. "An anniversary's a happy occasion."

"Not necessarily."

Marge turned to give her sister a sharp look. "You still haven't worked things out with Mac?"

"The only thing we agree on is not to agree. Would you believe Mac wanted me to ask Gus for the five hundred dollars I lent him right before he left Lake Eden? With thirty years of interest, no less! He even offered to do it for me. Can you believe it?"

"I believe it," Marge said, shaking her head. "Mac's never been shy about money."

"*Tell* me about it! But that's only one of the things we fought about." Patsy glanced over at Hannah. "I don't want to bore Hannah with the details. Hand me the onions and celery, will you, Marge? I'll chop them up and start frying them."

Hannah could see that Patsy was uncomfortable, and Marge didn't look exactly calm and serene, either. Since they were already upset, she figured she might as well introduce another upsetting subject.

"You know that I found Gus, don't you?" When both sisters nodded, Hannah went on. "Are there any questions that you'd like to ask me about how he died?"

Marge and Patsy turned to each other and frowned. "Not really," Marge answered. "The police told us everything we needed to know."

Hannah just stared from one to the other in surprise. Usually the victim's relatives wanted to know everything.

"To tell you the truth, Hannah, none of the relatives really liked him all that well," Patsy confided.

"Why?"

"Well . . ." Marge took over. "He just wasn't like the brother we remember. His personality was completely different."

"In what way?"

"He bragged a lot, and he flashed money around. People from Minnesota don't usually do that," Patsy explained. "And he seemed to think he was a lot better than we were. It was like he was *amused* by us."

"But he came back to see all of you when he saw the notice of the reunion in the paper."

Both Marge and Patsy shook their heads. "No, he didn't," Marge insisted. "Lisa and Herb didn't put any notices in the paper. All they did was mail out invitations to the relatives in our address books."

"So how did Gus find out about it?" Hannah was puzzled.

"We think he must have seen the posters that Lisa and Herb put up on Main Street," Patsy answered.

"You mean, he just stumbled on the reunion when he came back to see his long-lost family?"

"Came back to gloat is more like it," Patsy commented.

"Patsy!" Marge chided her.

"Well, it's true. We both know Gus wasn't like that when he left. He was a little wild, but that was because Mom and Dad spoiled him."

"The high school girls didn't help. The way they fell all

over him made him pretty full of himself." Marge gave a little sigh. "He was never a bad person, though . . . at least not
back then."

For the second time in less than an hour, Hannah kept her
expression perfectly blank. Maybe Gus hadn't been a bad
person when he'd left Lake Eden, but the years that had
passed had turned him into someone she wouldn't describe
as nice. A nice person didn't talk about all he had to the
have-nots in Lake Eden. A nice person didn't try to control
everything, or order other people to wait on him hand and
foot. A nice person would have made allowances for Jack
Herman when he learned that Jack had Alzheimer's. Gus
knew about it. Hannah had heard Marge mention it to her
brother. But Gus had still faced off against Jack the night of
the dance.

"Maybe Gus changed over the years," Hannah offered,
since they seemed to be waiting for her to say something.

Marge exchanged glances with Patsy. "Or maybe there's
another explanation," she said.

"What's that?"

"Neither one of us is sure he really *was* our brother Gus."

"You think he was *pretending* to be your brother Gus?"

"We don't know, for sure." It was Patsy who answered
this time. "We had a family meeting while you were in talking to Mike. Some of the relatives thought he was Gus, but
the others were positive he wasn't."

Hannah felt knocked completely off balance. She hadn't
expected this turn of events! "If he was an imposter, he was a
good one. He seemed to know a lot about your brother's
life."

"Not that much, really." Patsy shook her head. "We com-
pared notes, and all he really knew were the basics. We think
maybe he knew Gus and that's why he was so good at pretending to be him. Marge could pretend to be me around
people who hadn't seen me for over thirty years. Nobody
would know the difference."

"How about his appearance? Did he look like your brother?"

Marge nodded. "We think so, but Mac pointed out that any guy just under six feet tall with dark blond hair who was close to the same age could pass for Gus."

"Did Mac know him well?"

"Oh, yes. They were on several sports teams together at Jordan High."

"Did your brother have any distinguishing features, like moles or birthmarks, or anything like that?" Hannah asked Patsy.

"Nothing."

"How about scars from accidents or operations?"

"He didn't have anything other than the usual scrapes and cuts from playing baseball, and they would have healed a long time ago," Marge answered her. "And he never had surgery that we know about."

"Do you have any idea why someone would try to impersonate your brother?" Hannah asked the critical question.

"No," Patsy answered. "I mean, it's not like there was an inheritance for him to collect or anything like that."

"Marge?" Hannah turned to her.

"I don't know, either. But we all agree on one thing," Marge gave Hannah a long, level look. "We want you to find out for us."

FUNERAL HOTDISH
"Anniversary Hotdish"

Preheat oven to 350 degrees F., rack
in the middle position.
Or
Use an 18-quart electric roaster set
to 350 degrees F.

**Hannah's 1st Note: Joyce says this is easiest with three
people helping: one person to chop and sauté the celery
and onions, one person to brown the hamburger, and one
person to cook the pasta and mix the sauce.**

Start by spraying the inside of your pan, or the electric
roaster with Pam or another nonstick cooking spray. *(I
used a great big disposable turkey roaster sprayed with
Pam.)*

1 bunch of celery *(approximately 10 stalks)*
3 large onions *(We used four because we love onion)*
6 pounds lean hamburger *(We used 8 pounds
   because we like it beefier)*
2 two-pound boxes elbow macaroni *(for a total of
   four pounds—Joyce's Funeral Committee uses
   Creamettes Elbow Macaroni)*
1 large can *(50-ounces)* Campbell's tomato soup,
   undiluted
2 large cans *(46-ounces each)* Campbell's tomato
   juice

1 large bottle (*46-ounces)* catsup *(the Swanville Funeral Committee uses Heinz Ketchup)*
1 Tablespoon brown sugar
1 teaspoon ground black pepper *(freshly ground is
best, of course)*

Clean and chop the celery into bite-size pieces. Put them in a frying pan with a little butter and start cooking them over low heat, stirring occasionally.

Peel and chop the onions into bite-sized pieces. Add them to the frying pan with the celery and continue to cook them, stirring occasionally, until they're translucent.

Brown the hamburger over medium heat. Be sure to "chop" it with a spoon or heat-resistant spatula so it browns in bite-size pieces. *(Joyce and her committee do this in a pan in the oven.)*

Drain the browned hamburger, and rinse off the fat by putting the meat in a strainer and spraying it with warm water. *(We drained the hamburger, but we forgot to rinse it off with warm water—it was good anyway.)*

Cook the elbow macaroni according to the directions on the box. DO NOT OVERCOOK. *(Joyce's committee does not salt the water, but we did.)* Drain it and set it aside.

Combine the undiluted tomato soup, the tomato juice, and the catsup. Mix in the brown sugar and the pepper.

(Joyce's committee does this right in the electric roaster and then heats it before they add the other ingredients. We mixed up our sauce in the bottom of the disposable turkey roaster and didn't heat it before we added the other ingredients.)

Add the cooked celery and onions to the sauce and stir them in.

Stir in the hamburger.

Add the cooked, drained macaroni and mix well.

Once everything is thoroughly mixed, cover the disposable roaster with heavy duty foil and put it into a 350-degree F. oven for 2 hours, stirring occasionally so that it heats evenly and doesn't stick to the bottom. *(If you used an electric roaster, put on the lid, turn it up to 350 degrees F., and cook it for 2 hours, stirring occasionally so that it heats evenly and doesn't stick to the bottom of the roaster.)*

Joyce's Note: Joyce says to tell you that cooking the hotdish for 2 hours is mainly to blend the flavors since everything is precooked.

Hannah's 2nd Note: When we made this for the family reunion, we sprinkled shredded Parmesan cheese on the top before we served it. Marge says if she ever makes it at home, she's going to add pitted black olives to the sauce, because Herb and Jack like them so much. She's also going to make garlic bread to go with it.

Yield: The Swanville St. Peter's Lutheran Church Funeral Committee says this recipe will serve 75, but they always serve plenty of other side dishes with it. If you plan to use Funeral Hotdish as your only main course, I wouldn't expect it to serve more than two-dozen people, especially if they're really hungry.

Chapter Ten

"You're going to take the case, aren't you?" Michelle asked, looking young and gorgeous in white shorts to show off her tan and a pink camisole top that played peek-a-boo with her waistband. Her light brown hair was brushed back into a high ponytail held in place with a pink scrunchy, and she looked as if she were still in junior high, except for the fact that her figure was one that most junior high girls would envy.

"I'm taking the case. Lisa already asked me. And Marge and her sister asked for my help, too." Hannah took out another head of cauliflower and plunked it on the cutting board. Edna Ferguson, the head cook at Jordan High, had arrived to join the ladies in the Thompson cottage kitchen, and Hannah had gone to her mother's cottage to make the salad for the buffet table.

"I like Patsy." Andrea adjusted the straps of her gaily flowered, polished cotton sundress. It had an old-fashioned bolero jacket, and it was part of Claire's fifties collection. Hannah had seen it in the window of Beau Monde Fashions.

"We met Pasty when we were walking over here." Michelle explained. "She said she could tell at a glance that we were sisters."

Hannah didn't comment, but she knew it was true. Anyone who saw Andrea and Michelle together was struck by the family resemblance. And if you added Delores to the mix, you could tell they'd inherited their petite figures and lovely features from her.

"What size is that top?" Andrea asked Michelle.

"A five."

"It looks smaller than that. I wear a five and it looks too tight for me."

"It's a little too tight for me, too," Michelle admitted. "I washed it in hot water and it shrunk. I guess it's probably more like a size three now."

Hannah, who'd been listening to their conversation without comment, came very close to groaning. She hadn't worn a size three since preschool. While her sisters had gotten Hannah's share of their mother's petite beauty genes, Hannah had inherited her tall, gangly frame and tendency to be a bit overweight, right along with her frizzy red hair and freckles, directly from their father.

"You look nice today, Hannah," Michelle said, as if she'd suddenly realized that Hannah was feeling left out of the conversation.

Andrea, who was always socially aware, picked up on Michelle's cue. "Yes, you do. I like that shade of green on you."

"Thanks," Hannah said, glancing down at the forest green blouse that she'd paired with tan cotton pants. Forest green was one of her favorite colors. She looked up to see Michelle watching her, and she noticed again how much skin her youngest sister was exposing. "You're wearing sunscreen, aren't you?"

"Yes, and mosquito repellent, too. You don't have to worry about me."

"Right." Hannah exchanged a glance with Andrea. She was willing to bet that they were thinking the same thing. Sunburn and mosquito bites were the least of their worries. While there was nothing indecent about the way Michelle was dressed, her outfit would be certain to produce a loud chorus of wolf whistles if she walked past a construction site.

"Is Lonnie coming to the potluck tonight?" Andrea asked, mentioning the young sheriff's deputy that Michelle had been dating for over a year.

"Yes. And that reminds me . . . I'd better change clothes. Lonnie doesn't like me to wear this top around other men. He says it makes them slobber."

As Michelle headed off to the bedroom to change, Andrea and Hannah exchanged grins. "I think Lonnie's a good influence on her," Andrea commented.

"You could be right," Hannah agreed.

"Do you need some help chopping those vegetables?"

"Not really. This is the only good knife Mother has." Hannah crossed her fingers to negate the lie, a leftover habit from childhood. Their mother had a whole butcher block full of expensive knives on the counter, and every one was perfectly sharpened. But if she let Andrea help her, her younger, less-culinarily talented sister would probably chop off a finger. And Hannah would much rather tell a little white lie than be responsible for that!

"What are you making?" Andrea stepped closer and peered into the bowl. "I see cauliflower and broccoli chopped up into little pieces. It's got to be some kind of salad."

"It is. It's Sally's Sunny Vegetable Salad. I got the recipe from her last year. Lisa's doing a Caesar with black olives, Edna's fixing macaroni salad, and Marge is making coleslaw."

"And I've got my salad," Andrea said proudly. "It's got cottage cheese and grated onions in green Jell-O."

Hannah tried a few comments to that in her mind. *That sounds good,* was an outright lie, and *That's nice,* was too generic. She finally thought of something appropriate to say. "That'll look great with the rest of the salads," she said, just as Michelle emerged from the bedroom wearing white slacks and a lavender top with blousy, chiffon sleeves.

"Nice outfit," Andrea complimented their youngest sibling.

"Thanks. Lonnie loves it when I wear purple and white. I think it's because they're the Jordan High colors." Michelle walked over to stand next to Hannah. "Can I do anything to help?"

Hannah would have loved to ask Michelle to chop up some broccoli, but she'd already told Andrea the fib about the knives. "How about whisking up the dressing?" she suggested. "If Andrea will gather the ingredients, that is. And while you're doing that, I need to ask your opinion about something."

"What's that?" Michelle asked, as Andrea brought over the small cooler that Hannah had brought with her.

"Mike says he doesn't mind if I investigate as long as we exchange information. He sounded sincere, but I'm not sure."

"That's because you can't tell with a cop," Michelle said quickly. "They don't have to be truthful all the time. I think cop school teaches them how to lie to trick suspects."

Both Hannah and Andrea turned to Michelle in surprise. "Do you think Lonnie lies to you?" Hannah asked her.

"Absolutely." Michelle gave a little laugh. "Last night he told me that I was the most beautiful woman in the world."

"That's not a lie," Hannah said.

And at almost the same time Andrea asked, "What's wrong with that? You are."

"Thanks, guys," Michelle smiled at both of them, "but I know that's not true. Lonnie was lying, pure and simple."

"It wasn't a lie, strictly speaking," Hannah informed her. "Lonnie just exaggerated a bit to flatter you."

Andrea agreed. "Men are allowed to say things like that whether they mean them or not."

"But it usually means they want something," Hannah added.

"Oh, he did," Michelle said.

Andrea and Hannah locked eyes. It was clear that both of them were hoping the other one would ask. But the silence lengthened, and finally Hannah broke down.

"Okay, I'll ask," she said. "Are you willing to tell us what Lonnie wanted?"

Michelle laughed. "I was wondering which one of you would cave in and ask me. Sure, I'll tell you what he wanted. Lonnie asked me if he could buy me an engagement ring for Christmas."

"But you've got two years of college to go," Andrea pointed out.

"I know that. I told him it was too soon. And I said that if he still felt the same way next year, he should ask me again."

"Smart sister!" Hannah exclaimed, exchanging a high-five with Andrea.

"But the two years I've got left in school aren't the only reason I didn't want to get engaged now," Michelle went on. "There's someone else I might want to date."

"Someone here in Lake Eden?" Hannah asked, hoping that wasn't the case. Lonnie would be pretty upset if he had a rival he had to face every day in town.

Michelle shook her head. "Someone at school. And he hasn't even asked me out yet. But I think he will, and I want to be free to go if he asks me."

"That's probably smart," Hannah told her.

"I think so. I don't want to commit to anyone until I'm absolutely sure. I'm just like you, Hannah."

Hannah winced inwardly. What Michelle was admiring as a smart choice might actually turn out to be a flaw in Hannah's personality. There were some people who simply couldn't commit to anything. They sat on the fence all their lives, wavering between two choices, and ended up completely alone. Hannah didn't think that was what she was doing, but she wasn't completely sure. In any event, this wasn't the time for deep soul-searching. She needed their opinion of the alliance that Mike had suggested.

"We got off the track here," Hannah said. "We were talking about cops and lying. Do you think Mike was lying to me when he promised to give me access to information he learned if I'd do the same with him?"

Michelle looked thoughtful. "I don't know. Does he have anything to gain by lying to you?"

"Of course he does," Andrea answered the question. "He knows Hannah will play straight with him if she agrees to his deal. But she won't know if he's not playing straight with her."

"I'll know," Hannah said.

Andrea looked surprised. "How?"

"My sister's a member of the sheriff's wife network. Mike has to report everything he does to Bill, doesn't he?"

"Yes, but . . ."

"And it won't be too difficult for you to get a look at those reports, will it?" Hannah interrupted her.

Andrea began to smile. "It won't be hard at all. Tell Mike yes, and I'll check the reports so we can keep him honest."

Michelle manned the whisk while Andrea handed her the ingredients. Hannah chopped the last of the vegetables and as she was chopping, she thought of something she wanted to ask Andrea.

"When Mike interviewed me, he told me that the diamond pinkie ring Gus was wearing was paste, and he thought the Rolex was a fake, too. How about his clothes? Do you think they were fakes?"

"Are you talking about knockoffs?" Andrea asked.

Hannah shrugged, unable to place the word. "I don't know. What are knockoffs?"

"Designer styles that are copied by other manufacturers, mostly in foreign countries. When Bill and I went to Hawaii, we had a four-hour layover in Los Angeles. The taxi driver took us downtown, and I bought a fake Gucci bag for ten dollars. It even had the logo as part of the brass clasp."

"You mean the *G* and the backwards *C?*" Michelle asked her.

"That's exactly right. It was a clutch, really cute, and it smelled like real leather."

"But it wasn't," Hannah guessed.

"Bingo!" Andrea pointed her finger at Hannah. "Of course I knew it had to be hot, or a knockoff. Real Gucci bags sell for anywhere from ten to a hundred times that much. But I liked it, and Bill bought it for me."

"What happened?" Michelle asked.

"Well, the leather smell faded before I even got it home, and the second time I carried it, the clasp fell apart."

"Why didn't you have the clasp fixed?" Michelle asked her.

"Maybe I should have, but I didn't feel like going out of town to have it done."

"You could have taken it to Bud Hauge's welding shop," Hannah told her.

"No, I couldn't have. Bill was a deputy sheriff when we got married, and everybody in town thought he'd bought me a Gucci bag. How would it look for a deputy sheriff's wife to try to pass off an illegal knockoff of a designer bag as the real thing?"

"It would be bad," Michelle said.

"Fodder for the gossip hotline," Hannah added.

"Exactly. And that's why I tossed it in the trash."

"Wise move," Hannah complimented her, and grabbed the bowl with the dressing before Michelle could whisk the daylights out of it.

"Whoa!" Michelle exclaimed, staring at her oldest sister in shock as Hannah added the dressing to the salad. "Why are you doing that now? We're not going to set out the buffet for another two hours!"

"That's okay. There's nothing in this salad to wilt. You can dress it hours ahead of time. It's even a good idea, since it takes that long for the flavors to meld. All you have to do is toss it, cover it with plastic wrap, and stick it in the fridge. Then, when you're ready to serve, you just sprinkle on the bacon pieces and the salted sunflower seeds, and set it out on the buffet table." She stopped, took a deep breath, and got back to the subject at hand. "Now, back to Gus's clothing. Did either of you two fashion experts get a good look at them?"

"I did," Andrea said, which was nothing less than Hannah had expected.

"I didn't," Michelle admitted. "When everybody else was crowding around the car, I was saying goodbye to Lonnie in the church parking lot. He had to work, so I went out to the mall with a couple of my friends, and I wasn't invited to the Inn for the breakfast buffet. Then last night at the dance, Lonnie and I were sitting with Lonnie's parents, and Rick and Jessica. I saw Gus and I thought he looked really good, better dressed than anyone else there, but I didn't really get close enough to catalogue his outfit, if that's what you mean."

"Expensive, expensive, expensive," Andrea categorized, giving a little shrug. "I can't tell you how much exactly, but I'm sure the two ensembles I saw him wearing cost enough for a down payment on a Lake Eden fixer-upper. I'd bet my real estate license on that!"

Hannah just stared at her sister. That was good enough for her. Andrea valued her real estate license only slightly below her husband and her children. "Then the clothes were real even if the jewelry wasn't?"

"That's right."

"That proves that Gus Klein had some money . . . or at least he did until he spent it on master tailors, fine material, and shoes even Mayor Bascomb couldn't afford."

SALLY'S SUNNY VEGETABLE SALAD

5 cups chopped broccoli florets

5 cups chopped cauliflower florets

2 cups shredded cheddar cheese *(the sharper the cheddar the better the salad)*

½ cup golden raisins *(Sally says to tell you she's used sweetened, dried cranberries as a substitute for the raisins)*

⅔ cup minced onion *(Sally uses chopped green onions)*

½ cup white *(granulated)* sugar

1 cup mayonnaise *(Hannah uses Hellmann's—it's called Best Foods west of the Rockies)*

2 Tablespoons red wine vinegar *(I used raspberry vinegar)*

---

6 bacon strips, cooked and crumbled *(or ½ cup bacon bits)*

¼ cup *shelled,* salted, toasted sunflower seeds

Chop the broccoli and cauliflower florets into tiny bite-sized pieces.

Combine the broccoli and cauliflower in a large salad bowl. Add the shredded cheese and mix it up with your fingers.

Mix in the raisins and the minced onion.

In a small bowl, combine the sugar, mayonnaise, and red wine vinegar. Mix it with a rubber spatula, or a whisk until it's smooth.

~~Pour the dressing you just mixed over the top of the~~ salad. Toss it, or stir it with a spoon or spatula until the vegetables are coated with the dressing.

Sprinkle the bacon bits on top.

Sprinkle the sunflower seeds on top of that.

Hannah's 1st Note: You can make this salad several hours before serving. It's even better that way because the flavors blend. Just toss the vegetables and raisins with the dressing, cover the bowl with plastic wrap, and refrigerate it until your company arrives. Then all you have to do is sprinkle on the bacon bits, and the sunflower seeds, and serve.

Yield: 12 to 16 servings.

Hannah's 2nd Note: I made this for a 6-person dinner party once, and I ended up with about half of the salad left in the bowl. I refrigerated it to see what would happen, and it was every bit as good the next day!

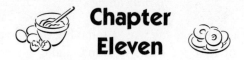

Chapter
Eleven

Hannah stifled a yawn as she loaded pots and pans into one of the industrial-sized dishwaters at the Thompson cottage kitchen. She had volunteered for the task to free up the other women who wanted to see the slide show that Lisa, Herb, and Norman had compiled from the old family photos that everyone had brought. Hannah had wanted to see the slide show, too, but she knew she was far too tired to keep her eyes open once she was snuggled down on a blanket on the beach, the alternate venue Lisa and Herb had arranged because the pavilion was still roped off as a crime scene. Norman had rented a giant-screen television, the kind they used for huge outdoor events, from a place in Minneapolis, and the men who'd delivered it had helped to run an extension cord from the nearest cottage. Even though she was across the road and up the equivalent of a city block from the festivities, Hannah could hear applause and laughter from the family members gathered on the beach.

The moths beat themselves silly against the screens as Hannah finished loading one dishwasher and poured in the heavy-duty detergent. Only one more to load and she could go home.

Hannah yawned again as she rinsed out the crock of a slow cooker and found a place for it on the bottom rack of the second dishwasher. She was short on sleep and long on worries. For one thing, she was still having trouble banishing the thought of that ice pick. It didn't make a whole lot of sense, since she'd found victims who'd suffered more violent and much gorier deaths in the past. But there was something about the fact that the killer might have used one of her grandfather's Christmas gifts to his customers as a murder weapon that really disturbed her. Perhaps it was because she had an ice pick just like it at home.

There was another reason Hannah was worried, and it had to do with Moishe. Would she arrive home to find that the cat she'd adopted had shredded every pillow and piece of stuffed furniture in her condo?

"Hannah?" a voice called out, accompanied by a knock on the wooden frame of the screen door. "I need to talk to you, Hannah."

Hannah recognized the voice. It was Ava from the Eden Lake Store. "Come on in, Ava. It's not locked."

"Do you need some help?" Ava walked over to the sink and stared down at a saucepan that was waiting to be scoured.

"Not really. I'm almost done. What's on your mind?"

"There's something I have to tell you. It's about Gus."

Hannah turned to look at her. Ava appeared extremely upset, and Hannah hoped she wasn't about to hear a confession! "What is it?" she asked.

"The Beesemans from Red Wing were in, and she mentioned that they weren't sure the body they found was really Gus."

"That's right. Marge had some doubts, and so did Patsy."

"And this Mrs. Beeseman . . . Betsy, I think her name was . . . said there wasn't any way to tell, since Gus hadn't had any distinguishing marks or scars on him when he left Lake Eden."

"That's right."

"Well . . . he did."

"He did what?"

"He did have a distinguishing mark on him."

"A scar?"

"No, a tattoo. It was two crossed bats and a ball, almost like that major league baseball logo they show on TV before every game."

"Are you sure?"

"I'm sure."

"But why didn't anyone else mention it?"

"I don't think anybody else knew."

"Not Marge? Or Patsy?"

"Neither one of them. It was a tattoo in . . . well . . . a kind of a private place."

Hannah didn't really want to ask, but she knew she should. "What kind of private place are we talking about here?"

"Backside private. On the left."

"You mean . . . ?" Hannah used her own anatomy to pat the area in question.

"That's it. That's exactly where it was."

"And this isn't just hearsay. I mean, you're sure this tattoo was . . . there?"

"It was there. I saw it with my own two eyes way back in high school." Ava stopped and looked highly embarrassed. "But it's not what you're thinking," she added quickly.

"I *wasn't* thinking. I was trying really hard *not* to think."

"Good. It's just that I went over to visit Marge and Patsy one day, and Mrs. Klein told me I could wait up in their room and read some of their movie magazines. So I went up there, and on the way I passed by Gus's bedroom. The door was open, and he was inside getting dressed. And his backside was to me."

"And you saw it?"

"Yes. That was when I saw it. He didn't see me standing there, so I hurried on down the hall as quiet as I could be.

And I went straight into Marge and Patsy's room. I'm absolutely positive he didn't know I was there, and that's all there was to it."

Ava finished her account in a rush, as if she'd rehearsed it several times before delivering it to Hannah. That made Hannah doubt that Ava was being entirely truthful, but she couldn't prove otherwise and it really didn't matter in the long run.

"Thanks for telling me, Ava," Hannah said. "And if Marge and Patsy knew, they'd thank you, too. It's one sure way to tell if the victim really was Gus."

Ava looked worried. "I'm not going to have to testify, or anything like that, am I?"

"I wouldn't think so. It really doesn't have anything to do with the murder. It's just a question of whether he was who he said he was . . . or not."

"Good! I was worried about that, but I thought I should tell you anyway." Ava headed for the door, but she turned back before she got there. "Thanks a lot, Hannah."

"That's okay. I'm really glad you told me."

"So am I, but that's not it."

"Not what?"

"That's not what I'm thanking you for. You see, Bill dropped by and paid Gus's bill out of the money they found in his wallet. So now I've got the money, and I don't have to be worried about that anymore."

"I'm glad," Hannah said, figuring that Bill had pulled some strings to do that. Everyone knew that Ava was on a tight budget and couldn't afford to absorb many losses.

"I'm getting a new Popsicle flavor in next week. Drop in and have one on me."

"Thanks, Ava. I'll do that." Hannah gave her a wave as she went out the door, and then she turned back to her dishwashing chores. At least now she knew how to tell if the body she'd found was really Gus Klein . . . *if* he hadn't had his tattoo removed after he'd left Lake Eden. She'd just finished adding several soup ladles, a bean pot, and two slow cooker crocks to the bottom rack when there was another knock, a very timid knock, on the frame of the screen door.

"Who is it?" Hannah called out.

"Barbara Donnelly. I need to talk to you, Hannah."

"Come in. It's open." Hannah made quick work of stashing a metal spatula on the top rack of the dishwater. She had no idea why Bill's secretary wanted to talk to her, but perhaps she could pump Barbara for information. "I thought you were at the slide show."

"I was, but Norman told me that my pictures of Marge and Patsy at Girl Scout Camp won't come for another half hour. And I wanted to see you, so I came right over." Barbara walked to the sink and picked up a scouring pad. "Do you need some help?"

"Not really, I'm almost through," Hannah said, experiencing a flash of *déjà vu*. "Why did you want to see me, Barbara? You look a little upset."

"It's what Marge said about Gus at the family meeting."

"And that was . . . ?" Hannah asked to encourage her.

"That they didn't have any way of telling whether Gus was really their brother. She said a lot of time had passed and they really couldn't tell by just looking at him. And then she mentioned that Gus didn't have any distinguishing marks."

"Right," Hannah said, that sense of *déjà vu* growing stronger.

"Well, he did except Marge didn't know about it. Patsy didn't either. Nobody did unless they happened to . . ." Barbara stopped and cleared her throat. "Maybe I'd better start again."

Hannah gave her an encouraging nod. "Go ahead."

"It was the summer right before my senior year at Jordan High. A bunch of us went out to the lake to swim, and we needed a place to change into our suits. You've seen the changing rooms, haven't you?"

"Yes." Hannah had used those same changing rooms when

she'd taken swimming lessons as a child. They consisted of a concrete slab enclosed by an eight-foot high block wall on three sides. The fourth wall did not complete the enclosure. Instead it ran parallel to the first wall making a passageway about four feet wide. It also stopped about four feet short of joining the second wall so that a swimmer could walk inside the hallway that was formed, turn the corner into the large part of the enclosure, and have privacy from anyone outside.

"You know how the changing rooms don't have a roof, and they're open on top?"

"I know."

"The Lion's Club had them built that way so they wouldn't get all moldy inside. My dad explained it to me. But the girls' changing room had a low spot on the floor right by the door. If it rained, there was a big puddle full of all sorts of nasty leaves and things and it didn't dry up for a couple of days."

"I understand," Hannah said because Barbara seemed to be waiting for her to say something.

"Well, we didn't want to walk through the leaves and yuck, so we decided we'd use the boys' changing room if nobody was in it. The only problem was that somebody had to check to see. I was the only one that could scale the wall, so I did and I peeked inside. And there was Gus Klein just ready to step into his swim trunks."

Hannah thought she knew what was coming next, but there was only one way to make sure. She clamped her lips shut and waited for Barbara to go on with her story.

"His back was to me, and I saw his tattoo. It was two crossed bats with a baseball in between. And it was on his left side, just about where his back pocket would have come if he'd been wearing pants. I jumped down in a hurry so he wouldn't know I'd seen him. And then we ran back to the car and held up the blanket my dad always kept in the trunk, and took turns changing in the backseat."

"Did you mention what you'd seen to anyone else?"

"Good heavens, no!" Barbara looked shocked. "I didn't want Gus to know I'd seen him and one of the girls would have told. Anyway, that's it, Hannah. I just thought I should tell you right away. I didn't want to mention it to Bill for the obvious reason."

"What obvious reason is that?" Hannah was curious.

"He'd think I was a snoop, or maybe worse. I did date Gus for a while, you know."

"I didn't know, but thanks for telling me." Hannah gave her a warm smile. "And don't worry. I won't mention what you said to anybody."

After Barbara left, Hannah turned back to the work at hand. She scoured two frying pans, a pasta pot, and a scoop encrusted with something that looked like scrambled eggs but probably wasn't. She stashed them in the dishwasher, poured in the heavy-duty detergent, and gave a final look around the kitchen to make sure everything was spotless. Then she turned both dishwashers on, gave a final wipe to the kitchen counters, switched off the lights, and headed for the door. She was just stepping out when she ran smack into Rose McDermott.

"Hi, Rose," Hannah said, wondering if she was going to get the tattoo story for the third time that evening.

"I was looking for you, Hannah. Hal's still at the slide show, and I wanted to talk to you alone."

"Sure, Rose." Hannah sat down in the old porch swing that graced the porch of the Thompson cottage, and pointed to a wicker chair. "Sit down and be comfy."

"Thanks. Your guy is sure doing a great job with that slide show."

Which guy is that? Hannah wanted to ask, but she didn't. She knew perfectly well that Rose was referring to Norman.

"Anyway . . . Marge called a family meeting this afternoon. Hal's her third cousin twice removed, you know, so we went. And she told us she wasn't sure that Gus was really her brother Gus, but since he didn't have any scars, or marks, or anything like that when he left Lake Eden, they had to wait for DNA testing to find out for sure."

"Right."

"Anyway . . . he did."

"Did?" Hannah prompted, even though she was sure she knew what was coming.

"Did have a mark. Gus had a tattoo. He had it when he was a senior in high school."

"And you know this for a fact?"

"I saw it!" Rose said, and Hannah knew she was nodding for emphasis, even though it was dark and all she could see was Rose's slightly darker shape in the chair. "Actually, I saw it twice. But I wouldn't admit it to anybody but you, Hannah. Hal would just die if he ever found out what Gus did."

Uh-oh! Hannah had all she could do not to groan out loud. She really didn't want to know the details of how Rose had seen Gus's tattoo. Twice. Tacked on top of her natural reticence to hearing something embarrassingly personal was the fact that Rose was at least ten years older than Gus, maybe more.

"Just describe the tattoo," she told Rose. "I don't need to know anything else."

"It's okay. I want to tell you. I've kept the secret all these years, and I know you won't say anything to anybody. It was right after Hal and I were married and he was running the café by himself. I was still working as head secretary at the school."

"I didn't know you worked at the school."

"I was there for four years. I started right after I graduated high school, when Mr. Garrison's secretary moved away. He was the principal before Mr. Purvis."

Hannah wasn't sure what being the principal's secretary had to do with Gus and seeing his tattoo, but asking wouldn't do any good. Rose liked to tell things her way.

"Gus was no stranger to the principal's office. He was always getting into trouble. Nothing big, but since the other guys looked up to him so much for being such a fine athlete, he was supposed to set a good example."

"And he didn't?" Hannah guessed.

"Not hardly!" Rose gave a little laugh. "Gus was a hellion, pure and simple. He was always getting into trouble. It was nothing big, just pranks and stuff, but there wasn't a week that didn't go by without Gus being sent to Mr. Garrison's office. And Mr. Garrison was an old Army man. He believed in corporal punishment if the occasion warranted."

"Go on," Hannah said, beginning to get a glimmer of things to come.

"Anyway . . . Gus did something particularly bad the week that school started. I don't remember exactly what it was after all this time, but it had something to do with the drama teacher and three dead frogs."

Hannah's imagination took off like a rocket, and she had all she could do to keep it in check. "And Gus got caught for what he'd done?" she prompted.

"That's right. Anyway . . . I was about to take some reports to the superintendent's office when Gus came in. I knocked on Mr. Garrison's door, showed Gus in, and then I went to deliver those reports. When I got back, Mr. Garrison's door was closed and all I could hear was a loud whacking noise."

"Corporal punishment?" Hannah guessed.

"And how! The first thing I noticed was that the Board of Education was gone. It was a paddle that hung on the wall right outside Mr. Garrison's office. It said *Board of Education* on it, and the *Board* part was in red because it was supposed to be a joke."

"I get it."

"Anyway . . . I knew right away what was happening. Mr. Garrison was spanking Gus with that paddle. And from the sound I was hearing, there was nothing between that paddle and Gus's behind."

"I understand."

"Now normally I wouldn't have done anything at all. I mean, I was only the secretary and Mr. Garrison had a right to punish the students however he wanted. It's different now, of course. But I was a little worried because Gus wasn't making any noise at all. So I went to the door, peeked through the keyhole, and saw the whole thing."

"What whole thing?"

"Mr. Garrison was spanking Gus. His pants were down, he was bent over, and his back was to me. I could see the tattoo as plain as day, Hannah. It was crossed bats with a baseball between them. Of course everything around it was inflamed and I knew Mr. Garrison had been paddling him for quite a while."

"What did you do?" Hannah asked, not able to resist.

"What *could* I do? I was Mr. Garrison's secretary, and I couldn't interrupt him. So I went back to my chair and I waited until he was finished and Gus came out of the office."

"And then you . . . ?"

"Offered Gus some lanolin. I had it in my desk drawer because my hands were chapped. And I figured that if it helped my hands, it might be good for Gus's you-know-what."

"Makes sense," Hannah said. "So you gave Gus some lanolin?"

"That's right. And next time he came in, a week later, he tossed the tube of lanolin on my desk and thanked me."

"That's nice."

"Not really. Because right after he thanked me, he dropped his pants and mooned me to show me that the Board of Education paddle hadn't left any marks."

"Oh." Hannah said, still slightly confused. "But I don't understand why you're so nervous about Hal finding out you gave Gus the lanolin."

"It's not that," Rose said. "It's just that Hal was in the Army with Bill Garrison, and if he ever found out that one of the students Bill disciplined mooned me to show that Bill's paddling had healed, he'd be really angry at me for not telling Bill about it."

"I understand," Hannah said, even though she didn't. It was another case of chalking it up to sensibilities she didn't comprehend. "Well, you don't have to worry. I'm not about to say anything to anybody."

"I know you won't." Rose stood up. "I'd better get back before Hal realizes I didn't just go to the ladies' room. Thanks, Hannah. And I really hope you catch Gus's killer . . . if it really *was* Gus."

Hannah sat there a moment after Rose left, just soaking up the peace of the night. The stars glittered brightly overhead and cast rippling streaks over the water. She could hear the mosquitoes buzzing, but her repellent was still working. It was a perfect summer night except for the puzzle of Gus Klein's murder.

When she felt capable of actually moving, Hannah got up and went down the steps to the path that led to the parking lot. She passed by the picnic area and heard sounds of merriment and clapping as the slide show continued. She walked on for a minute or two and finally arrived at the public parking lot. She was just about to unlock the door to her cookie truck when someone called out to her.

"Hannah! Wait!"

Hannah stopped with the key in her hand and turned to see Delores rushing down the gravel road. Her mother had exchanged the high-heeled sandals she'd been wearing earlier for a pair of ballet-type flats, but she was hobbling a bit, as if they didn't fit her.

"What's the matter with your feet?" Hannah asked, when her mother arrived at the cookie truck.

Delores sighed loudly. "They're Carrie's shoes. She always brings an extra pair. But they're too big and I have to curl my toes to keep them on." Delores stopped and took several short breaths. "I need to talk to you, Hannah. It's important."

"Are you going to give me a lecture about how embarrassing it is for you when I find dead bodies?"

"No."

Hannah reared back slightly in surprise. "You're not?"

"I'm not. I'm responsible for this one, Hannah. I asked you to go look for Gus, but I really didn't think you'd find him dead. It's all my fault!"

Hannah began to frown. In the bluish light cast by the arc lights that ringed the public parking lot, she could see that her mother was agitated. "Are you trying to tell me you had something to do with his death?"

"Of course not. The last time I saw him was when I left the dance with Carrie at midnight."

"But you look upset. What is it?"

"Marge and Patsy told everyone that Gus didn't have any distinguishing marks."

"That's right," Hannah confirmed it, "or at least they didn't *know* about any distinguishing marks," she amended, since she'd found out about one distinguishing mark from three sources so far.

"They wouldn't necessarily know. Marge's mother was death on body adornments. Marge really wanted to get her ears pierced, but her mother wouldn't let her. After Patsy got married, Marge and I went to visit her while Mac was training at Camp Ripley. He was in the National Guard. All three of us went to the doctor and got our ears pierced."

"That's interesting, Mother," Hannah said, even though it wasn't. And then, despite the fact she didn't really want to know, she asked, "But what does that have to do with distinguishing marks on Gus Klein?"

"Gus had a tattoo."

Hannah worked hard to appear unfazed by the question that flashed through her mind. *How did her mother know about Gus's tattoo?*

"This is highly embarrassing, but I feel it's my duty to tell you," Delores went on, "since you've agreed to investigate the murder."

"You don't have to tell me anything," Hannah blurted out.

"Yes, I do. You see, I dated Gus in high school, long before I met your father."

Hannah came close to groaning. The best thing to do would be to cut her mother off at the pass, before she could say anymore. "I don't need to know that, Mother. Was the tattoo two crossed bats with a baseball between them?"

"Yes!"

"And it was on the left of Gus's backside?"

"That's right! But how did you . . . ?"

"Three women already told me about it," Hannah interrupted her mother's question. "And there's probably a couple more waiting to catch me alone."

"And they *all* told you about his tattoo?" Delores looked outraged. "That rat! He told me he *loved* me! Who were they? I have to know."

"No, you don't. They all found out about the tattoo by accident."

"By *accident?* What do you mean?"

"One was visiting Marge and walked by his bedroom door when he was dressing, one peeked over the wall in the boys' changing room at the lake, and the other one . . ." Hannah stopped abruptly. She couldn't mention the principal's office because her mother would be able to identify Rose as the secretary. "He mooned the other one," she settled for saying, only recounting the second part of Rose's experience.

"Likely stories!" Delores gave a little snort. "I guess I shouldn't be surprised. I knew all along that Gus was a *rake-hell.*"

"Is that the same as a *bounder* and a *scoundrel?*" Hannah asked, exhausting her Regency Romance vocabulary.

"In a way, dear. It's a matter of degree. But it's water over the dam. It happened years ago, and I don't know why I got so upset."

"I do," Hannah said, before she could stop herself.

"You do?"

"Yes. You wonder how you could have been so naïve."

"And gullible. And you wonder how many people know you were that vulnerable back then."

"That, too." Hannah reached out and squeezed her mother's shoulder. Since she'd grown up in a family that seldom showed overt affection, this was tantamount to a hug. "The same thing happened to me when I was in school. But I was older and I really should have known better."

"Really?" Delores gave Hannah's hand a pat, the Swensen family way of returning a hug.

"There was someone in college, an assistant professor. He said he loved me, and I believed him, but I found out that he was engaged to somebody else."

Delores looked shocked. "That's just awful, dear!"

"It was. It took me a long time to get over it. It's one of the reasons I didn't want to go back to college after Dad died."

"Because he was still there?"

"That's right. He probably still is, for all I know."

Delores gave her a shrewd look. "You don't care enough to find out?"

"Not really."

"You're over it, then," Delores pronounced. "The strange thing is, I was sure I was over Gus when I started dating your father."

"But you weren't?"

Delores frowned. "I think I was. And I'm sure it wouldn't have bothered me a bit if your father were still alive. But he isn't. And seeing Gus again brought up old memories."

"I understand," Hannah said. And she did.

"But I almost forgot to tell you something. I talked to Iris Herman Staples this afternoon. She's Lisa's oldest sister, you know."

"I know."

"Well, she remembered some cookies that their mother used to make, and she said they were Jack's favorite cookies. She was just a toddler at the time, but she remembered them. Marge and Patsy did, too. They said their mother used to love those cookies so much, she'd hired Emmy to bake them whenever she had ladies over for meetings."

"What kind of cookies were they?" Hannah asked.

"Patsy said that Emmy called them Red Velvet Cookies. We were eating a piece of Edna's red velvet cake at the time, and they all agreed that the cookies were just like the cake, except that they had more chocolate in the batter and there were chocolate chips inside. They were even frosted with a cream cheese frosting. You've eaten Edna's cake, haven't you, dear?"

"Yes." Hannah thought she knew exactly where her mother's conversation was heading.

"I mentioned the cookies to Lisa, and she looked through her mother's recipe box, but she couldn't find any cookie recipe like that. Jack remembers them, though, and he told Lisa they were the best cookies he'd even eaten."

Hannah couldn't stay silent any longer. "So you want me to try to make a red velvet cookie that tastes like the one Jack remembers?"

"That's right, dear. It won't be too much trouble, will it?"

Hannah felt like laughing, but she didn't. Her mother had no concept of how many batches of trial-and-error cookies she'd have to bake before she found the proper balance of ingredients. And even when she arrived at a cookie recipe that worked, she still had no assurance that it would even remotely resemble the cookie that Jack Herman remembered.

"Dear?"

Hannah gave a tired little sigh and bowed to the inevitable. "I'll do my best, Mother," she promised.

"I asked Edna to write out her recipe for you." Delores

handed her a piece of notebook paper covered with Edna's fine, spidery writing.

"Thanks, Mother. This'll help."

"Then you think you can do it?"

"I'll give it my best shot."

"By tomorrow night? It's Jack's birthday, and I think it would be wonderful to surprise him with a batch of his favorite cookies. Unless, of course, you're too busy to bake them."

"I'll try, Mother," Hannah repeated, realizing that it would be another night with less sleep than she needed.

"Thank you, dear. Just let me know if there's any way I can help you."

Hannah was about to say there was nothing her mother could do, when she thought of something. "There *is* one thing . . ."

"You want me to help you *bake?*" Delores sounded even more panic-stricken than Andrea had when Hannah had once asked her to listen for the timer and take cookies out of the oven at The Cookie Jar.

"No, Mother. I can handle the baking part. It's just that I need to ask you more questions about Gus. Will you drop by the shop around ten for coffee tomorrow morning?"

"Of course I will."

"Good. I'll try to have a test cookie ready for you to taste. And could you ask Marge to let you into the library later tonight or early tomorrow morning to collect any Jordan High yearbooks you can find with pictures of Gus?"

"I'll do it right after the slide show's over. Marge wants to help you any way she can."

"Thanks. I'd better get going, Mother. I want to mix up some cookie dough tonight and bake it first thing tomorrow morning."

Chapter Twelve

Hannah wasn't quite sure what to expect when she opened the door to the condo, but when Moishe wasn't there to leap into her arms, she knew what she'd find wouldn't be good. He was hiding again and that meant trouble.

The living room looked fine at first glance. It even looked fine when she walked through it, eyeing anything that could be destroyed by a determined feline. The one remaining couch pillow was intact, and so were the couch, the crocheted throw from her Grandma Ingrid's farmhouse, and the bouquet of silk flowers Delores had given her for her coffee table. Her desk appeared to be fine, but there was something hanging over it, something new, something . . .

"Good heavens!" she exclaimed, stepping closer. Norman must have had time to deliver the Kitty Kondo because it was standing . . . perhaps *looming* was a better word . . . over her desk.

There was a sound, and Hannah turned to see Moishe sidling into the room. He stepped cautiously closer but stopped short of her, staring at his Kitty Kondo with narrowed eyes. Then he puffed up like a Halloween cat, and the hair on his back stood up. He made a low, growling noise Hannah had only heard him make a few times before, and she knew he was suspicious and fearful of the new piece of furniture that had invaded his living room.

"It's okay. Norman put it there for you," Hannah attempted to explain. "It's a Kitty Kondo, and it's an activity center for cats."

Moishe's ears canted back to flatten against his head, and Hannah knew he wasn't convinced. "Just look at this," she said, stepping up to the carpeted tower and batting at one of the jingling balls hanging from the pole on the second story. "Isn't that fun?"

Moishe's growl was not an assent, and Hannah was wise enough to know it. Some less savvy human roommates might have attempted to pick him up and put him on the activity center, but not Hannah. She valued the skin on her arms too much, and she didn't want to arrive at Jack's birthday party tomorrow night covered in Band-aids. Moishe would have to learn to like his new Kitty Kondo gradually.

"Let's go have some tuna," Hannah said, leading the way to the kitchen without checking the rest of the rooms for damage. Moishe had obviously been traumatized by the forest green Kitty Kondo that had invaded his living room, but a whole can of albacore tuna should take his mind off the carpeted intruder.

Two hours later, Hannah slipped on the oversized T-shirt she wore as a summer nightgown and crawled into bed. Moishe had cut a wide berth around the activity center when they walked through the living room on their way to bed, but he hadn't growled or bristled, and that was a good sign.

She certainly hoped the cookie dough she'd mixed up after two failed attempts would work. She'd read through Edna's red velvet cake recipe, balanced the wet and dry ingredients for drop cookie dough rather than a cake batter, and added more chocolate and some chocolate chips. There was no point in using the vinegar and baking soda, since the cookie dough would sit out on the counter and lose its fizz between batches. She couldn't use buttermilk, either, since she didn't have any in her refrigerator and she certainly didn't want to drive out to the Quick Stop to buy some.

The first batch she'd baked looked fine, but they were too flat and chewy. The second batch solved that problem, but they fell apart when she tried to take them off the cookie sheet. She thought she'd managed to mix up a winner with the third batch, but she was so tired her eyes were beginning to cross. She covered the dough and stashed it in her refrigerator. She'd be risking disaster by baking more cookies tonight. The third batch would have to wait until morning to bake.

" 'Night, Moishe," she whispered, reaching out to give her pet a scratch under the chin. Then she closed her eyes and fell asleep to dream of Red Velvet Cookies dancing around the floor of the Lake Pavilion while Frankie and the Frankfurters played the *Beer Barrel Polka*.

It wasn't morning. It couldn't be morning. But it must be morning, because a rooster was crowing in the living room.

Hannah rolled over and pulled the covers over her head, but that didn't help. The rooster kept right on crowing. Except it wasn't exactly crowing. It was more of a chirping sound, like a cricket on steroids, or a frog croaking in a falsetto, or a mouse being terrorized by a . . .

Hannah's eyes popped open. Her mind was working so hard to identify the origin of the sound she was hearing, it had awakened her. And it was the middle of the night. At least she *thought* it was the middle of the night. It was certainly dark enough to be the middle of the night.

There it was again, a sort of a high-pitched squeak. Perhaps it *was* a mouse being terrorized by a cat! "Moishe?" she called out, flicking on the light.

Moishe was nowhere in sight. He wasn't on the bed, and he wasn't in it, either, because there was no lump under the covers. He wasn't in the bedroom at all. The chirping had stopped, and Hannah knew that meant she had to get up. She gave a tired sigh as she pulled her slippers out from under the bed and put them on. It was a warm summer night, and she didn't need to protect her feet from cold floors. But her slippers were washable, and she did need to protect her feet from any tangible evidence of rodent carnage that might be scattered in her path.

There was nothing in the hallway. Hannah was careful as she walked. And there was nothing in the living room except . . .

Hannah stopped short as she spotted Moishe sitting proudly on the second floor of his Kitty Kondo. He was practically grinning at her, but not so widely that he might drop the prize in his mouth. It was a furry gray mouse with a string attached, and Hannah knew that string had been tied to the pole of kitty toys when they'd gone to bed. Moishe must have gathered his courage and gone up there in the middle of the night to get his prize. And he must be chewing on it right now, even though she couldn't see his jaw working, because it was making a new sound, an electronic beeping sound that seemed to be coming from her bedroom.

Realization dawned and with it, Hannah groaned. The beeping was coming from her alarm clock. It was time to get up and face the morning. She'd had a full four-hours' sleep, and that was all she was going to get.

There was a soft hissing sound from the kitchen, and Hannah sniffed the air. The last of the water had gone into her coffeemaker's basket and it was dripping down through the coffee grounds to join the fresh brew that awaited her in the carafe.

"I should have taught you to shut off the alarm clock," Hannah said, addressing her courageous hunter.

As Hannah turned to go back to the bedroom to shut off her alarm, Moishe made a sound that she took for agreement, but he didn't open his mouth. It was clear he wasn't about to give up his prey for an early-morning conversation.

It didn't take long for Hannah to shower and dress, and

she drained the last of her first mug of coffee as she walked down the hallway to the kitchen again. There she found Moishe still staring at the food in his bowl, the toy mouse held tightly in his mouth. "Can't have your mouse and eat it, too?" she asked, pointing to the food bowl.

Moishe made another pathetic closed-mouth sound, and Hannah took pity on him. "I tell you what . . . why don't I tie the mouse back on the pole, and you can catch him again later? That way you'll have twice the fun." With that said, Hannah reached for the mouse, and surprisingly, Moishe let her have it. As she headed for the living room to tie it back on the pole, she wondered if he'd really understood her and opted for twice the fun, or whether the food in the bowl had simply won out over the nonfood in his mouth.

She had time for one more cup of coffee. Hannah poured her last cup and leaned against the counter to sip it. Once she finished her coffee, all she had to do was retrieve the cookie dough, find her car keys, pick up her purse, and go out the door.

The phone rang, and Hannah mentally corrected herself. All she had to do was answer the phone, pick up the cookie dough, find her keys and her purse, and go.

"Hello," she said, answering normally since Moishe wasn't bristling.

"Hi, Hannah. You were up, weren't you?"

It was Norman, and Hannah laughed. "Of course I was up. I have to be at work in thirty minutes. I'm glad you called, though. I wanted to thank you for putting up Moishe's Kitty Kondo."

"You're welcome. I didn't think you'd mind if Sue from downstairs let me in."

"I don't mind at all!"

"Good. I think it's going to take a while before the Big Guy gets used to it. He made himself scarce while I was installing it, and when I tried to coax him closer, he hid under your bed."

"He's a faster learner than you think. You should have seen him this morning playing with that mouse on the pole. He managed to get it loose, and he looked really proud of himself."

"Great! I'll pick up some replacement toys the next time I'm out at the mall. The girl at the pet store said her cats tear up at least one toy a week."

"Thanks, again," Hannah said. "You're the most thought-ful person I know."

There was a silence, and Hannah knew Norman was a bit embarrassed by her compliment. "Well, you are," she told him.

"Thanks. You threw me off balance there and I almost for-got the reason I called. It's number fifty-seven."

"Number fifty-seven?"

"Five-seven. That's right."

"But *what's* five-seven?"

"The Animal Channel. For Moishe to watch. I asked around after the slide show last night. I thought you might want to turn it on before you left for work."

"Right. Thanks, Norman. I'll do that. And if you can, come in for cookies this morning. I'm trying out something new."

Hannah had no sooner hung up the phone than it rang again. She assumed it was Norman, who'd thought of some-thing he'd forgotten to tell her, so she answered, "Hello again, Norman."

"It's not Norman. It's Mike."

"Oops. Sorry about that. I just finished talking to Norman on the phone, and I thought he was calling back."

"Norman calls you *this* early in the morning?" Mike sounded shocked.

"Sometimes. He knows I get up early."

"How does he know *that?*"

"Because I'm always in the kitchen at The Cookie Jar by six at the latest, and he sees the lights on when he drives by on his way to the dental clinic. Anyway, how did *you* know I'd be up this early?"

There was a pause, and then Mike laughed. "Okay. Let's start over. Morning, Hannah."

"Morning, Mike. What can I do for you at the crack of dawn?"

"I don't think I'd better try to answer that. I just called to say that Ronni says to try seven-five."

Hannah was puzzled. "Try seven-five for what?"

"For the Animal Channel. Ronni turns it on every day for her dog. She's got a Pekingese."

"Ronni who?"

"Ronni Ward. Her engagement didn't work out, and she's back doing fitness training at the station. She just rented the apartment across the hall from me."

"Oh," Hannah said, wondering if she should start worrying about Mike and Ronni. The last time a woman from the sheriff's department had lived in Mike's complex, they'd been involved. And right after that unpleasant thought had crossed her mind, Hannah wondered if Andrea knew that Ronni was back in town. Even though Bill had sworn up and down that he wasn't the least bit interested in the winner of Lake Eden's bikini contest, Andrea had worried that they were more than employer and employee.

"Andrea knows," Mike answered Hannah's unspoken question. "Bill said he told her last night when he got home."

"Oh," Hannah said again, treading on eggshells. She wasn't about to tell Mike any sisterly secrets.

"Bill said Andrea thought they were involved when he went to Florida for that convention."

This time Hannah didn't even open her mouth for fear she'd say the wrong thing. Less was more, or silence was golden, or any one of several phrases that seemed to fit the situation.

"Anyway, I thought I'd tell you. Try seventy-five and see if it works. And if it doesn't work, try fifty-seven. Ronni sometimes transposes numbers."

"Good thing she doesn't do countdowns for NASA."

"Very funny, Hannah. Just try both numbers. It might save you money on couch pillows. And that reminds me . . . are you going to be at the lake this morning?"

"No, I have to work. I'll be at The Cookie Jar."

"Good. I've got a couple of things to do in town, anyway. I'll come in about eleven, and we can compare notes."

"Fine by me," Hannah said. "And thanks for telling me about the Animal Channel. I'm about to leave for work, so I'll try it right now."

Once she'd hung up the phone, Hannah headed for the couch and the remote control that she kept in the drawer of the coffee table. The drawer was fairly cat-safe, but she still pushed it all the way to the back and covered it with an old copy of the TV guide. Moishe had already killed one control, and it had cost her big bucks to replace it.

"Hi, Moishe," she greeted her pet as he jumped up to the seat of the couch and then even higher to perch on the back. "Just for fun, let's see if Ronni Ward got the number for the Animal Channel right."

When channel seventy-five came on the screen, Hannah let out a gasp of pure shock. She didn't know they were allowed to do things like that on television! She resisted the urge to cover her cat's eyes and wasted no time punching in fifty-seven. When a pride of lions replaced the scene that had shocked her on channel seventy-five, she smiled and reached up to give Moishe a scratch. "Okay, this is the Animal Channel. It's number fifty-seven and I'll leave it on for you."

Once she'd stashed the cable control in the drawer and collected her cookie dough, her keys, and her purse, Hannah noticed that one of the lions, probably the adult female, was stalking a zebra. " 'Bye, Moishe. Enjoy the show, but don't get any grandiose ideas," she said. And then she headed out into the early morning darkness to drive to The Cookie Jar and bake the day's cookies.

RED VELVET COOKIES

Preheat oven to 375 degrees F., rack
in the middle position.

2 one-ounce squares unsweetened baking chocolate
½ cup *(1 stick, ¼ pound, 4 ounces)* butter at room
   temperature
⅔ cup brown sugar, firmly packed
⅓ cup white *(granulated)* sugar
½ teaspoon baking soda
½ teaspoon salt
1 large egg
1 Tablespoon red food coloring
¾ cup sour cream
2 cups flour *(pack it down in the cup when you
   measure it)*
1 cup *(a 6-ounce package)* semi-sweet chocolate
   chips

Line your cookie sheets with parchment paper. Spray
the parchment paper with Pam or another nonstick cooking spray. *(If you don't have parchment paper, you can use
foil, but leave little "ears" of foil sticking up on the ends,
enough to grab later when you slide the whole thing on a
cooling rack.)*

Unwrap the squares of chocolate and break them apart.
Put them in a small microwave-safe bowl. *(I used an
8-ounce measuring cup.)* Melt them for 90 seconds on
HIGH. Stir them until they're smooth and set them aside
to cool while you mix up your cookie dough.

Hannah's 1st Note: Mixing this dough is easier with an electric mixer. You can do it by hand, but it takes some muscle.

Combine the butter, brown sugar, and white sugar together in the bowl of an electric mixer. Beat them on medium speed until they're smooth. This should take less than a minute.

Add the baking soda and salt, and resume beating on medium again for another minute, or until they're incorporated.

Add the egg and beat on medium until the batter is smooth *(an additional minute should do it.)* Add the red food coloring and mix for about 30 seconds.

Shut off the mixer and scrape down the bowl. Then add the melted chocolate and mix again for another minute on medium speed.

Shut off the mixer and scrape down the bowl again. At low speed, mix in half of the flour. *(That's one cup.)* When the flour is incorporated, mix in the sour cream.

Scrape down the bowl again and add the rest of the flour. *(That's the second cup.)* Beat until the flour is fully incorporated.

Remove the bowl from the mixer and give it a stir with a spoon. Mix in the chocolate chips by hand. *(A firm rubber spatula works nicely.)*

Use a teaspoon to spoon the dough onto the parchment-lined cookie sheets, 12 cookies to a standard-sized sheet. *(If the dough is too sticky for you to work with, chill it for a half-hour or so, and try again.)* Bake the cookies at 375 degrees F., for 9 to 11 minutes, or until they rise and become firm. *(Mine took exactly 9 minutes.)*

Slide the parchment from the cookie sheets and onto a wire rack. Let the cookies cool on the rack while the next sheet of cookies is baking. When the next sheet of cookies is ready, pull the cooled cookies onto the counter or table and slide the parchment paper with the hot cookies onto the rack. Keep alternating until all the dough has been baked.

When all the cookies are cool, peel them off the parchment paper and put them on waxed paper for frosting.

Cream Cheese Frosting

¼ cup softened butter *(½ stick, ⅛ pound)*
4 ounces softened cream cheese *(half of an 8-ounce package)*
½ teaspoon vanilla extract
2 cups confectioner's *(powdered)* sugar *(no need to sift unless it's got big lumps)*

Mix the softened butter with the softened cream cheese and the vanilla until the mixture is smooth.

Hannah's 2ⁿᵈ Note: Do this next step at room temperature. If you heated the cream cheese or the butter to soften it, make sure it's cooled down before you continue.

~~Add the confectioner's sugar in half-cup increments~~ until the frosting is of proper spreading consistency. *(You'll use all, or almost all, of the sugar.)*

A batch of Red Velvet Cookies yields about 3 dozen, depending on cookie size. They're soft, velvety, and chocolaty, and they'll end up being everyone's favorite.

Hannah's 3ʳᵈ Note: If you really want to pull out all the stops, brush the tops of your baked cookies with melted raspberry jam, let it dry, and then frost them with Cream Cheese Frosting.

"We're done!" Hannah said, carrying two mugs of coffee over to the stainless steel workstation in the kitchen of The Cookie Jar.

Lisa glanced up at the clock with a smile. "I know, and it's only seven."

"You got here at six. You really shouldn't have come in, Lisa," Hannah gently chided her partner. "I told you to take the week of the reunion off."

"I took yesterday off. That's enough. From now on I'm coming in at six to help with the baking."

"But that's a lot of work for you, with the reunion and all."

"It's a lot of work for *you*, too! You're baking cookies every morning and then coming out to the lake every afternoon to help with the dinner buffet."

"Okay, you win." Hannah held up her hands in surrender. "I appreciate the help. But don't feel you have to come in if you're too tired, okay?"

"Okay, as long as you don't feel you have to come out to the lake to help with dinner."

Hannah laughed. "Do we have a culinary standoff?"

"I think so." Lisa turned and pointed to the pan of bar cookies she'd baked. "The bars are cool enough to cut. Do you want to taste my new invention?"

"Sure. What do you call them?"

"Rocky Road Bar Cookies, because they remind me of rocky road ice cream." Lisa walked over to cut a piece and brought it back to Hannah.

"I see nuts, and marshmallows, and chocolate, and . . . I don't know what else."

"Go ahead and taste. And give me your honest opinion."

Hannah took a bite and chewed. The bars were delicious. "Yummy!" she pronounced. "On a goodness scale of one to ten, these are a twelve."

"Do they remind you of rocky road ice cream?"

"Yes. And they also remind me of S'mores. We used to make those on Girl Scout campouts."

"What's a S'more?"

"A graham cracker with a square of Hershey's milk chocolate on top. You toast a marshmallow over the campfire, plunk it on top of the chocolate square, and cover it with another graham cracker. Then you eat it when it's hot and everything just melts in your mouth."

"That sounds great! I think I missed a lot by not joining the Girl Scouts."

"Why didn't you?" Hannah asked.

"They met after school on Wednesdays, and I had to get right home. Mom was sick, and Dad worked an extra two hours four days a week so he could take Friday off to do all the stuff that was closed on the weekends."

Hannah kicked herself mentally for not realizing that Lisa would have a selfless reason for not joining the Girl Scouts. "You're talking about things like going to the bank?"

"Yes. And driving her to doctor's appointments and other medical stuff. She went in for dialysis on Fridays."

"That must have been hard on you, Lisa."

"Yes, but worth it. Mom had some good times when she was in remission and all my sisters and brothers would come to visit."

Hannah saw Lisa blink several times and knew she was remembering her mother and grieving for her. It was time to introduce a happier subject. "I've got something for you to taste," she announced.

"What's that?"

"Red Velvet Cookies."

Lisa stared at her in something close to shock. "You mean you've got Mom's recipe? The one Dad remembers?"

"No, but I put one together that I *hope* is like your mom's. My mother thought it would be a nice surprise for your dad's birthday."

"It's great! You're wonderful, Hannah!"

"Don't get too excited. They might not be like your mother's cookies at all. I understand she stopped baking them years ago."

"That's what Iris said when she told me about them."

"Do you remember them?" Hannah asked.

"No. I think she'd already stopped baking them. But I get to taste one anyway, don't I?"

"Of course. I haven't tasted one yet, either."

Mere seconds later, both partners had fresh mugs of coffee and a cookie on a napkin in front of them to taste. Hannah tried hers first and pronounced it good, but perhaps not the exact cookie Emily Herman had baked.

"It's better than good, it's superb," Lisa declared. "The chocolate melts in your mouth and the cream cheese in the frosting sends it off the top of that goodness scale you were talking about earlier."

"Thanks, Lisa. When you get out to the lake will you find your sister and ask her what she thinks? Have Marge and Patsy try them, too. If they taste like your mother's, I'll bake another batch before I come out this afternoon. Maybe they'll jog your dad's memory and he can tell us more about the night Gus left town and why there was bad blood between them."

"Do you really think your cookies can cure Dad's Alzheimer's?"

"No, but the chocolate is bound to be good for him."

"That's true." Lisa gave a little laugh. "And even if your cookies don't give us any answers, they'll be a lovely birthday present for him."

After Lisa left, Hannah got the coffee shop ready for customers. This meant filling the sugar and artificial sweetener containers that sat on each table and setting out dishes with coffee creamer. Once the napkin dispensers were filled and the tables were wiped down a final time, Hannah sat down at her favorite table in the back of the coffee shop and waited for Luanne to arrive.

Nothing was moving on the street except Jon Walker's old Irish setter, who was strolling from the drugstore up the block. Jon was nowhere in sight, so Hannah unlocked the front door of the coffee shop and went out to intercept Skippy. But just as she got there, Jon appeared at the end of the block with a leash in hand. A handsome man of Chippewa ancestry, Jon was the town druggist and the owner of Lake Eden Neighborhood Pharmacy.

"Hi, Jon," Hannah greeted him.

"Morning, Hannah. Skippy started without me this morning. By the time I grabbed the leash, he was halfway up the block and headed for your place."

"He must have smelled the cookies. Want to come in and have one?"

"Sure. Skippy, too? I can take him back to the drugstore if you don't want him inside." Jon bent down and snapped on the leash.

"Skippy, too. The health board's never around this early, and technically I'm still closed so it doesn't matter anyway."

Once Jon was settled in a chair with two of his favorite Molasses Crackles and a mug of coffee, and Skippy was sitting at his feet with one of the dog biscuits Hannah kept for visiting dogs, she asked the question she'd been planning to ask him ever since she'd seen the pill in the cottage Gus Klein had inhabited so briefly at the lake. "I saw someone take a pill the other night and I'm wondering what it was. I found another one the next day, so I got a good look at it."

"Do I want to know who took the pill and where you saw it?"

"Not really."

"Okay. What did it look like?"

"It was a capsule. One end was green and the other end was white."

"A green-and-white capsule," Jon repeated. "Was it a regular size capsule, or a really skinny one?"

Hannah thought about that for a moment. "I think it was a regular size. Mother used to take gelatin capsules to make her nails stronger. It was that size."

"Regular, then. How about markings? Did you see any?"

"There was something there, but it was blurred and I couldn't make it out."

"Do you know the difference between a capsule and a caplet?"

"I think so. Caplets are solid, right?"

"Right. But this capsule you saw was one you could have pulled apart like your Mother's gelatin capsules?"

"That's right. Do you have any idea what it was?"

"I may have, if you described it accurately." Jon leaned a little closer, even though the coffee shop wasn't open yet and there was no one else at the tables. "Does this have anything to do with the murder out at the pavilion?"

"Uh . . ." Hannah dithered for about two seconds and then she decided to play it straight. "It may have. I don't know for sure."

Jon covered his eyes with his hands. "I wish you hadn't said that, Hannah. You could be asking me to give you information that I should be giving to the sheriff's department."

"Have they asked you anything about green-and-white capsules?"

"No."

"I don't think they will, since I'm the only one who saw it and I flushed it down the drain so the frog couldn't get it."

Jon gave a little groan. "I'm not even going to *ask* you about the frog. It's too early in the day. You're going to owe me big time for this, Hannah."

"How about a dozen Molasses Crackles?"

"You got it. But you don't really have to give me cookies. As long as I'm not breaking any laws, I'll be happy to tell you anything I know."

"Great! Tell me, please?"

"It's like I said before . . . if your description is accurate, it sounds like an amphetamine capsule to me."

"Really!" Hannah began to frown. "What, exactly, does an amphetamine do?"

"It increases heart rate, decreases appetite, and makes you feel alert. It used to be prescribed as a diet pill, but it has addictive properties and some nasty side effects, like sleeplessness and occasional hallucinations. It's more tightly regulated now."

"Then the pill I saw couldn't have been an over-the-counter antacid?"

Jon shook his head. "I don't think so, not unless it's something so new I haven't seen it yet. I know I don't have any antacids like that at the store."

"Okay," Hannah said. "Thanks, Jon. You've helped me a lot. Hold on a second and I'll pack up some Molasses Crackles for you."

A few minutes later, Hannah saw Jon and Skippy out the door with a dozen Molasses Crackles, two more dog biscuits, and the steak bone she'd been saving for the Malamute who lived next to Lisa and Herb's neighbors. She still didn't understand what Gus had been doing with an amphetamine and why he'd called it an antacid, but she didn't have time to think about that right now. She had to bake another couple of batches of Red Velvet Cookies before the birthday party tonight, catch Gus Klein's killer without alienating Mike in the process, go out to the lake to make three batches of Wanmansita Casserole to serve at Jack's party, and check on her wayward cat to make sure he was still behaving. She knew she could do it, but it would take all the energy she had to give, and then some!

ROCKY ROAD BAR COOKIES
(S'MORES)

Preheat oven to 350 degrees F., rack
in the middle position.

24 graham crackers (*12 double ones*)
2 cups miniature marshmallows (*white, not colored*)
6-ounce package semi-sweet chocolate chips (*1 cup*)
1 cup salted cashews
½ cup butter (*1 stick, ¼ pound*)
½ cup dark brown sugar, firmly packed
1 teaspoon vanilla extract

Spray a 9-inch by 13-inch cake pan with Pam or other nonstick spray. (*If you like, buy a disposable foil pan in the grocery store, place it on a cookie sheet to support the bottom, and then you won't have to clean up.*)

Line the bottom of the pan with a layer of graham crackers. (*It's okay to overlap a bit.*)

Sprinkle the graham crackers with the marshmallows.

Sprinkle the marshmallows with the chocolate chips.

Sprinkle the chocolate chips with the cashews.

In a small saucepan over low heat, combine the butter and brown sugar. Stir the mixture constantly until the sugar is dissolved.

Turn off the heat, move the saucepan to a cool burner, and stir in the vanilla.

Drizzle the contents of the saucepan evenly over the contents of the cake pan.

Bake at 350 degrees F. for 10 to 12 minutes or until the marshmallows are golden on top. Cool in the pan on a wire rack.

When the Rocky Road Bar Cookies are cool, cut them into brownie-sized bars and serve.

If there are any leftovers *(which there won't be unless you have less than three people)* store them in the refrigerator in a covered container. They can also be wrapped, sealed in a freezer bag, and frozen for up to two months.

Yield: 2 ½ to 3 dozen yummy treats that will please adults and kids alike.

Chapter Fourteen

"This is a wonderful cookie, Hannah!"

"That's what Lisa said. But do you think it's anything like the cookies Iris told you about?"

Delores gave a dainty little shrug. "I'm not sure, dear. It certainly tastes like the cookie she described to me. But there's no way to tell unless she tastes it. Isn't that right?"

"That's right. Lisa took a few out to the reunion. I'm waiting for her to call and tell me what Iris thinks."

Hannah got up to refill her mother's coffee mug. They were sitting in the kitchen at The Cookie Jar, and Delores looked as fresh as the first daffodil of spring in a bright yellow linen suit with a lacy white shell. If Hannah were wearing the same suit, in a larger size of course, she'd look as wilted as an old banana skin.

"What is it, dear? You're staring at me."

"Sorry. You look wonderful this morning, Mother."

"Thank you, Hannah."

"I was just wondering if your suit is real linen."

"Of course it is. You know I don't like to wear synthetics."

"I know that, but . . ." Hannah stopped and sighed.

"But what?"

"I can't figure out how you can wear a linen suit when it's this hot and humid outside and still not get it wrinkled."

"I'm careful, dear. And I take off the jacket and hang it up on the hook in the back of the car when I drive."

"But your skirt isn't wrinkled, either."

"Well, I don't take it off and hang it up in the car, if that's what you're thinking!"

Delores gave a little laugh and Hannah joined in. Her mother was quick-witted this morning. "I'm careful about how I sit," Delores explained. "Your grandmother used to say, *Ladies don't wrinkle unless they assume unladylike positions.*"

Hannah nodded. Her maternal grandmother had been a stickler for proper etiquette, impeccable grammar, and a ladylike demeanor.

"You said you wanted to ask me some questions about Gus," her mother opened the discussion.

"I do. Did you manage to find a picture of him about the time the two of you were dating?"

Delores reached for one of four Jordan High yearbooks she'd stacked on the stainless steel surface of the workstation and flipped it open to a page that was marked with a pink strip of paper. "This is his formal senior picture."

Hannah stared down at the yearbook photo. Gus looked every bit as handsome as Marge and Patsy had claimed he was. She could understand why the high school girls had been wild about him.

"What happened to him after high school? I was going to ask Marge, but I forgot. Did he go on to college?"

Delores shook her head. "Good heavens, no. His grades weren't good enough. He got drafted."

"Into the Army?"

"No, into the minors. Didn't anybody tell you that Gus played baseball?"

"Marge and Patsy mentioned it, but I thought it was just in high school."

"No, Gus was really very good, and he was a first round

draft pick. He still holds the Minnesota state record for the highest batting average."

"Did he ever make it to the majors?" Hannah asked.

"I don't think so. I'm sure Marge would have mentioned it to me." Delores stopped and looked thoughtful. "Or maybe not. I was already engaged to your father by then, and she might have thought it wasn't appropriate to bring it up."

"Was Gus still playing baseball when he came back to Lake Eden to stay with Marge and his parents?"

"No. I know that for a fact. Gus came into the hardware store one day and he told your father he'd quit the farm team."

"Did he give a reason?"

"He said that life on the road with a baseball team just wasn't for him, that he wanted to get a good job and settle down. But I never believed that!"

"Why not?"

"Because it was his chance for a great career if he'd worked at it. I don't think he did. It just wasn't in his nature. For one thing, there were the women. I'm sure he had plenty when he was with the team, and he probably didn't treat them well. He certainly didn't in high school! And then there was the gambling. The Gus I knew when we were in high school made his spending money by cheating at cards and making rigged bets."

"Didn't he ever lose?" Hannah was curious.

"Only when he ran into someone who was a bigger cheater than he was. And when that happened, he just borrowed money from his sisters, or his current girlfriend, and kept right on gambling. He drank a lot, too. It was easy for him to buy liquor, because he looked older than most of the other boys."

"Did you ever lend him money when you were dating him?"

Delores gave a little sigh. "More often than I should have. And he didn't always pay me back. As a matter of fact, I think he still owed me twenty dollars when he left Lake Eden. Gus was a louse, pure and simple."

"Maybe he changed," Hannah suggested, playing devil's advocate.

"A leopard doesn't change its spots." Delores gave a little snort for emphasis. "I'm willing to bet that he was kicked off the team for drinking, or gambling, or romancing the wrong woman, or something like that."

Hannah bit her tongue and didn't say anything about sour grapes or a woman scorned. This was her mother, after all. Instead, she pulled the Jordan High yearbooks closer and smiled at her mother. "Show me the pictures?" she asked.

For long moments, Hannah looked and Delores pointed, giving a brief explanation for each photo she'd marked. The collection of Gus Klein pictures was extensive. There were at least a dozen photos in each book. It appeared that Gus had been awarded almost every high school athletic trophy, although Hannah didn't notice any academic honors.

"That's it, dear," Delores said, closing the last yearbook. "Is there anything else you need to know?"

"Just a few more things. Do you know anything about why Gus Klein left Lake Eden in the middle of the night?"

"I'm not sure why he left. I don't think he told anyone. And I don't know the details, but I heard there was a big fight between Gus and Jack Herman."

"Who told you that?"

"Your father. He was driving home from the store with Uncle Ed, and they stopped to break up the fight."

"What was the fight about?"

"I asked, but your father wouldn't tell me. Uncle Ed wouldn't say, either."

"So nobody knows?"

"Nobody knew except your father and Uncle Ed. And they're both gone now." Delores stopped and blinked hard, several times. "Of course Jack Herman knows, but . . ."

"But he might not be able to remember," Hannah finished her mother's thought.

"That's right. Poor Jack. Your father said he got the worst of it, and they dropped him off at Doc Knight's clinic to get stitched up. That was before the hospital was built. They didn't want to take Jack home that way and scare Emmy half to death. Iris was just a toddler, and Emmy was expecting Tim any day."

Hannah made a mental note to talk to Doc Knight about the night he'd treated Gus. Perhaps Lisa's father had said something about the fight.

"Is there anything else, dear?" Delores asked, glancing at the clock on the wall. "I need to pick up Carrie and go out to the mall. We want to find a little something for Jack's birthday party."

"There's just one more thing. Do you think there's anyone in town who had a grudge against Gus? Maybe somebody who might have wanted to see him dead?"

Delores's eyes widened. If she'd been depicted as a cartoon character, the little balloon over her head would have contained a drawing of a lightbulb. "Yes, I do! I don't know why I didn't think of it right away! Remember when I told you about Mary Sue Erickson?" She waited for Hannah to nod, and then she went on. "Well, that didn't last long. Gus only went out with her twice. But right after that, he dated Bert Kuehn's older sister."

Hannah was puzzled. "I've never heard of Bert Kuehn's older sister. Does she live in town?"

"She doesn't live anywhere, dear. Bert's sister is dead. She died the night of the senior prom in a terrible car accident."

"You told me Gus was a drinker. Was he driving drunk?"

"Not according to the accident report. It said that Bert's sister was at the wheel and her blood alcohol level was normal."

Hannah picked up on her mother's phrasing. "But there was some question about whether Bert's sister was actually driving?"

"Yes, there was. No one could prove otherwise, but the first person on the scene was the Jordan High baseball coach. He pulled both of them from the car before Doc Knight got there. Everyone in town wondered whether Gus had been driving and the coach had covered it up for him."

"Why would he do something like that?"

"To save Gus's career and his reputation as a coach. It was a feather in his cap to have one of his ballplayers drafted. As a matter of fact, he left Jordan High the next year and got a job in college baseball as an assistant coach. I seem to remember it was somewhere in Michigan, but I'm not sure exactly which college."

Hannah flipped open her stenographer's notebook, the one she'd designated as her murder book, to jot down the names. Bert Kuehn certainly had a reason to hate Uncle Gus, and both Bert and Ellie had been at the dance the night Gus was killed. They'd even brought six of their house specials from Bertanelli's Pizza for the potluck dinner. "What was the baseball coach's name, Mother?" she asked.

"Toby Hutchins. But I really don't know where he went when he left Lake Eden. All I can remember is that his new team was the wolves, or something like that."

"Wolverines?"

"That's it, dear. Do they play in Michigan?"

"Ann Arbor. The Wolverines is the team name for the University of Michigan athletic program."

"Really!" Delores looked impressed. "How do you know that?"

"It just stuck in my mind," Hannah said, settling for a half-truth. She wasn't about to tell her mother that she'd worked to memorize the team names from all the big colleges to impress a boy she'd hoped to date in high school.

"I really don't think you could track him down at this late date," Delores told her. "That was years ago, and I doubt he's still coaching baseball."

"If he's still alive, I'll find him," Hannah said, more confidently than she felt. "Is there anyone else who might have wanted Gus dead?"

"I'm not sure. Perhaps one of the girls he stopped dating in high school carried a grudge."

"Who would that be?" Hannah asked, mentally adding her mother's name to the list. Of course the way Delores told it, she'd dumped Gus when she'd caught him kissing another girl. That made her the dumper and Gus the dumpee, not the other way around.

"Oh, dear. I can't really remember all the girls that Gus dated. He was the love-them-and-leave-them type."

"Could you get together with Marge and Patsy when you get out to the reunion, and see if they remember any names?"

"Of course. You know I want to help, dear. I'll just take these yearbooks with me and see if they remember anybody. And I'll see whether I can find any of his old classmates to talk to. Lottie Borge is here. She married a Herman cousin. And she was only a year behind Gus in high school."

Just then Luanne Hanks stuck her head in the door. "Lisa just called and she said to tell you that Iris tasted a cookie. She said she thinks they're perfect."

"Great!" Hannah exchanged a high five with her mother.

"And Mike Kingston's here and he says he wants to talk to you. Should I send him back?"

When Hannah nodded, Delores picked up her stack of yearbooks and headed for the door. "What does *he* want?" she asked as she pulled it open.

"He wants to pick my brain." Hannah gave a little laugh and waved goodbye to her mother. "And since I want to pick his, it amounts to a draw."

"Hi, Mike," Hannah said when he came through the swinging, restaurant-style door that separated the coffee shop from the kitchen. "I'm a little short on time. Do you mind if I mix up a batch of cookies while we talk?"

CARROT CAKE MURDER 153

"I don't mind, especially if you feed me." Mike flashed her his famous grin.

Hannah glanced over at the trays of cookies ready to be packed up and taken out to the birthday party. "I've got Raisin Drops, Molasses Crackles, Red Velvet Cookies, and Party Cookies."

"What are Party Cookies?"

"These." Hannah held up one of the pretty four-color pastel cookies she'd made earlier this morning. "They're for Jack Herman's birthday party tonight, but I've got plenty."

"I'll take one of those and one of the Red Velvet Cookies. I've never had either one of them before."

"You got it!" Hannah said, grabbing the cookies and delivering them, along with a mug of black coffee.

"Thanks, Hannah. I expect you've been asking questions."

"Some."

"Did you find out anything?"

"Not much." Hannah started to melt chocolate for the Red Velvet Cookies to give her a few seconds to think. She didn't want to tell Mike too much, but she had to tell him something. "Marge and Patsy talked to me right before dinner last night," she said.

"And?"

"They had some doubt that the victim, the man who claimed to be Gus Klein, really was their brother."

"Really?

Mike's eyes widened slightly, and Hannah knew she'd handed him a nugget he hadn't panned. "I guess Marge and Patsy didn't tell you that."

"No. But it figures they'd tell *you*."

Hannah stopped in her tracks and turned, six squares of unsweetened chocolate in her hand. "I thought this was supposed to be an exchange of information, not a contest about who's going to get all the clues and catch the killer first."

"It *is* an exchange of information! At least that's what I want it to be." Mike looked very sincere. "Do you think I could be letting my ego get in the way?"

Duh! Hannah thought, but of course she didn't say it. "What makes you say that?" she asked instead, unwrapping the chocolate, which was beginning to melt in her hand, dumping it into a half-pint measuring cup, and popping it into the microwave.

"It's just that I pride myself on my interviewing techniques, and I can't believe I didn't pick up on something like that and pursue it."

Hannah glanced at him as she set the timer on the microwave. "Maybe it's a girl thing," she said.

"And maybe I'm losing my touch and you're just really good at this."

"Fat chance," Hannah told him, melting the chocolate squares and salvaging his ego simultaneously. "I'm just lucky, that's all. And people talk to me because I was raised here. I've got the hometown advantage."

Mike considered it for a moment and then he said, "You're right. That probably counts for a lot. I like these Party Cookies, Hannah. They remind me of something, but I don't know what."

"Old-Fashioned Sugar Cookies."

"That's right!"

"It's close to the same recipe, but with different flavoring and pretty colors."

"Right. So let's get back to the identity of the victim. Why did Mrs. Beeseman and Mrs. Diehl have doubts about it?"

Hannah was stymied for a moment and then she realized that Mike was talking about Marge and Patsy. "It's just that they hadn't seen him for so many years," she tried to explain. "And both of them thought that his personality had changed since he left Lake Eden."

"It probably did. He was pretty young then, wasn't he?"

Hannah did some mental arithmetic and came up with a figure. "He was in his twenties, I think."

"Point taken. You're not the same person you were when you were twenty, are you?"

"I hope not!" Hannah said, without thinking. And then she was a bit embarrassed over the vehemence of her answer. She'd been horribly naïve at twenty, and she preferred to think that she was wiser and more sophisticated now.

"I bet you were cute!"

Hannah felt her heartbeat speed up as Mike flashed his knee-weakening grin. How could one man affect her autonomic nervous system so drastically? Then she remembered that he'd used the past tense. She was about to call him on it, when he spoke again.

"They had enough time to get a good look at him," Mike continued. "Did they think his physical characteristics matched their brother's?"

"Yes, but they pointed out that any guy about the right age and height with blondish hair might have fooled them. Marge told me that Gus didn't have any distinguishing physical characteristics or marks." Hannah stopped speaking, but she quickly convinced herself that telling Mike about the tattoo couldn't hurt. "But he did," she said.

Mike's eyes narrowed. "How do you know?"

"You don't need to know that. Let's just say that four different people told me about one special physical characteristic that Gus had."

"And that characteristic would be . . . ?"

"A tattoo. It was two crossed bats with a ball between them and it was on his left buttock."

"And you know this for a fact?"

"Not me!" Hannah glared at him. "The people who told me about it said that he got it in high school and it was still there unless he had it removed in the intervening years."

"Hold on," Mike said, pulling out his cell phone. "I'll call

Doc Knight and find out. Thanks for telling me, Hannah. This could be important."

While Mike was waiting to be put through to Doc Knight at the hospital, Hannah began to assemble her cookie dough. She mixed the softened butter with the sugars and beat them together until they were light and fluffy. Then she mixed in the baking soda and salt, and added the egg. Once that was incorporated, she mixed the sour cream with the red food coloring and added them to her mixing bowl. As she mixed them in, she half listened to Mike's conversation with Doc Knight while she debated whether or not she should tell him about how Jack Herman and Gus had fought on the night that Gus left Lake Eden.

"Okay, then. Thanks, Doc." Mike clicked off his phone and looked over at Hannah. "The victim has an identical tattoo to the one you described."

"No," Hannah said, nodding her head.

"What does that mean? You said no, but you're nodding yes."

"That means I came to a decision about something else, and I was acknowledging the information you gave me about the tattoo at the same time.

"Then the no you said was for the decision."

"Yes," Hannah said, shaking her head.

"Hold on. This time you said yes, but you shook your head no."

"That's right. Yes, I came to a decision. And no, I won't tell you what it's about."

Mike drained the last of his coffee and stood up. "Thanks for the cookies. And thanks for telling me about the tattoo. I'll let the family know we have positive I.D. I'd better go now. I've got a meeting with my team in twenty minutes."

"Take these with you." Hannah reached for the box of cookies she'd packed up for him to take back to the sheriff's station. "And share them with your team. There's nothing like chocolate to perk you right up."

PARTY COOKIES

DO NOT preheat the oven yet. This
dough must chill before baking.

2 cups melted butter *(4 sticks)*
2 cups powdered sugar *(not sifted)*
1 cup white sugar
2 eggs
2 teaspoons vanilla *(or any other flavoring you
    wish)*
1 teaspoon baking soda
1 teaspoon cream of tartar *(critical!)*
1 teaspoon salt
4 ¼ cups flour *(not sifted)*
Food coloring *(at least 3 different colors)*

¼ cup white sugar *(for later)*

Melt the butter. Add the sugars and mix. Let the mixture cool to room temperature and mix in the eggs, one at
a time. Then add the vanilla, baking soda, cream of tartar
and salt. Mix well. Add the flour in half-cup increments,
mixing after each addition.

Divide the cookie dough into fourths and place each
fourth on a piece of waxed paper. *(You'll work with one
fourth at a time.)* Place one fourth in a bowl and stir in
drops of food coloring until the dough is slightly darker
than the color you want. *(The cookies will be a shade
lighter after they're baked.)* Place the colored dough back
on the waxed paper and color the other three parts. *(You
can leave one part uncolored, if you like.)*

Let the dough firm up for a few moments. Then divide each different COLOR into four parts so you have sixteen lumps of dough in all. Place a sheet of plastic wrap on your counter and roll each lump into a dough rope with your hands *(just as if you were making bread sticks.)* The sixteen dough ropes should each be about 12 inches long.

To assemble, stack the dough ropes, two on the bottom, two on the top, near the edge of the plastic wrap. Squeeze them together a bit and push in the ends so they're even. Flip the edge of the plastic wrap over the top and roll them up together tightly in one multi-colored roll. Twist the ends of the plastic wrap, fold them over on top of the roll, and refrigerate the rolls as you make them. When you're all finished, you'll have four rolls of multi-colored cookie dough chilling in your refrigerator.

Let the dough chill for at least an **hour** *(overnight is fine, too.)* When you're ready to bake, pre-heat the oven to 325 degrees F., rack in the middle position.

Put ¼ cup white sugar *(granulated)* in a small bowl and have it ready next to your greased cookie sheets.

Take out one dough roll, unwrap it, and slice it into ½ inch thick rounds. *(Each dough roll should make about 24 cookies.)* Place each round into the bowl of sugar and flip it over so it coats both sides. Position the sugarcoated rounds on a greased baking sheet, 12 to a standard sheet. Return the unused dough to the refrigerator until you're ready to slice more cookies.

Bake the cookies at 325 degrees F. for 12 to 15 minutes, just until they begin to turn slightly golden around the edges. Cool them on the cookie sheet for a minute or two, and then transfer them to a wire rack to complete cooling.

These cookies freeze very well if you stack them in a roll, wrap them in foil, and place the foil rolls in a freezer bag. You can also freeze the multi-colored unbaked dough rolls by leaving them in the plastic wrap and placing them in a freezer bag.

Yield: Approximately 8 dozen pretty party cookies.

Chapter Fifteen

By the time the hands on the kitchen clock met and pointed straight up at the ceiling, Hannah had finished baking and frosting the Red Velvet Cookies. She was about to call Norman to see if he was free to taste one, when Luanne pushed though the swinging door between the kitchen and the coffee shop.

"Norman just called," she told Hannah. "He's got an emergency patient in the chair, and he can't make it in to taste those cookies you told him about."

"Okay. Thanks for telling me. How are you holding out on cookies?"

"Just fine. It's been only the regulars so far. As far as take-out goes, Mrs. Surma came in for two dozen Orange Snaps for the Brownies, Reverend Knudson picked up some Viking Cookies for his grandmother since she liked them so much after church, and Mr. Purvis came in for five dozen Oatmeal Raisin Crisps for his teachers."

"But school's not in session yet."

"That's what I said, and he told me it's teachers' prep week. They come in a week early to get things done that they don't have time to do when they've got classes to teach."

A mental picture of her second grade teacher flashed through Hannah's mind. Miss Gladke was dressed in a pair of white overalls with a white painter's cap pulled over her curls. And she was up on a ladder with a brush in her hand, painting the walls of her classroom.

Hannah took a step back from the ridiculous image. She knew that painting wasn't the type of work done during teachers' prep week. Miss Gladke would be making up lesson plans, choosing textbooks, and other academic tasks.

"You can leave for the reunion now," Luanne told her. "I can take care of everything here. I'll lock up when it's time and be in tomorrow morning at nine to help you open."

Hannah was grateful for the extra work Luanne was putting in, especially because Delores and Carrie were spending the week at the lake and she was sure Luanne would much rather spend the time with her four-year-old daughter.

"You probably won't have many customers this afternoon. Why don't you call your mother and Nettie, and have them bring Suzie down here for cookies? It's a hot day, and I've got some Pecan Crisps made into ice cream sandwiches in the freezer."

Luanne looked absolutely delighted at the suggestion. "Thanks, Hannah. I'll do that. Suzie just loves to come down here with her grandmas and see all the different kinds of cookies. She says she wants to be a cookie baker when she grows up."

"Great! She can take over for me when I retire . . . unless she changes her mind and decides to be a nuclear physicist or a brain surgeon, of course."

Less than five minutes later, Hannah was zipping down the alley in back of her shop in her cookie truck. She turned west on Third and then made a right onto Main Street. Luck was with her and there was a parking spot directly in front of the Rhodes Dental Clinic. Hannah wasted no time pulling into the spot and shutting off her engine. She grabbed the pink box of cookies she'd packed as a care package for Norman, got out of the truck, and headed straight for the front door that nestled under the green-and-white metal awning that protected dental patients from the sun and rain in the summer and the snow in the winter.

A buzzer sounded somewhere in the interior of the building as Hannah opened the front door and stepped in. The sliding frosted glass windows at the reception desk were closed, but that didn't surprise Hannah. Norman usually hired a student from the Jordan High senior class work-study program to man the desk during the school year, and he took care of things himself during summer vacation.

"Please make yourself comfortable in the waiting room. I'm with a patient, but I'll be with you in just a minute or two."

Hannah smiled as Norman called out to whoever had come in the door. He had no idea who it was, and she decided to surprise him. Since he was expecting a reply, she settled for a one-word response that was unlikely to give away her identity.

"Okay," she replied, keeping her voice deliberately low. Then she walked over to the magazine rack and chose a current issue to read while she was waiting. Norman ordered magazines specifically for his waiting room, and they were delivered directly to the clinic. His patients weren't stuck perusing three-year-old news stories, or movie magazines that featured celebrity weddings that had already ended in divorce.

As Hannah flipped through a gourmet food magazine, she heard voices coming from the examining room just inside the inner door. She didn't consciously intend to eavesdrop, but there were no other patients that she could engage in conversation. That meant the waiting room was perfectly silent, except for the soothing music that was playing at low volume. She could hear every word that was spoken in the examining room.

"I waszh eating an apple and it juszht pulled out."

"That happens sometimes. How old it is?"

"Doc Bennett put it in sheventeen yearszh ago."

"He did a fine job. Most bridges need to be replaced long before that, especially if they're not made of modern amalgams. Just let me clean it up for you and I'll reattach it. It'll only take a couple of minutes."

"Good! I've got shurgery at two, and I need to get back to the hoshpital."

Hannah drew in her breath sharply. She thought she'd recognized that voice! It was Doc Knight, the very man she needed to see!

The sliding glass doors opened and Norman peered out. He seemed surprised but pleased to see her. "Hi, Hannah. I didn't know it was you out here. This isn't a dental emergency, is it?"

"No, it's a cookie deficiency emergency." Hannah carried the pink box over to the window and presented it to Norman. "Is that Doc Knight I heard back there?"

"Iszh me!" Doc Knight answered her. "What kind of cookieszh did zhu bring?"

"Something new I baked today. They're called Red Velvet Cookies. Would you like to try one, Doc?"

"Oh, no you don't!" Norman confiscated the box. "Not until I reattach his bridge."

"Sorry, Doc," Hannah called out.

"Not half aszh shorry aszh I am."

Hannah turned back to Norman. "Is it okay if I go back to keep him company while you're cleaning up that bridge? I've got some questions I need to ask him."

"Not a good idea. Doc's my patient, and I have to protect his right to privacy while he's under my care."

"Okay, but I just wanted to talk to him."

"Sorry, it's not allowed. If I let you back there, I'd be violating our patient-dentist relationship."

"Oh, nonshenszh! She'szh going to catszh me here or at the hoshpital, anyway. Might aszh well get it over wiszh."

Norman shrugged. "You heard him. He's waiving his right to privacy. Hold on a second and I'll let you in."

Hannah smiled as she went through the doorway to the inner sanctum and into the examining room. She liked Doc Knight, and he'd always been good about answering her questions. "Hi, Doc," she said, taking the chair against the wall.

"Hi, Hannah," Doc said, giving her a grin that showed several missing teeth. "Iszh a good thing your name iszhn't Shuszhana or Shally. Sheila would be okay, though."

"Not with me. I like my name," Hannah said with a laugh. "I need to ask you some questions about Gus Klein and Mary Jo Kuehn."

"That'szh easzhy. I don't know anything exszhept that they were girlfriend and boyfriend."

"How about the accident? The night of the senior prom when Mary Jo died?"

"I waszhn't here. I waszh in Boszhton for a two-week medical convenszhon. The county coroner took care of that and he'szh been dead for twenty yearszh."

Hannah came close to groaning. Doc Knight would be no help on that subject. "How about the fight Jack Herman had with Gus Klein? That was the night Gus left town for good, and nobody saw him again until the family reunion."

"I waszh here for that. Fire away, Hannah. I'm your captive audienszh. There'szh no way I'm leaving here until I get my bridge back."

"Mother told me that Dad and Uncle Ed broke up the fight and brought Jack to your office."

"She'szh right. Tha'szh what happened. Jack waszh in pretty bad shape. They didn't want Emmy to szhee him until I got him all cleaned up and looking aszh normal aszh I could. Didn't work, though. She went into labor and delivered that night."

"And the baby was Lisa's brother Tim, right?"

"That'szh right. And Tim waszh just fine. Iszh like I told Jack . . . she waszh ready to deliver, anyway. He didn't do anything wrong. He waszh juszht defending hiszh . . ." Doc

Knight stopped and shook his head. "You didn't hear me szhay that."

"Szhay . . . I mean, *say* what?"

"Szhay anything about defending anybody."

"You just told me that Jack was fighting to defend someone." Hannah peered closely at Doc. "Was it Emmy?"

"You didn't hear me szhay that, either."

Hannah's mind flew, attempting to fit the pieces she'd learned together. There'd been some important verbal salvos at the dance. When Jack had mentioned Mary Jo Kuehn, Gus had retaliated by mentioning Emmy. Then Jack had taken offense at the fact that Gus had used a diminutive name for his wife, and replied with Emily's full name. After that, Gus had mentioned Jack's sister Heather, but Marge had brought up their teacher, Mr. Burnside, and steered the conversation to safer ground.

"Do you know if Gus dated Emmy before she married Jack?" she asked.

"Yeszh."

Hannah gave herself a mental kick for asking an ambiguous question. "Yes, you know? Or yes, he dated her?" she asked, hoping to clear up the confusion.

"Yeszh I know. And that'szh all I'm going to szhay."

There was a knock on the door and Norman came in. "Just let me reattach this, and then you can have one of Hannah's cookies. The only stipulation is that you chew on the other side." He turned to Hannah. "Do you use nuts in your Red Velvet Cookies?"

"No. They have chocolate chips, but they melt when they bake and they're soft. There's nothing at all chewy, if that's what you're asking."

"That's exactly what I'm asking." Norman set the tray he was carrying down on the round shelf that was attached to the dental chair, and turned to Hannah again. "Excuse us for a couple of minutes. This won't take long."

Hannah watched while Norman tilted the chair back, positioned something she assumed was the bridge in Doc Knight's mouth and held it in place. A minute or so later, he removed his gloved fingers and stepped back.

"Okay," he said to his patient. "You're as good as new. I'll go get those cookies and we'll all have one."

The moment Norman left the examining room, Hannah seized her opportunity and moved her chair closer to Doc Knight. "Did the fight have something to do with Emmy dating Gus in the past?" she asked.

"Of course it did."

Now that Norman had reattached his bridge, Doc answered normally. For a brief second or two, Hannah was thrown for a loop. She's gotten used to the lisp. "Was it a love triangle?" she asked him.

"Only in Gus's mind. Emmy loved Jack, and Jack loved her. It was a good marriage, Hannah. Gus was a trouble-maker, and he didn't care who he hurt. To tell the truth, I was relieved when he left town. I felt sorry for his parents. It had to be hard not knowing what had happened to their son, especially since he left like a thief in the night, with no explanation and no good-byes. I still don't know which would have been more heartbreaking."

"Which?"

"The way he left and not knowing why. Or the grief he was bound to cause them if he'd stayed."

Hannah took a moment to digest Doc's statement. It was damning, but probably accurate. Doc Knight was a straight shooter, and he didn't equivocate. But there were more questions to ask, and Norman would be back any moment.

"You said Gus didn't care who he hurt. Does that mean there were people who hated him?"

Doc thought that over for a second. "I'm sure there were."

"And some of them were right here in Lake Eden?"

"Oh, yes. I can think of several. You've got to understand that the Gus we knew was concerned only about himself. He used people to get what he wanted. And then, when he didn't need them anymore, he discarded them like old candy wrappers. It was all about Gus, if you know what I mean. He had an ego that wouldn't quit."

"I know the type," Hannah said, remembering the assistant professor she'd dated in college. "Tell me more."

"Gus was a funny bird, at least that's what the psychiatric head at the hospital where I did my internship would have called him. I watched Gus grow up. He was in grade school when I was in high school, and it was all in one building. Gus was a manipulator from early on and everybody, including his family, gave him whatever he wanted."

"Marge and Patsy said he was spoiled."

"That may be too mild a way to describe it. Spoiled kids usually know better. Most of them know right from wrong, and they're aware that other children their age aren't treated the way they are."

"And you don't think Gus was aware of that?"

Doc Knight shook his head. "I'm almost sure he wasn't. Gus grew up with everything he ever wanted. That caused him to be amoral."

"Amoral?" Of course Hannah knew what the word meant, but she'd never actually heard it applied to someone she knew.

"Yes, amoral. I really don't think the question of right or wrong ever occurred to him. If Gus wanted something, he got it. And if something bothered him, he got rid of it. That went for material things, and it also went for people. He lived for the moment, and it was all about Gus. Nothing else mattered. I have no idea how many angry people he left in his wake. And even worse . . . I don't think Gus did, either."

"So you weren't surprised when he turned up dead at the family reunion?"

"Not really." Doc Knight gave a little shrug. "The big surprise is that it took two days for somebody to do it!"

Chapter Sixteen

"Whoa!" Hannah held up her hands in surrender as Michelle came barreling through the screen door at their mother's cottage. "Where's the fire?"

"Andrea's talking to Bertie Straub on the road, and I wanted to get here before she did."

"Why?" Hannah picked up the pepper grinder and prepared to grind pepper over the casserole she was preparing.

"Because I've got something I have to tell you. I wanted to talk to you yesterday, but every time I tried, you were with someone. And I don't want anyone else to hear."

"Not even Andrea?"

"*Especially* not Andrea!"

Hannah put down the pepper grinder with a thump. "Why?"

"Because she can be kind of . . . prudish."

"And I'm not?"

"Maybe a little, but nothing like Andrea! I think it's because she's married."

Hannah thought about that for a moment. "You'd think a married woman would be more sophisticated and worldly than a single woman. What you said seems counterintuitive."

"Maybe it seems that way, but it's not. Married women don't date anymore, and that means they don't do any wild and crazy things like single women do."

"I see." Hannah picked up the pepper grinder again and gave it a series of twists. "And since I'm single, you assume that I do wild and crazy things?"

"Well . . . no. Maybe you don't. But you *could,* if you wanted to."

"Hmm." Hannah made the most noncommittal comment of all. "So what did you want to tell me? Or did you change your mind?"

Michelle walked over to the counter where Hannah was working, and pulled up a stool. "It's about Sunday night and the murder. I think I saw the killer."

"Really?!" Hannah was glad she hadn't opened the bottle of cumin. If she'd been in the process of measuring it, the whole thing might have landed in her hotdish.

"Well . . . maybe. It was really quiet and there wasn't anyone else out. It just stands to reason that the person I saw go across the road and around to the front of the pavilion is the murderer."

Hannah drew in her breath sharply. "Did this person see you?"

"No. He didn't even know I was there. Or maybe it was a she, a woman wearing pants and a jacket. I was a long ways away, and I couldn't really tell."

Hannah glanced out the window over the sink. If Michelle had been in the kitchen of the cottage at two in the morning, she would have had a perfect view of the road and the entrance to the pavilion. "You were standing at the sink at two in the morning?"

"Not exactly."

"What does that mean?"

"It means that's not precisely correct."

"I *know* that's what it means!" Hannah gave a little sigh. That made twice today that she'd fallen into a semantic trap. "Why don't you just tell me where you were?" she suggested.

"Down on the dock with Lonnie. We were swimming and we climbed up on the dock to take a rest."

At two in the morning?! Hannah's mind shouted, but she didn't voice the sentiment. And she didn't ask about swimming attire, either, since she was supposed to be the non-prude.

"And you saw this person at two o'clock?" she asked instead of the thousand and one questions she really wanted to ask.

"I think it was about two. I met Lonnie on the dock at one-thirty. Mother and Carrie were asleep by then. And by the time we climbed back up on the dock and got our towels, it was probably close to two."

"But you don't know for sure, because you weren't wearing a watch."

"That's right. I don't have a waterproof watch. As a matter of fact, I wasn't wearing . . ."

"You said you saw this person walk across the road. Did he get out of a car?"

"There was no car. I would have heard it drive up. It was really quiet except for the crickets and the frogs and the mosquitoes. And the lapping of the waves against the dock, and the loons across the lake."

"Describe the person for me," Hannah interrupted her sister before she could hear more than she wanted to hear. "You said you couldn't be sure whether it was a man or a woman?"

"That's right. I just saw him or her through the trees. And this person went inside and didn't come out while we were sitting on the dock."

"And that was how long?"

"I was in bed by two-thirty. I know because I looked at the clock. Do you think I should tell Mike what I saw?"

Hannah shrugged. "You probably don't need to do that. I'm sure Lonnie has already told him."

"No, he hasn't. Lonnie didn't see the person. He was sitting with his back to the road. I was right next to him, facing the other way. I really don't want to tell Mike unless you think I absolutely have to. Mother's bound to hear about it, and I shouldn't have been out that late."

"Let me get this straight," Hannah said, reaching into her purse for her steno notebook and grabbing a pen. She really wanted to cut her baby sister a break, but this was a murder investigation. "Tell me *exactly* what you saw and when you saw it."

"I saw a person walk across the road, go around the side of the pavilion, and enter through the front door."

"You know, for sure, that this person went inside?"

Michelle nodded. "Light spilled out on the concrete when the door opened. A second later, the light disappeared, so the door must have shut again."

"Makes sense. And you were so far away you couldn't tell the identity of this person, or even if that person was a man or a woman?"

"That's right."

"Giving your best estimate, you think it was about two in the morning when the person went inside the pavilion?"

"I think so."

"Would you have seen the person if he or she had come back out while you were still sitting on the dock?"

"Yes. The light would have spilled out again when the door opened, and I would have noticed it."

"So you believe that the person was inside the pavilion for the entire period from two to two-thirty? And two-thirty is the time you left the dock and went back into the cottage?"

"A little before two-thirty. I already told you, I looked at the clock when I climbed in bed, and it was two-thirty. And I know the lights were still on inside the pavilion."

"How do you know that?" Hannah asked, remembering that when she'd checked the next day, the lights had been off.

"Because I saw light leaking out one of the shutters when I passed by the kitchen window on my way to the bedroom."

"Okay," Hannah said, flipping her notebook shut. "I've got it all down."

"So what do you think? Do I have to tell Mike?"

"No. All you saw was a shadowy figure entering the pavilion and not coming out again. That's not going to help in Mike's investigation. He already knows somebody went inside to kill Gus, because Gus didn't stab himself in the chest."

Michelle looked very relieved. "Thanks, Hannah! I'm really glad Mother won't know I was out so late. I'm too old to punish or anything like that, but she gives me that look."

"What look?"

"You know the one. It's her hurt look. And then she says, *Oh, Michelle! I'm so disappointed in you!* And then I know I've let her down, and it just about kills me."

"That's why she does it," Hannah said, remembering the very same phrase with her name in the culprit spot.

The screen door opened, and Andrea hurried in, carrying a Jell-O mold. She headed straight for the refrigerator, opened the door, and found a place for it inside. "I hope my Lemon Fluff Jell-O Mold didn't get hot and melt!"

"What's in it?" Hannah asked her.

"Lemon Jell-O, lemon pie filling, crushed pineapple, and Cool Whip."

"Cool Whip and not real sweetened whipped cream?"

"That's right."

"Then it should be fine. Cool Whip doesn't break down as fast as whipped cream. And even if your mold got a little runny, it'll firm up again before dinner. There's plenty of time."

"Oh, good. And you'll help me unmold it? I'm not very good at that."

"Of course I will," Hannah promised her. "Michelle said you were out on the road talking to Bertie Straub?"

"That's right. I was making an appointment for this weekend. She's going to give me a full weave, and this time it's going to be in four colors. I've never done more than three, but I want a reddish blond in the mix. And I'm having a layer cut to give my hair more body."

"A four-color weave's going to take all morning," Michelle commented.

"You don't know the half of it! I'm also booked for a manicure, a pedicure, and a full makeover. And when I'm all through with that, I'm heading down to Claire's to try on some of her sexy summer sundresses. The next time you see me, I'll be a new me."

"But I like the old you," Michelle said.

"So do I," Hannah added. "I think you look just fine the way you are. I really don't know why you want to be a new you, when . . ." her voice trailed off as the obvious reason occurred to her. Mike had mentioned it on the phone this morning. "Ronni Ward?" she guessed.

"Of course not! I just want to look good, that's all. When you've been married for as long as Bill and I have, you have to work to rekindle the romance every now and then, and . . ." Andrea stopped speaking and gave a little sigh. "You're right. It's Ronni Ward. Bill told me she was back in town when he got home last night. How did *you* find out about it?"

"Mike. He called me this morning to give me the number for the Animal Channel for Moishe, and he mentioned it."

"Did he also mention that Ronni rented the apartment across the hall from him?" Andrea asked.

"He did."

"Are you jealous?" Michelle raised the question.

"Mike and I don't have that kind of commitment. It's true that I date him, but I go out with Norman, too. That means I don't have any *right* to be jealous."

Andrea gave a nod of concurrence. "That's a perfectly reasonable point, but it's not what Michelle asked. Are you jealous?"

"What do *you* think?" Hannah faced them squarely.

"You're jealous." Andrea spoke for both of them. "You just don't know what to do about it, that's all."

LEMON FLUFF JELL-O

3 small *(3-ounces apiece)* packages of Lemon Jell-O
2 cups water
1 large can *(20-ounces)* crushed pineapple
2 cups cold water ***
1 small *(2-cup)* container Cool-Whip *(or any other whipped, non-dairy dessert topping)*
1 can *(enough to make an 8-inch pie)* lemon pie filling****

*** *This is approximate because it all depends on your can of crushed pineapple. You're going to drain the crushed pineapple and save the liquid. Then you'll add the cold water to the juice until it makes a total of 2 cups.*

**** *If you can't find lemon pie filling in a can (Andrea couldn't—Florence didn't have it at the Red Owl) you can use a 3.4 ounce package of lemon pudding and pie filling. Just follow the directions for pie filling and add it to your Jell-O mixture at the proper time.*

Drain the can of crushed pineapple. Save the liquid to use later.

Boil two cups of water in a small saucepan. Take it off the burner.

Empty the three packages of Lemon Jell-O powder into the recently boiled water. Stir until the Jell-O is dissolved. This step should take about 2 minutes. *(There's nothing*

worse than Jell-O powder that doesn't dissolve. It makes a layer of sweet lemon rubber at the bottom of your Jell-O mold and the mixture on top is runny. To tell if Jell-O powder is dissolved, reach in with your impeccably clean fingers and rub a bit of liquid between your thumb and your finger. If it's not gritty, it's dissolved.)

When the Jell-O powder is dissolved, combine the pineapple juice with cold water to make 2 cups of liquid. Add this to your saucepan and stir it in.

Refrigerate your saucepan until the Jell-O is partially set. *(This should take approximately 45 minutes.)*

Put the Jell-O mixture into a bowl and whip it with a whisk or an electric mixer.

Fold in the Cool-Whip.

Fold in the lemon pie filling. *(This is the time to make the instant pudding and pie filling and fold it into your Jell-O if you couldn't find canned pie filling.)*

Fold in the drained, crushed pineapple and blend thoroughly.

Spray a 2-quart Jell-O mold, or a standard-sized Bundt pan with Pam or another nonstick spray. You'll also need a second, much smaller bowl or mold to hold the Jell-O that won't quite fit in the first mold.

Transfer the Jell-O mixture to your molds and chill it in the refrigerator for at least 12 hours before serving.

Chapter Seventeen

The three sisters worked in silence, helping Hannah assemble the casseroles she was making for tonight's dinner. Andrea opened cans, Michelle chopped onions, and Hannah fried hamburger, enough for four batches of Wanmansita Casserole.

"To tell you the truth, Hannah, I really don't know what to do about Ronni Ward, either." Andrea broke the heavy silence that had fallen over them. "It's just that I thought a complete makeover might help. I shouldn't have said that about you being jealous."

"That's true. You were dead wrong, you know. The sinking feeling in my stomach and the overwhelming urge to wrap my hands around Ronni Ward's perfectly shaped throat and squeeze couldn't possibly be caused by jealousy."

Both Andrea and Michelle burst into laughter, and Hannah joined in. It was a good moment sandwiched in between all the bad things that had happened lately, and all three wanted to savor it for as long as they could.

When they'd quieted down again, Andrea turned to Hannah. "How about a makeover for you, too? I can run and find Bertie and make an appointment, my treat."

"No, thanks. I don't think it would help." Hannah carried the first casserole to the preheated oven and slipped it inside.

"Okay then. How about going out to Heavenly Bodies at the mall with me?"

"What's Heavenly Bodies?" Michelle asked.

"It's a new fitness club. Their motto is, *We'll make you look like a star*. That's because of the name. Do you get it?"

Michelle groaned and gave Hannah one of those *I-don't-believe-she-said-that* looks.

"We get it," Hannah answered Andrea. "You know how I feel about fitness clubs. They'd have to open at three A.M. for me to go there before work. And after work, I'm too tired to go anywhere that requires any effort. It would be a waste of money for me to join."

"But this one's different. They give you a key to the outside door and you can come in anytime, day or night, twenty-four seven."

"They have around-the-clock staff?" Michelle looked interested.

"No, but they've got an agreement with the guards at the mall to come in to check every hour."

"That doesn't sound very safe to me," Hannah said. "I wouldn't want to go there by myself at three in the morning, knowing that dozens of other people had keys and any one of them could unlock the door and walk in on me."

"I wouldn't feel safe, either," Michelle added her opinion. "It would be creepy to go to a gym alone at night."

Andrea shrugged. "Go during the day, then. You could always go on your lunch hour. Lisa would be happy to handle the coffee shop by herself for an hour or so, especially if she thought it was helping you."

"That's another point. I don't think it *would* be helping me." Hannah picked up another casserole and slid it into the oven. "I've never been able to stick with an exercise program, and there's no reason to think it would be different this time. I start out just fine, but after a week or so, I start making excuses for not exercising. And then, before I realize what I'm doing, it's been over a month since I've jogged, or used the treadmill, or whatever I planned to do. Besides . . ." Hannah paused to carry the remaining casseroles to the oven, and when she came back, she plunked down on the stool at the counter and sighed. "Look, Andrea . . . it doesn't really matter how cute the club's name is or the promises they make. Let's face reality here. We all know I'm never going to look like a star."

"Well, you *are* a star as far as I'm concerned!" Andrea looked very serious.

"With me, too," Michelle chimed in.

"Thanks," Hannah said. It was nice to get a vote of confidence from her sisters.

"Let's not talk about makeovers, or fitness clubs, or Ronni Ward anymore, then. It's just too depressing." Andrea reached into the briefcase she was carrying and pulled out an envelope. "Let's talk about murder instead."

There was perfect silence for a nanosecond, and then both Hannah and Michelle burst into a volley of laughter. Andrea looked slightly puzzled for a moment, and then she began to smile. "I didn't realize I made a joke," she said, handing the envelope to Hannah. "I brought these for you."

"What are they?"

"Crime scene photos. Bill brought them home with him last night, and I scanned them into the computer after he went to bed. I printed them out this morning as soon as he left for work."

"Thanks, Andrea. These will help me a lot." Hannah didn't mention that Mike had offered to give her a set of the crime scene photos. "Did you look at them?"

"No. You know I don't like gory things. I figured I'd let you look first, and you could show me the ones that aren't too awful."

Michelle began to frown. "Wait a second. How did you scan the photos and print them out without looking at them?"

"It was easy. They go face down on the scanner, so that was no problem. And then, when I brought them up on the screen to print them out this morning, I just peeked through my fingers, clicked on them, and sent them to the printer."

"But they came out face-up, didn't they?" Hannah questioned her. And then, when both of her sisters turned to look at her in surprise, she asked, "Why are you looking at me like that?"

"You've been using your computer!" Andrea exclaimed.

"Of course I've been using my computer. Norman's been giving me lessons. *Mother's* using a computer, for crying out loud! I don't want to be the only holdout in the family."

"It's a matter of pride," Michelle explained to Andrea.

"No, it's actually a matter of necessity," Hannah countered. "I got tired of asking Norman to look up things on the Internet for me."

Andrea gave a smile of approval. "Well, good for you," she said. "And speaking of good, those casseroles you put in the oven are starting to smell great. What are they called again?"

"Wanmansita Casseroles. It's Gary Hayes's recipe. You remember Gary and Sally, don't you? They used to live right across the street from Mother."

"Sally with the apron collection!" Michelle identified her. "You used to take me over there, and she'd let me look at her aprons while you talked about recipes and stuff."

"That's right."

"Wait a second." Andrea began to frown. "That doesn't make sense."

"Sure it does. I used to get home from school early because I had study hall last period. And I'd take Michelle over to Sally's with me."

"Not that. I remember that you went over there. It's just that Sally and Gary lived right here in Lake Eden. And if they lived here, why does Gary call it a casserole?"

For a moment Hannah was confused, but then she realized

what her sister was asking. "You mean, the word *casserole,* instead of the word *hotdish?*"

"Yes. Everybody in Lake Eden says *hotdish.* What's the difference, anyway?"

"I'm not positive, but I don't think there's any difference between a casserole and a hotdish. It's probably another example of regional dialogue," Hannah did her best to explain.

"You mean like *pop* and *soda?*" Michelle asked.

"Exactly right. Sally said it was an old recipe from Gary's family, and I think they came from Oklahoma. They must call a hotdish a casserole there. Or it got passed on to another relative who changed the word *hotdish* to *casserole.*"

Andrea gave a big smile. "That explains the rest of the name, then. There are a lot of American Indians in Oklahoma, and *Wanmansita* is probably an American Indian word. I should ask Jon Walker."

Hannah shook her head. "Jon's Chippewa, and I don't believe they got as far west as Oklahoma."

"Well, what American Indian tribe would it be?"

"It depends on when the recipe was named," Michelle told her. "And there are lots of Indian tribes in Oklahoma. They've got the Delaware, Arapaho, Miami, Iowa, Shawnee, Caw, Creek, Chickasaw, Cheyenne, Cherokee, Witchita, Patawatomi, Peoria, and Osage, plus a couple of others I can't remember."

Andrea looked impressed. "How do you know all that?"

"I took a course in Indian Studies last fall, and it was taught by a visiting professor from O.S.U. The names were so intriguing, I remember them. And besides, there's a mnemonic. It's *Donna Asked Mom In Secret, Can Wally Play Outside?* The first letter of each word stands for the first letter of an Indian tribe."

"But you named more *C*'s than that!"

Michelle laughed. "You're right. You have to remember that there are four *C*'s and two *P*'s. It's not as easy as the word *HOMES* for the Great Lakes."

"Or *Roy G. Biv* for the colors of the spectrum." Hannah added.

"Or *Mother Very Eagerly Made Jelly Sandwiches Under No Protest.*"

"The planets," Michelle said. "I never could remember them without that."

"But now you'll have to, since *Protest* is gone," Hannah reminded her.

"Pluto." Michelle gave a little sigh. "I forgot all about Pluto."

"*What* about Pluto?" Andrea asked.

"It's not a full planet anymore. It's been downgraded to a dwarf."

"Oh, no!" Andrea looked horrified.

"What's the matter?" Hannah asked her. "You look as if you just lost your best friend."

"It's Tracey. I just taught her the planets that way! And now she's going to get them wrong when she goes in to be tested for her Girl Scout badge."

"She's smart enough to remember to leave Pluto out," Hannah comforted her sister. "Just remind her before she goes to the meeting, or wherever they go to be tested."

"It's the school. The scouts are using the auditorium since school hasn't started yet. And Tracey's the youngest one going for a badge, and she really wants to get it right."

"She will," Michelle said with a smile. "But I thought Tracey was a Brownie Scout, not a Girl Scout."

"She is, but Bonnie Surma got a special exception for Tracey to study for her badges early. And it's a really big deal this year because one of the ladies from national is coming to award the badges."

"Tracey will be fine. Don't worry," Hannah reassured her sister again, and then she picked up the envelope and removed a file that was inside. "Let's go over the crime scene photos together."

"Don't look," Andrea instructed Michelle.

"What do you mean, *don't look?* It's not like I'm a child, you know. You don't have to protect me from the ugly side of life."

"You're too young to know anything about the ugly side of life. The ugliest thing you ever saw was the stuffed boar's head that hung over Grandpa and Grandma Swensen's couch!"

"I thought that boar's head was cute! All that bristly hair sticking up. He looked like a character in a cartoon. But getting back to the ugly side, I bet I've seen more ugly things than . . ."

"That's enough, girls!" Hannah interrupted, stepping in with her best big-sister-in-charge voice. "If you don't stop squabbling, I won't let you taste the new cookies I brought."

There was complete silence for a moment, a phenomenon that deeply gratified Hannah. She hadn't lost her big sister touch.

"New cookies?" Michelle was the first to speak.

"Yes. I made them for Jack Herman's birthday party tonight. Lisa's mom used to make a similar cookie years ago."

"Do they have chocolate?" Andrea wanted to know. "I'm going to need chocolate if I'm going to look at anything the least bit gory."

"They've got plenty of chocolate. There's chocolate in the cookie dough and more chocolate chips inside. And there's cream cheese frosting, too."

Michelle gave a little whimper of anticipation. "Cream cheese frosting is my very favorite. Sometimes I make up a batch and spread it on soda crackers."

"Is that *good?*" Andrea asked her.

"Yes, but make sure you buy salted soda crackers. Then you lay them out with the salt side down and frost the other side. You can spread it between two graham crackers, too. Or two chocolate cookie wafers. That tastes almost like Oreos."

With peace restored and cookie hunger kindled, Hannah wasted no time opening her box of Red Velvet Cookies and giving each of her sisters a sample. While they were tasting her newest creation, she paged through the crime scene photos. Since nothing was really gory, she left them all in the pile.

When she was finished censoring the stack of photos, Hannah almost called out, *You can look now,* the phrase her father had used on Christmas morning when they sat by the Christmas tree, eyes tightly shut, until he brought in the presents that had been too large to wrap. But the photos she held in her hand weren't presents. They were grim reminders of what could happen when the sanctity of human life was violated.

"I'm ready with the photos," she said instead.

"These are great cookies, Hannah!" Andrea complimented her, wiping her fingers on a napkin. She picked up the stack of photos, examined the one on top, and then she handed it to Michelle.

"Yuck!" Michelle commented.

"My cookies are *yuck?*" Hannah, who hadn't noticed the photo pass from hand to hand, was clearly astounded by Michelle's remark.

"Not your cookies. They're absolutely fantastic, and they remind me of red velvet cake. I meant this photograph. He was stabbed, right?"

Hannah nodded. "Keep your eye out for something unusual that I might have missed, or anything that doesn't fit with the way you remember the pavilion from the night of the dance."

"But you were right there," Michelle pointed out. "You found him. You saw everything with your own two eyes. How could you have missed something?"

"Hannah was probably in shock," Andrea reminded her. "Finding a dead body isn't fun."

"Okay. You're right," Michelle said, taking the next photo from Andrea and examining it.

Nobody said anything for at least five minutes, an unusual occurrence when the three Swensen sisters got together. But Hannah was busy watching her younger sisters, and Michelle and Andrea were absorbed in examining the photos. Finally the last one was placed facedown on the counter.

Andrea gave a big sigh. "I didn't see anything unusual," she said. "And I'm pretty sure that everything looked just the way it did when I left the dance."

Michelle gave a little nod. "I agree. I'm sorry we didn't learn anything new, Hannah."

"So am I, but I did learn *one* new thing."

"You did?" Andrea looked surprised.

"What is it?" Michelle asked.

"Everything was exactly as I remember it. And that means one of two things. Either being in shock doesn't affect my memory, or I'm getting much too used to finding murder victims!"

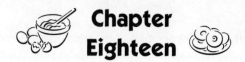

Hannah picked up the photos and returned them to the envelope. There was another file in the envelope that she hadn't noticed before. "What's this?" she asked Andrea. "A duplicate set?"

"No. Those are photos they took of the cottage where Gus was staying right before they searched it. It's standard operating procedure. I heard Bill talk about it once."

"It's a good procedure!" Hannah gave a little grin. "I've seen other places they've searched, and they always looked like the aftermath of a tornado."

"Not this time," Michelle spoke up.

"Why not?"

"Because they confiscated almost everything after they searched, and took it to the sheriff's station. Lonnie said they were going to go through it with a fine-tooth comb to see if there were any clues."

"There wasn't much more than a suitcase full of clothes and some personal items in the bathroom," Hannah said, thinking back in time to early Monday afternoon when she'd walked through the cottage searching for Gus.

"How about the closet? Did you look in there?" Michelle asked.

"The doors were open," Hannah did her best to bring back the mental picture. "I looked at the bed first. The suitcase was on it, and it was open. And then I turned to look at the closet. There was one of those little green frogs. You've both seen the type that lives at the lake. He hopped out of the closet and . . . it was empty inside. I remember now. There were no clothes on the hangers."

"That's because they were all in the suitcase," Michelle said. "Gus probably hadn't gotten around to unpacking yet."

"But why hadn't he? He'd already changed clothes twice." Hannah turned to Andrea. "That's right, isn't it?"

"Twice at the minimum," Andrea said, giving a definitive nod. "I saw him when he drove up at the church. He was wearing an eggshell white linen suit with an Egyptian cotton shirt . . ."

"You could tell his shirt's country of origin by just looking?" Hannah interrupted her sister's recital.

"Not exactly, but Egyptian cotton is distinctive, and it's always been the hot material. It was a wonderful shade of slate blue. You know the color. It's blue, but it's got a lot of gray in it, too. Very subdued, and it looks great with blond or gray hair. The shirt was open at the neck, and he had on a gold neck chain and . . ."

"Then he must have changed clothes, because that's not what he was wearing at the dance," Michelle interrupted her.

"You're right. The suit he wore at the dance was completely different. And he was wearing a different shirt. Not only that, he wasn't wearing a tie when I saw him at the church, and he wore a designer tie at the dance. It's right there in the crime scene photos."

Hannah was grateful that her sisters had noticed what Gus had been wearing when they saw him in the car at the church. She'd only caught a glimpse of him, and she would have been hard-pressed to describe any item of clothing he'd worn.

"There's one thing that really puzzles me." Andrea turned to Hannah. "It's the suit Gus was wearing the first time we saw him."

"What about it?"

"It was linen. I said that before. And linen wrinkles. He wore it to the brunch. I know that, because Mother mentioned it to me. But he had to have taken it off before he showered and changed for the dance. That was an expensive suit. I'd guess it was over five hundred dollars, maybe a lot more. He was staying at a cottage with a nice big closet. Why didn't he hang it up?"

"Are we sure he didn't?" Michelle asked.

"I'm almost positive he didn't." Hannah paged through the photos of the cottage, found the one of the bedroom, and handed it to Michelle. "Here's a picture that shows the closet. Check it out for yourself. It's as bare as Mother Hubbard's cupboard."

"Maybe he spilled something on it at the brunch and it needed to be dry cleaned?" Michelle suggested a possible explanation.

"Maybe, but there aren't any dry cleaners open on Sunday," Andrea pointed out. "And by the time they opened on Monday morning, he was already dead."

"So what would you do with an expensive suit you wanted dry cleaned?" Hannah asked them.

"Toss it on the floor of the closet so your wife will take it to the cleaners," Andrea said. "That's what Bill always does. I try to get him to stuff it in a laundry bag, but he forgets."

"Since there was nothing on the floor of the closet, maybe he just tossed it back in his suitcase," Michelle suggested.

"If he did, it would be right on top." Andrea paged through the photos until she came to the one of the suitcase. "It's not here, so he didn't. And since he was such a nice dresser, he probably wouldn't have thrown it in on top of his clean clothes anyway."

Something niggled at the back of Hannah's mind, and she shut her eyes to concentrate. A second or two later, she had it. "I just remembered something. When I went to the cottage to look for him, his car was parked in the driveway. And I'm almost sure there was a jacket hanging up on the hook in the backseat."

"Was it the jacket to his linen suit?" Andrea asked her.

"I don't know. I really didn't pay much attention. Is the Jaguar still parked in front of the cottage?"

Michelle shook her head. "Mike sealed it up and had it towed to the impound lot. It's going to stay there until they find out if Gus had a will, or any other family members back in Atlantic City."

"I wonder if the jacket's still in it," Hannah said. "I'd like to find out if it's the one to the missing linen suit."

"But why would Gus take it off inside the cottage and then carry it out and hang it in his car?" Andrea asked.

"Maybe he planned to take it to the cleaners, but he was killed first?" Michelle suggested.

Andrea shook her head. "Then he would have just tossed it in the backseat, or the trunk. He wouldn't have bothered to hang it up."

"Wait!" Hannah began to smile. "I know why he hung it in the car!"

"Why?" both sisters asked her, almost in unison.

"Because that's how you keep linen from getting wrinkled. Mother mentioned that this morning. She always hangs up her linen jacket when she drives the car."

"I get it," Michelle said, looking excited. "Gus didn't carry the jacket back out to his car to hang it up. He slipped it off when he left the brunch, and hung it up for the drive back to the lake."

"And forgot to take it with him when he went inside the cottage." Andrea finished the scenario.

"But where are the pants?" Michelle reminded her. "We still haven't found them." Then she turned to Hannah. "Do you think the missing pants are a clue?"

Hannah shrugged. "Search me. But it *is* interesting, and it might mean something. I'm just not sure what."

"Nobody's using the cottage, so you can go back and go

through it again," Andrea told her. "You might find something that the crime team missed."

Hannah gave her a grin. It wasn't the first time she'd found something the crime team hadn't thought was important, but that later turned out to be an important clue. "You say it's vacant?"

"Yes. Lisa thought maybe somebody else would move in, but none of the relatives want to use it."

Hannah was puzzled. "Why not? It's a nice cottage. And it's not a crime scene or anything like that. Why doesn't anybody want to use it?"

"Because Gus stayed there," Andrea explained.

"But he was only there for an hour or so. He didn't even have time to unpack!"

"That's true, but I guess they think it's bad luck." Michelle did her best to explain. "A lot of people are really superstitious."

"Maybe so," Hannah said, turning back to her cooking duties. She was glad that no one else was using the cottage. She intended to go back there at the very first opportunity, but her primary purpose wasn't to search for clues Mike's crime team might have missed. It had more to do with the frog. She hoped he'd hidden out somewhere when the crime team had searched the cottage, or hopped out the door to find a new place to inhabit. Maybe it was silly of her to be concerned, but she'd try to get over there later this evening to check.

WANMANSITA CASSEROLE

Preheat the oven to 325 degrees F.,
rack in the middle position.

2 pounds lean hamburger***
2 medium onions, sliced
1 cup diced celery *(that's about 3 stalks)*
1 green bell pepper, seeded and diced
1 large package of crinkle noodles *(I used egg noodles that were twisted in the middle.)*
2 cans *(14.5 ounces each)* of diced tomatoes with
juice
1 can *(5 ounces)* sliced water chestnuts**** *(Sally
uses chopped)*
1 can *(4 ounces)* mushroom pieces
2 teaspoons cumin
2 teaspoons chili powder
2 teaspoons salt
1 teaspoon pepper *(freshly ground is best, of course)*
2 cups grated cheddar cheese

*** *If you use regular hamburger instead of lean,
you'd better buy 2 ½ or 3 pounds, because there's a lot of
fat that'll cook off. If you buy extra lean hamburger it
probably won't have enough fat and you'll have to add
some.*

**** *Don't worry about the ounces on the water chestnuts—anything from 4 ounces to 8 ounces will do.*

Start by spraying a 9-inch by 13-inch cake pan, or a
half-size disposable steam table pan with Pam or another

nonstick cooking spray. If you choose to use a disposable pan, set it on a cookie sheet to support the bottom and make it easier to move it from the counter to the oven, and then out again when it's finished.

Pour 6 quarts of water into a big pot and put it on the stove to boil. You'll use this to cook the noodles. *(If you start heating the water now, it should be boiling by the time you're ready to cook the noodles. If it boils too early and you're not ready, just turn down the heat a little. If it's not ready when you are, crank up the heat and wait for the boil.)*

Crumble the hamburger and brown it over medium heat in a large frying pan, stirring it around with a metal spatula and breaking it up into pieces as it fries. This should take about 15 or 20 minutes.

When the hamburger is nice and brown, put a bowl under a colander so that you can save about ⅓ cup of fat to use with the onions. Dump the hamburger into the colander to drain it.

Put the drained hamburger into the prepared baking pan.

Pour the ⅓ cup of hamburger grease back into the frying pan.

Peel the onions and slice them into ⅛ inch thick slices. *(When you do this they may fall apart in rings and that's perfectly okay.)*

Place the onion slices in the frying pan, but don't turn on the heat quite yet.

Dice the celery. Add it to the onion slices in the frying pan.

Cut open the green bell pepper and take out the seeds, the stem, and the tough white membranes. Chop the remaining pepper into bite-sized pieces. Once that's done, add them to the onions and celery in your frying pan.

Cook the aromatic vegetables *(that's what they call them on the Food Channel)* over medium heat until they're tender when pierced with a fork.

Drain them in the same colander you used for the hamburger, and then mix them up with the hamburger in your baking pan.

Add some salt to your boiling water on the stove. Then dump in the noodles, stir them around, let the water come back to a boil, and then turn down the heat a bit so the pot doesn't boil over. Set your timer for whatever it says on the noodle package directions and cook the noodles, stirring every minute or so to make sure they don't stick together.

Drain the cooked noodles in the same colander you've been using all along, add them to your baking pan, and mix them up with everything else.

Add the diced tomatoes, juice and all, to your baking pan. Wait to stir. You don't want to mush your noodles by stirring too much.

Open and drain the cans of water chestnuts and mushroom pieces in the colander that's still sitting in the sink.

Dump the water chestnuts and mushrooms on top of the tomatoes in your baking pan.

Sprinkle the cumin over the top of your casserole.

Sprinkle the chili powder on top of the cumin. *(Gary says to tell you that if your chili powder has been sitting around for as long as theirs has, it's a good idea to buy fresh.)*

Sprinkle on the salt and grind the pepper on top of that.

Now is the time to mix it all up. This might not be easy if the baking pan's too full to stir with a spoon. If that's happened, just wash your hands thoroughly and dive in with your fingers to mix everything up. When you're through, pat the casserole so it's nice and even on top, and call it a day.

Wash your hands again, and then cover the baking pan with a single thickness of foil.

Bake at 325 degrees F. for 60 minutes, or until you peek under the foil and see that it's hot and bubbling.

Remove the pan from the oven. Remove the foil slowly and carefully to avoid burning yourself with the steam that may roll out. Set the foil on the counter to use again in a few minutes.

Sprinkle the 2 cups of shredded cheddar cheese over the top and return the baking pan to the oven. Bake it, uncovered, for another 10 minutes, or until the cheese melts.

Cover the pan again with that foil you saved, and let your casserole sit on a cold burner or rack to set up for at least 10 minutes, and then serve and enjoy!

Hannah's 1st Note: Sally says to tell you that she made 4 pans of this for a luncheon meeting. There were 25 people and she had one whole pan left over.

Hannah's 2nd Note: Gary says to tell you that they didn't serve seconds, though.

Yield: Judging from the above notes, I'd guess that one pan of Wanmansita Casserole would serve 8 to 10 people, especially if you served fresh buttered rolls and a nice mixed green salad on the side.

Norman gave a resigned sigh as he perched rather precariously on the top of Hannah's cookie truck. They were parked next to the chain link fence that surrounded Cyril Murphy's impound lot. Any cars that the city of Lake Eden, the Winnetka County Sheriff's Department, or the Minnesota Highway Patrol impounded were stored here. Hannah and Norman had driven here right after she'd unmolded Andrea's Jell-O, put it on a platter, and returned it to the refrigerator. Michelle had promised to remove the Wanmansita Casseroles from the oven when they'd finished baking, and to carry them to the dinner buffet. That meant Hannah was free to pursue the linen jacket lead they'd uncovered, and Norman had agreed to help her.

Hannah glanced at her watch. They had exactly one hour before dinner would be served, and they had to locate Gus Klein's Jaguar, look to see if the jacket was there, and drive back out to the lake in time to join everyone for Jack Herman's birthday party.

"I still think this is breaking and entering," Norman said as he began to climb up the chain-link fence.

"No, it's not. It might be entering, but there's no breaking involved. Go ahead, Norman. You said you could do it."

"I can. I'm just not sure I want to. Do you know for a fact that Cyril doesn't keep guard dogs inside?"

"I do." Hannah shaded her eyes with her hand as she stared up at Norman. He had reached the top of the chain link and was just about to climb over. "Cyril bought two guard dogs when he opened the impound lot, but he ended up taking them both home for pets."

"Okay. What do you want me to do now?"

"Just drop down on the other side and unlock the gate. The sooner we get this done, the sooner we can get back out to the lake."

Norman gave a brief nod and dropped down. Hannah noticed that he landed lightly on the balls of his feet, the exact opposite of what would have happened if she'd jumped from that height. She watched him head for the gate at an easy trot, and she was impressed. Norman had never been in bad physical shape, but he appeared to be more agile and fit than he'd ever been before.

"Got it!" Norman called out, opening the gate for her.

"You picked the lock that fast?"

"Not really. It wasn't locked."

"Sorry about that." Hannah stepped inside and watched as he shut it again. "I should have thought to check it before I asked you to climb over. And speaking of that climb you made, have you been working out?"

"You noticed!" Norman looked pleased. "I've been swimming out at the new fitness club. They've got a lap pool. You should come out with me sometime. Members can bring a guest."

"Are you talking about Heavenly Bodies at the mall?" Hannah guessed. And when Norman nodded, she was almost tempted to give it a try. But then she remembered that her old swimsuit didn't fit her anymore. That meant she'd have to try on suits in a department store fitting room, and that was always depressing.

"Do you want to split up to look for the car, or do it together?"

"Together, but separate," Hannah said, enjoying the apparent contradiction. "Let's do what the police do when they search for something in the woods."

"Walk forward in parallel and meet at a designated point?"

"Exactly. That way you'll hear me if I spot it, and I'll hear you if you do. Let's pick a starting point and walk straight down the rows. Then we'll meet at the fence in back and start up another two rows."

It took three rows out of what must have been at least twenty, but they lucked out. Norman called out from the middle of his row, and Hannah darted between the cars to join him. She found him standing next to Gus Klein's Jaguar with a smile on his face. "This has got to be it. It's probably the only Jaguar in the lot."

"It's the one Gus was driving," Hannah confirmed it, "And there's the jacket I remembered."

"Linen," Norman commented. "I think that's the same one he was wearing when he drove up in front of the church."

"Mother said he wore it to the brunch he hosted at the Lake Eden Inn. He must have hung it up so that it wouldn't wrinkle for the drive to the lake."

Norman stepped up to the window, pressed his nose to the glass, and peered in. When he stopped back, he was shaking his head. "I don't think so," he said.

"Why not?"

"Because his pants and shirt are there, too. They're hanging behind the jacket. And I really don't think he drove out to the lake in his underwear."

Hannah and Norman stood there staring at the expensive linen suit. For long moments, the only sounds were the humming of insects and the far-off drone of cars on the highway.

"This just doesn't make sense," Hannah said at last. "Gus changed clothes at the cottage. His suitcase was open on the bed. And the closet was right there, no more than three or four steps away. I just can't figure out why Gus went outside and hung his suit up in his car."

Hannah smiled across the picnic table at Norman. "It was so nice of you to make Clara and Marguerite's Mexican Hotdish for Jack's birthday party."

"Maybe not. You haven't tasted it yet. I doubled the spice. Marguerite says it's even better that way. She felt so bad about not being able to bake it for Lisa and Herb's family reunion, and I volunteered to do it for her."

"That was really nice of you, Norman."

"It was fun, and really easy. Taste it and tell me what you think."

Hannah took a bite and smiled. "It's excellent, but it's a little spicier than I remember."

"Then Clara must have made it the night you went over there for dinner. She uses only one packet of taco seasoning. When Marguerite makes it, she uses two packets."

"The sour cream on the side is a nice touch."

"That's a little trick I picked up in Puerto Vallarta. We went to a place that was famous for its fish tacos and they were too spicy for Bev. The waitress brought her some sour cream to cut the heat."

"That's nice to know," Hannah said, referring to the sour cream, not to the fact that Norman had taken his ex-fiancée, Beverly Thorndike, to Mexico.

"We should go sometime. You'd love it down there. We could stay at the La Jolla de Mismaloya resort."

"Isn't that the location John Huston used in *The Night of the Iguana?*" she couldn't resist asking.

"That's right. Of course it's all modern and restored now, but they really did a good job of keeping the original ambience."

"Nice," Hannah said, deciding that one-word responses were best. She really didn't care to hear much more about Norman's Mexican vacation with Beverly.

"They run the movie continuously in the bar. The first night Bev and I were there, we sat through it twice."

"Really."

"You'd love the place, Hannah. It's very relaxed, and you can practically live in your swimsuit."

Swimsuits again. It was the second time in less than an hour that she'd been reminded of swimsuits. "Great," she said, not mentioning that if she agreed to go anywhere with Norman, and the way she felt right now the odds of that happening were drastically reduced, it certainly wouldn't be somewhere he'd vacationed with his ex-fiancée.

"I wonder what's wrong with Lisa," Norman said, changing the subject abruptly. "She looks worried."

Hannah turned to look. Her friend and partner was making her way through the crowd toward the picnic table where they were sitting.

"I don't know, but she's definitely upset." Hannah glanced around for Jack Herman and was relieved to see him smiling and laughing with Marge and a full table of relatives. Whatever the problem was, it wasn't with Jack. But there was definitely something wrong.

"Oh, Hannah! I've got to talk to you!" Lisa said, rushing up.

"Of course. What is it?"

"Not here! Mac and Herb are waiting on the dock for us. It's private there. I promised to come and get you right away. You too, Norman."

Hannah and Norman exchanged glances as they got up to follow Lisa. Hannah's glance said, *Uh-oh. This is something big!* And Norman's answering glance said, *You can bet the farm it is!*

The sun had lowered in the sky, changing from a bright yellow ball high in the sky to a huge orange orb at the edge of the horizon. The surface of Eden Lake gleamed with color. Red, yellow, orange, and pink streaks rippled with the waves across its surface, forming a riotous canvas for the darker reflections of the pines that lined the shores. The dock protruded, a dark carpet rolled out to greet the approaching evening. Two motionless figures in silhouette stood at the end of the dock, and as they drew closer, Hannah could see their tense postures and serious demeanors.

"Norman," Herb reached out for his hand. "You've met my Uncle Mac, haven't you?"

"Yes." Norman reached out to shake Mac's hand.

"And thank you for coming, Hannah. You've met my Uncle Mac?"

"Yes, at the dance." Hannah gave him a nod and a brief smile. "Nice to see you again."

For several moments that followed the polite greetings, no one moved or spoke. It was as if they'd been turned into carved pieces on a chessboard, waiting for someone or something to move them.

"So what's wrong?" Hannah asked at last, taking a step closer and breaking the grip of inertia.

"It's Dad," Lisa said, sounding tearful. "We're afraid he killed Uncle Gus!"

CLARA & MARGUERITE HOLLENBECK'S MEXICAN HOTDISH

Preheat oven to 350 degrees F., rack
in the center position.

4-ounce can Ortega diced green chilies *(with the juice)*

2 cups shredded Jack cheese *(approximately 8 ounces)*

2 cans *(14 ounces each)* diced tomatoes *(with the juice)*

1 medium onion, chopped

2-ounce can sliced black olives *(with the juice)*

1 large green bell pepper, seeded and chopped

2 cups UNCOOKED white rice

2 packages *(approximately 1-ounce each)* Taco seasoning *(Clara buys Lawry's)*

3 cups cubed cooked chicken

1 can *(14.5 ounces)* chicken broth

½ cup cold butter *(1 stick, ¼ pound, 4 ounces)*

2 cups Fritos corn chips

2 cups *(approximately 8 ounces)* shredded Mexican cheese *** *(I used the kind with four cheeses mixed together)*

*** *If the cheese selection at your grocery store is limited, just use shredded Monterrey Jack for the first cheese, and shredded sharp cheddar for the second cheese to melt on top of the Fritos. If you can't find Monterrey Jack, use Mozzarella, or Swiss.*

Spray a 6-quart roaster with Pam or other nonstick cooking spray. *(Clara buys disposable half-size steam table pans at CostMart and uses one of those. She says to be careful to set it on a cookie sheet before you fill it, though. The disposable foil could buckle and you could end up with uncooked Mexican Hotdish all over your kitchen floor!)*

Hannah's 1ˢᵗ Note: This hotdish is easy to make because once you've got the cubed chicken, all you have to do is open a bunch of cans. You don't even have to drain them. Just dump them in your baking pan, juice and all!

In the bottom of the pan or roaster, mix together the diced green chilies, the Jack cheese, the two cans of diced tomatoes, the chopped onion, the can of sliced black olives, the chopped bell pepper, and the UNCOOKED white rice. *(Marguerite told Norman that she washes her hands and then just mixes everything up with her fingers, but that's only if no one's around.)*

Sprinkle the Taco seasoning over the top, add the chicken cubes, and mix again.

Add the chicken broth and stir everything up with a wooden spoon. *(You can also get in there with your impeccably clean hands and mix it up that way.)*

Cut the cold stick of butter into 8 pieces and put the pieces on top of the hotdish.

Cover the pan with heavy duty foil *(or a double thickness of regular foil)* and turn down the edges to seal them.

Bake the hotdish for 1½ hours *(90 minutes)* at 350 degrees F.

Take the baking pan out of the oven BUT DON'T TURN OFF THE OVEN YET. Remove the foil carefully as steam may escape.

Sprinkle the Fritos on top of the hotdish, spreading them out as evenly as you can.

Sprinkle the cheese on top of the Fritos as evenly as you can.

Don't cover the hotdish. Return it to the oven to cook for another 10 minutes, uncovered, or until the cheese has melted.

Let the baking pan or roaster sit for at least 10 minutes so the hotdish can firm up before you serve it.

Hannah's 2nd Note: When I first had this hotdish at Clara and Marguerite's condo, they served it with white wine margaritas. If you don't want to serve alcohol, it would also be good with ice cold lemonade.

Hannah's 3rd Note: Norman served this with sour cream on the side for those who wanted to put a dollop on top of their serving. (I really liked it that way.) I think it would also be good with guacamole on the side for those who want to add that.

Chapter Twenty

Mac took out a handkerchief and wiped his brow. "It was a little after one-thirty. Patsy was already sleeping, but I was still wound up from the dance and talking to all the people I haven't seen for years. I knew there was no way I was going to be able to sleep, so I got up to get a glass of water and take a couple of those aspirins with the sleep aids."

Hannah knew the type of over-the-counter medication he was talking about. "How did you come to see Jack?"

"I was running water at the sink in the kitchen, and I looked out the window. It faces the pavilion, and I saw Jack walking down the road from his cottage. He cut across to the pavilion and went around to the entrance. I think he went inside, but I don't know that for sure. You can't see the entrance from the window."

Mac stopped speaking and cleared his throat. "I thought about going out to get him and walking him back to his cottage. I was already in my pajamas, but I figured I'd just get dressed again and go out after him. But then I realized that there was somebody inside the pavilion. One of the shutters was still open, and the lights were on. I figured whoever was in there would take care of Jack if he couldn't find his way back, so I took the tablets and went back to bed." Mac stopped speaking again and sighed. "I sure wish I'd gone after him now, but you know what they say about hindsight."

Hannah glanced at Lisa. Her friend looked as if wanted to break down and sob. Hannah wanted to assure her that her father couldn't have killed Gus, but what Mac had just told them fit perfectly with what Michelle had seen from the dock. Of course Michelle hadn't known that the person she saw was Jack Herman.

"Did you tell this to the police?" Hannah asked, not knowing which answer she'd prefer. If Mac had already told Mike, the matter was out of her hands and she didn't have to worry about when she should tell him, or even *if* she should tell him.

"Of course not!" Mac shook his head. "I haven't told anybody except you four. I didn't even tell Patsy. Since I didn't see Jack go into the pavilion, I don't know for sure if he did, or not. I just saw him walking outside. The awful thing is Jack probably doesn't even remember leaving his cottage."

Lisa bit her lip. "You're probably right, Uncle Mac."

"But don't you get too upset, Lisa. I've known Jack for years. He was almost like a brother to me. He's kind, and loving, and . . . there's no way he'd do anything violent to anybody."

Hannah was silent, but her mind raced. The fight her mother had told her about between Jack and Gus wasn't exactly nonviolent. And Doc Knight had backed up that story.

"I knew if I told the cops about Jack, it would just muddy the waters." Mac reached out and took Lisa's hand. "Besides," he said, giving her hand a squeeze, "we're family. And family's got to stick together."

"She's a real trooper," Norman said, watching Lisa stick candles on top of the birthday cake she'd made for her father while Herb stood by, ready to light them.

"Yes, she is. And she loves Jack with all her heart." Hannah thought about how Lisa had given up her college scholarship, two years ago, to stay at home with her father who'd just been diagnosed with Alzheimer's. She'd wanted to become a doctor and Hannah was convinced she would have made a good one. On the other hand, Lisa seemed happy and content with the hand life had dealt her, especially now that she'd married Herb.

"What?" Norman asked, noticing Hannah's determined expression.

"I've got to clear Jack. I just have to do it for Lisa!"

"I know you do, and I'll help any way I can. How about Mike? Will you tell him what Mac told us?"

"I promised him that I'd share information."

"That's not what I asked you," Norman said with a chuckle. "Let me ask again . . . will you tell Mike?"

It was Hannah's turn to smile. "I don't know. I haven't made up my mind yet."

"And you'll put off making that decision to give yourself time to clear Jack?"

"That's probably right. I just hope my conscience doesn't get in the way." Hannah broke into applause as Lisa walked to the table where Jack was sitting, set the cake down in front of him, and led them in singing *Happy Birthday.*

"Make a wish and blow out the candles, Dad," Lisa said, kissing him on the cheek. "It's like you used to tell me when I was a little girl. If you blow out all the candles, your wish will come true."

Jack smiled as he bent over to blow out the candles, and everyone applauded when he extinguished every one. "Marge always tells me I'm full of hot air," he said, and everyone laughed again.

"That was great, Jack," Herb said, patting him on the back. "Now your wish will come true."

"It already did. I wished for enough of Lisa's Chocolate Peanut Butter Cake for everybody. And Marge and her sister are at the back table right now, dishing it up on the plates."

* * *

"Why are we here?" Norman asked, following Hannah inside as she opened the door to the cabin Gus Klein had used so briefly.

"I just want to check on the frog."

"What frog?"

"The one I saw yesterday when I came here looking for Gus. I'm just hoping the crime scene people didn't trample him, or anything like that."

"So you're going to check to make sure he's all right?"

"Yes. Don't worry. It'll just take a second and then we'll rush right back for the cake."

Norman chuckled as Hannah turned on the lights and began to look for the frog. "I'm not worried about that. I just thought we were here to check something for your investigation. And now I find out it's for the frog."

"Sorry."

"Don't be. I think it's nice of you to be concerned. Do you want me to check the bedroom?"

Hannah turned to smile at him. "Yes. I'll get the kitchen. That's where he was when I left him."

While Norman looked in the bedroom, Hannah went into the kitchen. She looked in every cupboard and checked the counters and the sink. There was no little green frog hiding anywhere that she could see.

"Hannah?"

Hannah turned to face Norman as he came into the kitchen. He was holding his hands in front of him and they were cupped around something.

"You've got him?" she guessed, hoping that she was right.

"He was under the bed."

"Is he all right?"

"He's fine. Where do you want me to put him?"

"Up here on the counter. I'll run a little water in the sink. I know he can hop down, because he was up here when I saw him the last time."

Norman placed the frog on the counter while Hannah turned the faucet on and off. "Anything else?" he asked her.

"Can you open one of the windows a little in case he wants to hop out?"

"I already did," Norman said with a smile.

"Okay, then. We can go now."

They turned off the lights and started down the road toward the scene of the party. Jack's birthday celebration was still going strong if loud voices and laughter were any indication. Norman held the flashlight in one hand, and he held Hannah's hand with the other. "Have you figured out a time line for Gus?" he asked.

"I think so. Herb took a run to the house after church and found Gus waiting. It's the old family house. Marge and Herb's dad took it over after her parents died. Gus didn't know that she gave it to Lisa and Herb, of course."

"The old family home was the logical place to go."

"That's right. Herb brought Gus to the church, and then he took everyone out to brunch at the Inn. Mother said the brunch ran late and Gus was still there when they left at two. By the time he paid the bill and left, it had to have been at least two-thirty. Then Gus drove back to Lisa and Herb's house and looked through the trunk his parents packed from his old bedroom. It was probably four thirty by the time he left there. It's thirty minutes from Lisa and Herb's house to the lake, so Gus couldn't have gotten to the cottage until almost five. Then he changed clothes and went to the dinner buffet at the pavilion."

"And that started at six. I know. I was there to take pictures. So that means he spent all of an hour at the cottage?"

"That's right, give or take thirty minutes or so." Hannah was almost sorry as they approached the lights and music of the party. She really enjoyed the time she spent alone with Norman. "I'm sorry I didn't explain about the frog, Norman."

"You shouldn't be. I think you've got your priorities straight, Hannah."

"I do?"

"Yes. Maybe a murder investigation is more critical, but the welfare of a frog is important, too."

It was almost nine in the evening by the time the party began to break up. Tomorrow would be what Lisa and Herb were calling, "Games Day." There would be the usual summer picnic games, like kickball, three-legged races, sack races, biking expeditions, tricycle parades, and team softball. There would also be water games, like swimming and diving competitions, water polo, canoe and rowboat races, and even a synchronized swimming demonstration by three junior-high girls who hoped to make their high school team. Anyone who didn't want to or couldn't play in the games was recruited to be a volunteer judge. Others were encouraged to sit in lawn chairs and cheer on the contestants.

Hannah glanced at her watch and turned to Norman. "I'm going to help clean up, and then I'm heading home. I'd invite you over, but I really need to get a good night's sleep. I haven't had my full six hours for at least a week."

"Why didn't you tell me when I called this morning?" Norman sounded surprised.

"Tell you what?"

"That Moishe acted up again. I thought the Kitty Kondo did the trick."

"I think it did do the trick. He certainly enjoyed playing with the mouse this morning. And the fact that I lost sleep last night has nothing to do with Moishe. It's Mother's fault."

"Your mother called you in the middle of the night?"

"No, she gave me a deadline for Jack's Red Velvet Cookies, and I promised to do my best to have them by tonight. When I got home last night, I researched them and mixed up three different test batches. I didn't get to bed until midnight, and Moishe started playing with the squeaky mouse at four in the morning, a minute or two before my alarm went off."

"But he didn't tear up any pillows or race around inside your bathtub?"

"No. I'm beginning to think you were right, Norman, and he was acting up because he was bored."

Once Norman had hugged her and they'd said their good-byes, Hannah started to pick up paper dessert plates and put them in the trash. In the space of fifteen minutes, the picnic tables had been wiped down and the dishes had been scraped and put into the dishwashers. Hannah was more than ready to drive home and go to bed, but there was one more thing she had to do first.

It took a while to find Lisa. Hannah finally spotted her alone at a picnic table under a pine tree. No doubt her partner wanted to be alone to think about what Mac had told them, but thinking alone wouldn't solve the problem.

"Lisa?" she said, sitting down across from her partner.

"What is it?"

Lisa's voice sounded thick, as if she'd been crying, but Hannah didn't mention that. "I need to talk to your dad for a minute," she said. "Do you think you could find us a nice quiet spot?"

"He's in a nice quiet spot right now. Herb took him back to the cottage so they could watch what's left of the ball-game. The Twins had a doubleheader with the Angels today."

"Will he mind if I interrupt him?"

"He won't mind. It's probably over by now, anyway." Lisa got up and led the way. "Are you going to ask him questions about the night of the murder?"

"Yes. I need as much background as I can get. Don't worry, Lisa. I'll do my best not to upset him."

"I don't think you'll upset him. You never have before. And I know that he really likes you."

Lisa opened the screen door and they stepped into the small cottage where Jack and Marge were staying. "Hi, Dad," she greeted her father with a kiss on the cheek, and then moved over to Herb. "How did the ballgame go?"

"Twins won the first, but the Angels won the second," Herb told her.

"Oh, well." Lisa sat down next to her father. "Hannah needs to ask you some questions, Dad. Herb and I are going to leave you with her for a couple of minutes. Hannah's our good friend, and you can tell her anything, okay?"

"Okay." Jack nodded and watched his daughter walk off. "She's a good girl," he said.

"Yes, she is. You're lucky to have her, and she's lucky to have you." Hannah moved a little closer to keep his attention and asked her first question. "Is it possible you went for a walk on Sunday night after the dance?"

"Yes, it's possible. It was the first night in a different bed. I always sleep better at home, you know."

"And you might have gone for a walk if you couldn't sleep?" Hannah asked him.

"I might have . . . Hannah. It's Hannah, isn't it?"

"That's right. You remembered!"

Jack shrugged. "It comes and goes. I just try not to get too . . . what's the word that's the opposite of calm, Harriet?"

Hannah resisted the urge to correct him. "Agitated? Frustrated?"

"Both of those. If I stay quiet, I've got a better shot at remembering. Say, Helen . . . he wasn't shot, was he?"

"No, he was stabbed with an ice pick."

"Too bad. If he'd been shot, I'd be in the clear."

"Really?"

"That's right. Emmy wouldn't let me have a gun in the house. She was always afraid the kids would get hold of it and shoot each other, or some such thing. And now my little girl's a trophy winner in that cowboy game with Herb. Life's iron . . . iron . . . what's the word?"

"Ironic?"

"That's it. Life's ironic, Hazel."

"It's Hannah," Hannah corrected him before she could think better of it.

"I know you're Hannah. I just wanted to see how many times I could call you the wrong name before you corrected me. That must have just about killed you!"

Hannah gave him a startled glance and then she started to laugh. "You're like the guy who got a hearing aid and didn't tell his family he was wearing it."

"And changed his will a dozen times," Jack finished the old joke. "You'd be surprised what I remember and what I don't. There's no rhyme or . . . whatever that other *R* word is . . . to it. Sometimes a smell will spark something I haven't thought of in years. And other times it's something I eat, or a car I see in an old movie, or an antique around the house."

"You told me that once before," Hannah said. "I was hoping those Red Velvet Cookies I made for your birthday would bring back the memory of the fight you had with Gus the night he left Lake Eden for good. I think that's one of the keys to this whole thing, Jack. I wish you could remember what that fight was about."

"So do I. But I've tried and I can't."

"Don't try so hard. Just eat another couple of the cookies tomorrow. You daughter, Iris, said Emmy used to bake them when Iris was really little."

"They *did* taste familiar. It's probably why I thought they were so good. I miss her, you know."

"Your wife?"

"That's the hardest thing about getting old. Everybody you knew when you were young is dead."

"It must be horribly depressing," Hannah commented, feeling horribly depressed just thinking about it.

"It is. But then there's the upside."

"What's that?"

"You get to outlive your enemies. That's the good part . . . unless you're the guy that killed them, of course."

CHOCOLATE PEANUT BUTTER CAKE

Preheat oven to 350 degrees F., rack
in the middle position.

WARNING: THERE ARE PEANUTS IN THIS
RECIPE. MAKE SURE YOU ASK IF ANYONE IS AL-
LERGIC TO PEANUTS BEFORE YOU BAKE AND
SERVE THIS CAKE!!!

Hannah's 1st Note: Lisa says she got the idea for this
cake by watching Marge make her Cocoa Fudge Cake.
Since Herb is crazy about Reese's Peanut Butter Cups,
Lisa's cake combines peanut butter and chocolate.

Butter and flour a 9-inch by 13-inch sheet cake pan.
*(You can also spray it with Pam or another nonstick cook-
ing spray and then just lightly dust it with flour. You can
also do what Lisa did and spray it with a product that
mixes nonstick cooking spray with flour.)*

Hannah's 2nd Note: I was really leery of the nonstick
cooking spray mixed with flour, but Lisa says it works just
fine.

2 cups white *(granulated)* sugar
2 cups flour *(don't sift—just level it off with a knife)*
———————

1 cup butter *(2 sticks, ½ pound, 8 ounces)*
1 cup peanut butter *(Lisa used Skippy creamy
    peanut butter)*
1 cup water
———————

213

½ cup cream *(or evaporated milk, if you're all out of cream)*

1 teaspoon vanilla extract

1 teaspoon baking soda

2 eggs, beaten *(just whip them up in a glass with a fork)*

Hannah's 3rd Note: Lisa used the mixer down at The Cookie Jar to make this cake. She says you can also do it by hand if you don't have an electric mixer.

Mix the sugar and the flour together at low speed.

Put the butter, peanut butter, and water into a medium-sized saucepan. Turn the burner on medium heat and bring the mixture ALMOST to a boil. *(When it sends up little whiffs of steam and bubbles start to form around the edges, take it off the heat.)*

Pour the peanut butter mixture over the sugar and flour, and mix it all up together.

Rinse out the saucepan, but don't bother to wash it thoroughly. You'll be making a frosting and you can use it again before you really wash it.

Whisk the cream, vanilla extract, baking soda, and eggs together in a small bowl.

SLOWLY, add this mixture to the large mixer bowl and combine it at medium speed. *(You have to go slowly with*

this step because you have the hot peanut butter mixture in your bowl and you're adding an egg mixture. This cake wouldn't be wonderful if you ended up with peanut butter flavored scrambled eggs!)

Scrape down the mixing bowl with a rubber spatula, remove it from the mixer, and give it a final stir by hand.

Pour the batter into the 9-inch by 13-inch greased and floured cake pan.

Bake at 350 degrees F. for 30 to 35 minutes. When the cake begins to shrink away from the sides of the pan and a long toothpick inserted in the center of the cake comes out clean, it's done.

Hannah's 4th Note: Lisa uses my Neverfail Fudge Frosting on this cake. It's given as an alternative frosting at the end of Marge's Cocoa Fudge Cake recipe, but I'll write it down again here.

NEVERFAIL FUDGE FROSTING

½ cup *(1 stick, ¼ pound, 4 ounces)* salted butter
1 cup white *(granulated)* sugar
⅓ cup cream
½ cup chocolate chips
1 teaspoon vanilla extract
½ cup chopped salted peanuts *(optional)*

Place the butter, sugar, and cream into a medium-size saucepan *(You can use the one from the cake that you didn't wash.)* Bring the mixture to a boil, stirring constantly. Turn down the heat to medium and cook for two minutes.

Add the half-cup chocolate chips, stir them in until they're melted, and remove the saucepan from the heat.

Stir in the vanilla.

Pour the frosting on the cake and spread it out quickly with a spatula. If you're pouring it on a warm cake or a cold cake, just grab the pan and tip it so the frosting covers the whole top.

Sprinkle the chopped salted peanuts *(if you decided to use them)* over the top of the frosting.

If you want this frosting to cool in a big hurry so that you can cut the cake, just slip it in the refrigerator, uncovered, for a half-hour or so.

Hannah's 5th Note: Lisa says to tell you that this cake is absolutely yummy if you serve it slightly warm. It's also wonderful at room temperature. If you keep it in the refrigerator, take it out 45 minutes or so before you plan to serve it.

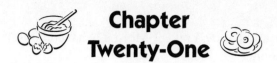

Hannah had an odd thought as she unlocked her door. If her condo complex had been built next door to the Palace of Westminster, she would be hearing Big Ben strike ten. Of course that didn't account for the time change.

It had been so long, Hannah had almost forgotten to brace herself for the furry orange-and-white cat bombardment. She staggered slightly as he landed in her arms, but she was smiling all the while. "Hi, Moishe!" she said, nuzzling him as she carried him over to his favorite perch on the back of the couch and gave him a pat before she set him down. Things were back to normal. All was right with her world.

But before she could give her pet the scratch behind the ears he'd always expected, Moishe jumped down from the back of the couch and made a beeline for the Kitty Kondo. He whisked inside, and a second later came out on the penthouse floor.

"Oh, that's your favorite perch now?" Hannah asked, walking over to give him the scratch that was part of her coming home ceremony.

She stood there petting him and listening to him purr until the phone rang. Then she hurried to the base station on the end table by the couch to get the receiver. "Hello?" she answered.

"You sound happy. I take it Moishe behaved himself while you were gone?"

It was Norman, and Hannah began to smile. "Thanks to you, he did. All I lost was another squeaky mouse, and I'm sure it's around here somewhere."

"That's the reason I called. The girl from the pet store called me on my cell phone. Their shipment of mice came in, and I stopped out there to pick up some more. If you're not too tired, I'll bring them over. But if you are, it can wait until the next time I see you."

Considerate. Norman was so considerate. And despite the fact that she'd gotten very little sleep this week, Hannah felt energized by the fact that Moishe was back to his old self.

"Come on over," she said. "I just got my second wind, and I'll put on the coffee."

Hannah put on the coffee. And while she was there in the kitchen, she gave Moishe a full bowl of food and fresh water. Then she headed straight to the pantry. She needed to serve something with the coffee when Norman arrived at her condo. It was a Minnesota tradition. The obligation to serve a kind of sweet treat was still in force, even though they'd both eaten generous portions of Jack's birthday cake less than two hours ago. A good Minnesota hostess could not serve coffee all by itself!

It took Hannah all of thirty seconds to evaluate the supplies on her pantry shelves. The *something* would be Scandinavian Almond Cake. It would make her whole place smell wonderful while it was baking, and it was easy to assemble and serve. She even had some sliced almonds to sprinkle on top of the batter. What could be easier?

Ten minutes later, Hannah slipped her loaf pan into the oven and set the timer. She was about to pour herself a cup of the coffee she'd just made when there was a knock at her condo door.

"Already?" Hannah said to Moishe, whose head had emerged from his food bowl when he'd realized that there was someone at the door. She glanced at the clock, calculated the time, and shook her head. "It's not Norman. It couldn't be. Even if he broke the land speed record, there's no way he could make it here this fast!"

Always cautious, especially when she was working on a murder case, Hannah didn't simply open the door. The fish-eye peephole that had been in the door when she'd bought her unit was practically useless. It distorted her visitors' features so much she couldn't even recognize her own mother! From force of habit, Hannah looked through it anyway, and what she saw made her rear back with a start. It *was* her own mother. At least she *thought* it was Delores.

"Uh-oh!" Hannah whispered under her breath. Delores didn't visit her at the condo. She'd stopped when Moishe had shredded her tenth pair of pantyhose. There must be something drastically wrong to have brought her here this late in the evening. But perhaps it wasn't Delores. It could be another woman with dark hair. She wasn't going to open the door until she knew for sure, so she called out, "Who is it?"

"Don't you recognize your own mother?" Delores asked. "We're sweltering out here, not to mention we're getting eaten alive by the mosquitoes. Open the door, Hannah."

Hannah opened the door and saw why her mother had answered in the plural. Delores had Michelle and Andrea in tow.

"I thought you went home after the party," Hannah addressed Andrea.

"I did, but Grandma McCann had everything under control. She said Bill called to say he'd be tied up until late, and then Mother called, and . . . here I am."

"Me, too," Michelle added. "I was getting ready for bed, but Mother decided we needed a family meeting, so she dragged us all over here."

"Well, the family's about to get bigger," Hannah said, ushering them into the living room. "Norman should be here in ten minutes or so."

Delores smiled. "That's just fine. Norman's practically family, anyway. And we don't have any secrets from him . . . do we, dear?"

Hannah was saved from the necessity of a response by an orange-and-white blur that streaked through the living room, tore through the opening in the bottom floor of his new Kitty Kondo, scrambled up two floors, and emerged at the penthouse floor to glare at his archenemy.

"Oh, how cute!" Delores exclaimed, not even noticing that Moishe was puffed up and practically spitting. "You got one of those wonderful Kitty Kondos for my darling grand-cat. You must have been saving your pennies, dear."

"I always do. And that's what it cost me. They're having a twofer sale at the pet store in the mall, and Norman bought one for Cuddles. This one cost just a dollar, so he got it for Moishe."

There was total silence for the count of ten, and then Delores cleared her throat. "Who told you that, dear?"

Hannah's eyes narrowed. "Norman did," she responded. "There *isn't* a twofer on the Kitty Kondos at the pet store?"

"Well . . . I haven't checked recently, but . . ."

"Mother!" Hannah interrupted her. "I need to know if there was a twofer on the Kitty Kondos two days ago."

"Well . . . actually . . . I'm not really sure that . . ."

"Give it to me straight, Mother," Hannah demanded. "I can take it."

Delores gave a big sigh and shook her head. "I don't think so, dear. Of course he may have negotiated a special price for some reason or other, but . . ."

"But Norman lied to me about the twofer," Hannah interrupted what was going to be another excuse.

"That would be my guess, dear. But you've got to admit that it was sweet of him to buy it."

"It *was* sweet," Hannah admitted, "but he lied to me."

"You could be right. What are you going to do about it?"

Hannah stared at her mother in shock. "Well . . . I'll just have to pay him back, that's all. I'll find out what it costs, save the money and . . ."

"And make Norman feel really bad that he gave Moishe such a wonderful present," Michelle jumped into the mother-daughter conversation. "Are you really sure you want to do that?"

"Of course I don't want to make Norman feel bad!" Hannah was outraged at the assumption. "But I don't want to accept charity, either. I own a successful business. I can pay."

"But you'd spoil all his fun," Andrea said, frowning at her older sister. "Norman thinks he put one over on you. He's proud of himself, and he's happy he found something to give you. And he's crazy about Moishe, and he wants to give him something, too. And now you want to ruin it all for him?"

"And make him feel bad for even trying to please you?" Michelle added.

"Of course not. But . . ." Hannah stopped and thought about it. Maybe her mother and sisters were right. Maybe she ought to let Norman think he'd put one over on her. And maybe she should be grateful that he cared enough about Moishe and enough about her to try to give them both a present.

"Well?" Delores raised her eyebrows in a question.

"You're right," Hannah said, giving in as gracefully as she could. "I won't say a word about it."

"Good for you!" Michelle said.

"You're doing the right thing," Andrea added.

"It's very smart of you, dear," Delores had the final word on the matter as she took a seat on the couch. "What's that divine scent?"

"Almonds," Hannah told her. "I'm baking Joyce's Scandinavian Almond Cake."

Delores looked pleased. "Is that the recipe Joyce gave me from her friend Nancy?" she asked.

"That's the one. The only difference is that I used clarified butter instead of margarine."

"When will it come out of the oven?" Andrea asked her.

Hannah turned to glance at the clock on her end table. "In about five minutes. And then it has to cool a bit, but I'll serve it warm."

"Marvelous!" Delores gave a nod. "I suppose you're wondering why we're here, dear."

"The thought did cross my mind."

"It's about Gus, of course. Marge and I got together this afternoon and made a list of all the women Gus dumped. And we called every one of them this afternoon. They all have alibis."

"*All* of them?"

"That's right. But I didn't come here just to tell you that. I stopped in at Ava's store when I left Jack's birthday party, and she told me that she talked to the credit card company. It seems the gas card Gus used to fill his tank wasn't valid."

"Uh-oh!" Hannah said, as a couple of the puzzle pieces clicked together. Gus had worn what Mike thought was a fake Rolex on his wrist, and a diamond pinkie ring made of paste. If he had been living a lie and only pretending to be rich, how many other merchants along his route from Atlantic City to Lake Eden, Minnesota, would discover they'd been defrauded?

"When did he gas up his Jaguar?" she asked, recognizing the loose end. She wasn't sure if it was important, but she knew from experience that murder cases were usually solved by asking questions and remembering the answers.

"He filled his tank when he came back from the brunch at the Inn," Delores told her. "And that was a Sunday, so Ava couldn't call in the card. She did it today, and that's when she found out that the gas card he used was no good."

"No good? Does that mean it was stolen?' Hannah asked.

Delores shook her head. "Ava said it was canceled, not stolen. The lady she talked to told her they canceled his account because the bill hadn't been paid."

"That doesn't sound good," Hannah said, taking a moment to digest the information she'd been given. Then she turned to her mother again. "Will you go out to the Inn tomorrow morning and see if Gus's charges for the brunch were accepted on his credit card? Sally must have called them in by now."

"Of course," Delores agreed.

"Great." Hannah turned to Michelle. "Will you ask Lonnie if Gus's Rolex was real? Mike told me he was pretty sure it wasn't, especially when the guys in robbery said the diamond in the pinkie ring he was wearing was paste."

"I'll do it right now," Michelle said, pulling out her cell phone and ducking into the kitchen to place the call.

Andrea began to frown. "What's going on here, Hannah? Do you know yet?"

"Not yet," Hannah told her, wishing her answer could be more definitive. "All I know is that Gus wasn't what he said he was."

"Fake," Michelle said, poking her head through the doorway. "Lonnie got a call from the jeweler today. I'll be with you in a minute, okay?"

"Do you think Gus was deliberately trying to defraud his friends and relatives?" Delores asked Hannah.

"I don't know. I didn't know him when he was growing up, but you did. What do you think?"

Delores thought about that for a long moment and then she sighed. "It's possible," she said. "I don't really want to believe it, but it's definitely possible."

SCANDINAVIAN ALMOND CAKE

Preheat oven to 350 degrees F., rack
in the middle position.

Before you start to mix up this recipe, grease *(or spray with Pam or another nonstick cooking spray)* a 4-inch by 8-inch loaf pan. *(Mine was Pyrex and I measured the bottom.)*

Cut a strip of parchment paper *(or wax paper if you don't have parchment)* 8 inches wide and 16 inches long. Lay it in the pan so that the bottom is covered and the strip sticks out in little "ears" on the long sides of the pan. *(This makes for easy removal after your cake is baked.)* This will leave the two short sides of the pan uncovered, but that's okay. Press the paper down and then spray it again with Pam or another nonstick cooking spray.

1 stick *(½ cup, ¼ pound, 4 ounces)* salted butter
1 ¼ cups white *(granulated)* sugar
1 egg *(I used an extra large egg)*
½ teaspoon baking powder
1 ½ teaspoons almond extract
⅔ cup cream *(you can also use what Grandma Ingrid used to call "top milk" or what we now call Half 'n Half)*
1 ¼ cups flour
¼ cup sliced almonds *(optional—they make your cakes look pretty)*

If you decided to use the sliced almonds, sprinkle a few in the very bottom of your paper-lined loaf pan. *(This cake is like a pineapple upside down cake—the bottom will be the top when you serve it.)*

Hannah's 1ˢᵗ Note: Now don't let this next step scare you. It's extremely easy and it will keep your cakes from turning too brown around the edges.

Place the stick of butter in a one-cup Pyrex measuring cup or in another small microwave-safe bowl. Zap it for 40 seconds on HIGH, or until it's melted. *(You can also do this in a small saucepan on the stove.)* Now pour that melted butter through a fine-mesh strainer, the kind you'd use for tea, *(or a larger mesh strainer lined with a double thickness of cheesecloth.)* After the melted butter has dripped through, dump the milk solids that have gathered in the strainer in the garbage *(or throw away the cheese-cloth, if you've used that method.)* What you have left is clarified butter.

Set your clarified butter on the counter to cool while you . . .

Mix the white sugar with the egg in a medium sized bowl, or in the bowl of an electric mixer. Beat them to-gether until they're light and fluffy.

Add the baking powder and the almond extract. Mix well.

Cup your hands around the bowl with the clarified butter. If you can hold it comfortably and it's not so hot that it might cook the egg, add it to your bowl now and mix it in. If it's still too hot, wait until it's cooler and then mix it in.

Hannah's 2nd Note: In the following steps, you're going to add half of the cream, and then half the flour. You don't have to be precise and measure exactly half. Just dump in what you think is approximately half and it'll be just fine.

Add half of the cream and mix it in.

Add half of the flour and mix it in.

Now add the rest of the cream, and mix.

And then add the rest of the flour, and mix thoroughly.

Pour the batter into the loaf pan you've prepared and smooth the top with a spatula.

Bake the cake at 350 degrees F., for 50 to 60 minutes, or until a toothpick inserted in the center comes out clean.

Let the loaf pan sit on a wire rack or a cold burner for 15 minutes. Then loosen the cake from the short sides of the pan *(the non-papered sides)* with a metal spatula or a knife.

Tip the cake out on a pretty platter, and remove the parchment paper. Let it cool and then dust the top with powdered sugar if you wish.

Hannah's 3ʳᵈ Note: Mother's friends, Joyce and Nancy, have special half-round loaf pans especially for baking Scandinavian Almond Cake. Joyce's cake bakes for the same length of time as mine does. Nancy's pan has a dark nonstick surface. It's heavier than Joyce's pan and the dark surface makes it bake faster. Nancy bakes her cake for 35 to 40 minutes, or until a toothpick inserted in the center comes out clean.

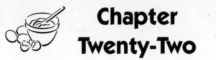

Chapter
Twenty-Two

"This is delicious cake, dear," Delores said, sipping the coffee Hannah had brought her and taking a bite of her slice of almond cake. "I think I prefer it warm . . ."

"Thank you, Mother."

"A man would be lucky to have you for a wife. You're such a good cook."

"It's my business, Mother."

"You keep a nice home, too."

"Thank you, Mother," Hannah said again. Then she took a deep breath because she knew that two compliments in a row from her mother were usually followed by a lecture about how she should settle down, get married, and start a family.

"I know you think there's plenty of time for a husband and family, but your . . ."

The start of her mother's biological-clock-is-ticking lecture was interrupted by a knock at the door. Hannah sent up a quick prayer of thanks for Norman's timely arrival and held up her hand.

"Hold that thought, Mother. I've got to get the door."

With that said and her mother momentarily silenced, Hannah hurried over, bypassed the nearly useless peephole, and called out, "Who's there?"

"Mouse delivery for Moishe," Norman announced, and

Hannah opened the door. "I can just drop them off if you're tired."

"Come in and join the party," Hannah said, opening the door all the way so he could see the assembled crew of Swensens.

"Good thing you got your second wind," he said just loudly enough for Hannah to hear him. And then he turned to them. "You came to help Hannah tie squeaky mice to Moishe's Kitty Kondo?"

"Not exactly," Michelle said, laughing. "We were just eating and discussing murder."

"Sounds like a good combination to me. Eating what?"

"Scandinavian Almond Cake," Hannah told him. "Find a seat, and I'll get you a piece with your coffee."

"Moishe's purring, Hannah," Norman remarked, after Delores, Andrea, and Michelle had left. "I can hear him all the way over here."

"That's because Mother's gone. He probably thought I was punishing him when I let her in the door."

"Or he's just glad everything's back to normal and you've forgiven him for past transgressions. You *have* forgiven him, haven't you?"

"Long before you got here. And long before Mother and the girls got here, too. Thanks to you, that's one problem solved. Now all I have to do is figure out who killed Gus."

"If you're not too tired, tell me what you've got so far." Norman took a sip of the coffee Hannah had just refilled.

"I've got lots of motives, but not many suspects. Gus wasn't a very nice person, and there's a long list of people who had a reason to dislike him, even hate him."

"And they are . . ."

Hannah grabbed her shorthand notebook and opened it to the suspect page. "I'll start at the beginning. There are a lot of girls he dated in high school and then dumped for someone else. Mother and Marge made a list. Unfortunately, every single one of them has an alibi."

"Okay. Who else?"

"Bert Kuehn. There's speculation that Gus was driving drunk and he got into the car accident that killed Bert's sister, Mary Jo. The official police report states that Mary Jo was driving, but Gus's high school baseball coach was the first on the scene, and he could have helped Gus put Mary Jo in the driver's seat."

"Did you talk to the coach?"

"No. He left Jordan High and went to coach college baseball at the University of Michigan. I haven't had time to track him down yet."

"I'll help you do that before I leave. Anyone else?"

"There's the possibility of a robbery gone bad. Gus was flashing around money and telling everyone that he was rich."

"But didn't you say that the money in his wallet was still there?"

"Yes. Mike thinks the robber might have panicked when he realized he'd killed Gus, and he fled without anything."

"But you don't agree?"

"Not really. He could have grabbed the Rolex. He wouldn't have had any way of knowing that it was a fake."

"You're sure the Rolex was a fake?"

"Positive. Michelle checked with Lonnie before you got here tonight, and he said he talked to the jeweler. It was definitely a fake, and the ring Gus was wearing was paste. Mike told me that it wasn't unusual for rich people to wear fake watches and jewelry and keep their expensive things in a safe at home. That's what he thinks Gus did."

"But you don't agree?"

"No, but I have more information now. Ava told me that Gus charged gas on a gas card that had been canceled by the company for nonpayment. Mother's going to check with

Sally tomorrow to see if the credit card he used to pay for the brunch went through okay."

"And Mike doesn't know about the canceled gas card yet?"

"No."

"Are you going to tell him?"

"I don't know yet. I'm afraid that if he thinks there aren't any valuables in Gus's apartment in Atlantic City, he might delay sending someone there to check it out. It wasn't high on his list of priorities, anyway. It's really doubtful that someone from New Jersey followed Gus here and killed him."

"That's probably right," Norman said, but he didn't look completely convinced. "But a hired killer could have hidden himself in the crowd of people here for the reunion, bided his time, and killed Gus when nobody else was around."

"Impossible."

"Why? There's got to be at least a hundred and fifty people at the lake."

"And they all get together and talk," Hannah explained. "Somebody who's not a relative would be found out in a hurry. I walked through that crowd enough to know everybody asks everybody else about how they're related, and their background, and the other relatives they know."

Norman thought about that for a moment. "You've got a point. It would be a lot harder than trying to crash a convention or another event like that."

"Back to the suspects," Hannah said, flipping the page. "There's Jack, of course. You already know about that. And then there's the gambling Gus used to do. It could be someone who thought Gus cheated him, someone who carried a grudge all these years. Or it could be someone he borrowed money from and never paid back. Mother told me he was terrible about that. He still owed her twenty dollars from high school when he left Lake Eden for good."

"He sounds like someone I'm glad I met only once," Norman said, shaking his head.

"Well put!" Hannah complimented him. "But that doesn't mean he deserved to die."

"True. Anybody else on your suspect list?"

"Ava."

Norman looked shocked. "Ava Schultz from the store?"

"That's right."

"Because of the canceled gas card?"

"No, Ava didn't know she'd been cheated until today, when she called in the charges. She doesn't have the kind of automatic pumps that accept or reject gas cards. She just writes the number on a form, has the person sign it, and calls them in."

"Okay, but why would Ava want to kill him if she didn't know about the canceled card?"

"Because he didn't stay with her."

"Ava asked him to spend the night?" Norman asked, looking surprised.

"I don't know for sure. What I do know is that she was very quick to tell me that when Gus came back to the store with her after the dance was over, it wasn't what I was thinking. She assured me that the only thing he wanted was to get some groceries."

"Maybe that's all it was."

"Maybe, but I added her to the suspect list anyway. A woman scorned is a prime suspect."

"So Ava's still a suspect?"

"No, I cleared her when Andrea brought me the crime scene photos. Gus is a couple of inches over six feet tall, and Ava's more than a foot shorter. She's also much lighter. I don't think she can weigh more than ninety pounds dripping wet."

"That's about what I'd guess," Norman said.

"So there's no way Ava could stab him in the chest with

enough force to kill him . . . unless she stool on a step stool, of course."

"And there was no step stool?" Norman asked.

"None in the whole pavilion. I know because Patsy was looking for one so she could replace the lightbulb over the back door."

"How about if she knocked him down on his back and then stabbed him?"

"How?" Hannah asked him. "He outweighed her by at least fifty pounds."

"Right. Well . . . you were probably right to take her off the list. She's a pretty unlikely candidate. Anybody else on there?

"Just one. And I'm beginning to think this last one is the one who did it."

"Who's that?"

"The unidentified suspect who killed Gus for some unknown reason. I don't know about you, Norman, but this case has really got me stymied."

"You'll solve it. You always do. Something will happen to put a few of the pieces in place and then the rest will follow."

"Thanks for the vote of confidence."

"You're welcome. Maybe that baseball coach is a piece of the puzzle. Fire up your computer, and let's see if we can find out more about him."

Once the computer was online and Norman was sitting in what Hannah thought of as the driver's seat, he turned to her. "What's the name?"

"Toby Hutchins."

"Is that *Toby* as in *Tobias?*"

"I don't know, and Mother didn't either. I asked. Before I wrote it down."

"Okay, let's go with Toby. I'm going to load the University of Michigan Web site and see what's there."

Hannah watched while the Web site loaded. "There's a place to click for athletics," she said, pointing at the screen.

"Right. We'll try that first." Norman waited, and when the athletics page loaded, he clicked on the link for baseball. Once that page came up, there was another link for history, and then one for coaches.

"We might have something here," Norman said, letting the page for baseball coaches load. But when it came up on the screen, he gave a little groan.

"What is it?" Hannah asked.

"It only gives head coaches and the years they headed up Wolverine Baseball. Didn't you say Toby Hutchins was an assistant coach?"

"That's what Mother said."

"This is a dead end, then." Norman went back to the original screen. "At least we know he lived in Ann Arbor at one time. Maybe there's something about him in the local papers." A few moments later, he asked, "Do you want to try the *Ann Arbor News*? Or the University paper, *Michigan Daily?*"

"Let's try the *Michigan Daily*. Mother was pretty sure he coached there."

Norman pulled up the Web site and did a search for Gus's high school baseball coach. There were several mentions in sports coverage, but then Norman's search took them to another page.

"Uh-oh," Hannah breathed as she saw the heading on the page. Toby Hutchins was dead and had been for three years now. He'd been killed in a boating accident. According to the obituary, there were no survivors and no one to contact. "Another dead end," she sighed. "Literally."

"Let's try the Atlantic City yellow pages," Norman suggested.

"For Toby Hutchins?"

"No, for Gus's nightclub. I want to find out if Mood Indigo actually exists."

It didn't take long to pull up the Yellow Pages and find the address for Mood Indigo. Norman printed it out, along with the phone number, and glanced at his watch. "Too late to

call," he said. "They're two hours ahead, and they're probably closed by now."

"What are you doing now?" Hannah asked as Norman
typed something in and started loading another Web page.

"Making reservations. Maybe someone at Mood Indigo
knows why Gus came back to Lake Eden."

"You're going to fly to Atlantic City?" Hannah was dumbfounded.

"Why not? Doc's filling in for me tomorrow, anyway. I'll
drive to the airport, catch the red-eye, sleep on the plane, and
get there before noon."

"But don't you have to go back home to pack a suitcase?"

"Not really. I'll pick up what I need at the airport."

"How about clothes?"

"I've got what I'm wearing, and I can pick up another
shirt. If Gus's nightclub really is as fancy as he claimed it was,
it'll probably have a dress code. I'm just glad I've got my suit
hanging in the car, and I can take off for the airport from
here."

Hannah just stared at him for a moment as the gears in her
brain whirred and then meshed. Pieces of the puzzle clicked
into place, and she reached out to hug him. And then, because that wasn't enough, she placed a big kiss on his lips.

"Wow!" Norman said when she released him. "If I'd
known that flying to Atlantic City would affect you that way,
I would have done it a long time ago!"

"That's not it," Hannah said, still slightly breathless from
the way Norman had returned her kiss.

"Then what is it? Not that I'm complaining, of course."

"Remember the suitcase on the bed?" she waited until
Norman nodded. "And the empty closet at Gus's cottage?"

"Yes."

"And the linen suit hanging in the Jaguar?"

"Of course I remember. I'm the one who climbed the fence
at the impound lot. But what does that have to do with me?"

"Gus didn't unpack and hang up his clothes, because he

knew he wasn't staying. And he hung his linen suit in the car when he changed clothes for the dance because he was planning on leaving later that night."

"How do you know all that?"

"Everything adds up. Ava told me he gassed up his car before he even found out which cabin was his. That tells me he was planning to take off again before Ava opened up in the morning."

"Okay. Anything else?"

"There's the pill I saw him take at the dance. He said it was an antacid, but I described it to Jon Walker and he thought it was a type of amphetamine. Gus wanted to be alert so he could drive back to Atlantic City. That's why he bought all those candy bars and snacks. He told Ava they were for his breakfast, but they weren't. That's why he bought the disposable cooler, too. And made his ham and cheese sandwiches at the bar in the pavilion. He was going to take them with him in the car and drive all night."

Norman thought about it for a moment. "That *does* make sense. But why did he want to leave after only one day? The reunion doesn't end until Saturday night."

"My guess is that he never planned to come to the reunion in the first place. He just saw the posters Lisa and Herb hung on Main Street and thought it was a handy excuse. He came for another reason."

"To see his family?"

Hannah shook her head. "I really doubt that. If he'd wanted to reconnect with his relatives, he would have stayed for the whole reunion. My guess is that Gus came for a purpose. And he must have accomplished it before he hung that linen suit in his car and took that pill to keep him awake."

"Okay," Norman said, standing up and giving Moishe a scratch behind the ears before he headed to the door. "I'll find out why he came here. And I'll check out his apartment to see if he really had a safe with watches and jewelry."

"Be careful," Hannah warned, feeling strangely bereft as he pulled her into his arms for a hug.

"I will be. Where's your cell phone?"

Hannah got her purse and rummaged around until she found her cell phone in the bottom. "Here it is," she announced, handing it to him.

"The battery's low," Norman said, turning it on and pressing some buttons that emitted squeaky sounds.

"Moishe likes those sounds," Hannah said, noticing that her cat had perked up his ears. "It probably sounds like a mouse symphony to him."

Norman laughed as he shut the phone and handed it to her. "Put it on the charger tonight, and don't forget to take it with you tomorrow. I'll call you when I get to Atlantic City, but you have to remember to turn your cell phone on so it'll ring."

"I will. I'll charge it up the second you leave, and I'll take it with me when I go to work tomorrow. And I'll turn it on and leave it on in my purse."

"Good. Don't forget. And be careful, Hannah."

"I will be."

"Do you promise?"

Hannah smiled. Norman really *did* care about her. "I promise," she gave her word.

"If you figure out who killed Gus before I get back, don't take any chances. And whatever you do, don't go after his killer alone. Call Mike and make sure he's got your back."

"Okay."

"Do you promise, Hannah?"

It was a much harder promise, but Hannah could see how much it meant to him. "I promise, Norman," she said.

Chapter Twenty-Three

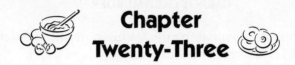

The coffee was on, Moishe's food and water bowls were filled, and she'd checked to make sure the little locks that Bill had installed on every window were engaged. All she had to do was wash her face, brush her teeth, put on the over-sized T-shirt she used for a nightgown in the summer, and crawl under the covers.

"Come on, Moishe," Hannah said, picking him up from his perch on the penthouse floor of his Kitty Kondo. "It's getting late, and I really need to . . ."

She was interrupted by a knock on the door, three sharp raps that she thought she recognized. A second later, there was a second series of similar raps.

". . . answer the door," Hannah finished her sentence, and put Moishe back on the penthouse floor. "Who's there?" she called out, even though she thought she knew.

"It's Mike. I need to talk to you. You're still up, aren't you?"

No, I'm sound asleep! Hannah felt like saying, but of course she didn't. What she said was, "I'm up. Hold on a second, and I'll get the door."

"Thanks, Hannah." Mike stepped into her living room. "I figured you were still up. I saw Norman driving out."

"Did you talk to him?" Hannah asked, hoping that he'd

say no. Norman was a law-abiding citizen. If Mike had asked him where he was going, Norman would have told him.

"I just waved. I was in a hurry to get over here."

"Is there a break in the case?" Hannah asked, sending up silent thanks to her lucky stars that Mike had been in a hurry.

"Nothing new." Mike did a double take as he saw what was on the wall by her desk. "What's *that?*"

"Moishe's new Kitty Kondo activity center. Norman installed it yesterday." Hannah stopped and thought fast. She didn't want to make Mike feel bad for not thinking of getting one for Moishe. "Thanks to the Animal Channel number you gave me, and his new activity center, Moishe's not destroying things anymore."

"Great! I've got something for him in the cruiser. I'll go down and haul it up here before I leave. I just stopped by to ask you if you learned anything I should know about."

"Actually . . . yes," Hannah said, leading him over to the couch. And then, because she was a good hostess, she asked, "Coffee?"

"Thanks, but I'm all coffeed out. I think it's because I've been drinking the swill at the station. But I wouldn't mind something sweet if you've got it."

"I've got it. I baked almond cake tonight. How about a slice with a glass of milk?"

"Sounds great!"

"Make yourself comfortable and I'll get it." Hannah made a quick trip to the kitchen. When she came back, Mike was sitting on the couch with Moishe in his lap.

"Here you go," she said, setting the cake and the milk on the coffee table. "Try the cake and see how you like it."

Mike took a bite and nodded. "I like it a lot, unless you've been watching *Arsenic And Old Lace.*"

"I haven't seen it for years, and my almonds aren't bitter," Hannah said, referring to the fact that arsenic tasted like bitter almonds. "How did they discover that, anyway?"

"You mean about the bitter almonds?"

"Yes. You can't ask dead people how the poison that killed them tasted."

Mike threw back his head and laughed. "You're right. Somebody must have tasted it without swallowing. Or reported the taste before they died."

"Gruesome. And that reminds me, did Doc Knight run a tox screen on Gus Klein?"

"Yes. It's standard operating procedure."

"Did he happen to find any traces of amphetamine?"

"Why do you want to know *that?*"

Hannah sighed. Mike wasn't being very cooperative. "I saw Gus take a green-and-white capsule at the dance. When I asked him if he should mix alcohol and medicine, he said it was an over-the-counter antacid."

"And you didn't believe him?"

"I believed him at the time. But then I started thinking about it, so I described it to Jon Walker and asked him what it could have been."

"And he told you it could have been an amphetamine?"

"Yes."

"Jon's right. It was an amphetamine. It showed up on the tox screen."

Hannah felt a sinking feeling in her stomach. "When did the tox screen come in?"

"With the autopsy. Doc put a rush on it, and I had it first thing Tuesday morning."

"But I saw you late Tuesday morning at The Cookie Jar! Why didn't you tell me about it?"

"Because it's an official document. It's against regulations for me to share official reports and documents with you."

"So there are things you're not telling me?" Hannah asked him, feeling betrayed.

"A few, yes, but only if they're something confidential that only authorized personnel can know. Besides . . . the amphetamines didn't kill him. He was stabbed with an ice pick or similar object."

The lightbulb of suspicion that had been flickering in Hannah's mind ever since she'd talked to her sisters about sharing information with Mike turned into a steadily glowing globe. She knew the truth now. Mike was holding out on her. Perhaps he didn't mean to. She'd give him the benefit of the doubt. He might truly believe that he was honoring the pact they'd made.

"What about the suitcase on the bed?" she asked. "Were there any more pills in it?"

"Come on, Hannah." Mike gave a weary sigh. "The suitcase is in the evidence room."

"And only authorized personnel can know what's in it?"

"That's right. Some of the contents could be important during the trial."

"*What* trial? You haven't arrested anyone yet."

"No, but we will. And there's no way I want the killer to walk on a technicality because I've been careless with the evidence."

"I understand," Hannah said, and she did. Mike had never said much about it, but Hannah knew that the gang member who'd shot and killed Mike's wife when she was pregnant with their first child had gotten off on a technicality. Bill had told her all about it. It was one of the reasons Mike was so determined to follow police procedure to the letter. No criminal he caught was going to walk free on a technicality if he could help it.

"I'll tell you what I can, Hannah. You know I will."

"I know." Hannah knew that Mike was sharing some information with her. But the information she would get from him wouldn't be critical to the case. He was treating her like an outsider, not a member of his team. And while he might honestly want things to be different, they wouldn't be.

"What's the matter?" Mike asked, frowning slightly.

Nothing that you'd understand, Hannah almost said, but she bit the words back. It was silly of her to be disappointed. She should have known all along that Mike's two-way street was really one-way. He might want to break the rules for her, but he wouldn't.

"Hannah? What's wrong?" Mike asked again.

"I'm just tired," Hannah said, uttering the first thing that popped into her head.

"I'd better go, then. Lock the door behind me, and I'll run down and get that present for Moishe I told you about. I'll knock when I come back up."

Hannah waited, her eye to the peephole. She was expecting to see a distorted image of Mike as he came up the stairs, but instead she saw something huge, bright pink, and fuzzy.

"Okay, Hannah. It's me."

The huge, pink, fuzzy object had Mike's voice, so Hannah opened the door. And then she started to laugh as she saw what he was carrying.

"It's a flamingo," Mike explained unnecessarily. "Didn't you tell me that Moishe liked flamingos?"

"I probably did. He loves to watch them on the Animal Channel. How big is that thing, anyway?"

"It's taller than I am, so it's six and a half feet, at least. And its name is Fred. Where do you want it?"

"Right there," Hannah said, pointing at the corner by the couch. "Will Fred fit there?"

"Sure, if we fold his wing in a little." Mike did just that as Hannah watched. "Too bad Fred doesn't have a tray in its beak, or something. You could use him as a couch table."

Just what I need. A six-and-a-half-foot table shaped like a flamingo, Hannah thought, but of course she didn't say it. Even though Fred wasn't to her taste and he looked dreadful in her living room, she was touched that Mike had thought to get the toy for Moishe.

"Thanks, Mike," she said for lack of anything better to

say. And then, because it sounded so sparse, she added, "Wherever did you find it?"

"Oh. Well . . . actually Fred's recycled. I hope Moishe won't mind."

"I don't think he does," Hannah said, watching her cat approach the big bird and rub up against it. "Is it something the police confiscated?"

"No, it's something I had at my place. Ronni brought Fred back from Florida. She bought him on that trip she took with Bill. And then she moved and she didn't have room, so I kept him at my place. I offered to give him back when she moved in across the hall, but she said she didn't want Fred anymore because he didn't match the colors in her living room."

"I see," Hannah said, wishing she hadn't asked.

"Well, I'd better go. I'm really glad Moishe likes Fred. I got a new 50-inch television and he was in the way."

Hannah walked Mike to the door, thanked him again, kissed him briefly, and sent him on his way. Then she closed and locked the door, and turned to stare at the fuchsia Phoenicopterus.

"I know you like Fred, now," Hannah said, watching her cat rub his head up against the flamingo's legs, "but do you know what he eats?"

Moishe turned to look at her, and Hannah thought he seemed concerned about the diet of Ronni's second-hand shorebird.

"Fred eats shrimp, Moishe, lots and lots of shrimp. Maybe you'd better shred him up now. Then the next time I thaw a bag of shrimp for you, you won't have any competition."

"Rowww!" Moshe responded enigmatically, staring at her with his big yellow eyes.

"You're right." Hannah gave him a smile. "Maybe I'd better take a lesson from you when it comes to Fred's first owner, and shred her, too."

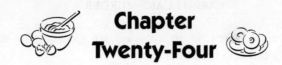

Chapter
Twenty-Four

"Bye, Moishe." Hannah tossed him a few salmon-flavored kitty treats as she headed toward her condo door. "Try to be a good boy again today. I'll be home early this afternoon to feed you."

Her hand had just connected with the doorknob when the telephone rang. Hannah muttered a phrase she wouldn't have used around her nieces in any circumstances and headed back to the kitchen to answer it. The hair on Moishe's back wasn't bristling, so it probably wasn't Delores.

"Hello?" she said, wondering who'd be calling her this early.

"Hi, Hannah."

"Norman!" Hannah began to smile as she recognized his voice. "Where are you?"

"At the airport in Atlantic City. We landed about twenty minutes ago. I'm just waiting to rent a car with GPS, and then I'll be off to find Mood Indigo."

Hannah glanced at the clock. It was five forty-five in the morning. That meant it was seven forty-five in Atlantic City. "It won't be open this early," she reminded him.

"I know. I'll just drive over and take a look at it. Then I'll have some breakfast."

"When are you coming home?" Hannah couldn't help but

ask. It was silly since Norman had been gone for less than a day, but she already missed him.

"If things go the way I hope they will, I should be back early tomorrow morning, maybe sooner if everything works out."

"Well, come by here first thing," Hannah told him. "I don't care how early it is. I want to hear all about it. Or if it's past six in the morning, stop by The Cookie Jar. I should be at work by then."

Hannah had just taken the last two trays of Cherry Winks from the oven and slid them onto the baker's rack when the back door opened and Lisa came into the kitchen.

"Lisa! What are *you* doing here? I thought you were frying pancakes for the big Game Day breakfast this morning."

"That was the plan, but it changed. I got your mother and Carrie to fill in for me."

"Uh-oh!" Hannah winced visibly. "I'm not sure about Carrie, but I know for a fact that Mother's never fried a pancake in her life. Dad always fixed breakfast for all of us."

"Don't worry. Your mother and Carrie are just setting the tables and mixing up the orange juice. That frees up Patsy to help Marge with the pancakes."

Hannah gave a big sigh of relief. "But that still doesn't explain why you're here. I finished the baking, so I really don't need any help."

"Yes, you do. I'm going to help Luanne open so that you can go out to the lake. Dad remembered something this morning, and he won't tell anybody except you."

"Is it about Gus's murder?"

"I don't know. Herb's with him at the cottage, and they're waiting for you to drive out. You don't think Dad might have . . . I mean . . . I just can't believe that . . ."

"Neither can I," Hannah interrupted her, "and I'm positive that he didn't. But maybe he remembered something from the past that'll help catch the killer."

* * *

Less than twenty minutes later, Hannah was knocking at the door of the cottage. She'd pushed her cookie truck to the limit on the highway and paid no heed to the health of her shocks as she'd flown over the gravel road that ran around the perimeter of Eden Lake.

"Hannah!" Herb greeted her, looking surprised. "How did you get here so fast?"

"Lisa said it was important."

Herb began to frown, and Hannah knew he was mentally calculating the distance and figuring out her average speed. As the only traffic enforcement officer hired by the city of Lake Eden, he'd given out enough speeding tickets to know when someone had broken the law.

"I hope you didn't speed through town," he said.

"I didn't. I did take the gravel road around the lake a little too fast, though."

"How fast?"

"I didn't look at the speedometer, but it was fast enough to bump my head on the top of the truck three times."

"That should teach you to slow down," Herb said, looking very stern. "I really ought to give you a ticket, but it's not my jurisdiction."

"But Lisa *said* it was important," Hannah repeated.

"That's what Jack told us. Come on in, Hannah. Jack's at the kitchen table. He wants to talk to you alone, so after I take you in to him, I'll go down and see if I can help with the breakfast."

Hannah stepped in, and Herb led her to the table where Jack was sitting with a cup of coffee and the box of cookies she'd given him for his birthday. "Here's Hannah to see you, Jack."

"Hi, there," Jack said, smiling at Hannah. And then he turned to Herb. "Thanks for keeping me company, son. Hannah will walk me down to the breakfast when we're through here . . ." he turned to Hannah, ". . . won't you, Hannah?"

"Of course I will."

Jack waited until Herb had left, and then he gestured toward the counter. "Would you like a cup of coffee? Marge made a full pot."

"I'd love a cup, thanks. I'll get it," Hannah filled the clean cup that was sitting by the coffeepot and carried the carafe over to refill Jack's cup. Then she sat down in the chair across from him and waited.

"Your cookies did it, girl!" Jack grinned at her. "I remembered the last time Emmy made them, and that made me remember the reason I got into that fight with Gus. I'll tell you, but you've got to promise me you won't tell anyone else, not even Lisa."

"I promise," Hannah said firmly. What Jack was about to tell her might give her a lead to follow, but it was unlikely that his memories from over thirty years ago would have a direct bearing on the events that had transpired after the dance on Sunday night.

"Gus asked me to lend him some money on the night he left town for good," Jack told her. "We were friends, and I would have given it to him if I'd had any extra, but Emmy and I were barely making it on my salary. Iris was almost two years old, and Emmy was due to have Tim any day. Emmy couldn't work, and it was hard to make both ends meet."

Hannah nodded. She could understand how a young married couple with a toddler and a baby on the way would have trouble paying the bills on only one salary.

"I told Gus I was sorry, but I couldn't help him. And then he said I had to help him because he owed money from a card game, and they'd come after him if he didn't pay it back. I felt awful, but I didn't have anything to give him. All Emmy and I had was the little bit of money we'd put away for Doc Knight to deliver Tim."

"I understand."

"Well, Gus didn't. He wanted me to give him our savings for the new baby. I told him I couldn't. And then I suggested that he ask Patsy. She was working, and she had a pretty good job."

"Did he?" Hannah remembered Patsy saying something about a loan she'd made to Gus that Mac had wanted to collect.

"He said he couldn't, because he hadn't paid Patsy back for the last loan. He owed Marge money, too. And his parents wouldn't help him out again. The last time he borrowed money from them, they'd told him it was time he grew up and accepted responsibility for his own debts."

Hannah was beginning to understand exactly what the fight had been about. "And you got into a fight because Gus wouldn't take no for an answer?"

"In a way, but that's putting it mildly. Now, you need a little background here, or you're not going to understand this next part."

"Okay." Hannah took another sip of her coffee. "Go ahead."

"Well . . ." Jack swallowed hard. "You're sure you won't tell anybody?"

"I swear I won't," Hannah promised.

"Okay, then. I was kind of shy around the girls in high school, but Gus wasn't. We were friends, so I asked his advice about asking Emmy to go out on a date with me. But before I could get up the nerve, Gus asked her out."

"That rat!" Hannah breathed.

"That's right, but it was okay because Emmy only dated him a couple of times and then she said she wouldn't go out with him anymore. When I asked Gus why he'd asked her out in the first place, especially when he knew I wanted to, he told me he was just testing the waters and they were pretty cold."

"That scum!" Hannah stated, a little louder this time.

"Another good word to describe him." Jack gave her a smile. "Of course I didn't believe Gus, but it didn't really matter because the next day Emmy asked me out."

Hannah clapped her hands. "Wonderful! And you fell in love and got married."

"That's right. Not quite that quick, of course, but we got married right after we graduated from high school. Emmy was always a good cook. I think that's where all my girls get it. And her specialty was . . . what did you call these things again?"

"Red Velvet Cookies."

"That's right. Red Velvet Cookies. People used to beg her to make them, and then they started offering her money to bake. Marge's mother hired Emmy to bake for her sewing circle. What do they do at those sewing circles, anyway?"

Hannah blinked. She'd been so wrapped up in Jack's story of the past, his question was a jolt. "I don't know. I've never been to a sewing circle, but maybe it's the same thing they do at the Lake Eden Quilting Club."

"And what's that?"

"They quilt a little, and then they eat cookies and drink coffee. And after that, they gossip about whoever's not there."

Jack threw back his head and laughed. His laughter made Hannah feel good. Except for brief moments with Marge and his children, he'd been solemn and dour for the entire duration of the reunion.

"Go on, Jack," she said, nudging him gently. "Tell me the rest of the story."

"Sure thing. Well . . ." Jack stopped, and all traces of his smile disappeared. "I'm sorry, my dear. I forget."

For a brief moment, the term of endearment puzzled Hannah. Then she remembered that Lisa had taught her father to use *my dear* when he couldn't remember a woman's name.

"That's okay," Hannah said, giving him an encouraging smile. She felt like groaning in disappointment, but of course she didn't. It would have hurt Jack's feelings and served no positive purpose. Instead, she tried to set the scene for him and take him back to the time he'd been describing. "You were just telling me how Emmy used to bake for people," she prompted. "And you said Marge's mother asked Emmy to bake cookies for her sewing circle?"

"That's right! I don't know how I could have forgotten. Anyway, Emmy baked those . . . what are they called again?"

"Red Velvet Cookies."

"Yes. She baked Red Velvet Cookies for the sewing circle. We only had the one car, and she took me to work that morning because she had to deliver them. Her mother was there for a visit, so she was taking care of . . . of . . ."

"Iris?" Hannah prompted.

"Yes, Iris. Our daughter, Iris." There was so much love in Jack's voice that Hannah felt a lump form in her throat. "And when Emmy got to Marge's mother's house to deliver the cookies, she ran into Gus. He wasn't supposed to be there. Everybody thought he'd left the night before. But he missed the bus, and he was waiting around for the next one to take him to camp."

Jack stopped and Hannah could see that he was confused. "What is it?" she asked him.

"That doesn't make any sense. I must be remembering it wrong. Gus was too old for camp. We're the same age, and I was already married to Emmy. Say . . . did I tell you we got married right out of high school?"

"Yes. I think you were talking about baseball camp," Hannah said quickly, before Jack could get off on a tangent. "Wasn't Gus supposed to leave for his Triple A baseball training camp?"

A huge smile spread over Jack's face. "That's it! Gus was supposed to leave the night before, but he missed the bus so he was still home. I bet he was out playing poker and didn't watch the time. He did that a lot. And if you're late for that kind of training, they fine you, and . . ." Jack stopped and looked confused again. "Where was I?"

"You were telling me about the cookies Emmy delivered to Marge's mother. And when she got there, she ran into Gus."

"That's what happened. How did you know that? Say . . . you weren't there, were you?"

"No, but Emmy was. And Gus was. What happened when Emmy saw Gus?"

"She said hello. Emmy was always polite. And then she gave Marge's mother the cookies. Right after that, she went out to the car to come home, but it wouldn't start. And that's when Marge's mother told Gus to take their car and give Emmy a ride home."

This time Hannah had even more trouble stifling a groan. From what she'd learned about Gus and the women he fancied, this couldn't be a good thing.

Jack took a sip of his coffee, and it was clear to Hannah that he didn't want to go on. But she needed to know, and perhaps he needed to tell the story to someone who'd promised never to repeat it. "What happened when Gus took Emmy home?"

"He didn't take her home." Jack's eyebrows met and knit in an angry line.

"Will you tell me? I promise you I won't repeat it. You can trust me, Jack."

"I know. Everybody says that. I didn't know anything, my dear. I was completely in the dark. Emmy didn't tell me about it until I got into that big fight on the night Gus left Lake Eden for good."

"Tell me what Emmy told you." Hannah reached out and took Jack's hand.

"She said Gus got fresh with her and she slapped him and walked over four miles home. Do you know why she didn't tell me about it?"

"She didn't want to worry you?" Hannah guessed.

"No, she didn't want me to kill Gus and go to jail for the rest of my life. She said she needed me and she loved me. And since nothing really happened, she didn't want to tell me about it." Jack stopped talking and blinked back tears. And after a moment, he seemed ready to go on. "Say . . . do you think that's what'll happen? "

"What do you mean?"

"I could have killed him. I was out there walking. Mac saw me from their cottage."

Hannah's eyes widened. "How do *you* know that?"

"Mac told me. He didn't know what to do about it. He said he didn't tell the cops, but he had to tell me."

Hannah was caught off guard. Mac hadn't mentioned anything about telling Jack. She regrouped quickly and asked her own question.

"Do you remember going out for a walk after the dance?"

Jack shook his head. "Marge took her sleeping pill, and we went to bed, the same as we do when we're at home. But I don't sleep very well if it's a different bed. I could have gone out for a walk. That's what I do when I can't sleep."

"You really don't remember walking that night?"

Jack shut his eyes and bowed his head. He kept that position for a long moment and then he raised his head and looked her straight in the eyes. "No, I don't remember," he said. "But there's no reason Mac would say it if I didn't. Will I go to jail if I killed Gus?"

"You didn't kill anybody," Hannah said, purely on instinct. And then, after giving it thoughtful consideration she confirmed it. "I know you didn't."

Jack looked grateful, but dubious. "I hope you're right, my dear. Anyway, I didn't know anything about this Gus getting fresh business until he threatened to tell lies about Emmy."

Hannah felt something niggling in her memory. It was something she heard, and Gus was there. Jack was there, too. It was something from the night of the dance.

"He said if I didn't give him our savings, he'd tell everybody in town that Emmy had . . . Emmy had . . . I can't say it."

"Been unfaithful to you that afternoon?" Hannah guessed, and suddenly she remembered part of the conversation she'd heard in the booth between Jack and Gus.

"Yes! But that wasn't the worst. The worst was . . . was . . . I'm sorry. I forget."

Hannah almost gasped as the section of dialogue between Jack and Gus came back to her in its entirety. Gus had said, *I met another pretty girl today, Jack's oldest daughter, Iris.* And then he'd turned to Jack and said, *She doesn't look at all like you, so I guess she must take after her mother.*

"What is it?" Jack asked, looking confused.

"I just figured it out."

"Figured what out?"

"What your fight with Gus was about. Did Gus claim Iris was his baby?"

Jack's eyes widened, and he clenched his hands into fists. "Yes! That's exactly what he said! I knew he was lying, and I told him so, but he just laughed. And then he said that if I didn't give him our savings, he'd tell everyone in town!"

"So you punched him?"

"You bet I did! Nobody can lie about Emmy like that! Emmy's my wife! I hit him, and I hit him, and I hit him, and the next thing I remember is waking up in the clinic. Doc was stitching up the cut on my face so I wouldn't scare Emmy."

"And Tim was born that night," Hannah said, hoping to bring him back to a more pleasant memory.

"That's right." Jack started to smile. "I was right there. I held her hand until Doc told me to go outside and walk around. And when I came back, there he was! My son, Timmy!"

Hannah knew she should try to bring Jack back to the present. Reliving the memories of his fight with Gus had been painful for him, and it was time to move on. "Timmy's here, you know."

"Timmy's here?" Jack looked disoriented for a moment

and then he smiled. "I know that. He came with his wife and my three granddaughters. They're in that big house thing . . . what's it called?"

"A motor home?"

"That's right. Timmy and his family are in that big motor home parked down by the picnic grounds. He drove it all the way from Chicago for our reunion."

"Actually . . . they're not in the motor home right now. Timmy and his family are at the pancake breakfast with Iris and Marge, and everybody else. Lisa's probably back by now, too. Would you like me to walk you down there?"

"Good idea. I'll join them for breakfast. I hope I didn't eat too many of these cookies and spoil my appetite. What did you call them again?"

"Red Velvet Cookies."

"That's it. Just like the ones Emmy used to bake."

Hannah got up and pushed in her chair. What she'd known all along was confirmed. The only way to clear Jack was to catch the real killer. She motioned for Jack to join her, and when he did, she took his arm.

"Say . . ." Jack said. "Did Emmy give you the recipe?"

Hannah smiled. "Emmy gave me the recipe," she replied. And, in a manner of speaking, she had.

"Good pancakes!" Hannah declared, forking up another bite. "What's the recipe, Patsy?"

"It's just the basic recipe you can find in almost any cookbook. There's nothing special about it."

"But they taste a lot better than that."

"It's because we age the batter," Marge explained. "We mix it up the day before and keep it in a covered bowl in the refrigerator overnight. Then all the flavors blend together, and all you have to do is give it a stir the next morning."

"Look at the one I made, Aunt Hannah," Tracey, Hannah's five-year-old niece, pointed to the pancake sitting on a square of wax paper next to her breakfast plate. "Aunt Patsy helped me make it."

Patsy turned to Andrea. "I told her it was all right to call me Aunt Patsy," she explained. "I hope you don't mind."

"I don't mind at all. Tracey has lots of aunts and uncles that aren't really family members."

"They're pretend aunts and uncles," Tracey told Patsy. "Aunt Hannah is real, because Mom and Aunt Hannah are sisters. And Aunt Michelle's real, too. I don't have any real uncles, but I pretend with Uncle Norman and Uncle Mike and Uncle Herb."

Since Patsy looked thoroughly confused, Hannah stepped

in to change the subject. "That's an interesting pancake, Tracey. Does it taste as good as it looks?"

"I think so. It's from the same bowl as the one I'm eating, so it should be the same."

"And the one you're eating is good?" Andrea prompted her.

"Really, really good. It's the best pancake I ever had. Maybe, if I'm not too full, I'll have one more, but not *this* one." Tracey pointed to the pancake she'd fried.

"You're not going to eat your own pancake?" Michelle asked her.

Tracey shook her head so hard her blond ponytail bounced from side to side. "I have to save it, because it's the first pancake I ever made."

"But food spoils after a while," Hannah reminded her. "You won't be able to keep it forever."

"Yes, I will. Aunt Lisa figured it out for me. She's going to take my pancake home and dry it in her . . ." Tracey stopped and glanced across the table at Lisa. "Would you tell me the name of that machine again, Aunt Lisa?"

"It's a dehydrator. It removes the moisture from fruit and vegetables so that you can store them longer."

"You're going to try to dry Tracey's pancake?" Michelle looked amused.

"Why not?" Lisa gave a little laugh. "And once I dry it, I'm going to shellac it so it won't fall apart."

Herb looked dubious. "But is that going to work?"

"It worked with the cookie ornaments I made for our Christmas tree down at The Cookie Jar. Isn't that right, Hannah?"

"Right. We used those ornaments last year, too, and they held up beautifully." Hannah winked at Lisa. "Of course Norman had to work overtime fixing all the teeth our customers broke trying to get a free cookie from the Christmas tree."

Tracey's eyes widened. "Really?" she asked.

"No, I was just kidding. But it could have happened. Those are real cookies under that shellac."

"And mine's a real pancake," Tracey said, turning to smile at Lisa. "Aunt Lisa's never dried a pancake before. My pancake will be the very first one."

"If anyone can do it, Lisa can," Jack said, leaning over to give Tracey a hug. "What are you going to do with your fine-looking pancake when it's dried?"

"I think I'll hang it on the wall in my room, so I can remember how much fun I had today."

"That's a good idea, but I think you need a fallback position."

"What's a fallback position, Uncle Jack?" Tracey asked him.

"How about calling me *Grandpa Jack?* I'm a little too old to be your uncle."

"Okay," Tracey gave him a smile. "What's a fallback position 'Grandpa Jack'?"

"It's what you do when the first thing you try doesn't work. Do you see that dentist with the camera around here anywhere?"

"He's not here," Hannah spoke up. "Norman had to go out of town, and he won't be back until tomorrow morning."

"Too bad. He could have helped us out. Does anybody else have a camera?"

Lisa gestured toward her husband. "Herb has a digital, Dad. Do you want him to take a picture for you?"

"Not for me, for..." Jack reached out and patted Tracey's shoulder. "... for my dear, here."

"Tracey," Tracey provided her name before anyone else could do it. "But you can call me *my dear*. I like it, and nobody else calls me that."

"I'm glad you like it, because I'll probably forget your name again." Jack laughed at himself, and everyone else joined in. It was a good moment, and Hannah hoped that he'd forgotten the conversation they'd had and the painful incident he'd remembered.

"So Herb . . ." Jack looked over at him. "Will you take a picture of the . . . the . . ."

Tracey leaned close and whispered something in Jack's ear.

"Right. Will you take a picture of the pancake?" Jack finished his question. "That way Tracey can have the picture framed if the pancake doesn't turn out right."

"I'll do that," Herb promised. "Good idea, Jack."

"Are you through with your breakfast, Grandpa Jack?" Tracey asked him.

"I'm through. How about you?"

"I'm through, too. I wanted another pancake, but I'm too full. Do you want to go to the store for dessert?"

"Did you say *dessert?*" Jack asked, laughing when Tracey nodded. "People don't usually have dessert after breakfast."

"But there's no rule that says you can't," Tracey said, and then she looked a little uncertain. "Is there?"

Jack shook his head. "I don't think so. What did you have in mind?"

"We could get a double Popsicle and ask Mrs. Schultz to split it for us. She's really good at it, and she never breaks them the wrong way."

"Sounds good to me as long as it's not a root beer Popsicle. I don't like root beer Popsicles."

"Me, either. Maybe she'll have lime. That's really good. Or cherry. That's even better." Tracey turned to Andrea. "Is it okay if I go with Grandpa Jack, Mom?"

Andrea smiled. "It's fine with me."

"How about you, Marge?" Jack turned to her. "Is it okay if I go to the store with Tracey?"

Marge laughed. "It's fine with me. I have to start in on the cleanup anyway."

"We'll be right back, so don't worry about us." Tracey stood up and took Jack's hand. And then they walked off together down the road to the store.

"Popsicles for breakfast!" Patsy gave a little laugh as she stood up. "I'd better get started. I have to be down at the lake at eleven to judge the swimming races. I just hope I don't topple off the judge's raft and fall in the lake!"

Andrea laughed. "Falling in the lake with all your clothes on isn't what I'd call fun. That's a nice outfit, and you might ruin it."

"Thanks," Patsy said, glancing down at her light green pantsuit. "It's not just the clothes I'm worried about, though."

"Patsy can't swim," Marge explained.

Hannah was absolutely amazed. The Lake Eden school district had a mandatory water safety program for all of its students. They'd built one of the very first indoor pools, and swimming instruction started in grade school and continued right up until senior lifesaving. "You went to school in Lake Eden and you can't *swim?*"

"That's right, and it's not for lack of trying." Patsy smiled ruefully. "Tell them Marge."

"She can't float," Marge said. "And since she can't float, she can't swim. Patsy can paddle and kick like crazy, but she can't keep her head above water for long."

"They taught me all the strokes and the kicks in the shallow end of the pool. I was really good at those. I know *how* to swim, but I just can't do it. After three or four strokes, I go straight down to the bottom of the pool."

"The swimming teacher came to the house to explain it to our parents," Marge told them. "We were supposed to be playing outside, but we came in and listened. It has something to do with bone density, or specific gravity, or natural buoyancy, or maybe all of those things."

"All I know is, everybody in the whole school tried to teach me to swim, and nothing worked," Patsy said.

"We dressed alike in grade school," Marge went on. "We looked exactly alike, and we had matching pink swimsuits. The swimming teacher couldn't tell us apart."

Patsy gave a little laugh. "Until she told us to get in the pool and float. Marge floated. I sank like a stone. I think that's the reason I don't really want to get out on that raft and judge the swimming races. I get really nervous around deep water. I tried to get Mac to take over for me. He was on the swim team at Jordan High, and he won all sorts of awards. But he's coaching the red softball team, and they've got practice."

"I'll take your place," Michelle offered. "I love to swim, and it won't bother me a bit. You said it starts at eleven?"

"That's right."

"And ends when?"

"It's for all ages, and over a hundred kids are entered. You should be through in two hours."

Michelle gave a little groan. "Uh-oh. I have a conflict. I'm supposed to help with the tricycle parade from noon to two. Unless you want to take my place helping kids decorate their tricycles?"

"I can do that. It's perfect for me. I love kids, and Mac and I never had any of our own. He never really cared one way or the other, but I always wanted to be a mother."

"You would have been a good one," Marge told her. "You sure were good with mine. How about you two?" She smiled at Andrea and Hannah. "What are your plans for the day?"

"We're going out for pizza," Hannah said, motioning to Andrea.

"You're hungry? You can't be hungry! You just had a big pancake breakfast!"

"We're not going for the food," Andrea said, catching on to her sister's agenda. "We're going fishing."

"For information?" Michelle asked.

"Exactly right," Hannah said. "It's about Mary Jo Kuehn and the night she died in that car crash. There are still some people around town who think that it was Gus's fault."

Marge looked sick. "We heard that back then. And he *said* he wasn't driving, but . . ."

"Looking back on it, we think he could have been." Patsy

gave a little sigh. "Do you think that Bert could have killed Gus because he believed that Gus was driving that night?"

"It's a possibility," Andrea said.

"And we won't know until we check out his alibi," Hannah added. "We need to ask Bert where he was between one and three on Monday morning."

"I'll watch Tracey," Michelle promised. "And if you're not back by eleven, I'll take her out to the raft to judge the swimming races with me."

Patsy looked horrified. "Oh, don't do that! What if she falls in the water?"

"It's okay. Tracey can swim," Andrea reassured her. "As a matter of fact, she's entered in the kindergarten races."

"She learned to swim this early?" Marge asked.

"Oh, yes. When Tracey was in preschool, Janice Cox taught the whole class to swim. And this year Tracey's in kindergarten, so she gets to use the school pool."

"I'll make sure I go to the races to cheer her on," Marge promised.

"How long do you think you'll be gone?" Patsy asked, stacking up the plates on the table.

"An hour at the most," Hannah told her.

"You should be fine then," Patsy said with a nod. "I looked at the schedule when I thought I'd have to be a judge, and the kindergarten race is the last one."

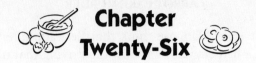

Chapter Twenty-Six

When Hannah and Andrea pulled up in Bertanelli's parking lot, it was far from packed. It was clear that pizza was not the breakfast of choice in Lake Eden. Hannah parked her cookie truck near the door, and they hopped out.

"How are we going to do this?" Andrea asked her.

"We'll just wing it. Do you think you can eat a pizza?"

Andrea thought about it as they went through the door and headed to the main room to find a booth. "I think so," she said. "But only if it's sausage, pepperoni, and extra cheese."

"No anchovies?" Hannah teased her.

"Not before noon. There's something about anchovies in the morning that's just not right, you know?"

Hannah knew. It was a lot like orange juice on corn flakes, a combination she'd once seen a friend attempt to eat when she was out of milk. It wasn't that it was so awful. It was just that it wasn't right.

"Hi, ladies," a waitress came over to greet them a moment after they'd taken a booth near the back of the room. "Can I get you something to drink?"

"Coffee would be good," Hannah told her.

And almost simultaneously, Andrea said, "I'll have coffee, please."

"Two coffees coming right up."

Andrea waited until they were alone again, and then she leaned closer to Hannah. "You mentioned that Norman was out of town. Did he go where I think he went?"

"That depends on where you think he went."

"Atlantic City?"

"That's right."

"To check out Mood Indigo?"

"Right, again. He said he'd call me on my cell phone just as soon as he found out anything at all."

"And you've got your cell phone with you?"

"I do," Hannah said, patting her oversize purse.

"And you remembered to plug it into the charger last night?"

"I did."

"And you've got it turned on?"

"I do."

The waitress came back to their booth with two mugs of coffee. "Here you go," she said, setting a mug in front of each of them.

"Thanks." Hannah decided that there was no time like the present to find out about Bert. "Is Bert in?"

"Not yet."

"How about Ellie?" Andrea asked.

"She's not here yet, either. They're still catching up on sleep from Sunday night."

Hannah and Andrea exchanged glances. "What happened on Sunday night?" Andrea asked.

"The weekly cash register tapes didn't tally with the orders from the kitchen, and we had to find the error."

Hannah picked up on the collective pronoun. "Who's *we?*" she asked.

"Bert, Ellie, and me. I'm the head waitress, so I'm responsible for the others. We went through everything until we found it."

"What was it?" Andrea asked her.

"One of the new waitresses transposed a couple of numbers. It was an honest mistake, but the register was short and we had to account for it."

"So how late were you here?" Hannah asked the critical question.

"Until a quarter to three. We close at midnight on Sundays, so it took us two hours and forty-five minutes to find it."

"I'm glad you found it," Hannah said. And in her mind she added, *in more ways than one.*

"So am I! I'm just glad that nobody had a hand in the till. That happens sometimes in the restaurant business. Would you ladies like a menu? Or do you know what kind of pizza you want?"

"We'd like a medium sausage with pepperoni, and extra cheese." Hannah ordered what Andrea had dictated.

"And mushrooms," Andrea added. "And black olives, too. What other toppings do you have?"

The waitress looked up from her order pad. "How about onions, fresh tomatoes, and anchovies?"

"Yes on the onions and fresh tomatoes," Hannah told her, "but no anchovies." She motioned toward Andrea. "She doesn't like anchovies before noon."

"Can't say I blame her for that!" the waitress said, grinning at Andrea. And then she looked down at her order pad again. "That's a medium sausage pizza with pepperoni, extra cheese, mushrooms, onions, ripe olives, and tomatoes. Is that right?"

"That's right," Hannah said.

"Can I give you ladies a little tip?"

Hannah began to smile. "Absolutely. And if it's a good tip, we'll give you a good tip, too."

"Believe me, it's a good tip!" the waitress said. "You ordered a medium sausage pizza with six extra toppings. Each extra topping is fifty cents and that means you've got an extra three dollars tacked onto your one-topping pizza, okay?"

CARROT CAKE MURDER 265

Both Andrea and Hannah nodded.

"A medium garbage pizza is only a dollar fifty more than a one-topping pizza. And a garbage pizza has all the toppings you just ordered plus anchovies. Do you follow me so far?"

"I think I'm beginning to," Hannah said, starting to smile. "What are you telling us?"

"Why don't you just order a garbage pizza and tell me to hold the anchovies? If you order that way, it'll save you a dollar fifty."

"Good tip!" Hannah said.

"It sure is." Andrea looked delighted. "We'll be sure to double that and add it on to what we would have given you anyway."

"I can't believe we ate the whole thing!" Hannah said, staring down at the empty pizza pan.

"Neither can I. I don't know what got into us."

"That would be pizza," Hannah said, laughing as she glanced around the room. It was filling up for lunch and . . .

"What is it?" Andrea asked, when Hannah's laughter stopped abruptly.

"Déjà vu. Again."

"Very funny," Andrea said, but when she caught sight of Hannah's face she began to frown. "What's wrong, Hannah?"

"Remember the time we came in here for lunch and we spotted Mike with Shawna Lee?"

"I remember. You were really upset."

"That's what I meant about déjà vu."

Andrea looked truly mystified. "What are you talking about, Hannah? Mike *can't* be here with Shawna Lee. She's dead!"

"I know that. It's not Shawna Lee. It's somebody else, but it's like déjà vu because they're sitting in the same booth and she's wearing a tight yellow sweater."

Andrea glanced over at the booth in question. "It's silk,"

she said. "I can tell from here. She's got clothes sense, who-ever she is."

"Do you recognize her?" Hannah asked.

"No. All I can see is the back of her head. Nice hair, but she could be anyone. We'd better look away, Hannah. We're staring too much."

"Why should we look away? They're sitting with their backs to us. They won't know we're staring."

"You don't know that for sure. They might."

"How? Do you think they have eyes in the backs of their heads?"

"Of course not, but maybe one of them is sensitive."

"Sensitive?"

"Like Grandma Elsa," Andrea explained. "I had to sit next to her at church, remember?"

"I remember."

"Well, she used to whisper to me if she thought someone was staring at her, and I'd turn around and look. She was always right. She said she could feel their eyes boring right into the back of her head."

"And you think Mike and that woman, whoever she is, might be able to feel us staring at them?"

Andrea gave a little shrug. "Maybe."

"Okay. We won't stare then. We'll just get up and go over there to see who it is."

"But . . ." Andrea hesitated, and then she shook her head. "I don't think that's a good idea."

"Why? We're all adults here."

"Maybe, but your voice is tight. "

"What does *that* have to do with anything?"

"It means you're all wound up. It's like that windup frog toy Mother bought for Bethany. You wind it and it puffs up. And when you let it go, it spins all over the floor and croaks."

"And you think that if I walk over to find out who that woman is, I'll spin all over the floor and croak?"

Andrea thought it over for a moment, and then she sighed deeply. "Well, maybe not the croaking part."

That did it. Hannah started to laugh. The mental image was just too much to handle.

"Shh!" Andrea warned her. "If you laugh too much, everybody's going to look at us."

Of course that made Hannah laugh harder. And since laughter was contagious, it was too much for Andrea to resist. She began to laugh, too, until both of them were nearly howling with mirth.

"Ronni Ward!" Andrea gasped, clutching Hannah's arm.

"What?" Hannah asked, still in the throes of laughter.

"She's in the booth with Mike. She turned around to look at us, and I saw her face."

If ever there was a sobering thought, a thought that could erase all traces of Hannah's laughter and even her smile, it was the thought of Ronni Ward.

"Are you sure?" she asked, hoping Andrea had laughed herself into a massive hallucination.

"I'm sure. Are you okay, Hannah? You look a little funny."

"That's because I'm turning green. You might have been wrong about the croaking, you know?"

Andrea looked worried. "You mean . . . you're so jealous, you want to die?"

"Not me. I was thinking more of Ronni Ward. And maybe Mike, too."

"Are you serious?" Andrea's worried look grew into something approaching panic.

"Relax. I'm not *that* jealous. I'm just teasing you, that's all."

Andrea let her breath out in a relieved sigh. "For a second there, I thought you were serious. Jealousy can make you . . . who's double-oh-seven?"

"What?"

"Whose ring tone is that?"

"What's a ring tone?"

"I'll explain later. Your cell phone's ringing, and the person who's calling you has the James Bond theme for a ring tone."

"I was wondering where that music was coming from." Hannah reached into her purse, pulled out her cell phone, and answered it. She talked for a moment, and then she turned to Andrea. "It's Norman, calling from Atlantic City."

"Uh-oh!"

"What's an uh-oh?"

"Mike's headed this way. Get up and go to the ladies' room. I'll keep Mike busy, and you can talk to Norman in there."

"It's weird knowing that I'm talking to you in the ladies' room at Bertanelli's," Norman said.

"I know. It feels strange to me, too." Hannah glanced around. The bathroom was neat and clean, but it certainly wasn't a place for lounging or socializing. There was only one place to sit, and Hannah took it. "What time is it there?"

"Almost two in the afternoon."

"Where are you?"

"At Mood Indigo."

Hannah was surprised. "It's open this early?"

"It's open a lot earlier than this. Alison lets them in every day at eleven in the morning. She said they do a lot of business with the lunch crowd."

"Who's Alison?"

"Alison's the . . . uh . . . headliner act at the club."

"Her name is on the marquee?"

"That's right." Norman stopped talking for a moment, and then he came back on the line. "Hold on a second, Hannah. They're about to start the next act, so it's going to get really noisy. I'll try to find a quieter spot."

Norman must not have put her on hold, because Hannah heard a blast of music, followed by raucous shouts from the audience. She couldn't quite make out the words, but it sounded like a boisterous crowd.

"This is fine, thanks," Norman said to someone there.

"Another drink?" a female voice asked.

"No, this orange juice should do it," Norman told her, and then Hannah heard a door shut and the music faded to a dull roar.

"Sorry about that, Hannah," Norman said, picking up where they'd left off. "There's a big lunch crowd today. The construction crew that's been working down the street got paid."

"So they went to a nightclub on their lunch hour?"

"That's right. Except it's not . . ." A blast of music drowned out the rest of Norman's reply, and Hannah began to frown.

"I can't hear you!" she said.

"I know. Hold on again, okay?"

There was a popping sound over the blaring music, and then Hannah heard Norman say, "Thanks, but I didn't order champagne."

A female voice replied, but Hannah couldn't hear her. She did hear Norman's laugh, however, and he sounded fascinated by whatever she'd said.

"It's nice of you to offer, but I'd better pass. I'm talking to my girlfriend."

There was another inaudible utterance by the female, and Norman laughed again. And then the door shut and the music was muted once again.

"What was all *that* about?" Hannah asked.

"You don't want to know. She came in to bring me champagne. It's what Gus told her to do whenever anyone came into his office and shut the door. It was some kind of signal, I guess."

"Do they know he's dead?"

"Not yet. And his name wasn't Gus here at the club."

"Then the detective Marge hired was right, and he *did* change his name."

"That's right. If he hadn't mentioned Mood Indigo, I never would have found a trace of him."

"What was his name there?" Hannah was curious.

"Grant Kennedy. Sounds impressive, huh?"

"Yes, it does. When are you going to tell his employees at the club that he's dead?"

"I'll tell Alison this afternoon when she takes me over to their apartment."

"Alison shared an apartment with Gus?"

"That's right. She says they've been together ever since she came to work here."

"And that was . . . ?"

"Three years ago. She's very good at what she does . . . if you like that sort of thing, of course."

"You don't like blues singers?"

There was silence for a moment and then Norman spoke. "Alison doesn't sing," he said.

"What *does* she do?"

"Uh . . . she dances."

"She dances," Hannah repeated, still having trouble meshing the two mental pictures she had of Mood Indigo, one from Gus and the other from Norman. Gus had described his club as upscale and exclusive, catering to a moneyed clientele. It certainly didn't sound exclusive to Hannah when construction workers came in on their lunch hour!

Since the two mental pictures weren't compatible, Hannah decided to ignore what Gus had told her and concentrate on what Norman had said. Mood Indigo was a place construction workers came on their payday lunch hour to watch the dancers and . . . "Exactly what does it say on that marquee?" she asked Norman.

"Um . . . I told you. It has her name, ALISON WONDER-LAND."

"Oh, boy!" Hannah breathed. She was beginning to understand precisely the type of club Gus had owned. "What else does it say on the marquee?"

There was a long silence and then Norman sighed. "Okay. I was going to tell you anyway, except not on the phone. "It says, FULL FRONTAL NUDITY."

"You're in a *strip* club?"

"Not exactly, if you're thinking of strippers like Gypsy Rose Lee. The talent at Mood Indigo is . . . uh . . . a few notches down on the socially acceptable scale."

Hannah couldn't help it. She started to laugh. She laughed so hard she couldn't talk.

"What's so funny?" Norman asked.

"I was just wondering what your mother would say if she knew you were in a sleazy strip club, drinking champagne."

"I'm not drinking champagne."

Hannah started to laugh again. It reminded her of Andrea's reply to the toy frog comparison, and that made her laugh even harder.

"Do you want me to tell you what would happen if Mother found out about it?" Norman asked, sounding very serious.

Hannah stopped laughing abruptly. Norman sounded grim. "What would happen?" she asked him.

"Even if the people in Lake Eden knew, it probably wouldn't affect my dental business. But Mother would be mortified. She'd be so embarrassed and hurt, she'd want to move away from Lake Eden. And then your mother would lose a partner and a friend. Does any of that sound familiar to you, Hannah?"

"Yes," Hannah said, realizing that Norman had used almost the same words when he'd told her about the Seattle police report and why he didn't want it to be made public.

"You got busted in a strip club when you lived in Seattle?" Hannah could hardly believe she was saying the words.

"That's right. It seems Goldie was running a little side business in the back."

"Goldie?"

"Goldie Lox. She owned the place."

Hannah was beginning to see a pattern here, with names

like Alison Wonderland and Goldie Lox. What was next? Candy Cane? Betty Will? Helen Back? Lotta Moves? And then, because she was getting sidetracked from something much more important, she asked, "What was the side business? Drugs? Prostitution?"

"Numbers. It was just a small operation, mostly sports bets from what I was told. But Goldie got raided, and everyone there was taken into custody."

"But they let you go right away, didn't they?"

"Not until I posted bail for being drunk, disorderly, and resisting arrest."

Hannah was dumbfounded. "You? I've never even seen you take a drink!"

"I did back then. It was my first year at the dental clinic, and we all went out for a drink after work on Fridays. Goldie's place was just down the block, and since she was a client of ours, we used to go there."

"You were Goldie's dentist?"

"It was more than that. She'd bring her girls in to see us whenever they had a dental problem. People might not approve of her line of business, but she was a good boss. I don't think most strip club owners give their dancers free medical and dental care."

It was something that Hannah had never considered before, and it took her a moment to respond. "You're probably right," she said.

"Anyway, that's what happened. They let my partners go because they were smart enough to cooperate with the police. I wasn't, so they kept me overnight."

"Were you convicted?" Hannah asked.

"I pled no contest and paid a fine, but the record stands. And that's why the double scotch I was drinking at Goldie's place was the last drink I ever had."

"Wow!" Hannah said, for lack of something better to say. If someone else had told her that Norman had a drunk, disorderly, and resisting arrest conviction, she would have accused that person of lying. It seemed totally out of character for Norman, and she still had trouble believing it, but she'd heard it straight from the horse's mouth. The Norman he must have been back then was totally different from the Norman he was now.

"So do you understand why I didn't want to tell you about it?" Norman asked.

"I understand. You said you were afraid I'd look at you differently."

"Right."

Hannah heard Norman take a deep breath. "So do you look at me differently?"

"Yes. It makes you seem less perfect and more of a normal person with foibles. And I feel as if I know you better, and I like you even more for telling me about it."

There was dead silence for a moment, except for the muted music in the background. And then Norman chuckled. "Well, that's a relief! I still can't believe you like me better because I've got clay feet."

"Clay is good," Hannah said. "I've got them, too. And so do most of the people I like best."

There was another blast of music, and Hannah knew the door to Gus's office had opened. A second later, it closed again and Norman came back on the line.

"I've got to go, Hannah. That was Alison. She's taking me over to their apartment now."

"And you're going to tell her about Gus?"

"Yes. And I'll ask her if she has any idea why Gus came back to Lake Eden."

"Good. Don't forget to ask her if he had any enemies and if there's anyone from there who might have wanted to kill him."

"Will do. I'll call you right after I leave the apartment. Love you, Hannah."

"Love you too, Norman." The words were out of her mouth before she stopped to think. But she *did* love Norman, so it wasn't a lie. It was possible for a person to love more than one person at once. She was living proof of that!

She punched the button to end the call, and stood up. On her way past the mirror, she fluffed up her hair and pulled her blouse down in back to cover one of her figure faults. Then she hitched up her pants at the waist to hide another figure fault and went out the door to see how Andrea had fared with Mike.

Chapter
Twenty-Seven

"Hurry, Hannah! Tracey's race is about to start!" Andrea practically streaked across the sand toward the chairs that had been set up on the lakeshore for the audience. Hannah followed, wishing she hadn't eaten that last piece of pizza, and they reached the chairs just in time to hear the whistle blow.

"Which one is she?" Hannah asked, shading her eyes with her hand.

"She's wearing the green bathing cap, the one with the little white flowers on it."

"How far up in the pack is she?"

"She's second." Andrea sounded very proud. And a moment later she let out a little squeal. "She's . . . in the lead! Do you see her? Tracey just passed the boy that was out in front!"

"I see her!" Hannah bounced up and down on the chair. "She's widening the gap, pulling way out in front, and . . . she won, Andrea! Tracey just crossed the finish line!"

"Fantastic! I knew she could do it!"

The two sisters hugged for a moment, and then they sat down again. Both of them were grinning from ear to ear.

"She's just got to join the swim team at Jordan High!" Hannah exclaimed.

Andrea laughed so hard, tears of mirth rolled down her

cheeks. And when she managed to stop laughing, she just stared at Hannah and chuckled.

"What are you laughing about? She'd be great on the swim team. She's fast, and competitive . . ."

"And only six years old," Andrea reminded her. "Tracey's in kindergarten, Hannah. She can't join the Jordan High swim team for at least eight years."

"Right," Hannah said. "Well . . . their loss, kindergarten's gain."

"Did you see me?" Tracey shouted out, racing across the beach to them.

"We saw." Andrea hugged her, wet swimsuit and all.

"You were great, Tracey," Hannah echoed her praise. You outdistanced every one of them."

"Yeah. And Calvin Janowski's pretty fast. I heard his mother say he's got an ear infection and that's why he lost, but I don't believe it. I talked to him before the race, and he was bragging about how he was going to beat me." She stopped and looked up at her mother and her aunt. "Isn't that just like a boy?"

Andrea and Hannah shared a smile, and then Hannah answered. "Pretty much, I guess. But some girls do it, too."

"I know. Karen said that if I got too confident, I was going to come in dead last."

"I think that was just a friendly warning, honey," Andrea said, taking the towel that Tracey was carrying and slipping it around her shoulders.

"Well . . . maybe."

"Karen probably wanted you to be careful not to count your chickens before they were hatched," Hannah added.

"But why not, Aunt Hannah?"

"Why not what?"

"Why not count chickens before they're hatched? You can, you know. Our whole class went out to Egg World on a field trip last year, and the egg lady showed us how to tell a fertilized egg from one that wasn't."

"Really?" Hannah felt dazed. She hadn't known they'd covered all that in kindergarten.

"How did they do that?" Andrea asked, jumping off into deep waters.

"Oh, they put them through the candle machine, and we saw the little baby chicks on the monitor. You could count those, and you'd know exactly how many chicks there would be."

"Well . . ." Hannah was momentarily at loss for words. "I guess you could do that."

"I even asked the egg lady if there was another way to know, because Grandma and Grandpa Todd don't have one of those candle machines."

"What did she say?" Hannah was curious.

"She said that all you had to do was keep the hens away from the roosters, and you wouldn't have any fertilized eggs."

Hannah exchanged glances with Andrea. They were a bit out of their depth, and it was time to change subjects.

"So, honey . . ." Andrea said, doing her best but coming up with nothing.

"Your Mom and I were just wondering what you want to do next?" Hannah bailed her younger sister out.

"I need to change out of my swimsuit and get into my regular clothes. And then I have to find Grandpa Jack, because he said he'd buy me a grape Popsicle and split it with me if I won."

"Do you want to change at Grandma's cottage?" Andrea asked her.

"No, my clothes are in the girls' changing room. If you wait right here for me, I'll just change in there."

Tracey started to scamper off, but she stopped and made her way back. "I almost forgot," she told them. "Mrs. Schultz gave me a message for you, Aunt Hannah. She said that when you got back from your lunch, you should go over and see her."

"I wonder what that's about?" Andrea commented, once Tracey had run off to the changing rooms.

"I don't know, but if she told Tracey it was important, it probably is. I'll head over there now and hook up with you later."

The Eden Lake store was deserted. Everyone was at Games Day. Hannah pushed open the door, and the bell that announced customers tinkled emptily inside. "Ava?" she called out.

Ava emerged from the living quarters in the back, wiping her hands on a dish towel. "Sorry about that. There hasn't been anyone in for an hour, so I washed my lunch dishes."

"Tracey said you wanted to see me?"

"Not really, but I thought I should. It's about the murder, Hannah. It's been eating at me, and I didn't really want to tell you, but then I started thinking about how maybe if I kept quiet some perfectly innocent person would get convicted, and . . ." Ava's voice trailed off, and she gave a little sigh. "He didn't do it, Hannah. He couldn't have. We all went to high school together, and he was the gentlest, the kindest, the nicest . . . I feel like I'm betraying an old friend!"

"Why don't you let me worry about that," Hannah soothed her. "I'm not the police. I don't have to tell them if we decide it's not important."

"You're sure? I don't want to get him in trouble."

"I'm sure. Tell me, Ava."

"It was the night Gus got killed. I did what I told you. Once he left and went back to the pavilion, I got ready for bed. I was about to climb under the covers when the bell rang in front."

"You had a customer?"

"Right. My father installed that bell in case somebody had car trouble or they were running out of gas. Nobody's used it for twenty years, but it worked, and I put on my robe and went to the front door."

"And it was . . . ?"

"Jack. Jack Herman. He was standing there looking confused, so I unlocked the door and let him in. I know about his troubles, and I figured that if he was sleepwalking or something like that, I'd take him back to the cottage and wake Marge."

"So what happened?"

"He wasn't sleepwalking. He was perfectly normal, at least I thought he was. He said he knew it was late, but he saw the light on and he hoped I'd open up and sell him a jar of pickled pig's feet for Marge."

"And you said . . . ?"

"I told him I'd be happy to, but why did he want to buy them now? It wasn't like Marge would want to eat them for breakfast, was it?"

"What was his reaction to that?"

"He laughed and said no, they weren't exactly breakfast food, but they were going to be really busy tomorrow with the family photos and all, and he thought he'd buy them now and have them on hand."

"Did he pay you?"

"Oh, yes. Jack always pays his bills. Even when he and Emmy were poor as church mice, they never charged anything as far as I know."

"Okay. Thanks for telling me, Ava." Hannah fought a feeling of defeat as she turned and headed for the door. She'd hoped that Mac was lying about seeing Jack, but now it seemed that Jack had been out at the time of Gus's murder.

"Hannah!" Patsy looked delighted to see Hannah when she appeared in the kitchen of the Thompson cottage to see if Andrea was there. "I've been looking all over for you."

"Well, you found me." Hannah made herself at home by walking over to the thirty-cup coffee pot the ladies kept going in the kitchen, and pouring herself a cup.

Patsy looked around. The kitchen was crowded with

ladies loading the dishwashers and washing pots and pans in the sink by hand. She motioned to Hannah to follow her into the deserted living room, and they took a seat on the couch.

"Marge just told me what Mac told you last night. You don't think Jack did it, do you?"

Hannah hesitated. What Ava had told her seemed to substantiate Mac's story, but she was on an emotional keel with Ava. There was no way she could believe that Jack had killed Gus. "No. Or at least I'm hoping that Jack didn't do it. I talked to him, and he doesn't remember confronting Gus."

"Would he remember it?" Patsy looked sick as she asked the question.

"I'm not sure, but I'm afraid his memory of that night doesn't count for a whole lot."

"That's what I thought." An angry expression crossed Patsy's face. "I'm so mad at Mac for telling you and Lisa that he ran into Jack on his walk. They were buddies in high school, and I thought they were still good friends. A true friend wouldn't have said anything to anybody."

"Hold on a second," Hannah's mind spun and then screeched to a shocked halt. "You said something about Mac being out on a walk when he ran into Jack?"

"That's right. Mac goes for a walk every night before bed. The doctor told him it was good for his circulation. If he misses his walk, he gets muscle cramps in the middle of the night."

Hannah felt her confusion grow at the two stories she'd heard, one from Mac and one from Patsy, that didn't jibe. "Maybe I'm confused, but this doesn't make sense. Mac told me he saw Jack through the kitchen window at the cottage."

"He did?" Patsy looked shocked. "Where did he say Jack was when he saw him?"

"Coming up the road. And Mac watched him cross over to the pavilion and walk around the side. He said it was the side with the entrance, but he couldn't see whether Jack went inside or not."

"But that can't be right!" Marge looked shocked.

"What do you mean?"

"Mac couldn't have seen Jack walk to the pavilion. There's a big pine tree in the way. We can't see the pavilion at all from the kitchen window. Mac must have run into Jack on his walk. That's the only explanation."

"I don't understand." Hannah was horribly confused. "Why would Mac lie about being out for a walk?"

Patsy just shook her head. "Oh, *that's* easy. Mac hates being in the middle of trouble, and I'm sure he didn't want to answer a bunch of questions from the police. If he admitted he was out for a walk when he ran into Jack, the police might have thought Mac went into the pavilion and killed Gus over the money."

Hannah felt as if her brain was an unfinished sweater that was starting to unravel. Nothing seemed to make any sense. "What money?" she asked.

"I told you before. It's that old loan I made to Gus. Mac wanted to go to Gus and demand that he pay back the money with interest."

"Did he ask Gus to do that?"

"He'd better not have! It was money I earned before we were married, and it was mine to spend as I wanted. I lent it to Gus to keep him from getting into trouble over a big poker game he lost. And I told him he didn't have to pay it back as long as he stopped gambling."

"Did he?"

"For a while, but it was in his blood. Some people are born to take chances, and Gus was one of them. But Mac had no right to try to collect my money. And that's exactly what I said when he told me he was going to do it. It wasn't his business in the first place, and if he'd succeeded, he just would have spent it on the stock market anyway."

"Mac invests in the stock market?"

"He doesn't invest. Investors make money at least part of the time. Mac speculates, and he loses. He's been doing it ever since we were married, and he hasn't made any money yet!"

Hannah decided it was time to get back to the subject. Patsy was getting frustrated, and that wouldn't help. "So Mac didn't want to admit that he was out for a walk, because the police might think he had something to do with Gus's murder?"

"Exactly. And it would be even more suspicious if the police found out about the loan and the fact that Mac had wanted to try to collect it. Mac was afraid they'd take him in for questioning and lock him up. That's why he asked me to lie for him if they came around asking questions. He asked me to say he was home and we were together all night."

"But you weren't."

"No."

"What did you tell him when he asked you to lie for him?"

"I told him I wouldn't, not if they asked me directly. It's just not right to lie. I said I wouldn't volunteer the information, but if someone asked me, I'd have to tell the truth."

Hannah was silent for a moment, adding up the information she'd gotten. "Was Mac angry with you when you told him you wouldn't give him an alibi?"

"He didn't seem to be." Patsy gave a little shrug. "Mac said he could understand how I felt, and he just hoped the police wouldn't nose around."

"He took it *that* well?" Hannah was surprised. "I would think he'd be upset with you for not supporting him."

"I don't think so. Of course with Mac, it's hard to tell. He can smile on the outside and seethe on the inside. We've been married long enough for me to know that."

Chapter
Twenty-Eight

Hannah was walking down the road from Ava's store to the grassy area that Lisa and Herb had designated for the nonwater games when she heard the James Bond theme again. For a moment she ignored it, assuming that it was someone's radio, but then she realized that it was coming from her purse. Norman was calling her again. She grabbed her cell phone, flipped it open, and answered. "Is it Rhodes, Norman Rhodes?" she asked in her best James Bond voice.

"Hannah! You recognized my ring tone."

"I did. It's the only one that doesn't play the default."

"What's the default?"

"It rings just like a real telephone. Why is yours different?"

"I set it that way before I left for Atlantic City. You can have personal sounds or songs for everyone in your phone book. That way you know who it is before you answer. I'll program it for you when I get back."

"And that'll be tomorrow morning?" Hannah asked, hoping that nothing had delayed him.

"That'll be later tonight. I'm at the airport right now, and I'm catching a flight in twenty-five minutes. It lands at a little after nine. "

"Your time, or my time?" Hannah asked, feeling a bit like a world traveler.

"Your time. Do you want me to meet you at your place?"

"Absolutely! And if I'm not home yet, just go downstairs and get the key from Sue or Phil again," Hannah said. And then she wondered if she'd sounded too eager. "I mean . . . if you want to, that is."

"I want to. Let me tell you what I learned from Alison."

Hannah detoured off the road and into the picnic area. It was deserted since lunch was long over, and she took a seat at a picnic table under a shady tree.

"Okay, shoot," she said.

"Let's start with no safe," Norman said, "and no money, either. The apartment was in an okay area, but it wasn't anything like the penthouse Gus bragged about."

"Then it was all lies?"

"Yes, and that includes the masseuse and manicurist on call, the dinner parties catered by a four-star restaurant, and anything else he mentioned. Everything about Gus was fake. Mood Indigo pulls in enough money to stay in business and pay living expenses, but that's about it."

"How about the Jaguar?"

"Leased. Alison said Gus had one valid credit card when he left, and that was canceled yesterday. She got the notice in the mail. Even worse than that, a month ago he borrowed money from the kind of people who break arms and legs if you're late paying them back, and they charge a lot more than the prime lending rate. Do you get my drift?"

"Oh, yes," Hannah breathed, actually feeling sorry for Gus.

"Alison said they came around looking for Gus at Mood Indigo right before he left. He gave them the money from the till, but they said that if he didn't come up with the rest by the end of this week, they'd have to think of some way to encourage him."

"Uh-oh!"

"Uh-oh is right. Alison said Gus was pretty worried when they closed the club that night, and she tried to distract him

CARROT CAKE MURDER   285

with some programs she'd taped. One was an antiques show
with appraisers that travel around the country and do appraisals for people."

"I know the one she's talking about. It's one of Mother's
favorite shows."

"Well, Alison and Gus were watching it, and all of a sud-
den Gus got up and started to pack his best clothes. He told
Alison that he had to go back to his old home town, because
he'd left something there that was worth a whole lot of
money."

"What was it?"

"He didn't tell her, but she's almost sure that something he
saw appraised on the television show gave him the idea."

"What was on the show that night?" Hannah asked the
logical question.

"Alison wasn't sure. She said she was tired and she kept
falling asleep. The only things she could remember were a
black teddy bear, some kind of famous photograph, and
some baseball cards."

Hannah pulled her notebook out of her purse and rummaged in the bottom for a pen. "Okay," she said. "The Antiques Show with a black teddy bear, a famous photograph,
and baseball cards. I'll find Mother and Carrie, and ask them
if they saw that episode."

"Great. I think we're getting close, Hannah."

"Me, too," Hannah said, although she still didn't have any
definitive answers. "You did a great job, Norman."

"Thanks. Just remember what you promised me about
calling Mike to watch your back . . . okay?"

"Okay," Hannah said, stacking a second promise on top
of her first, and wondering if the penalty was exponential for
breaking a double promise.

Hannah spotted her mother on the edge of the crowd,
looking like the queen at Ascot. She was sitting up ramrod
straight in a green Adirondack lawn chair, and she was

dressed in a white chiffon gown that tied at the waist with a wide red sash. As a concession to the bright summer sun, or perhaps as a tribute to outmoded fashion, she wore a wide-brimmed white hat with a red chiffon band around the crown. The band was adorned with red and white flowers, and Hannah began to smile as she approached. No other women in Lake Eden would have the nerve to wear such an outlandish hat, but Delores carried it off with panache.

"Hi, Mother," Hannah took the empty chair next to her mother and turned to Carrie. "Hello, Carrie. I've got a question I need to ask both of you."

"First I've got some information for you," Delores said, leaning closer, even though there was no one close enough to hear. "Carrie and I drove out to the Inn this morning, and we asked Sally about that credit card Gus used for the brunch."

"The charges went through just fine," Carrie picked up the story. "Sally said she always runs it through right away when it's a credit card from someone out of state."

"I'm glad Sally was so prompt," Hannah said. "If she'd waited a few days, she would have been out of luck."

"The credit card's been canceled?" Delores guessed.

"Right. You two watch the Antiques Show on television, don't you?"

Delores nodded. "Every week. Stan says we can deduct it as a legitimate business expense so we watch it live, and then we order the whole season through our Granny's Attic account. Since we own an antique store, it's research for us."

"Makes sense," Hannah said. "Did you watch it last week?"

Carrie laughed. "Of course we did. We haven't missed an episode yet."

"That was the one with the black Steiff bear, wasn't it, Carrie?" Delores asked.

"Yes. And the heart-shaped jewelry box with real diamonds and rubies on the top. There was a signed Ansel Adams, too."

"Maybe I'd better tell why I'm asking," Hannah said. And she proceeded to tell them part of what Norman had uncovered in Atlantic City. Naturally, she didn't mention Mood Indigo's true character. She just said that it wasn't a fancy nightclub the way Gus had described it to them. In her version of events, Mood Indigo was merely a cheap bar, and Alison was Gus's manager.

"So that's why I need to know what was on the show," Hannah wound up her story. "Gus's manager said they watched the show together, and then he told her that he had to go back to Lake Eden because he'd left something there that was worth a whole lot of money."

"And Norman uncovered all that?" Carrie asked, looking very proud of her son.

"Yes, he did," Hannah told her.

"Maybe he should have gone into the detective business. He certainly seems to be good at it."

"Don't even say something like that!" Delores warned her. "Just think of how you'd worry if Norman had to chase around after dangerous criminals."

"You're right," Carrie said, giving a little nod. "I didn't even think of that part of it."

Hannah decided it was time to get off that train of thought before Delores remembered that her own daughter had come into contact with the very same criminals she was warning Carrie against. "Anyway, we're sure that Gus came back here to get something valuable he left behind. I know he went through some of his old things. That night at the dance, he was talking about going through the trunk in Lisa's attic and looking for keepsakes from his childhood. He said he took a teddy bear and the baseball bat he used in high school."

"Maybe the bear was a Steiff," Carrie suggested. "A genuine nineteen-oh-seven black alpaca Steiff was worth a fortune, and it wasn't even in mint condition."

Delores agreed. "There's the bat, too. It could have been signed by a famous baseball player."

"But there weren't any baseball bats on that episode," Carrie reminded her. "There was the young boy with the baseball cards, but no bats."

Hannah realized that they were getting nowhere fast. "Let's go find Marge and Patsy," she said. "You can tell them what items were on the show, and they can tell us if they think Gus might have had something like that in his old room."

They sat around the kitchen table in the cottage where Marge and Jack were staying, sipping fresh coffee that Marge had just made. A plate of the Red Velvet Cookies Hannah had baked for Jack sat in the center of the table, contributed by Jack before Tim had come to take him off to the softball game.

"A Steiff bear?" Marge exchanged glances with Patsy and they both burst out laughing.

"Believe me, it wasn't an antique Steiff!" Patsy said, still chuckling. "The bear Gus took was from Uncle Carl's Five and Dime. Aunt Minnie and Uncle Carl gave every one of us a teddy bear when we were born."

Hannah listened while her mother and Carrie described the items on the show. She was amazed at how much they remembered, but Marge and Patsy kept shaking their heads.

"And then there were the baseball cards the little boy brought in," Delores said.

"They were appraised at eight hundred dollars for insurance purposes, but you wouldn't get more than half of that if you sold them at auction," Carrie said. "That wouldn't be enough to bring Gus back to Lake Eden, would it?"

Marge shook her head. "He spent more than that while he was here. Gus treated over twenty relatives to champagne brunch, and that didn't come cheap."

"Gus did have Grandpa's baseball cards, though," Patsy reminded her. "Dad gave them to him when he made the team at Jordan High."

"He didn't happen to have . . . I mean . . . it's not possible that there was actually a . . . um . . . do you remember if he had . . ."

"Wait!" Hannah interrupted her mother. Delores was so excited she couldn't seem to get the words out. "Take a deep breath, Mother. And then tell us what you're trying to say."

Delores took a deep breath. And then she exhaled with a whoosh. "Honus Wagner," she said.

"You're right!" Carrie's mouth dropped open for a moment, and then she closed it with a snap.

"After the little boy left with his baseball cards, the appraiser mentioned that there was a holy grail of baseball cards. That's what he called it. The last time that card came up for auction, it sold for over two million dollars."

Patsy made a little sound, and they all turned to gaze at her. She looked dazed, almost as if someone had bopped her over the head.

"What is it?" Hannah asked her.

Patsy just sat there motionless, staring at the wall and not blinking. Hannah was wondering if she should call for medical help, but then she seemed to snap out of it.

"Oh, my!" she said. "It's just . . . I think I *remember* that card. Honus Wagner is a really unusual name."

"Do you remember what the card looked like?" Delores asked her.

"I'm . . . I'm not sure. It's been over thirty years, but . . ." Patsy stopped and took a deep breath. "I think it had a picture of short-haired man with a black collar and "PITTS-BURGH" written across his chest in block letters."

"That's it!" Carrie shouted.

And at almost the same time, Delores exclaimed, "Gus actually has a Honus Wagner baseball card?"

"*Had* one," Hannah reminded her mother.

Marge drew in her breath sharply. "Do you think that's the reason Gus was killed? For the baseball card, I mean?"

"It could be," Hannah told her. "If it's worth that much money and the killer knew it, it's certainly a compelling reason."

"Then that means the killer has the Honus Wagner card!" Carrie looked very excited. "If we can find the Honus Wagner card, we'll find the killer!"

Hannah knew she could punch several elephant-sized holes in Carrie's logic, but she chose to refrain. What Carrie had said would work to her advantage.

"The killer doesn't know we found out about the card," Hannah told them. "And that means we can't breathe a word about it."

"Because anybody here could be the killer?" Delores guessed.

"Exactly. And even if you tell someone you *know* couldn't possibly be the killer, news like this is bound to get out. Just one wrong word could do it. Or even a suspicious reaction to something someone says. And if you actually mention it, someone could overhear you, or the person you tell could inadvertently let something slip. We have to keep our guard up and pretend we don't know a thing about it."

"Very true," Delores said with a nod. "Your father used to say that three men can keep a secret, but only if two of them are dead."

That lightened things up a little, but Hannah wasn't through. She had a plan, and she wasn't about to let loose tongues ruin it.

"Just think about how wonderful it'll be if we can recover that baseball card," she said. "I'm sure Mother and Carrie would be happy to help you sell it."

"Of course we would!" Delores said quickly.

"Naturally," Carried echoed. "And since we're friends, our fee would be just a tiny bit of what some antique dealer who didn't know you would charge."

"Of course all that goes up in smoke if the killer gets a whiff of what we know," Hannah reminded them. "It would be a real pity if he tossed a two-million-dollar Honus Wagner card in the lake to keep from being incriminated!"

There were collective sighs around the table. Patsy and Marge exchanged glances, and Hannah knew they'd keep mum. Carrie and Delores would, too, especially since she'd reminded them of the stakes. If the killer thought that they were hot on his trail and ditched the Honus Wagner card, they could be the antique dealers who'd *lost* the sale.

"Let's meet right here after the talent show," Hannah said. "Michelle, Andrea, and I won't be there. We're going to come up with a plan to smoke out the killer, and that's when I'll tell you about it."

Chapter
Twenty-Nine

The mosquito lotion had been slathered on, her coffee cup had been filled, her cell phone was in her hand, and Hannah sat on the end of the dock at their family cottage. To call, or not to call . . . that was the question. She'd made that infernal promise to Norman, not once, but twice. If what they were planning to do was dangerous, she was honor bound to tell Mike. But was it dangerous? Hannah wanted to believe it wasn't, but they were about to search the cottages. The thief who had the two-million-dollar Honus Wagner card had already killed once to get it. There was no reason to doubt that he'd kill again to keep it!

She had to tell Mike. Hannah punched in his number and waited for her call to connect. She half-hoped he wouldn't answer, but of course he did.

"Hi, Hannah," Mike said, before she could even open her mouth.

"How did you know it was me?"

"I could tell by your ring tone."

Prudence warred with curiosity, and curiosity won out. "What's my ring tone?" she asked.

"Oh. Well . . . actually it's . . . an old Beatles song that I like."

Mike sounded embarrassed, and Hannah couldn't resist following up. "What's the name of the old Beatles song?"

" 'Here Comes The Sun.' "

"Why did you choose that one for me?" Hannah asked, although she was secretly relieved that it hadn't been "Eleanor Rigby."

"It's kind of crazy, but whenever I'm around you, I feel like the sun is shining. Whether it is or not, I mean."

Hannah came close to tearing up, it was so sweet. She really didn't know how to respond, but she was saved by an electronic beeping that came over the line.

"Can you hold on a second?" Mike asked. "That's Lonnie, and he's out in the field."

Hannah told him she would, and she sat there contemplating the dusk. The sun had gone down, but the moon appeared brilliant tonight, looming over the opposite shore like a huge silver globe in the sky. It was a full moon, or very close to it, and Hannah thought that if she had a book or a magazine, she could probably read it in this light.

"Sorry about that." Mike came back on the line. "Lonnie's at Bertanelli's Pizza to check on Bert's alibi, but Bert and Ellie took the night off."

"They're out here at the lake for the children's talent show," Hannah told him.

"Thanks. I'll call Lonnie back and send him out."

"Don't bother. Andrea and I checked it out when we were in there for lunch today, and Bert had an ironclad alibi."

"But Bert wasn't there. I asked. That's the only reason I took Ronni out to lunch."

I'll bet! Hannah thought, but of course she didn't say it. She was still too flattered at learning the ring tone Mike had chosen for her.

"How did you substantiate his alibi?" Mike continued, and Hannah knew he'd opened his notebook and was sitting there, pen poised to write down what she said.

"We talked to the head waitress. When they checked the tape from the register after they closed at midnight, it didn't match the total from the order slips. The head waitress, Bert, and Ellie were there until a quarter to three in the morning, looking for the error."

"Bert was there the whole time?"

"Yes. You can cross him off your list." Hannah decided it was time for a gentle nudge. "If you'd mentioned that you suspected him, I would have told you to cross him off right away."

Mike sighed. "My mistake. What else did you find out?"

"Some things you probably know already."

"Like what?"

"Like Gus didn't own any upscale nightclubs. Mood Indigo is a strip joint, and he lives in a little apartment with one of his dancers."

"How did you . . . ?"

"Never mind," Hannah cut off the question. If he didn't ask it, she didn't have to answer it.

"Okay. What else do you know?"

"He changed his name to Grant Kennedy."

"We knew that. It was on his driver's license."

Hannah wanted to ask why he hadn't told her, but she figured she'd just get the runaround again. "Gus borrowed money from some well-connected thugs who have some scary ways of collecting."

"That figures. Go on."

"The night he left Atlantic City, Gus and his girlfriend were watching the Antiques Show, the one where they do the appraisals. She said that before it was over, he got up and started packing a suitcase. And he said that he left something valuable in Lake Eden, something that could get him out of money trouble, and he had to go back and get it."

"Of course!" Mike sounded amazed that he hadn't thought of that himself. "He came back to Lake Eden to get the Honus Wagner trading card. Our appraiser said it was worth over two million."

Hannah gulped audibly. "You *know* about the Honus Wagner baseball card?"

"Sure. We've got it in the evidence room. It was with a bunch of other baseball cards in his suitcase."

"And you didn't *tell* me about it?" Hannah began to do a slow burn.

"It's *evidence,* Hannah. I can't give you a list of the *evidence* unless you're a sworn peace officer."

Hannah counted to three. And then, because she was still seeing red, she counted on to ten. She should have known that Mike wouldn't bend any rules for her. "Do you think Gus was killed for the Honus Wagner card?" she asked.

"I doubt it. If the killer knew about it, he would have searched the cottage, looked in the open suitcase, and grabbed the card. It may be the reason the victim came back to Lake Eden, but it wasn't the reason he was killed."

"Do you have any idea why he was killed then?"

"Not really, now that you cleared Bert Kuehn. But we're working on it. Somebody picked up that ice pick and stabbed him."

"You know for sure it was an ice pick?"

"Not conclusively, no. But Doc Knight found some tiny flecks of red and green paint. That matches what you told me about the ice picks that your grandfather gave for Christmas gifts. I had Rick check with the tool companies, but he couldn't find any that manufactured an awl with red and green paint on the handle, so I figure it's got to be one of your grandfather's ice picks."

"Grandfather wouldn't be happy about that," Hannah said with a sigh. "Did you find the ice pick?"

"Not yet. We got a bad break on that. If the killer was smart, he ditched it in the lake. That's almost impossible to drag."

"Why?"

"Because it's too big, and the murder weapon is too small. It would take months, and if it's under a submerged branch or buried point down in the mud, we'd never find it anyway."

"So where did you look?" Hannah asked him.

"We went through the dumpsters at the pavilion in case the killer dropped it there, but we didn't find it. And then we used a metal detector in the bushes surrounding the building." Mike chuckled slightly. "We found nine beer can openers, too many bottle caps to count, a rusted license plate from nineteen-fifty, and eleven dollars and forty-eight cents in change."

"How about the cottages? Did you search them?"

"Only the one Gus was staying in. I knew getting search warrants would be tricky since we didn't have probable cause, and I decided it would be wasting my team's time to search any of the other cottages. The killer would have to be crazy to hang onto the murder weapon."

"You're probably right," Hannah said, but she wasn't so sure. While it might be true that a cold-blooded killer would get rid of the murder weapon immediately, it might *not* be true for someone who struck out in the heat of the moment and then panicked when he saw what he'd done.

There was another series of electronic beeps, and Mike sighed. "I've got to take that. It's Rick Murphy from the crime lab. He's observing."

Hannah said goodbye and snapped her phone shut to end the call. There was no longer a reason to search for the baseball card, but they could search for the ice pick. Mike wasn't going to do it, and they didn't need search warrants, not if they did it while everyone was at the children's talent show.

The dark shadows from the pines loomed overhead as dusk turned into night. Hannah watched the reflection of the moon on the water and mulled over everything she'd learned until she felt the vibration of footsteps on the dock.

"We're back," Michelle announced, dropping down into a sitting position next to Hannah. "Everyone from the cottages you want us to search is in line to get into the pavilion."

"Let's review to make sure," Hannah said. "Marge and Jack?"

"They're with Herb and Lisa," Andrea reported.

"How about Patsy and Mac?"

Michelle nodded. "They're a little farther back in line, ahead of Edna and her sister."

"Mother and Carrie?"

"They were . . . we're not going to search Mother's cabin, are we?" Michelle sounded thoroughly shocked.

"No. I just wanted to make sure you were paying attention."

In the next minute or two, Hannah cited six more names. When she'd been assured that her sisters had spotted all of them in line at the pavilion, she turned Andrea. "Did you bring the flashlight from your car?"

Andrea patted the Red Owl Grocery bag she'd placed next to her on the dock. "Got it. And we got the two mag lights from your cookie truck. So the search is on, right?"

"It's on, but the objective has changed." Hannah felt a bit like a general, giving instructions to his troops. "We're not going after the Honus Wagner baseball card anymore. I talked to Mike, and he told me it was in Gus's suitcase, and it's locked up in the police evidence room. What we're going for now is an ice pick with a red-and-green painted handle."

"Like the antique ones Grandpa Swensen gave out in his hardware store?" Andrea asked.

"Exactly like that. Doc Knight found flecks of red and green paint and we're pretty sure that one of Grandpa's ice picks is the murder weapon."

"Searching is boring work when you don't find anything," Michelle grumbled as they came out of the pink cottage.

"I know," Hannah said. They'd found two ice picks, but one had a metal handle, and the other one had an orange plastic handle.

"We've searched five places already, and the only even vaguely interesting thing I found is that one of Lisa's brothers and his wife use different brands of toothpaste," Michelle complained.

Andrea shrugged. "It's not that bad. Don't forget that we could be suffering through the children's talent show."

"You've got a point," Hannah said, glancing over at the pavilion, which had been released as a crime scene this morning and reopened for Lisa and Herb to use. "Only two cottages to go."

"Let's get it done," Andrea said, opening the door to the cottage where Patsy and Mac were staying and stepping inside.

Hannah headed straight for the kitchen. "Remember to keep your flashlights pointed down below window level. We don't want anyone to see a light and decide to check it out while we're here."

She didn't turn around to look, but she knew that Michelle was going to the bedroom and bathroom, while Andrea searched the living room. They'd developed a routine, and it was working well for them. Hannah pulled open the drawers, one by one, and examined the contents. Most of the rental cottages had similar items in their kitchens. One drawer held mismatched silverware that had been moved to the summer cottage when the owner had purchased a new set for the house in town. Another drawer contained cooking utensils that had been relegated to the cottage when better ones had replaced them. The pots and pans were from yard sales or closeouts at CostMart.

Hannah moved on to the drawer next to the refrigerator. That was where most summer cottage owners kept the minimal set of tools used to tighten doorknobs, hang pictures, or pry things open. She made her way through a light hammer, two screwdrivers, one of each type, and a pair of pliers. And under those tools was something that made her gasp and step back in surprise.

There it was, one of her grandfather's ice picks. The paint on the red-and-green wooden handle was flaking off, but the point was sharp and wicked looking. Was this the ice pick that had killed Gus Klein? And if it was, what was it doing in the kitchen of the cottage that Mac and Patsy had rented for the reunion?

"Hannah?" Michelle called out. "There's nothing in the bedroom or bathroom."

"Nothing in the living room, either," Andrea added.

"Are you almost done?" Michelle asked.

Hannah was silent. She hadn't heard the question. Her mind was racing, trying to put the pieces together. Was it possible Mac had stabbed Gus when Gus refused to repay the old loan that Marge had told her about? And had he lied about seeing Jack from the kitchen window because he wanted to throw suspicion on someone whose memory was failing, someone who couldn't defend himself?

"Hannah?" Michelle called out again.

"What's wrong?" Andrea asked.

This time their voices broke through the busy workings of her mind, and Hannah whirled to see both of her sisters standing just inside the kitchen door.

"I've found the ice pick," she said. "It's in the tool drawer. And I think I know who killed Gus."

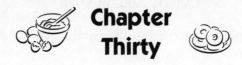
"Where are you, Hannah?" Mike answered on the first ring.

"Outside the pavilion with Andrea and Michelle. I found the ice pick, Mike."

"Where?"

"In Mac and Patsy's cottage. And I think Mac killed Gus."

There was a moment of silence, and then Mike sighed. "But that doesn't make sense, Hannah. If Mac killed Gus with the ice pick you found, why would he *keep* it?"

"I don't know. Maybe he was afraid that the owner of the cottage would notice it was missing. And since Gus was killed with an ice pick, somebody like you would put two and two together and come up with him as the killer."

"Okay. It's circumstantial, and we don't even know if the ice pick you found was the murder weapon, but I can see why you're suspicious. Do you have anything else to point a finger at Mac?"

"Yes! Mac told me he looked out the kitchen window in the cottage where he's staying with Patsy, and he saw Jack Herman out for a walk right around the time Gus was murdered. And he was lying."

There was a long silence, and Hannah began to frown. "Mike? Did I lose you?"

"You didn't lose me. It's just that Mac told us the same thing. Why do you think he's lying?"

"Patsy told me Mac went out for a walk that night. He goes for one every night, doctor's orders. He couldn't have seen Jack through the cottage window. There's a big pine tree in the way. He saw Jack on the road, all right, but they were *both* out there. And all this time, I've been afraid that Jack killed Gus."

"Me, too," Mike said, "and there's no way I wanted to believe that."

"But you didn't bring him in for questioning," Hannah reminded him.

"No. I probably should have, but . . . why? We all know Jack's memory goes in and out. And . . . well . . . there's no real proof he did it."

"You're a good man, Mike," Hannah said, meaning every word of it.

"Thanks. But maybe I'm not. Maybe I just didn't think I could get anything useful out of questioning somebody with Alzheimer's."

"There's that, too," Hannah said, "but I prefer to think that you cut him some slack because you thought it was the right thing to do."

There was another silence, and then Mike cleared his throat. "You said you found the ice pick. Where was it exactly?"

"It's in the kitchen tool drawer."

"You didn't touch it, did you?"

"Of course not! I left it right where it was."

"Okay. Everything you told me is circumstantial, but it's the best we've got unless we actually find traces of blood on the ice pick. Do you think Patsy will testify that Mac went out for a walk?"

"I'm almost sure she will. She told me that Mac came to her and asked her to lie for him. He wanted her to say he was with her all night, but Patsy refused. She told Mac she wouldn't volunteer the information, but if you asked her directly, she wouldn't lie for him."

"Good for her! I'll be right out to pull Mac in for further questioning. He's definitely a person of interest, if not more. Where is he right now? Do you know?"

"He's watching the children's talent show, and Patsy's with him. Andrea and Michelle saw them in line, waiting to get inside the pavilion."

"Good. Go on in and watch him ~~for him~~, and don't say anything to anybody. I don't want him to know we're interested in him. I should be there in less than fifteen minutes to take him in for questioning."

"Okay. We'll go inside and watch him. What do you want us to do if he leaves?"

"Don't follow him. If he *is* the killer, it could be dangerous if he thinks anybody's on to him. Just let him go, and we'll find him later."

"Okay. Anything else?"

"Keep an eye on his wife, too. If he thinks she might mention that walk he took, he could try to silence her."

Hannah gulped. "You mean he might . . . kill her?"

"That's *exactly* what I mean." Hannah heard an engine roar into life. "I've got to go, Hannah. I'm on my way, and I need to keep this line open."

Once Hannah hung up, she turned to her sisters and related what Mike had said. "He said he'll be here in fifteen minutes," she concluded.

"Let's go find Mac and Patsy," Andrea led the way to the door of the pavilion. "If we fan out, it'll be easier for us to see them in the audience. Lisa said they were making three aisles. There's one in the middle and one on either side."

"I'll take left," Michelle said.

"And I'll take the middle and look on both sides," Andrea said. "It'll take me a little longer, but that way I can double check for both of you."

"That leaves me with the right," Hannah said. "We'll just walk down the aisles, turn around, and walk back. Then we'll get together right outside the door to see which one of us spotted them."

When they entered the pavilion, the Beeseman sisters were ending their five minutes of song with "Gary, Indiana" from *The Music Man,* a perfect choice since it was their hometown.

The next act started the moment the Beeseman sisters left the stage. It was a group of twelve girls with lighted batons, performing an act to a Sousa march. All eyes were on the stage to see who could twirl her baton the longest without dropping it, and it was the perfect time to canvas the audience without being noticed. Once her sisters had arrived at their starting points, Hannah motioned them forward.

Hannah's eyes scanned the rows as she moved slowly forward, down one row to the end, up to the row in front of it, and then all the way back to the aisle. Like the carriage on an old-fashioned typewriter, she wove her way to the front of the room, and then she started the return trip.

Where only the backs of heads had been visible on her way to the front of the room, Hannah could see actual faces on her return trip. She saw her mother and Carrie, Jon Walker and his wife, Earl Flensburg, and Marge's cousins from Florida, but she didn't spot Patsy or Mac.

Hannah finished first, and she ducked out the door to wait for her sisters. Michelle came out next and she was shaking her head.

"You didn't spot them?" Hannah asked her.

"No, and there were no empty chairs, so they weren't in the bathrooms or anything like that."

"Good for you!" Hannah complimented her foresight. "Let's just hope that Andrea spotted them."

It seemed to take forever, but it probably wasn't more than a minute or two before Andrea came out.

"Anything?" Hannah asked her.

"No. I checked both sides, and they weren't there. I'm sure of it, Hannah."

"What now?" Hannah asked, the sinking feeling in her stomach growing into a full-blown panic. "You saw them in line."

The door opened again, and the three sisters turned to stare as Marge stepped out. "Hi," she said. "I saw you come in, and then I saw you leave. Is something wrong?"

Hannah gave a little sigh. "It could be. We were looking for Mac and Patsy, but we didn't spot them in the audience."

"They decided to skip the talent show," Marge reported, and she looked happy. "They were waiting in line, and Patsy said Mac had a change of heart. He begged her to give their marriage one more chance, and he said he wanted to take her to the water lily garden to propose to her all over again."

"The water lily garden in the middle of the lake?" Hannah asked, feeling her panic grow.

"That's right. It's where he proposed to her the first time. Isn't that just too romantic for words?"

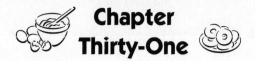

Chapter
Thirty-One

Things happened so fast that Hannah's mind spun, even though she was the one who was making them happen. Hannah and Michelle raced for a canoe, while Marge and Andrea waited on the road for Mike so that they could tell him where they'd gone.

No more than two minutes passed before Michelle and Hannah were paddling out in one of the rental canoes. Lisa and Herb had lined them up on the shore for the relatives to enjoy, and Michelle and Hannah had claimed the one on the end for their own.

"Do you know where the water lily garden is?" Michelle asked her.

"It's just off Sandy Point," Hannah told her. "Norman took me there."

It was a still night, and sounds carried across the water. There was the sound of the waves lapping against the shore, the occasional cry of a night bird, and a splash as some creature of the lake surfaced and then dove back down again.

Hannah held her finger to her lips, and Michelle nodded to show she understood. Their words would carry a great distance if they spoke aloud.

Another minute or two of steady paddling and they could hear voices. At first they were indistinct. Only the intonation was heard. It sounded conversational, rather than confrontational, and Hannah took heart. She couldn't tell how far away they were, but she knew it would take them at least five more minutes of paddling to get to the water lily garden.

Then the tone of the voices changed, and the words became distinct. The woman, Hannah was almost certain it was Patsy, sounded angry.

"I don't understand!" her voice floated over the water. "What difference does it make if the police know you went for a walk? They can't arrest you for murdering Gus if you didn't do it!"

Mac gave a mirthless chuckle. "Oh, but I did," he said.

"You . . . *did?*" Patsy sounded horrified.

"That's right. I told you I wanted to get that money back, and I went over to the pavilion to get it. Gus said *you* gave it to him. And since it was *your* money in the first place, he didn't have to pay *me* back."

"He was right. It wasn't your money."

"Sure it was. You're my wife. I earned it by being married to you all these years."

Patsy didn't say anything. Hannah could imagine how hurt and frightened she was.

"When I told him he had to pay it back, he *laughed* at me. And he wouldn't quit laughing, so I stabbed him to shut him up."

"You . . . killed him," Patsy said, and Hannah could tell she was close to a state of shock.

"That's right, and I'm not sorry I did. The only problem I've got now is you."

"But I won't tell anybody you killed him! I promise, Mac!"

Mac laughed, and it wasn't a pleasant sound. "Oh, sure. You won't tell anyone until I take you back to shore and you can run for help. Don't try to lie to a liar, Patsy. I'm a lot better at it than you are."

"But I love you, Mac!" Hannah could tell by the tone in Patsy's voice that she was desperate.

"Well, that's nice. Too bad I don't love you, huh?"

There was a moment of silence while Hannah and Michelle paddled hard. Mac was going to kill Patsy. Hannah was convinced of it. She just hoped that they could make it to the water lily garden in time!

We're on the way. Just keep him talking until we get there! Hannah urged her silently. And that was when Patsy spoke again.

"I can't testify against you, Mac."

"What do you mean?"

"Even if I wanted to, I couldn't."

"Why not?" Mac sounded suspicious.

"Because a wife can't testify against her husband. And I'm your wife, Mac. Even if I tell somebody what you said, they can't use it against you. That would be hearsay. And hearsay's not admissible in court."

"You're sure about that?" Mac sounded as if he were considering her argument, but Hannah had her doubts. It was more likely he was playing with Patsy like Moishe played with a mouse.

"Of course I'm sure," Patsy said, and to Hannah's ears she sounded desperate again. "I've been a legal secretary for almost thirty years."

"Well that *is* interesting. I've got to admit that. You're positive you're right then?"

Hannah motioned for Michelle to hurry. The water lily garden was just ahead. They'd be on the scene in less than a minute.

"I'd stake my . . ." Patsy stopped suddenly and gave a little sob. "It's all true, Mac. There's no way I can say anything in court to hurt you."

Mac gave a little chuckle and the hair stood up at the back of Hannah's neck. She could tell a crisis was coming with the force of a speeding freight train.

"Patsy, Patsy, Patsy," Mac mock chided her. "You're talking

about a trial here. But there's not going to *be* any trial. There's not even going to be an arrest."

Hannah could hear Patsy crying. They were very close now.

"We're all alone out here, and this canoe is going to flip right over." Mac chuckled again. "And you can't swim, can you, Patsy girl?"

"Stop!" Hannah shouted out, giving a mighty lunge on her paddle to hurtle them forward. "Stop or I'll shoot!"

Michelle gave her a startled glance, but she leaned on her paddle and the canoe leaped forward into the clearing that contained the water lily garden.

Mac didn't wait to see who it was. He just flipped the canoe and Patsy hit the water with a cry. Michelle and Hannah arrived just in time to see her go down into the watery depths.

"I'll get her," Michelle shouted.

"Take her to the point." Hannah gestured toward Sandy Point, which was only a half mile away. "I'll get him."

Hannah watched as Michelle grabbed Patsy and started to swim to shore with her. Patsy didn't panic the way most non swimmers do. Instead she let Michelle support her in the water and kicked with her feet to help them move. Once Hannah was sure they were going to make it, she turned to locate Mac. But before she could do more than glance at the overturned canoe, her own canoe began to tip.

Hannah used an expression she would not have considered around her two nieces, but half of it came out underwater. She was being dragged down to the bottom by Jordan High's champion swimmer.

If you get dumped in the water with all your clothes on, the first thing to do is get rid of your shoes. The words of Hannah's first swimming teacher came back to her in a rush. It was good advice. Hannah hated to lose her favorite sneakers at the bottom of Eden Lake, but it was better than losing her life at the bottom of Eden Lake.

If a drowning person gets you in a stranglehold, don't hold back. Pinch, gouge, bite, do anything you can to get out of it.

The moment that second piece of advice came to mind, Hannah started to fight. She dug her elbow into Mac's ribs, gouged at his eyes, pinched in a place she hoped would do real damage, and bit down on his arm.

The result was explosive. There was a yelp she could hear underwater, and suddenly she was freed. Hannah didn't stick around to see what would happen next. She kicked out with all her might and shot away several feet. After two deep breaths to restore her oxygen, and kicking all the while, she dove underwater, changed directions ninety degrees, and swam as far as she could.

When she came up, she saw she'd been successful. Mac was looking for her about ten feet from where she'd emerged. He hadn't expected her to change directions, but she couldn't play this hide-and-seek game for long. It was like rolling dice and betting on the outcome. She'd keep changing direction, he'd keep guessing where she would surface, and eventually he'd be right. It was the law of averages, and nobody could break that law. And then he'd grab her again and hang on, prepared for her to put up a fight. The element of surprise would be gone, and she'd end up at the murky bottom of Eden Lake with no air in her lungs.

"I see you!" His voice floated across the water to her. "You're a sitting duck, Hannah."

He'd spotted her! Hannah almost groaned. The moon reflecting off the water was just too bright tonight. She waited until he was about six feet away and then she ducked under the water again. She'd run the same pattern she'd run before. He wouldn't expect that . . . she hoped.

Her lungs were burning when she came up for air and discovered that she'd won another round. Mac hadn't expected her to make exactly the same ninety-degree turn underwater. But he would the next time she dove down. And he'd be waiting for her when she surfaced.

"Ah! There you are! Why don't you just give it up, Hannah? You're in lousy shape, and I'm not."

He was trying to distract her. Hannah knew she shouldn't listen. She had to plan out what to do next.

"I can keep this up all night. You know I'll get you eventually. And then I'll get her. And your sister. But you won't be around to see that."

Straight line. Try it, her mind shouted out. *What have you got to lose?*

My life, Hannah answered. But it was a good idea, and she decided to go with it.

A curious thing happened as she dove beneath the surface of the water. She thought she heard something droning in the distance, something like a motor. Was someone coming to help her? Or was she so scared that she was imagining things?

She snagged something with her hand, and for a moment, Hannah thought he'd come under the water to grab her. But it was something slippery like the stem of a plant or . . .

She was on the edge of the water lily garden! Hannah hadn't realized that she was so close. And then she remembered something that she'd said to Norman in what now seemed like eons ago. *I could always be a floating face in the middle of any of Monet's water lily paintings. It would be like* Where's Waldo? *and nobody would even spot me.*

A quick mental picture of the water lily garden the way she'd seen it that afternoon with Norman, and she knew it was about twenty feet across. Could she dive down even further to get under the shallow roots and swim ten feet in to come up in the middle?

What do you have to lose? her mind asked again, and this time she didn't bother to answer. She had something to gain if she made it. And if she didn't, what she'd lose would be lost anyway.

Her lungs felt like they were bursting, but she forced her feet to kick as she propelled herself under the surface, straight for what she hoped was the middle of the water lily garden. She had to surface without a sound. No gasp for breath or splash allowed.

Hannah forced her body on until she knew she couldn't swim another stroke. And then she wound her body through the maze of floating roots, tangled stems, and blossoms. Once she was close to the surface, she willed herself to remain perfectly stationary and silent, and not to gulp at the air her lungs needed so desperately.

She floated and her nose came up. She breathed the beautiful slightly sweet-smelling air. She took two breaths, and then she let her face just break the surface. There were plant stalks around her, taller than her head. That was very good. She straightened her body and let the top part of her head emerge. Carefully, cautiously, she surfaced up to her nose, no further. And nothing, absolutely nothing, happened!

Of course he was looking for her. Hannah expected no less. But he hadn't spotted her here in the middle of the water lily garden. She was part of a Monet exhibit, and he wouldn't think to look for her here.

As she remained there, grabbing roots around her with her legs to keep herself stable, she watched for any sign of him. If he started to swim toward Sandy Point, she'd dive down out of her cover in the water lily garden and grab the nearest canoe. She knew how to right it, and she'd head off after him. A canoe paddle could be a lethal weapon, and she wouldn't hesitate to use it.

But she could see him there, his head bobbing about the surface of the moonlight-clad water, looking for her in all directions. And then she saw something else coming from Sandy Point. It was a speedboat, and the motor was loud across the surface of the lake. There was a searchlight skimming the water, and Hannah knew that help had arrived.

They'd spotted him! Hannah saw someone dive into the water and haul him to the boat. She was safe. And Michelle and Patsy were too, since the speedboat had stopped at

Sandy Point and whoever was on it must know that they were okay.

"Hannah!" an amplified voice called across the surface of the water, and Hannah recognized Mike's voice. "Hannah!"

It was like Marlon Brando yelling "Stella!" in *A Streetcar Named Desire,* and Hannah responded to the anguished cry. "I'm here in the water lily garden."

"Hannah!" Mike yelled again. And this time it was a joyful cry.

Hannah took that as her cue, and she dove down under the garden, deep enough to bypass the roots, stems, and blossoms that had served her so well. This time when she surfaced, there was a smile on her face, and she gave a little wave as she swam out into the bright path of the searchlight that seemed as welcoming as sunlight.

Chapter
Thirty-Two

It was Sunday evening, the Beeseman-Herman family reunion was over, and they were gathering in the lobby at the Inn, waiting until they'd all arrived to be seated in the dining room. Andrea, Hannah, and Tracey were sitting on a couch by the mammoth stone fireplace when Michelle walked in.

"Wow!" Michelle said, gazing at Andrea. "You look absolutely fantastic!"

"Thank you," Andrea gave her a smile.

"I love your hair. That four-color weave is amazing. And your outfit's gorgeous, too."

Hannah felt the pangs of guilt begin. Andrea had mentioned she was having a complete makeover this weekend. It was time for a sisterly act of contrition.

"I'm sorry, Andrea," Hannah apologized. "You *do* look wonderful. I just didn't notice."

"Neither did Bill," Andrea said, and she didn't look happy.

"Maybe that's because you always look like you just walked out of a modeling session," Michelle told her, covering the situation smoothly. "I'm sure that's why Bill didn't notice."

"Well . . . maybe." Andrea looked slightly mollified. "You like the dress then?"

"Gorgeous," Hannah said, seizing the opportunity and jumping in quickly.

"Hello, darlings!" Delores breezed in with Carrie and Norman. "Bill and Lonnie just pulled into the parking lot, and Lisa and Herb were right behind them." She turned to smile at all of them and her gaze stopped on Andrea. "You look lovely, dear. Is that a new dress?"

"Yes." Andrea began to smile.

"Well, it's perfect for you. And I like your new hairstyle." Delores turned to Tracey. "Doesn't your mother look wonderful?"

"Mommy's always beautiful," Tracey replied, earning a hug from Andrea.

Once Bill, Lonnie, Lisa, and Herb had joined them, they made their way to the largest table in the dining room of the Lake Eden Inn. As usual, Delores had arranged place cards, and Hannah found hers. She was seated between Mike and Norman again. She gave a little sigh, decided it wasn't worth making a fuss about, and pulled out her chair to sit down. But before she could take her place at the table, Tracey rushed up to her.

"Aunt Hannah?" Tracey looked anxious. "Will you go to the ladies' room with me?"

Hannah nodded and slid her chair in again. There was more to this request than met the ear. Tracey was one of the most independent very-soon-to-be first graders in her class. If she'd needed to visit the ladies' room, she would have told Andrea where she was going, and gone by herself.

Hannah waited until they got out into the carpeted hallway outside the dining room, and then she asked, "Okay, what is it?"

"I want to get three more Girl Scout merit badges before the awards program, and one of them is for cooking. You have to make lunch all by yourself. The only part I can't do is dessert, and I want to have cookies."

Hannah thought she knew what was coming. "And you want me to teach you how to bake cookies?"

"Yes, Aunt Hannah. Will you, please? I can't ask Mom. You know why. I can't ask Grandma Delores, either. I know she doesn't bake. And if I ask Grandma McCann, I might hurt Mom's feelings."

"And you don't think it'll hurt your mom's feelings if I teach you to bake?"

"Why would it?" Tracey shrugged, and it was a miniature duplicate of Andrea's shrug. "You're the professional, Aunt Hannah. Everybody knows that."

Flattery will get you everywhere, Hannah thought, *and that's something you* did *get from your mother!* But of course she didn't say that. She said instead, "I'll be happy to teach you to bake, Tracey. It'll be fun."

"Chocolate Chip Crunch Cookies?" Tracey asked her. "They're Mom's favorites and then I can bake them for her."

"Good idea. Do you want to go on to the ladies' room? Or was that just a ploy to get me alone to ask me?"

"It was just a ploy. Let's go back in, Aunt Hannah. I want to use Mom's cell phone to talk to Bethany. She couldn't come because she's too little for one of Grandma's dinner parties, but I promised I'd call and tell her good night."

It was a lovely meal. Delores had ordered something new on the menu. It was called "A Taste of the Lake Eden Inn," and it was a meal of ten small samples of Sally's best dishes.

"That was great!" Bill said, putting down his fork after eating the last morsel of Sally's Flourless Chocolate Cake. And then he turned to Andrea. "That tasted almost as good as you look tonight. I've got the most beautiful wife in the world."

For one brief second Andrea looked shocked, but then she started to smile. "Thank you, honey," she said.

Thank you, Bill, Hannah thought, but she didn't say it. She was glad Bill had taken her advice when she'd cued him in about Andrea's makeover. "Thank you, Mother," she said instead. "That was a wonderful meal!"

Everyone else jumped on the bandwagon, thanking Delores for inviting them and complimenting her on her menu choice. When the thanks had died down, Delores rose to her feet and gestured toward Carrie. "We have some very good news, but I'll let Carrie tell you. And after she does, I have some personal good news of my own."

Delores sat down, and Carrie stood up. Hannah had a feeling they'd rehearsed this. "I'm not sure you know this, but Marge and Patsy asked us to hold a silent auction for the Honus Wagner baseball card that belonged to their brother, Gus. We sent out notices yesterday morning, and as of two o'clock this afternoon, our Granny's Attic Web site had received five firm offers."

"Tell them about the minimum opening bid," Delores prompted.

"The minimum opening bid for the card was one million, five hundred thousand dollars," Carrie said. "That's the least it could sell for. And the fact that we've received five bids in less than forty-eight hours shows that there are a lot of interested parties out there. I wouldn't be surprised if the winning bid is over two million dollars."

"When does the bidding close?" Andrea asked.

"Next Saturday morning at ten. We gave them a week to discuss it with their clients and enter a bid."

"That's wonderful!" Hannah clapped her hands. And then she asked the question she knew was on everyone's mind. "Who gets the money?"

"It'll be divided evenly between Marge and Patsy," Delores told them. "Gus never married, and he had no children. Marge and Patsy are his only surviving siblings."

Herb gulped so loudly, they all heard it. "You mean Mom and Aunt Patsy could each inherit almost a million dollars?"

"That's right," Carrie told him, "minus our commission, of course. And now Delores has something to tell you."

"It's the real reason we're celebrating tonight," Delores said, smiling at all of them, "but not even Carrie knows why."

Carrie nodded. "It's true. She wouldn't tell me. She said she wanted to tell everyone all together."

All eyes were on Delores, and she clearly reveled in the moment. Hannah decided to ask the critical question. "What are we celebrating, Mother?"

"Remember when we all got together at the Inn the last time?" Delores asked.

"I remember."

"And I said I was working on a secret project, and I'd tell you if it actually happened?"

"I remember," Hannah said.

"Well . . . it happened."

"*What* happened?" at least four of them asked at once, and Delores laughed.

"The secret project was my book. And a big New York publisher bought it."

For a moment they were all shocked speechless, and Hannah was the first to recover. "Congratulations, Mother! Is it a book about antiques?"

"No, it's fiction."

Carrie's mouth dropped open in surprise. "A Regency Romance?" she guessed.

"You're right!" Delores told her, looking very proud of herself. "And I used every one of you for characters. Isn't that marvelous?"

Uh-oh! Hannah said under her breath. "You used all of us?" she asked aloud.

"Of course, dear. One must write from life, you know. My three dear daughters are in it, of course, and I think I did a good job of depicting your true characters." She turned to Carrie. "Naturally you're in it, Carrie. And so is Mike, and Norman, and Lisa, too. You're there, Herb. And Bill. And

Lonnie. I even put some members of my Regency Romance group in it."

"How about me, Grandma Delores?" Tracey asked.

"Of course, darling. I couldn't write a book without putting you in it. You might not be the age you are now, though, so don't look for a six-year-old girl."

"Okay, Grandma. I won't."

"You know what they always say about real people in books, don't you?" Delores asked them, her eyes scanning the crowd.

"No, what do they say?" Hannah finally asked, when no one else spoke up.

"They say that people don't recognize themselves because they don't see themselves the way others do."

Uh-oh! Hannah's mind said again. *This could be very bad.*

"I did my best to be entirely truthful and take off the rose-colored glasses I normally wear to view my friends and loved ones," Delores went on. "I wrote you the way you truly are, the way someone who didn't know and love you like I do, would describe your flaws and your strengths."

"Oh, brother!" Hannah breathed, a little louder than she had intended. She was rewarded by a smile from Norman and a gentle nudge of approval by Mike.

"I didn't quite hear you, Hannah. What was that again?" Delores asked her.

Hannah thought fast. "I said *Oh, Mother* to get your attention. I wanted to ask you when they're going to publish your book."

"Sometime next year."

Perfect, Hannah thought. *That should give me enough time to sell The Cookie Jar and move hundreds of miles away.*

"Will you let me know exactly when?" she asked.

"Of course. Are you going to hold a launch party for me, dear?"

"Oh, definitely!" Hannah said, wondering how much

money it would cost to launch her mother straight to the moon.

As she walked to her cookie truck, still sandwiched between Mike and Norman, Hannah had a sneaking suspicion that the last of the summer evenings had come and gone. There was a crispness to the air that spoke of leaves turning colors, pumpkins ripening on the vine, and chrysanthemums triumphing as the last flower of autumn before winter's icy fingers sprinkled snow on the flowerbeds.

"What time is it anyway?" Hannah asked, since she'd forgotten her watch on her dressing table.

"Almost eight," Norman answered her.

"How about a movie at my place," she suggested, now that she'd finally caught up on her sleep. "I rented two of the newest releases at the video store, and I've got the leftover Black Forest Brownies."

Mike shook his head. "It sounds great, but I've got to pass. I dropped Ronni at the mall on my way here, and I have to meet her and drive her home. Her car's not working right."

A *likely story*, Hannah thought. As a matter of fact, it was the very same story Shawna Lee had used when she'd lived in Mike's apartment complex. "Ronni's out there shopping?" she asked, just barely managing to keep the pleasant expression on her face.

"No, she's job hunting. She doesn't make that much at the sheriff's station, and she needs to get part time work."

"Well, I hope she finds something. Tell her I wish her luck."

"That's nice of you, Hannah." Mike gave her a warm smile. "I'll tell her."

Hannah was grateful that Mike couldn't read her mind and know that the real reason she hoped Ronni would find work was so that she'd spend less time at the apartment complex with Mike. But some things were better left unsaid, and

Hannah turned to Norman. "How about you? Would you like to watch a movie with me?"

"I'd love to, but I can't. I promised Mother I'd meet them at Granny's Attic and check their Internet connection. Your mother tried to get online this afternoon, and she kept getting error messages. It's probably just a loose connection or a reset problem, but they want to keep up with the bids on the Honus Wagner card."

"You can't blame them for that!" Mike said, grinning at Norman. "It's hard to believe that a little piece of cardboard with a picture on it could go for that much."

They arrived at her cookie truck, and Norman reached out to touch Hannah's shoulder. "See you for coffee tomorrow, Hannah."

"Me, too," Mike said, reaching out to pat her other shoulder. "Bake some more of those Black Forest Brownies, okay? They're the best brownies I ever ate."

And with that the two men in her life walked away toward their respective vehicles. No kisses. No hugs. Nothing but pats on her shoulder.

"Rejected," Hannah said, sighing theatrically as she climbed into her cookie truck. It was an attempt to make light of it, but if she were to be entirely truthful, she did feel a bit abandoned.

She started the engine and gave a little wave as she passed Norman and Mike. Then she drove down the gravel side road that wound through the stand of trees, and turned onto the access road toward the highway.

She zipped along at good speed. There was no traffic to speak of. When she turned on Old Lake Road, it was also deserted, and she was just turning in at her complex when the cell phone in her purse rang. Her first instinct was to ignore it, but it rang again, and then again. Hannah stopped at the gate and pulled out her cell phone. It could be some sort of emergency. Not that many people had her cell phone number.

"Hello," she said, hoping it wasn't a random sales call.

"Hannah. I'm so glad I caught you! I tried your condo, but I got your answer machine."

For a moment that lasted no longer than a heartbeat, Hannah was puzzled by the identity of her caller. Then she recognized his voice, and a smile spread over her face. "Hi, Ross," she said. "Are you in California?"

"No, I'm in Minneapolis."

"That's wonderful! Are you coming to Lake Eden?"

"I'd love to, but I can't. I'm only here for eight and a half hours. I was flying to New York and we had to land here, some kind of mechanical problems. They're transferring us to another flight, but it won't leave here until four-thirty in the morning."

"So you're stuck at the airport until four-thirty?"

"Not the airport. Since the delay is longer than eight hours, they put us up at the Airport Hilton. Do you know where that is?"

"Sure," Hannah said, her smile growing wider.

"How about driving down? I haven't seen you in a long time, Hannah. And I've missed you."

"I've missed you, too," Hannah said.

"So how long do you think it'll take you to get here?"

Hannah did some fast calculations, taking into account the light Sunday night traffic and the fact that she'd just filled her gas tank. "Forty-five minutes," she told him.

"Great! There's an all-night diner across the street at the end of the block. I'll get a table and meet you there. I'm hungry, and all I've had is airplane food."

"I'll be there," she said. " 'Bye, Ross."

She clicked off the phone and tossed it back in her purse. And then she did something she'd never done before. She slid her gate card into the slot, drove in when the wooden arm rose to admit her, did a sharp U-turn over the flowerbed that acted as a center divider, and drove right back out again.

"Not rejected after all," she said, grinning as she stepped on the gas and headed for the highway.

BLACK FOREST BROWNIES

Preheat oven to 350 degrees F., rack
in the middle position.

4 one-ounce squares semi-sweet chocolate *(or the
   equivalent—¾ cup semi-sweet chocolate chips
   will do just fine.)*
¾ cup butter *(one and a half sticks)*
1½ cups white *(granulated)* sugar
3 beaten eggs *(just whip them up in a glass with a
   fork)*
1 teaspoon vanilla extract *(or cherry extract)*
1 cup flour *(pack it down in the cup when you measure it)*
½ cup pecans
½ cup chopped dried cherries (or *½ cup well-drained
   Maraschino Cherries finely chopped)****
½ cup semi-sweet chocolate chips *(I used
   Ghirardelli)*

*** *I used dried Bing cherries in one batch, and
chopped maraschino cherries in a second batch. People
loved both batches, but all agreed that the ones with the
dried cherries were chewier.*

Prepare a 9-inch by 13-inch cake pan by lining it with a
piece of foil large enough to flap over the sides. Spray the
foil-lined pan with Pam or other nonstick cooking spray.

Microwave the chocolate squares and butter in a microwave-safe mixing bowl for one minute. Stir. *(Since choco-*

late frequently maintains its shape even when melted, you have to stir to make sure.) If it's not melted, microwave for an additional 20 seconds and stir again. Repeat if necessary.

Stir the sugar into the chocolate mixture. Feel the bowl. If it's not so hot it'll cook the eggs, add them now, stirring thoroughly. Mix in the flavor extract *(vanilla or cherry.)*

Mix in the flour and stir just until it's moistened.

Put the pecans and dried cherries in the bowl of a food processor and chop them together with the steel blade. If the dried cherries stick to the blades too much, add a Tablespoon of flour to your bowl and try it again. *(If you don't have a food processor, you don't have to buy one for this recipe—just chop everything up as well as you can with a sharp knife.)*

Mix in the chopped nuts and cherries, add the chocolate chips, give a final stir by hand, and spread the batter out in your prepared pan.

Bake at 350 degrees F. for 30 minutes.

Cool the Black Forest Brownies in the pan on a metal rack. When they're thoroughly cool, grasp the edges of the foil and lift the brownies out of the pan. Put them facedown on a cutting board, peel the foil off the back, and cut them into brownie-sized pieces.

Place the squares on a plate and dust lightly with powdered sugar if you wish.

Jo Fluke's Note: The ladies at Delta Kappa Gamma deserve credit for this recipe. After I spoke to them in Camarillo, CA, they gave me a huge box of dried fruit that included the dried Bing cherries that I used in these brownies.

Hannah's Note: If you really want to be decadent, frost these with Neverfail Fudge!

Index of Recipes

Baking Conversion Chart

These conversions are approximate, but they'll work just fine for Hannah Swensen's recipes.

VOLUME:

U.S.	Metric
½ teaspoon	2 milliliters
1 teaspoon	5 milliliters
1 tablespoon	15 milliliters
¼ cup	50 milliliters
⅓ cup	75 milliliters
½ cup	125 milliliters
¾ cup	175 milliliters
1 cup	¼ liter

WEIGHT:

U.S.	Metric
1 ounce	28 grams
1 pound	454 grams

OVEN TEMPERATURE:

Degrees Fahrenheit	Degrees Centigrade	British (Regulo) Gas Mark
325 degrees F.	165 degrees C.	3
350 degrees F.	175 degrees C.	4
375 degrees F.	190 degrees C.	5

Note: Hannah's rectangular sheet cake pan, 9 inches by 13 inches, is approximately 23 centimeters by 32.5 centimeters.